MASK ME

THE ATLAS COLLECTION (BOOK 1)

SAPPHARIA MAYER

Ebook ISBN: 978-1-64893-000-3

Audiobook ISBN: 978-1-64893-002-7

Print ISBN: 978-1-64893-001-0

MASK ME

AUTHOR'S NOTE

Dear reader,

I am so glad you picked up my book, and I hope you enjoy the story it weaves. Please remember, theses books are works of fiction. The timelines are compressed, the interactions are dramatic and characters often jump into things for want of adventure.

You, dearest reader, live in a reality where the world is often stranger than fiction and a good dominant or submissive is hard to find. When you do find one, it is quickly evident they are imperfect humans who can't read minds, are less observant than one might prefer, and the interaction with them takes time. Like all things in life, communication is the key to any good interaction. The more authentically open you can be with a partner the more fulfilling the relationship.

Remember you are in charge of your life. Use your safe word, let others know where you are, know what aftercare looks like for you, use protection and have fun. The goal is to live in a beautiful safe, sane and consensual relationship with all parties pulling their weight. It is my hope you all find your special someone, just like the characters in my books. *~Sappharia*

WARNINGS & DISCLAIMERS

WARNING:

This book contains sexually explicit scenes and adult language. It may be considered offensive to some readers. This book is for sale to adults only, as defined by the laws of the country in which you made your purchase.

DISCLAIMER:

Please do not try any new sexual practice, without the guidance of an experienced practitioner. Neither the publisher nor the author will be responsible for any loss, harm, injury, or death resulting from use of the information contained in this book.

CHAPTER ONE

The long leather whip swings by my side and tears stream down my cheek. Bright red welts form in lengthy stripes around each arm. My entire body trembles. His breath falls on my neck.

"Stop it. Right now. Emotions have no place in this business. Confidence is on the outside first. I don't care how you feel, I care what you exude. Do it again," he hisses against my ear.

The whip flies across the room at the snap of my wrist...

A LOUD ALARM STARTLES ME FROM THE ODD DREAM. HIS WORDS haunt me, and I stare at the ceiling, working to settle the jumble of images.

"Good morning, James."

"Good morning, Ma'am. I noticed that you only got four point two four hours of sleep. This is not adequate to support a healthy lifestyle." The disembodied British voice reverberates through the speakers overhead.

I roll my eyes at the automated voice.

"Set status to morning program."

"Present status changed to morning program."

The thick window blinds slide open, ushering in the dawn as it lights the sky. The room changes as it increases in the incremental brightness.

"Ma'am, the current time is six zero two am. Inside Temperature: sixty-six degrees Fahrenheit, new inside Temperature setting to sixty-nine degrees Fahrenheit. Outside Temperature: sixty-eight degrees Fahrenheit, feels like sixty-six Fahrenheit. They forecast today to be near the same temperature as yesterday. Showers possible. It is partially cloudy with winds from the northeast at five miles per hour. The humidity is thirty-seven percent and the Barometric Pressure is twenty-nine point seven five and falling. Sunrise: six-thirteen am. Sunset: seven fifty-eight pm. Air quality: good. Ozone: satisfactory. Pollen: high. House status: coffee is complete. Current Mode: Awake," he says, completing the computerized report.

"Set oven to broil," I call back.

"Oven Temperature confirmed to broil."

"Start shower. Set Temperature to one hundred and five."

"Shower started." James affirms the command.

For a few minutes I stare up at the ceiling as the light of the day increases and it inches its way over the horizon. Finally, throwing off the covers, I walk into the bathroom and start my morning routine as the steam wafts into the bedroom.

I roll my shoulders and stretch, struggling to drag myself into the day. I ponder on the dream that haunted me on the edge of slumber as I step into the shower.

Life was once simple. Get up, go to school, eat, party, repeat. The not-so-simple part was the constant push and struggle to succeed. My dad meant well, but his expectations were always impossible to meet. With him gone, how will I know when I've achieved enough? I sigh at the thought. I am still numb at the reality—part of it still hasn't registered.

Six months ago my cell phone rang at seven thirty in the morning.

James announced my dad was on the phone. I thought it was odd he was calling so early, but when I took the call, it wasn't him, and I realized in that moment I would never hear his voice again. His best friend's cry rang through the speakers in my penthouse, a place my dad had never seen because my success was not 'traditional.' It didn't come from a 'real job,' so I hid my entire world from him and tried to make him proud in other ways. That day I recognized it would never happen.

The scorching water sluices the dark thoughts from my mind as the steam engulfs me like the hands of a caring lover. I scrub away the last vestiges of sleep and try to focus on the day ahead.

"Shower off," I demand, frustrated that it didn't settle me.

The water works into a trickle as the stream dies.

I dry off and dress in one of my favorite 'bum around the apartment' outfits and head to the kitchen.

The smell of dark roast coffee greets me at once, making my lips stretch into a grin. I pour it into a large mug and add heavy cream along with a couple spoonfuls of sugar. It is a decadent cup, but its richness settles me, helping me wake up my lagging senses.

Turning to the stove, I grab a skillet before beginning to beat the eggs with Parmesan, salt, and pepper. I put the mixture in the pan and let it sit while I shift my attention to the last preparations of the frittata. My mind drifts to the story on my writing desk as I continue to chop the ham and asparagus. I put the rich egg dish in the oven.

A forty minutes later, the aroma blooms in the kitchen. The light fluffy texture and golden brown top of the frittata makes my mouth water. I cut a piece and place it on the tray along with my coffee pot and head for my writing studio.

"Open all patio doors," I call out along the way.

"Patio doors opening."

The early breeze of the dawn blows through the condo. The sheer curtains billow in a soft undulation. I set the tray on the side table, then survey my writing desk, struggling to find a place to start. For the next hour I do everything else but write.

I pull up the most recent reports for the club and the PR firm, sort through emails I don't read, then click on a game of solitaire. My mind tries to find inspiration to jump start my current story, but I lack focus.

Draining my coffee mug, I fuss at myself for the procrastination. Without thought, I reach for the coffee pot, then lift the spoon of darkened organic sugar, watching it fall through the air like the sands of a faraway desert. I drop the spoon into the cup, turn to my computer, and type.

He looked down at her kneeling form. The sapphire collar gleamed in the waning sun while the matching leash draped down her ample bosom and into his hand.
"You look gorgeous, kneeling helplessly before me," he whispered, winding his hand through her hair. He tightened his grip, pulling her head back and lifting her to her feet.
"You'll look even more glorious under my lash."

I READ THE LINE AND SHAKE MY HEAD AT THE SAD PROSE, BUT AT least it's a start. The ideas slowly flow. My pen doodles across the notebook as part of one snippet flows into the next and lets me get lost in a world of my creation. In vain I try to ease the frustration. Normally, words flow like a film. They give me a place to slip from the harsh realities of life. Each idea weaves an ever more complex pattern with threads of my vivid imagination, forming a universe where there's at least a happy for now ending.

"Ma'am, Miss Kingston is here. Shall I let her up?" asks James, his computerized voice reminding me he's a talking box no matter how *friendly and warm* he often sounds.

"Yes, James." I release a sigh as I brace for the onslaught that is Samantha Kingston.

"Excellent, Ma'am," he replies.

Several clicks and soft whirls work their way through the house as the front door prepares for her arrival.

"Good afternoon, Miss Kingston. Miss Devereaux is in her writing studio." James' voice resounds through the penthouse.

Moments later, Samantha comes bounding into the room like a tigger on springs.

"Atlas, darling," she says in an exaggerated Staten Island accent, falling into a fit of giggles seconds later.

I raise my head, glancing up from my writing desk, attempting to appear annoyed, so she'll get the hint and leave me alone. All I want to do is sit here in my hermit state, creating the book, so I can meet the rapidly approaching deadline.

"Samantha." The acknowledgment is more curt than I intend.

She looks me up and down.

I am suddenly conscious of my appearance. My hair is pulled back from my face with pins, my dusty blue T-shirt has holes in it as if moths had a feast, and my jeans are ripped in all the wrong places, or the right ones, depending on why you're wearing them.

"And what brings you by my ever so humble abode today, Miss Kingston?" I ask without looking up from my notebook.

"That," she says. A frown is clear in her voice. "You sound like one of your books every time you open your mouth."

My eyes shoot up, and I glare at her.

"You're the one who's pushing me to get it finished. It's not like my schedule is empty and I'm lying on a sunny tropical beach sipping Mai Tais while the warm Caribbean water laps at my toes like a foot fetishist who's suffered a long winter."

Samantha rolls her eyes. "You just compared the Caribbean Sea to a foot fetishist."

The laugh she attempts to hold back erupts, and she doubles

over. I shake my head and exhale while Samantha pulls herself back together.

"Atlas, in all seriousness, girlfriend, you are burning the candle at both ends and in the middle. I know you need to work to keep your mind off of things, and no offense meant, but you're looking worn."

"No offense taken, but my world doesn't stop just because I'm overwhelmed. We've found that out far too recently. People depend on me and I'm not one to drop it all for some rest and relaxation, or just because I'm weary of all the things going on in my life."

My tone is pointed, but even I think it sounds tired. I don't want to imagine how raggedy I appear.

"Besides, I get the basics to keep *Alexandra's* appearance up."

"Yeah, and a few people at the club have been talking about how *Alexandra* doesn't seem up to her normal polished presentation. I'm serious, Atlas, I appreciate you have this whole self-sacrifice, you've got no needs and must save the world attitude, but it will send you to a premature grave. And for the record, there's nothing wrong with hanging out in the Caribbean sipping Mai Tais when you've already achieved an appreciable amount of success. Take a breather, for god's sake!"

Her exasperated tone causes me to pause, and then her words hit me.

"What do you mean people are saying *Alexandra* isn't her polished self? Do those people appreciate the things that woman does for them? She works her ass off to give them a place to *play their little fantasy games* and makes it all look sexy and effortless. Then she has to drive her sorry ass home—no... wait... she has a driver."

A smile creeps across my lips as the rant flows freely. I can't help letting the laugh escape when I'm finished.

"After all these years, it's still hilarious to listen to you talk about yourself in the third person, like your *persona* is someone unique. It cracks me up every time."

The tension in the air breaks, and I nod in agreement.

"But to them she is a distinct individual. Just like the author, Sam

McKenzie, for whom I slave away to ghostwrite her next brilliant novel."

I peer down at the notes and Post-its scattered across my desk. The blinking cursor on my writing software demands that I devote it the attention it deserves right now.

"Since you've interrupted my morning, what did you have in mind for today?"

"I don't know — something along the lines of kidnapping Ms. McKenzie's writing slave and having a spa day. We'd spend the day on grand extravagances with her credit card. Enough to force her accountant to wonder why he bothers trying to rein in her spending habits. Then I'll take said writing slave out on a magnificent night on the town where *Alexandra's* driver will take us bar hopping and everybody will wonder why the famous Ms. McKenzie is hanging out with such rabble."

Samantha's mischievous grin is infectious, and I grin back at her with a conspiratorial look.

"You know, rumor is *Alexandra* is a bitch on wheels when she finds out someone else commandeers her resources without permission."

"I know, right? But she swings a mean whip and I'm okay with taking a lashing for the both of us... if we get caught, of course." Her face is an attempt at sober resignation as she nods her head. "I mean, I am a team player."

"Yeah," I snicker. "Self-flagellation is far easier than self-whipping. Well, unless you are learning."

Samantha grinned at me and nods.

"Outstanding, let's go. I arranged for *Alexandra's* driver to pick us up out front. Her security team has been alerted that she'll be resting all day, and isn't to be disturbed."

Samantha nonchalantly picks up her bag and heads to the door.

"James, set for Alexandra Do Not Disturb. Forward all emergencies to Atlas' number," Samantha calls out to the house.

"Miss Kingston, I can only comply with Miss Devereaux's

commands at that level. You only have guest access," James replies in a monotone.

"James," I say, prompting the computer to be ready for a set of commands. "Set Alexandra to Do Not Disturb, set Miss McKenzie to Do Not Disturb, set emergency contacts for Atlas."

"Done," James replies. "Confirming current settings: Alexandra—DND, McKenzie—DND, Atlas available. Atlas—emergency referral for all DND. Please confirm."

"Confirm," I say heading for the door, only to be met with a glare from Samantha as I round the hallway entrance.

"Really?" her tone drips with sarcasm. "Two-thirds of you is set for DND but you're available. Didn't we just have this chat?"

"Let it go."

I try to move past, but her Amazonian figure steps in my way.

"Turn. It. Off," she says, her expression daring me not to comply.

I shake my head in resignation. This is the Samantha Kingston that has assured my sanity for the past several months. I love having a friend who pushes me when I can't seem to get there on my own, even if it creates the most irritating of moments.

"James." I glare at Samantha.

"Yes, Ma'am?"

"Set Atlas for DND—emergency on all faces only."

"Confirmed. Alexandra, Sam McKenzie, and Atlas Devereaux are set for Do Not Disturb status. Atlas' number is the emergency number on all faces," the computer confirms.

"Goodbye, James," I call out.

"Have a marvelous day, Ma'am. Alarm set to away in thirty, twenty-nine, twenty-eight, twenty-seven..."

I nod to the door and follow Samantha into the hallway, listening to the shuttering blinds. Things click and whirl as various settings in the house move into a new configuration. The final beeps ping as the security alarm sets. Without a doubt, I know she's already got everything lined up, and all I can do is brace for impact.

"I've got the day all planned out," Samantha twitters on excitedly.

"First, we'll go find you a fabulous new dress and amazing shoes. Then we'll search for a matching bra and garter belt, with the finest hose to encase those amazing legs. I'm thinking facial, nails, hair... definitely hair."

"What's wrong with my hair?" I cock my head and twirl a ringlet above my ear.

"You pull it back so much the poor stuff is breaking off like mad. Seriously? Atlas, when did you last take care of it?" She grabs a handful of the ends and shoves it in my face. "It's like straw!"

I huff out a sigh. My life is too busy to take great care of myself. It's enough that I am clean and well put together, when the occasion demands it. Besides, I'm nothing near what one would consider high maintenance.

"Earth to Atlas." Samantha's voice echoes through the hall, and I glance up to see her holding the elevator doors.

"Good lord, you think too much. What is racing through your brain now?"

I laugh, stepping into the elevator.

"I was thinking how funny it sounds when we talk about my *other personas* like they are actual people, with genuine lives, and if anyone knew they were all me, they'd think I was a little..." I shrug.

"You're one of the most compartmentalized people I've ever met. I don't understand how you keep it all together so flawlessly. However, the weight of the world is causing you to fray and tatter. Take some *me* time. Do something to enjoy your significant success." Her voice is soft and full of worry.

She knows that I'll pacify her and not change a thing. My life is full of responsibilities. When it slows down, then I'll take her advice.

The elevator dings. We walk arm in arm across the lobby, both of us breaking out in a fit of silly giggles when we see Alexandra's driver and a black limo waiting in front of the building.

"Good morning, Miss Devereaux and Miss Kingston," he says with a slight bow of his head, a ghost of a knowing smile on his lips as he opens the door.

"Thank you, Adam." I nod and climb into the car without the usual style and grace of Alexandra.

In that role I am invincible. Untouchable. Everyone shows deference, respect, and I rarely hear the word *no*. However, as Atlas, I'm just Alexandra's friend. The acquaintance no one quite understands but doesn't dare question for fear of Alexandra's notorious wrath and her hard-as-nails attitude.

Samantha climbs in after me and raises the privacy glass. Once she settles, she picks up the open champagne bottle and pours two glasses. The car slowly glides away from the curb and smoothly slides into traffic. Samantha holds a glass of bubbling liquid towards me, but I hesitate.

"It's a little early in the morning to drink, don't you think?"

"Why not live a little? Why not be reckless, even a bit, for once?" she says, shoving the glass toward me.

I accept it, eyeing the bottle suspiciously.

"Dare I ask which one you took from Alexandra's stock?"

She spews champagne at my deadpan question.

"Oh, she'll kill me without a doubt." Samantha turns the label toward me, and my eyes widen in shock.

The Armand de Brignac Ace of Spades Brut Gold label shines in the dim light, and I shake my head.

"Oh, she's not happy, I can assure you."

"It's not like she ever takes time to enjoy her vast collection, so someone should do it for her."

She tips her glass back and savors a long sip.

I follow suit. The aromatic liquid embraces my tongue, covering my palate with a bouquet of honeysuckle, nectarine, and pear. I let it sit there, savoring the blanket of essences. The bubbles play across my mouth, and I close my eyes, savoring the expensive sip.

"Everyone should see that expression on your face at least once in their life," Samantha whispers.

"What?" I see her staring at me.

"It expresses pure enjoyment. One where you are carried away yet living in a single moment with the greatest appreciation rather than just existing." She smiles, taking a less delicate sip of her own glass. "This is an excellent vintage. Besides, Alexandra has no idea who took it."

"But I'm..." I start.

"You are Atlas. I'm sorry, but *Alexandra* is DND, and there's no way for you to tell her." She snickers at her own constant joke.

I laugh and shake my head.

"You're impossible!"

"Yep. That's why we get along so famously," she replies, lifting her glass in a salute. "Cool, we're here."

I glance outside.

The opulent day spa screams torture of every kind instead of the relaxation Samantha promised. Adam opens the door, holding out his hand as I step from the car. I watch the attendants school their looks when they see my state of dress and begin a mental ping pong match between me, the car, and my well-dressed uniformed driver.

It must truly be a sight. I can imagine the rags-to-riches theme running through their heads. The inexorable Ms. McKenzie taking a poor girl under her wings for a make-over day. The irony isn't lost on me since she's using my account to pay for it. The entire thing makes me shake my head.

"Perfect! Let's do this," Samantha says and steps forward, then pauses. "Hold on, let me grab our drink."

She reaches into the limo and lifts the bottle from the ice bucket.

"I'm positive they don't serve champagne like this here. No matter how amazing the place is at everything else."

I chuckle. "No, Samantha, I'm positive they don't serve a three hundred dollar bottle of champagne to their guests," I mumble under my breath.

She moves smoothly toward the door, ushered inside by the confused attendant. I watch her calm confidence as she confirms a list of things on their clipboard before I turn to take in my new surroundings.

CHAPTER TWO

"Wow, that dress looks amazing on you!" Samantha calls from the couch for what seems like the hundredth time, as I turn on the dais.

I get a confidence boost from the lavish treatment and the designer clothes, but not everything can be spectacular on this figure.

"You've got to get that one, Atlas, and I saw the sexiest pair of red-soled shoes over there. They would look amazing with it." She motions to the clerk before her sentence is even finished.

"You mean the Louboutins?" I ask, rolling my eyes.

"Yeah, those." She grins, winking at me.

It drives me crazy when she acts less cultured than her background, and she knows it. Which is why she does it whenever she thinks I will rise to the occasion. This time is no exception.

Samantha's eyes go wide, and she mouths something to the sales clerk while I evaluate myself in the mirror. I twirl this way and that to get a view of every angle. On the hanger, it is everything I would choose. It's a plain ebony dress which lets me hug the shadows, but on, it skims my body in all the right places. The soft jersey knit is elegant and cuts a perfect silhouette.

In mere moments, the black smooth kidskin materializes and embraces my foot. My toes peek out of the front of the shoe as the intertwined laces run in a delicate pattern across the top of the near-vertical five and a half inch platform stiletto heel. The image staring back at me is amazing, sophisticated, and stylish. It's the opposite of the strict, stern style I use for Alexandra's club persona.

It is delicate feminine version of myself I have never allowed forward for fear of appearing weak. It is the femininity that men think is fragile. The image in the mirror appears anything but weak. There is an undercurrent of power and yet a soft openness. I feel sexy, amazing, and confident in my own person.

What brings the entire outfit down is I am barefaced, my hair is pulled back with pins, and my fingernails are due for a manicure fill. As Alexandra, I wouldn't have even graced this place without perfect hair and flawless makeup, but at the moment I'm not her, I'm just Atlas. I'm the girl behind the curtain, the soul that keeps all the masks running in perfect harmony, and suddenly I'm facing myself in a whole new light. I am the part who is responsible, prudent, calculated, and planned, but the image staring back at me makes me wonder where in the world that girl has gone.

"Perfect. I've got you a new pair of jeans, a T-shirt, and a more casual pair of sexy heels."

Samantha throws me a wide grin.

"I mean, those jeans would be hot to cut off of you, but they won't do here, girlfriend."

Her playfully accusing tone dares me to reply. I stare at her open-mouthed.

"Miss Kingston, I believe it was you who showed up upon my doorstep, whisked me out in a limo, fed me champagne far too early in the morning, and now complains about the way I was dressed?"

The elaborate reply must have been what she was hoping to get because her grin grows wider, and she nods to the clerk.

"Told you."

Samantha looks back at me and nods toward the dressing room.

"I can't wait to send those rags away so we can get on with our sexy adventures, in case you decide to step out of your work world and — oh, gasp — see a man." She tripped on that last sentence, her fingers silently tell me she was talking about someone who didn't pay me for my expertise in 'torture.'

"Whatever." I turn, storming into the dressing room.

A few minutes later, I step out in a well-fitted pair of jeans, designer T-shirt, and heels.

"You call this — casual?"

"Yep, casually expensive. Now we've got the basics, let's finish the rest of you. Come along, deary," she says in a shaky, high-pitched voice. "I'm getting old here waiting on you to figure it all out."

She walks off toward the spa area, and I'm left hurrying to catch up.

"By the way, I also got you a shaping bra, matching panties, garter belt, and silk nylons. I had to do something while you tried on a thousand dresses."

"Do something? A thousand dresses? You were the one who kept piling them into the damn dressing room!"

She turns to face me with playful lines creasing her face.

"You really need to lighten up. It used to be much more of a challenge to get a rise out of the calm, cool, collected Atlas Devereaux. Told you you're stressed."

Before I can reply, she turns and walks into the spa area.

"Ah, Miss Kingston, it's so good to see you again," a man greets her with an overzealous manner, leaning in to put air kisses near both cheeks.

"And who do we have here?"

He eyes me up and down and settles on my hair.

"Frederick, this is Atlas. The project I told you about," she says with a smile.

"Oh, my, you were so right." He says it to Samantha as if I'm not even in the room.

"But we have the technology. This can be fixed."

His index finger points up like he's had a flash of genius.

I watch Samantha and Frederick assess all my needs, commenting about this and that before deciding on what needs to be done. I stare off, letting my mind wander, and the world around me fades away.

"Yes, I agree. Get her off to that wonderful massage," I hear as Frederick's hand gently pushes against my shoulder. "I'll assemble the rest of the team while you two enjoy yourselves. You'll be so relaxed when you're done, beauty will overflow from the inside out."

Samantha is in her element and loving the fact that I'm not. With good-natured enthusiasm, she steers me toward the massage treatment rooms and instructs me to undress, then lie on the table under the sheet.

"Yes, ma'am," I reply with dripping sarcasm.

"Now we're getting somewhere, girl," she replies in a mimicking sarcastic tone of her own.

"You know, I have had a massage before," I say, pushing open the door to the massage room.

"With you it's so hard to tell. It ranks up there in the indulgent, non-puritanical category. I hear that *Alexandra* barely uses the spa facilities at her place. I'm just saying, but that's sad. All that goodness at her disposal and the woman is such a bitch she won't even use them."

"Maybe she's busy. You should cut her some slack." I smile softly and walk into the treatment room.

I undress and lie down on my back across the table, the meditative music playing softly in the background and the flicker of candlelight creating a warm glow across the room. A woman walks in dressed in a white Asian-inspired tunic and pants. It reminds me of the club's spa uniforms. My mind wanders off to the thousand things that need to be taken care of at the club. I can imagine the work piling up on my desk and hate feeling like I'm wasting time here when I should be working. Why in the world did I let Samantha talk me into this?

"Good morning," I hear the woman say, and it brings my focus back to the present moment. "My name is Ann. Tell me what's going on with your body today."

I paste on a smile. "I'm tense in the shoulders, neck, and jaw. My lower back is tight too."

She nods, repeating back the symptoms. "Now relax and let me do all the work."

Ann massages my face and works down my neck. Each movement is slow and subtle. Little by little, the muscles give in to her touch — knots releasing, joints popping here or there.

At some point in the process she has me roll over onto my stomach, working my back and legs. My entire body is relaxed, and I sigh in gratitude when the sheet settles across my shoulders.

"I could do this for hours, you're so tense, but that's good enough for today. I hope you'll think about getting regular massages. It could really help those muscles out. Take your time, and when you're ready, there is a robe for you on the back of the door. You can use it for the rest of your stay. Your next appointment is waiting for you, but there's no rush."

Her hand smooths the muscles across my back one last time, then the door opens and shuts with a soft click.

I pull myself out of my relaxed reverie and realize the bag with my clothes is gone. Walking over to the door, I pull on the soft, luxurious robe and slide my feet into the incredible slippers. I stretch one more time and walk into the hallway.

"Ah, Atlas darling, you appear so much more relaxed," Frederick coos softly. "Now, let's get you the soft, glowing skin you deserve."

I follow him down a short hall. He opens the door into another treatment room.

"Renee will be with you in a few minutes. She's the best aesthetician on staff."

Before long, I'm arranged on another table. Renee is massaging my face, spreading various potions and lotions on different areas. My closed eyes are pressed with soft cool disks and I'm left alone to relax to the same ambient music from the massage room. I doze off until Renee begins to gently wipe away the mask. Once again, her fingers move across my face, anointing it with various types of creams.

"Beautiful," she declares with her last stroke. "They are ready for you in the hair salon. Frederick is waiting outside to take you to his chair."

I step out of the room, and Frederick greets me, hustling me down the hallway to his salon chair. I am soon wrapped in a black nylon cape and facing away from the mirror. He consults with a couple of other stylists, comparing various colors until they all come to an agreement.

He paints my hair from the plastic containers on his rolling tray. Each stroke ends with the hair being wrapped in tin foil before proceeding to the next section. I sit, listening to the chatter of the other patrons and stylists as I surrender control to Frederick's capable hands. Two hours later, he declares me done, handing me over to the shampoo girl. The warm water is delightful, her hands massaging my scalp, rinsing the chemicals from my hair, then finishing up with a delightful concoction that smells of a tropical breeze and coconuts.

Once I settle back into Frederick's chair, he pulls a comb and scissors from the tool belt wrapped around his waist. The blades slide through my hair as pieces flutter down the nylon cape. Periodically he stops, pulling up pieces from both sides to measure, then goes back to snipping. When he's satisfied with his work, he pulls out the hair dryer and busies himself with various round brushes. Some of them he rolls in my hair, leaving them while the hairdryer blows from one side to the other.

When he's done, he steps back and stares at me in the mirror.

"Gorgeous. Now for nails and makeup," he says, holding out his hand to help me from the chair.

I try to turn to the mirror, but he grabs my shoulders.

"Not until we're done. Samantha's orders."

He grins at me conspiratorially, escorting me to my next stop.

My feet are placed in a large whirlpool tub of water and he sets a beautiful afternoon tea plate across my lap. While I savor my lunch, a young man attends to my feet, eventually painting a delicate pattern over the top of the French pedicure. When he pronounces my feet perfect, I'm led to a low manicure table, and the process starts all over on my hands. Finally, I'm taken to my last stop. A young woman works her magic on my makeup and smiles at me with pride.

I admit to myself that I have neglected the details of my appearance as of late. Usually I am far more fastidious, but I still can't seem to find a reason to focus on the details again.

"Now, off to get dressed," Samantha says as she rounds the corner.

I step out of the dressing room and do a little turn as Samantha cat calls me. I glare at her.

"Really, you must act more refined." I regard her with dismay.

"Really," she mimics, "you must lighten up and live a little."

I glance in the mirror to see what all the fuss is about and stand dumbstruck. As *Alexandra*, I've always had a polished but severe appearance to give me that 'bitchy' edge which works well as a professional female dominant. But this... this is so different.

"You look amazing," Samantha says, walking up beside me. "Now, let's do this thing!"

She pulls me by the hand, waving to the attendants as we head out of the salon. Adam is waiting with the car door in his hand.

"Miss, um, Devereaux," he stutters and stares at me.

I smile as I gracefully turn to sit and swivel my feet into the limo.

As Samantha walks up, Adam collects himself.

"Um, Miss Kingston. I'm so sorry."

Samantha laughs.

"It's okay, Adam. That was the right reaction."

CHAPTER THREE

The limo moves deftly through traffic as the evening lights reflect across the calm Potomac waters. We head over the Fourteenth Street Bridge. Adam glances in the rearview mirror often enough to make me uncomfortable, and I debate raising the tinted screen. My fingers slide restlessly over the button, but I don't apply pressure.

"Have you ever crashed a gala?" Samantha says casually as she watches the short, stout Washington skyline come into view.

Silence stretches between us. Its long fingers wrap around my throat and fill me with anxiety that almost stalls my beating heart.

Samantha turns toward me.

"My God, Atlas, you're white. What on earth is wrong?"

Her hands cover mine, stroking them slowly. Her face is full of worry.

"I've never crashed anything before," I whisper.

The whole concept of being caught, kicked out, and reprimanded leaves me cold. My life is all about rules. They govern my perspectives, relationships, and business decisions. The thought of violating them for fun is terrifying.

Concern transforms into amusement.

"You always have such a puritanical streak. It's such a juxtaposition when I know what you do in your other *job* and what you write about in *my* books."

She shakes her head and smiles.

"We've got tickets." She pulls the papers from her bag. "One of our clients thought we could use some *networking* time, so he sent them over this morning."

I glance at the logo emblazoned across the top.

"Those tickets go for a thousand dollars apiece. It's supposed to be the event of the season. The who's who of the DC political, philanthropic, and social circles show up to give over three million dollars in charity. Why in the world would he send us a pair of tickets?"

"He bought a table sponsorship for his company, which gave him ten tickets. Two of the people couldn't make it, and we've done great work for him in the past, so he thought he'd toss them our way."

"So why didn't you tell me this morning?" I say, the accusation clear in my tone.

"Simple. Would you have come if I had?"

"No." I shake my head.

Samantha smiles.

"And there we have it." She continues, as if my simple answer explains the entire mystery of the day, "The theme this year is an exotic paradise with the name *Midnight Oasis*. Themed dancers, vibrant fabrics, and best of all—masks!"

She hands me a black satin bag. The delicate script lettering proclaims the maker to be Italian. My hands tremble as I open it and pull out a delicate metal mask. The elegant lines create the outline of a face. When it's worn, it will look as if it is painted on my skin. Small crystals catch the dimming sunlight and cast sparkling rainbows across the dark black ceiling of the limo like hundreds of stars twinkling above our heads.

"Put it on," she prompts.

I place the mask to my face. I feel hidden in plain sight, and it gives me an odd sense of daring sensuality and confidence. The metal conforms to every contour as the left side sweeps up high above my temple, then curls back down toward my eye, giving an air of subtle power.

Samantha looks back at me in her own mask. The bright Swarovski crystals adorn the silver metal, giving way to a set of ornate silver chains just under her eyes. It creates a refined elegance and sensual mystery as she stares back at me with intense anticipation.

"Breathtaking." The word forms across my dry tongue, and I know she will capture every male's attention, both eligible and ineligible, the minute she steps from the car.

Large spotlights search the sky above the building. The car pulls up to the curb, and a long red carpet lies just outside the door. On either side, throngs of people line up behind metal barricades, cameras in hand, hoping to glimpse a member of the politico or a celebrity. A lengthy line of limos reaches down the street.

Adam opens the door and offers his hand to Samantha. With confidence, she navigates her way onto the red carpet. Cameras pop and flash around her, and my apprehension takes over. The sounds of distant sirens mix with the laughter and shouts of the crowd as an excited energy hangs in the air, and I hesitate.

His hand reaches back through the door to coax me out. The dryness in my mouth feels like looming desert sands swirling in front of an oncoming storm. My body tenses, forcing me to take a deep breath. Adjusting my posture, I move through the door. Adam's hand steadies me as I find my bearings on the tall stiletto heels. With a nod, he releases me and hands me to the crowd.

Samantha navigates the crush with confidence as she waves to the people along either side of the carpet and makes her way toward the gala entrance. It feels like a bizarre dream as I force my feet to move with practiced steps. The whole scene is disjointed and out of place, yet I feel safe behind the thin piece of metal.

"Over here," a photographer shouts to my left.

I place my hand on my hip, draping the other arm across the front of my body, and pull my feet together, shifting my weight to accentuate my hourglass proportions. With a tilt of my head I look at the crowd through the extra-long lashes and give a sensual half-tilted smile until the flashes cease. When the maelstrom ends, I turn and walk up the stairs toward to the double door entrance.

The riotous smells of the Middle East float in the air. My stomach rumbles in response.

Samantha comes up beside me and grins like a cat who has just eaten a canary. Her relaxed body shows she's in her element.

"You can thank me later," she says loud enough to be heard over the din, but not enough to draw attention.

Together we enter the grand ballroom. Overwhelming activities surround us. Large drapes hang from the ceiling in long columns of fabric and lights, creating small niches of intimate areas and larger performance arenas around the vast ballroom. On each table, tall oriental flowers add to the scale and exotic atmosphere.

On the large stage in the front center of the room, dancers from around the world perform. I watch in fascination as dance troupes take the stage in a multicultural display. There are the undulating movements of belly dancing of the Middle East to the free-swinging hands and hips of the Chinese Hmong dancers. Next, the Moia dance to the accompanying drumbeats. The powerful rhythm increases the speed and strength of their dancing, creating a jubilant mood. The melding of movement and melody along with the jingling jewelry creates a ringing that is infectious and elevates my mood.

The finale brings all the dancers together in their various dance styles. A beautiful display of disjointed unity. At the end of the exhibition, the crowd erupts in riotous applause.

When it dies, the lights lower. Spotlights highlight five long red lengths of fabric, creating four corners with one in the center. The soft music holds me captive in anticipation. On the first strong downbeat, four aerialists take death-defying falls from the top of the ceiling down the silks. I release an audible gasp.

Above our heads, they continue to suspend, swinging and falling through the fabric in various positions as their bodies gracefully move in unison. On the last beat of the music, the crowd once again shows their deep appreciation for the spectacle.

Together, Samantha and I circulate through the crush. Uniformed wait staff work their way with passed hors d'oeuvres. Plates of crudités with aioli garni, smoked trout with horseradish crème fraîche on toast points and eggs with caviar and salmon rosettes pass as we work our way to the table.

I grab a glass of champagne when a waiter walks by. Samantha chit chats, stopping at this table or that group of people.

Everywhere there are masked faces. Some are elegant and refined, while others are garish and crass. The room assaults every sense at once.

"Ladies and gentlemen—" A man speaks into the microphone from the large front stage. "If I could have your attention. Please make your way to your seats."

The roar of the crowd increases, and Samantha grabs my elbow, moving us toward our ultimate destination. Her face lights up when she sees a gorgeous man in a well-fitting, black tailored tuxedo standing next to a table set for ten. His black hair glows under the table's spotlight, and a smile brightens as Samantha approaches.

"Ian," she coos.

"Samantha." His voice rumbles from his chest. "I'm so glad you could make it."

They embrace more intimately than a simple business acquaintance would imply.

"Ian Breckenridge, may I present Atlas Devereaux."

"Lovely to finally meet you, Atlas. Samantha talks about you all the time."

He smiles, placing a soft but chaste kiss across my knuckles.

"That's a scary thought," I say, smiling back while glancing sideways at Samantha.

Ian's deep laugh carries over the din, and he nods his head knowingly.

"What are you doing with yourself these days?" Samantha inquires, sitting next to him when he motions to the seat with his hand.

"I'm the congressional campaign manager for Elizabeth Davies." He smiles.

"Well, look who's moving right on up the political ladder," Samantha jokes easily with him. "What do you think of your chances?"

"At the moment we're in the lead, but only by two percent. It will be a tight race. We're a strong incumbent, but we can't really afford any political bobbles. So here's hoping it will go smoothly."

"Ladies and gentlemen, please take your seats," the man with the microphone announces, causing the room to fill with the sound of conversation as chairs scrape lightly across the floor.

Once everyone is settled, an army of wait staff descends on the ballroom with the first course. For the next hour, the conversation flows around the table. Samantha flirts lightly with Ian when the conversations turn to politics or another heated topic of debate, causing the table to return to easier subjects.

In a final extravagance to the amazing five-course meal, the wait staff places a dark chocolate soufflé in front of each plate in unison. The beautiful dessert encases the delicious molten center which oozes out of the light, springy exterior when my fork pierces the edge. It is pure chocolate decadence.

"It is said..." The man on the stage speaks into the microphone once more. His dark, sharp-looking tuxedo molds across every muscle in his body. I am instantly captivated by his baritone voice, as is the rest of the room, since he has the attention of every person in the crowd.

The woman next to me leans over and whispers, "Oh my God, isn't he gorgeous? The most eligible bachelor here, and no one can seem to capture his attention."

She smiles, licking her lips.

"It is simple to take notice," he continues when the room goes silent, "but it is more difficult to put forth effort and take action. Tonight we want to celebrate a person who not only took action, but did so with the greatest of enthusiasm, placing her whole heart and commitment to the cause. She is a force to be reckoned with, in her tireless efforts in helping society understand and support the autistic population.

"Her imagination, fire, and drive is an inspiration to all who have the privilege to encounter her. There will never be a time when anyone will ask if she could have done more. She blazed a path where so many people have feared to travel. There were times of uncertainty, unexpected obstacles, and unanswered questions. Each time she refused to take no for an answer.

"In the words of Elbert Hubbard, 'A little more persistence, a little more effort, and what seemed like a hopeless failure may turn to glorious success.' Thank you for showing us the truth of these words.

"Ladies and gentlemen, may I present this year's Autism Foundation Lifetime Achievement Award winner, my sister, Elizabeth Davies."

Her simple sophisticated strapless black gown exudes classic glamour while the silhouette hugs her figure, falling to a flaring skirt. Her dark rich mahogany hair drapes elegantly across her shoulders, flowing in waves as she makes her way up to the stage.

While she is stunning, my eyes follow the form of the most breathtakingly gorgeous man I've ever seen, his stoic grace moving him across the stage as he hands Elizabeth the crystal award, then leans in to give her a soft kiss on the cheek.

Stepping to the small acrylic podium, she takes a deep breath and lets her eyes run across the audience in the room. "I am deeply humbled and honored to be receiving this award tonight. I would like to offer my sincerest gratitude to the hundreds of people who work tirelessly to help work through the various struggles of families with autistic members. To the Autism Foundation, thank you for your continued support in our collective cause."

Her speech continues, but my focus isn't on her; instead, my mind enjoys the gorgeous eye candy that introduced her.

I am startled from my thoughts when the award recipient says, "Again, thank you." The crowd erupts in a standing ovation.

Ian turns to Samantha and smiles. "And that is why she will win in the upcoming election."

CHAPTER FOUR

Once the room settles, the activity picks up in the ballroom. This time there are hoops hanging from the ceiling as women twirl and spin above us, their elongated bodies flowing gracefully from one position to the next.

On the far side of the room, couples dance the tango across a parquet floor, while on stage, acrobats perform daring moves, the same music producing distinct forms of artistry all around the large ballroom.

The hustle and bustle has me on edge. At the limit of my desire to do small talk, I catch Samantha's eye and motion to the bar. Concern brushes across her face, but I wave it away, smiling, and make my way through the crowd.

Usually I prepare for days to go into such a large social situation as *Alexandra*. This morning I had planned on curling up all day to write, not on ending up at the gala of the year. Glad for the respite, I lean against the bar.

"What can I get you?" the bartender asks, his eyes appraising me.

"Dealer's choice," I quip. "Something a little sweet and a bit unusual."

I smile, then turn to lazily scan the room, taking in the exotic scene. It doesn't take any time to recognize the who's who of the DC society and political circles, mixing and mingling. It might be a masked ball, but most of them are working their political agendas.

"Here you are, miss," the bartender says, placing a blue glow-in-the-dark cocktail in front of me.

I look at the drink, my face a mixture of confusion and amusement.

"You said you wanted something unusual." He grins at me.

"Yes, I think this most definitely falls into the category of unusual," I reply, picking up the glass and taking a tentative sip. The cool liquid coats my tongue, a hint of pineapple chased by a mixture of rum and citrus.

"It's superb," I say and lift the glass toward the bartender in a show of appreciation before turning back toward the ballroom.

Pinpricks light up across my body and I try to chalk it up to my uneasiness when I see a pair of piercing gray eyes staring at me from behind an intricate leather mask molded perfectly against a male face.

"Good evening."

The deep baritone slips across my senses, pulling my nerves taut. It is the same voice that announced the award.

"Might I join you?" he asks, nodding to the high-top table a couple steps away.

I smile and nod, not trusting my voice. He motions to the bartender, who nods and prepares his drink.

"Quite the unusual cocktail."

"Yes," I reply, smiling. "This happens when you put your drink choice in the bartender's capable hands."

To my surprise, he chuckles, picking up the dark amber liquid the bartender has placed in front of him.

"Shall we?"

I nod, and he leads the way over to a table. I gaze down to his firm ass. He is a marvel of animalistic grace and killer good looks. I follow closely behind and sigh, thinking how it would feel to cup his ass cheeks in my hands and pull him closer. Shocked at my own thoughts, I feel a warm blush rise in my cheeks.

"That was quite the speech you gave earlier," I comment, trying for light casual conversation.

"Thank you. My sister really has done an amazing job. They honored me when they asked me to present the award." His gray eyes look back at me with a studied intensity, and he smiles.

"How long has your family supported the Autism Foundation?"

"Since my nieces were both diagnosed about five years ago. My sister has been amazing with them." He beams, the devotion to his family obvious in his tone. "How about you? What brought you to the gala tonight?"

"Well—" I start thinking over the day. "I didn't exactly know I would attend when I woke up this morning."

His forehead wrinkles. "How does one not know they are going to the biggest gala of the year on the morning of it?"

I laugh. It sounds almost ridiculous when I say it out loud. "It's a long story, but it starts with a well-meaning friend and ends with two tickets to the gala."

"I'd love to hear it sometime." His genuine smile reaches his eyes, and they dance in the dim light. "How about we step out of here and into a smaller room where conversation is easier?"

I nod in agreement, and we pick up our drinks and move through the crowd. Passing Samantha, I smile, and she gives me a quiet thumbs-up, causing me to shake my head at the crowd of men surrounding her.

We make our way through large double doors that lead to a small enclave, softly illuminated with dim lights and glowing candles. The fragrance of spices wafts through the room from the trays of chocolate-covered fruits and truffles being passed by the servers. My body tingles with a sense of uneasiness and excitement. I give myself permission to silently devour him. His impeccable suit hugs his body in a perfect understated elegance, each line drawn perfectly without being too tight.

"Why me?" I ask boldly, my normal shy graceful tack off-kilter by the constant changes of the day.

Those gray eyes dance with a mix of surprise and amusement. "You seem different somehow. Watching you watch the room with a certain intensity intrigued me, and yet you attempt to fade into the shadows."

His soft voice is like a warm caress and yet the words are a complete juxtaposition. Bold and confident without being overly arrogant.

I'm not sure what to say after such a declaration. The awkward silence sits between us. My fingers fidget with my napkin. After a moment, I glance up to see him leaning casually against the high-top table, watching me. The muted light casts shadows across his face, leaving his eyes unreadable as it illuminates the slight tilt of his strong jaw line. His powerful hands wrap around the rock glass, and I wonder what it would be like to feel them around my waist as those lips firmly crushed against mine in a passionate kiss.

"Um, sorry, I'm not much of a conversationalist tonight. You must think you've made quite the mistake and that I'm terribly..." I stammer, shocked at my own wayward thoughts. Samantha's right, I have been spending too much time in my fantasy world. There's no way a man like this would ever want me. These masks just make everything so much more sensual and intriguing.

"Terribly what?"

"Boring. At the moment, not quite a wonderful conversational partner." My eyes meet his, and my shoulders straighten.

An abrupt bark of laughter escapes from those sensuous lips.

"Boring is not a word I would use to describe you."

"I'm not sure how you could say that," I retort.

His low, warm chuckle stirs something inside me.

"It seems we are conversing now."

"You know what I mean." I roll my eyes. "You shouldn't belittle someone who is openly admitting their current social ineptitude."

"Rolling your eyes is impolite and social aptitude, as you put it, can readily be taught when the lessons are motivating enough." He steps mere inches from me, his lips hovering just above mine, the air between us exchanging with one another as we both breathe.

"I wonder what would motivate the likes of you, young lady. You are one of the sexiest women I've ever met. There's something about you that's indescribable."

Taking a steadying breath, I inhale. The clean muskiness of his cologne surrounds me. It speaks of a man who knows he has his entire world firmly in his grasp. I stifle a moan when my mind races with a wide range of naughty things to motivate me. The image of being bent over his knee because I've failed in my lessons comes unbidden to my mind. Unfortunately, my body doesn't get the memo of the off-limits topic as the dampness slowly forms between my legs.

"You seem to be a woman well in control of her world."

His breath caresses my cheek.

"I'm always in control."

I meet his hard intense gaze, mentally pushing him to back down, but my chest rises and falls in shallow intakes of air while I focus on those lips, begging for a daring taste. In my mind I scream to be reckless just once and live a little. Everything in me wants to embrace the false sense of security the mask gives me. Closing my eyes, I focus on each inhale, desperate to control the erratic reaction of my body.

"I love a delightful challenge," he whispers.

When my eyes open, he's already moving, and it takes a second too long for me to understand his intent. I watch in slow motion as his head bends and his lips brush against mine.

The kiss is neither long nor deep, but my entire body lights in a buzz of sensations. Desire licks from my core, daring me to throw my arms around him and press into his lean, broad chest. His soft mouth caresses my lips, his scent filling my nostrils, and I suppress the moan begging to vocalize my flaming desire.

He raises his head and steps back, those gray eyes boring into me as if he could reach in and captivate my soul with the slightest touch.

"I bet you would look even more amazing completely out of control," he says as his voice drops to a whisper.

"That will never happen," I reply, forcing the air through my teeth while my mind and body war in opposite directions.

He leans in, the heady smell of his body taking over my senses as the roughness of his tongue slides across the outer edge of my ear.

"Your arousal smells so..." He inhales deeply. "Mmm... such a wonderful fragrance."

The air is already charged, I can't imagine—don't want to imagine—what I'll do if he touches me again.

I take a sudden step back, working to release myself from the spell that seems to have taken complete control of my sanity.

"I'd better go find my friend."

It sounds lame, but I need to clear my head before I do something I will regret. Turning, I straighten my posture and head for the entrance to the ballroom.

"I don't believe I caught your name," he blurts out, rising to follow me.

"That's because I didn't give it." I smile, turning to cross the threshold before moving swiftly into the circulating crowd. Spotting Samantha, I make a line straight toward her, silently telling her I am leaving. Then I make a turn straight for the door.

Punching Adam's number into my phone, I tell him to meet me out front. Once inside the safety of the car, I collapse against the seat.

My body screams in rebellion as I work to control my labored breath and tremble at the unexpected encounter. Images of his eyes and the electric way we kissed haunt my thoughts.

Power and control go hand in hand in my world. To give up either could send the whole thing tumbling down, and I refuse to let that happen no matter the pull of contradictory desires.

Leaning forward, I pour a finger of scotch as Adam weaves through the city traffic.

CHAPTER FIVE

It is ten o'clock in the morning as I wind my way through traffic toward the PR firm. I should be bright and alert by this time, but my body swears it's far earlier, as I once again debate the positives and negatives of a deep-tissue massage on a tense body. Accompanied by a lack of sleep, the result means my mood is sitting right on the edge of sour. Add to it the reason of the lack of sleep was a constant barrage of images of those lips and gray eyes peering at me from behind a mask. A man who made my body light up in a desire I thought long dead, at a gala I didn't even know I was attending, the conclusion becomes that burying myself in the pile of work on my multiple desks will either help me sleep or lead to something productive.

I maneuver my Mercedes SL65 up the drive toward the tall gleaming ornate metal gates of Empyrean. Without reducing my speed, the gates swing open. The vast paddocks surround either side of the tree-lined drive as the bright green grasses blow in the morning breeze.

I marvel at the impressive sight. No matter how many times I see it, I don't think I will ever grow tired of the view.

The large estate building, inspired by classic Italian villas, expands on the horizon. The broad entry, arched windows, and columns create a powerful statement while the barreled tile roof lined with deep carved brackets creates an unrivaled elegance. It is an awe-inspiring sight of splendor and power, but not the normal kind of power. This building holds secrets behind its façade.

There is a compact building just to the right of the huge manor. Originally designed as a separate guest living quarters for the estate house, it boasts a small placard gleaming in the sunlight, announcing it to be the headquarters of McKenzie Kingston, Ltd., a small boutique PR firm developed when Samantha and I were just out of graduate school, specializing in unique and alternative lifestyles.

A large, tall, bald man approaches my car with a tattoo that creeps up his neck and peeks out of the collar of his black shirt. His styled suit tailored to hug his body just tight enough grazes across the hard muscles underneath. His tan skin glows in the sun. At six foot seven inches with a high and tight cut and intense brown eyes, he should intimidate. Many would wilt under his massive appearance, but I smile and nod to him.

"Good morning, Miss Devereaux," he says, lowering his eyes as he opens my driver's side door.

I turn my legs in unison, and his hand is out ready to help me up from the car. Placing my hand in his, I rise from the soft black leather seat.

"Thank you, Steven." My voice is in obvious appreciation of such a fine specimen.

He holds out his arm and I place my hand in the crook of his elbow, allowing him to escort me to the door.

"I'll take excellent care of her, ma'am," he says, nodding back to my car, and gives a slight bow before turning to take care of his task. I know the car will come back with a full detail and polish. It will shine like it just rolled off the factory floor.

The columns on either side of the small portico rise around me, and I hesitantly place my hand on the handle of the red door leading into the office. The polished silver trim shimmers in the sun, not even a cloud to dampen its shine.

Opening the front door, I walk through the reception area, turn left, and step into a sizable room with four desks arranged in the corners facing toward the middle, each with two chairs placed in front of them facing the desks. The arrangement has always reminded me of a car dealership, but it works for the open concept of the office.

The fact that the desks are an eclectic mixture of antiques, modern glass, and expansive wood says everything about us in one grand eyeful. Each desk represents the person who sits there, letting visitors know this is no ordinary firm.

I make my way over to my desk, setting my briefcase on the floor next to it. The modern steel and glass desk is organized. Each area is sorted, and every item has a distinct purpose. The calm order of the desk makes me smile as I walk around it before melting into the contemporary high back office chair.

The front door opens, and a discombobulated Samantha turns the corner into the office, passing my desk on the way to hers. With a dramatic plop, she places her various bags on top of the paperwork scattered across her desk.

"What a grand time last night." She smiles with a dreamy look on her face. "I can't believe you left early."

"It was an overwhelming day. You know me, I can only party for so long. Besides, I'm out of practice to keep up with the crowds like you do, or catch the attention of a mass of men."

"Oh, you attracted attention all right. I can't believe you're so oblivious to it, Atlas." She scowls at me. "And what was that whole Cinderella move at the end?"

I look up at her. "What are you talking about?"

"What aren't you telling me?" She looks back at me and I feel like I'm in the middle of an interrogation. "Why was Mr. Reece Gabriel chasing after you? More importantly, why did he look like a hungry wolf after his prey?"

"I don't know what you're talking about," I sputter.

She stalks around to my desk and leans over the front. "Atlas Devereaux, what are you hiding? A man goes chasing after you and when you disappear, he stalks up demanding to know your name."

"He what!" I'm stunned at her revelation. "What did you tell him?"

"I told him you worked for me and gave him Sam McKenzie's business card." Samantha gives me a sly smile. "He was hot!" Her eyebrows wiggle. "What did you do with him?"

"Nothing," I shoot back. "We talked. I realized I was tired, made my excuses, and left. End of story. I didn't even get his name."

"A man does not chase after a woman, demand to know her name, and look for her all over a crowded ballroom after a nice little *chat*."

Internally, I plead for her to drop it, but the look on her face tells me she won't. All night I spent tossing and turning, thinking about that intense gaze and those lips. I don't need to hear that I affected him just as much.

A loud knock breaks our staring contest, and Samantha stalks to the door and flashes a glare at me.

A few minutes later she walks back in carrying a vase of flowers and a box under her arm.

"Looks like someone had an admirer last night," I tease. "I'm surprised you didn't get more than one, based on the level of court you were holding."

"These aren't for me, sunshine. Well, the flowers are, but this is for you." Her eyes narrow and I feel the heat of a flush creep over my skin.

My eyes drift toward the black box with a delicate silver ribbon knotted artfully on the top. Not a typical bow, but an actual set of knots. My brain goes spinning. Those are the knots I use in rope bondage, though they are also well-known by rope artists and sailors. I force my mind to focus on boats and the practical applications of well-crafted knots in the nautical world while trying to ignore the more dangerous line of thought that is forming, unbidden, below the surface.

"Oh, how sweet," she says, reading the card attached to her bouquet.

Thank you, Cinderella's fairy godmother, for telling me which cottage to look in for the right fit to the glass slipper. RG

SHE LOOKS UP AT ME AND DRAWLS, "WELL, TELL ME WHAT YOUR card says, Cinderella."

"I'm no Cinderella. My world is already complete, and I don't need a man to add to the already riotous complexity." I roll my head across my shoulders to relieve the sudden tension.

"You deserve fun," she says thoughtfully. "Why not go with it? Go out, have a few drinks, see where things lead? Where's the harm in that idea? I mean, he's obviously attracted to you."

She nods toward my box. "Open it. Let's see what Prince Charming sent over."

I smile mischievously.

"Oh, I'm sure it's a total thanks for the chat, but your friend is way hotter, here's a consolation prize because I'd feel like a jerk for sending her flowers when I talked to you first."

The snicker can't be contained.

"Atlas." The warning tone only makes me laugh harder.

I work the ribbon off the box without untying the knots. I lift the lid and fold back the tissue paper. A black mask stares back at me, along with a single red rose, thorns still on the stem. I gasp as my eyes scan the note.

That which yields is not always weak.
-Phedre no Delaunay de Montreve.

You're an enigma, wrapped in a mystery surrounded by a riddle and I
want to see what lies at the heart of such a labyrinth. -RG

———————

"That's the second time I've seen that look in as many days, Atlas." She walks over to peer into the box. "Oh. I see."

"I have never met such a presumptuous man in all my years—" I stop the sentence before it can get any worse.

"Oh yes you have, but you've just never met a dominant one who saw you, or at least *thinks* he sees you. Though he could be a womanizing ass who thinks all women are submissive, but I didn't get that vibe off him last night." Her hip leans against the corner of my desk, her arms cross. "I believe you may have met your match, Miss Devereaux."

"I don't have time for a relationship, Miss Kingston. My client lists are full both here and at the club, not to mention the mounds of work I have to do if I can even hope for the sleep James keeps harping on me to get."

My shoulders slump and I turn to my computer.

"And a book I need to finish at some point," I mutter.

From the corner of my eye, I see uncertainty marring Samantha's face.

"Sometimes we have to step off the edge and trust the next step to be there, for no other reason than the thrill of the moment."

"I don't do moments. I do planning, control, risk management. It's a Saturday morning and now I'm neck deep in work."

I try to blow her off by busying myself with emails and checking up on various client issues while trying not to think of those gray eyes which seem to haunt every moment. I pause and turn.

"Why would anyone send flowers on a Saturday?"

"Oh, I told him you'd be here. Especially after I made you play hooky yesterday. Besides, the look on your face last night when you ran out of the gala told me I'd at least find you at the club today. You have a power problem, Atlas. Just go with it for once," she says, pushing away from the desk. "It's not like you're so young and dewy-eyed you'll fall for any domineering ass who has money and looks at you with desire."

She makes a face and bats her eyelashes.

"Oh, yes, Sir, please, Sir, I'll do anything you say, Sir, because you are amazing with your great big bank account and brooding personality, but as soon as you want to hurt me for our mutual pleasure I will run away screaming and blame you for horrible things." Her high-pitch imitation echoes through the office.

I grab a piece of paper, throw it, and watch it bounce off her shoulder.

"What?" She looks at me, her face an attempt at emotionless innocence.

"You're terrible."

"Yeah, that's why you love me," she says with a grin.

CHAPTER SIX

The blinking cursor on my computer taunts me, telling me, in a passive aggressive way, I should be working. My fingers fidget as my pen taps in a staccato rhythm against the desk. I imagine the feel of his lips brushing against mine. It has been far too long since I let a man kiss me. Then again, I didn't really *let* him do anything, he just kissed me. He seized the moment and lived it.

My eyes drift to the clock on the front of my desk. The little statuette holds a timepiece as a stick man kneels head down in a praying position. It is a combination of reverence and control of time. Nowhere in the small piece is there anything about seizing a moment, but rather alludes to slaving away, and he, like me, is conscious of the passage of time. Yet this *masked man* seized something in me and has ruined my ability to get anything done in the time. Instead, our moments together run in a continuous loop through my mind.

I give my head a hard shake to clear the thought, but my body is already going down the path. I picture his hands sliding down my back, his palm brushing across my ass. In my ear he whispers, *It turns me on thinking about seeing my hand print here and here.* His desire is clear as he presses his hard length against my thigh to tell me the effect is mutual.

My breath comes in ragged pants. I close my eyes and lean back against my chair, attempting to look like I'm taking a break from work rather than indulging in a sexy daydream.

The images come unbidden. His hands caress my breasts as he whispers against my ear, *Your body is stunning wrapped in rope. I love watching it wind around you so I can embrace you everywhere at once.* At the word *everywhere,* he grabs me between the apex of my legs, and I gasp.

My eyes fly open.

Samantha is staring at me.

"Are you okay?" She edges the questions with amusement rather than concern.

I nod and turn back toward my computer as I try to calm my erratic heartbeat.

The rest of the morning passes in a mass of frustration. The more I try to work, the less I seem able to concentrate. Each task requires that I double-check my work because of the lack of focus.

My mind keeps flashing back to the handsome stranger behind the mask who caused me to momentarily lose a grip on my sensibility. It was so unlike me. I never slip in my control. But as long as the relationship remained casual, there was little harm in it.

What troubles me the most is my almost instantaneous connection with a complete stranger. Those soft lips consume my thoughts. His light-hearted teasing holds a promise of strength and tenderness, of control with compassion. I shake the thoughts from my head for what feels like the thousandth time.

"Want lunch?"

I stand up and look over at Samantha. For the last two hours, I've gotten nothing done except driving myself to distraction.

"Sure." Samantha looks up. "We can pop over to the club and grab something in the bar and watch the pool servers do their thing in those hot uniforms you make them wear."

The grin on her face is one of pure delight.

"I need to go change personas. Alexandra has a ton of work on her desk and her inbox is probably overflowing by now. Give me twenty minutes and I'll meet you in the bar."

I walk around my desk and make my way to the back exit.

"No way. If I let you out of my sight, I'll be eating alone or starve." She fakes a frown.

Smirking, I turn back.

"You would neither starve nor eat alone, but if you want to eat with me, then you'd better come help me *find* Alexandra."

The bookcase lines the back wall at the far end of the office. Hooking my finger on the top of *The Art of War*, I pull it toward me, as if to remove it from the shelf. A soft click resounds as the locks disengage. Gradually, the bookcase rotates to reveal a passage.

Stepping forward, I make my way down the stairs toward the connecting underground tunnel. Lights run along the sides of the narrow corridor, the shag carpet dampening footsteps as we make our way toward 'Alexandra's' dressing room in the club's basement. Soft music echoes off the walls to help ease the confining space. At the end of the passage, I reach out and twist a metal ring, pushing the door open.

"Lights," I call out in a lilted practiced Southern drawl, far different from my normal non-accented voice when I am just Atlas.

"Welcome back, Alexandra," the familiar computerized voice greets me as the lights increase in increments to allow our eyes to adjust from the darkened passage.

"Transformation."

Cabinet doors lift to reveal a line of severe looking black wigs. Across the room, the lights on the dressing table illuminate and the wardrobe door slides back to display a seemingly endless variety of severe business suits beside latex and leather outfits matching the massive line of shoes and boots on the opposite wall.

Samantha shuts the passageway door as I make my way to the dressing table before opening the drawer and lifting out the airbrush.

With a practiced hand, I add a couple of drops of color then blend it across my face. Occasionally I stop to change colors and start again. I do this routine so often I barely think about the process.

Contouring creates more structured features, shadowing the face into harsher angles while lightening others. The heavy eye makeup and long additional lashes gives a glamorous, retro feel to the look. I turn on the stool when I'm finished and smile at Samantha.

"I don't care how many times I watch you do it, I'm still amazed at how different you look when you are done," she comments, staring at my face.

"Oh, my dear Samantha," the heavy drawl rolls off my tongue as I make my way over to the line of straight black wigs. "I do believe that you are mistaken at any transformation you believe you may see. For it is by magic that the great Alexandra appears and disappears throughout the club."

A smile pulls on the edge of my lips as I tuck my hair under the wig stocking and apply a line of glue right at the edge of the hairline. Once the glue sets, I pick up a black china doll wig with long heavy bangs and flip it into place. The effect is a natural hairline adding to the look, and I settle into the new projected persona.

Stepping to the wardrobe, I hit the switch and the circulating rack moves a line of clothes in front of me. I stop it on a navy blue lace dress with a deep V surplice bodice, matching back, and long sheer fitted sleeves. The fitted waist flows into a skirt that skims against my hips, covered in a blue floral lace ending just above the knees. Over at the wall of shoes, I put on a pair of nude suede almond toe platform stiletto heels, adding five inches to my height, and reach down to adjust the ankle strap.

"How do I look, Miss Kingston?" I place my hand on my hip, jutting it out slightly, allowing one leg to fall gracefully in front of the other.

"In that dress, you look soft and feminine, but there's nothing soft about the way you carry it off." She shakes her head. "That long Southern drawl coming from a woman that looks like she belongs in a

New York penthouse who knows her word is law, messes with my brain."

Tilting my head down a little, I look up at her from under the long dark lashes.

"Why, Miss Kingston, I do declare that would be the point."

"Yes, ma'am," she returns in an equally impressive New Jersey accent, making me laugh.

"Shall we adjourn this dreary sight for a more appropriate view?"

"Let's. Please lead the way, Alexandra."

"Close," I command the room and listen to the clicks of doors sliding shut as we exit out onto the plush carpet-lined hallway.

Together we make our way down the corridor. On either side, closed doors lead to private play spaces. Outside each one, a light displays if it is in use or available for members. At the end of the hall, we bypass the elevator. I push open the fire door and walk up the service staircase.

Together we exit and turn the corner toward the bar. All around us there is a hum of conversation and a bustle of activity. The warm spring breeze wafts through the massive bi-fold doors spanning the enormous room which leads out to the pool's patio. Small groups are sitting everywhere, in a mix of casual and fetish clothing, chatting, drinking, eating, and socializing.

I smile every time I come here. It is opulent and lush without being overbearing. Hours of dreaming and planning the perfect luxurious space with sensual undertones comes to life.

We turn and walk into the bar and settle at a high-top table. Samantha's eyes scan the crowd around the pool area.

"I swear, Alexandra, you make those pool boys and girls look like they stepped off of Mount Olympus with those tight-cut outfits. I mean, look at the ass on that boy."

Her eyes follow one of the male servers who's bent over handing a drink to a guest.

A cocktail waitress walks to our table. Her metallic lace bodice is decorated with small sliver chains and scattered with crystals. The entire ensemble gives the illusion of a corset flowing into a short ivory skirt as the sheer chiffon overlay runs to the floor from her hips.

"Good afternoon, Alexandra, how may I be of service today?" Her eyes lower and a soft smile spreads across her face.

"Merlot please, Kristin. And Miss Kingston will have—" I give Samantha a playful poke.

"What? Oh, a Shiraz please." Her guilty smile tells me she knows I will once again advise her against harassing the servers. "Don't give me that look, Alexandra. Who they do off the clock..." she starts.

"Is still my business. We are never off the clock here. You know the rules, please don't make me remind you of them."

"Fine," she huffs.

"Afternoon, ladies."

I turn toward the familiar voice, watching Kade walk toward our table. He leans over, placing a kiss on each cheek, then doing the same to Samantha.

Kristin places the wineglasses on the table and water in front of Kade. I smile at the fact she has been so observant to our table's addition.

"Want to join us for some lunch?" I smile up at Kade. "Samantha here was just getting ready to break at least a half a dozen club rules, so I might as well bring security up to speed, just in case."

Kade holds my gaze knowingly when I pause in my rant.

"What! Alexandra, I would never do such a thing. Kade, darling, there's no reason to waste your precious time..." She stops mid-sentence when we both laugh in unison.

"Paybacks are hell, darlin'," I drawl.

"I like you better as Atlas," she mutters under her breath. "The nuns were easier to get one over for goodness' sake."

"Well, I help dearest Atlas settle her scores whenever necessary. You know how close we are, like two peas in the same pod."

"Yeah, whatever." She rolls her eyes.

Kade chokes on his water at the exchange. I look up in concern, but he waves it away, shaking his head.

"By the by, the general manager has advised me of a recent stock reduction in the champagne collection. An Armand de Brignac Ace of Spades Brut Gold, if I remember the inventory alert correct." I take a sip of my merlot, letting the question hang in the air. "You wouldn't know anything about it, would you, Samantha?"

"I'd check with Atlas on that one, ma'am." She grinned.

"So that's how you'll play it." I try to deadpan.

"Your move, madam." She laughs, saluting me with her wineglass, knowing she's got me on this one, before taking a long sip.

"You two are a riot, you know that." Kade leans back, watching our banter.

"Dearest Kade, could your security team kindly pull the recent security footage and access to the wine lockers. Please have the report on my desk in an hour." I turn and smile at Samantha. "Checkmate, darlin'."

"Well played," she retorts.

Lunch goes by with a familiar banter. The three of us have been friends for so long the inside joke threads are constant. There is an easy camaraderie and it helps take my mind from the images that have done nothing but distract me as I try to keep Samantha from sexually harassing my staff.

With a glance at the clock and a sigh, I watch Kristin clear the last of our dishes.

"I ought not tarry here any long for fear I'll get no work done today." With a slight turn toward Kade, I smile. "She's your responsibility now, Kade." Nodding toward Samantha, I stand to push my stool back under the table.

Kade gives me a death stare. I inhale and blink.

"Boy, don't let your eyes try to tell me to do something unless your ass wants the results."

His eyes cast down in respect before he looks at me again. "Yes, ma'am, my apologies."

"Now that is settled, I need to get to my office and do some work."

I turn to Samantha, who's flirting with one of the female cocktail waitresses. "Samantha!"

Her head snaps around and she tries to look innocent. "Yes?"

I sigh with dismay. "We have rules, and they apply to you more than anyone else because of your association with me."

"How is that fair?" she whines. "Why don't I get some kind of *get out of Alexandra jail free* card?"

"Because you like the feeling of bars when you're in the cage," I say with a raised eyebrow.

"Too true."

A smile blooms across Samantha's face as she turns to Kade. "Oh, darling, we will have the most amazing, glorious time together."

"Alexandra, you can't do this," Kade remarks without looking at Samantha.

"Heel, Samantha. Make sure she doesn't mess up the carpet, Kade." I smile, turning on to see my assistant Katie walking toward me.

"By the way, Alexandra, a friend of mine is coming by this afternoon," Kade says behind me.

"Ma'am, we have a delivery problem with the new leather toys for the charity auction next week. I got the call they won't be ready in time," Katie fires off, her voice full of nervousness as I follow her back to my office.

CHAPTER SEVEN

The day wears on into early evening as the emails pile up. I work to clear them. Each one acts like it's the biggest problem facing man. I coordinate and organize teams, mobilize response, and strategize how to stay out of these situations. I focus on my latest problem and almost miss the soft knock on my door.

"Come." The word rolls off my tongue, without me looking up to acknowledge the person at the door, my eyes scanning the club reports. There have been issues lately, but nothing I can't handle. I make a note to discuss the security concerns of the members with Kade.

"Ma'am, pardon my interruption, but there's a gentleman here to see you. He says Kade referred him." Her calm voice stays steady when my piercing eyes rise to meet hers. Katie is a brilliant assistant, but her submissive tendencies are often challenged by the more dominant members who refuse to accept it when she denies their requests.

My aggravation is evident. I've told her I wasn't to be disturbed. She trembles under my gaze—she knows I am not happy about the interruption.

"Referred for what?" I demand, annoyed that this situation will cause me to be here far longer than I think I can stand.

"He didn't say," she says, her voice right above a whisper.

My glare doesn't waver. I take a deep breath.

"Send him in. Please make a note on my calendar for us to discuss the meaning of *do not disturb*." I nod toward the door.

Her shoulders sag.

"Yes, ma'am, as you wish," she says, backing through the door rather than turning around. Her gaze falls to the floor.

I rise from my chair, straightening my dress with a slight downward tug, my back stiffening as I pull my shoulders back. Standing up straight, I huff in slight exasperation without looking up.

"While I can appreciate your ability to recognize the submissive nature of my assistant, and use it to your advantage, I don't appreciate the interruption," I state without looking up from my paperwork.

He approaches the chair in front of my desk and stops without saying a word. Dramatically, I draw my eyes to meet his, aiming to make this a quick meeting so I can get back to work.

The minute I see his face, every nerve ending in my body electrifies. My heart pounds, making it hard to breathe as my entire body goes on high alert.

It's him, my brain screams. The first glimpse of his full face without the mask causes my mouth to go dry. I feel light-headed and paralyzed. With an effort, I work to appear impassive, but there's nothing impassive about how I'm feeling that gives me the slightest thing to hold that ground.

I nod toward the chair in front of me, demanding my brain to work my mouth post-haste. For a long minute I stare at him staring at me. The palpable tension bounces around the room, but neither of us moves. The intensity of his gaze shifts something inside, and I demand a shift to my hidden needs.

He stands with a relaxed casualness as he observes me. In this moment I pray to everything divine that he can't see past the very distinction of Alexandra vs the *masked woman* he met at the gala last night. The sudden internal panic makes keeping my cool outward demeanor hard to control while inwardly something pushes on my desire to either kiss this man for all I'm worth or to fall to a kneel at his feet. The collision of the two opposite desires is like drowning without water.

"Good evening, Alexandra." The smooth deep husky voice that haunts my dreams fills the office.

My racing thoughts stop dead in my head, creating a pileup of enormous proportions. The internal stuttering continues, and I tell my body I'm in complete control and that it will listen right now before I blow this persona and look like an absolute loon.

"My apologies for the use of your first name, but Kade didn't give me a last name. He only told me to ask for Alexandra."

He reaches his hand out.

I force my legs to propel my body forward and raise my hand to meet his. Instead of a business-like handshake, he places a soft kiss across my knuckles, his gaze never leaving mine.

Oh my God, he really is just a womanizer who thinks every woman will give in to his personal whims. I use the thought to dash all others and gain a foothold of much-needed control.

"And you are?" I ask in a dead monotone, holding on to that last thought like a drowning shipwreck survivor. Everything in me demands that I stay strong.

"Of no consequence usually," he quips, yet his intense gaze does not waver, creating an odd juxtaposition as it sends my mind reeling in calculating confusion. "Or at least that's what Kade tells me."

What is this man playing at? I continue to work for my mental footing.

He stands eye to eye with me, but I'm wearing five-inch heels, so it's an unfair comparison. The handsome bespoke suit draws my eyes to the well-cut waist and the tie placed in a perfect trinity knot around his neck.

There is something understatedly breathtaking about the man standing here as he exudes an air of complete control. His short black hair lies without any of them out of place and just enough growth across his firm jaw to be more than stubble, but it is his eyes that hold me captive. The intensity that glimmers right under the surface is like a god holding a bucking bronco on rein.

A silent war of wills passes between us like electric sparks jumping off every surface. The first one to break contact will lose this round. One side of his mouth lifts in a semblance of a smile as he glances down to focus on the seat in front of my desk.

"I'm sorry to stare, but you look familiar somehow," he relents, dissipating some tension.

"Please have a seat, Mr..." I let the question dangle for him to fill in his name when the phone on my desk trills. I look down to see the name Edmund Hurter display across the caller ID and hit reject.

"Kade has told me so much about you and your club," he says as he unbuttons his suit jacket without hurry and settles into the seat. "It, like its proprietor, is beautiful, from what I've observed so far."

"Thank you." I pause, schooling the eye roll which is my normal reaction to such comments.

The door opens, startling me and kick-starting my brain back into motion. Katie glides through the room with a carafe of ice water and two glasses. She sets them on the table between the two chairs in front of my desk without a sound.

"How do you know Kade?" I force the question out. It takes every bit of internal focus to steady my breath and maintain my exaggerated accent to sound authentic yet relaxed.

I walk around to the front of the desk and lean against it. My hand wraps around the edge to steady me as he follows every move.

The conversation stalls as Katie pours two glasses of water, placing one on my desk and one on the table beside him. I nod a curt dismissal when her eyes rise, and she backs out of the office.

His gaze burns into me, but I refuse to return it until we are once again alone. He stretches back in the chair, making himself more comfortable while I demand every fiber in my body to stand straight and still.

"Kade and I have been friends for several years. We have similar backgrounds and eccentric tastes. He recommended your establishment," he replies without seeming the least bit bothered by my obvious power play.

I nod for him to go on, not yet trusting my voice as the explosion of emotions courses through each nerve ending. His gaze is taking in every movement. Never in my existence as Alexandra have I felt so awkward, nor has a man affected me so much.

"And what are these eccentric tastes of yours?" My mouth works the words into the air to fill the descending silence. Picking up the glass of water, I take a sip to moisten the arid wastelands that have overtaken my mouth.

Laughter lights up his dark features.

"My tastes run dark. They are rather more particular, as do yours, from what I hear." His head inclines toward me. "Since I moved back to the area, Kade thought I might find some stress relief here."

"So you're a submissive," I say in a matter-of-fact tone.

Most of my personal clientele are high-stress, high-paid men looking for a place to let go of some control. Since Kade recommended that this man talk directly to me, it is the best assumption I have for the awkward situation.

"No, Alexandra." He tries my name again, as if it doesn't seem to match the person standing in front of him. "My tastes are dominant. The play of power entices me. It is the elegance of this setting which Kade thought might meet my desires. From what I've seen, not only does your club fit into that category, but it seems to offer a rich variety of other diversions. I would love a tour if you are available."

"We cater to a wide variety of appetites. I am sure you will find something that appeals to you and quite a few willing *victims* in which to share your unusual pleasures, whatever they might be." I try to sound casual. "Are there any ones in which you are most interested?"

"Are you this inquisitive of all your clients, Alexandra?"

"Clients? Yes. Members, it depends. I find the better I know those who walk through the doors of my establishment, the better I am at ensuring they find the things they need to satisfy their tastes." I raise an eyebrow.

"Ah, so you are a control freak." He smirks.

"I'm always in control." The automatic phrase falls across my lips. It is something I learned early and practice often. It was drilled into me until it became part of my personality.

His eyebrows shoot up, making me shift uneasily and wondering what caused such an unusual reaction.

"I'll look over your membership application. You should have my decision by the end of the day. My assistant, Katie, can show you the upper facilities if you'd like." The words come out in a clipped tone. I push hard off my desk to signal the end of the conversation, suddenly uncomfortable in my office, and incline my head toward the door.

"Why did you need to see me?" I ask, stopping my progression back to the office chair.

His eyes take in every movement as if he's trying to work out a troublesome problem which should have an obvious answer but doesn't.

"I had to see the woman that seems to capture so much of Kade's attention. He speaks very highly of you."

I furrow my brows, looking confused at his statement.

"Kade speaks of so few people on a personal level, but you already know that." He answers my silent question. "It was a pleasure to meet you, Alexandra." His mouth twists as if the name is still, somehow, uncomfortable.

I give a curt nod of acknowledgment as I sit down behind my desk, and he turns to walk out the door.

"I don't believe I caught your name," I blurt out.

"That's because I didn't give it." He smiles and turns to cross the threshold.

My mind races over the conversation and I stare at the door in horror. It has to be a strange, twisted coincidence that he walked away without giving his name the same way I walked away last night.

There's no way he could have known it was me. My entire look, accent and persona is so different, even those who know often have difficulty remembering I'm the same person. There's no way he's figured it out from our brief time together last night. Besides, I calm myself, I was behind a mask.

I flick on the monitor, pulling up the images of the security system and watch while Katie takes him on a tour of the facility. Every once in a while he laughs or says something which makes her body tense as she flirts. On the other hand, he seems unaffectedly relaxed as their conversation plays silently on my screen.

They turn away from the camera, giving me a chance to admire his tight ass and truly one of the sexiest walks to ever grace my club floor. I slowly relax, enjoying my private show as I watch them walk in and out of various rooms in the upper level areas in the club.

My mind wonders what it would be like to see him in the lower private rooms. To feel those lips sucking across my hard nipples as his hand snakes down toward my... I mentally slap myself out of the daydream and refocus on the monitor's image.

Kade and Samantha are motioning them over to their table, and the groan that escapes my lips echoes off the office walls. Then he turns and looks straight at the camera. Those piercing eyes tell me he knows I'm watching.

CHAPTER EIGHT

The silhouette of the rising sun plays across the desert horizon. His hands possessively roam across the lush curve of her hips, down the side of her leg and back up to the soft folds nestled between her legs. A long, languid movement, telling her he's in no hurry to end her suffering or burning desire. Goosebumps form across her flesh, even her skin responds to his soft touch.

He lowers his head to her neck, brushing his lips down the soft delicate skin before...

THE SOUND OF THE FRONT DOOR CLOSING REVERBERATES through the lower office, and I mentally brace for the coming storm. Heel clicks echo off the stairwell. I gaze at the screen, hoping beyond all hope she'll leave me alone.

Samantha walks across the room. Her steps are purposeful, her designer suit hugging her curves in a sultry yet professional way as her perfectly styled short, dark hair undulates between red and black in the morning light. She makes her way to the coffee bar, picking up a white mug with a gaudy gold crown that proclaims *It's good to be the Queen!* and filling it with the inky black liquid.

"You're in the office early," she notes. "Do you ever sleep anymore?"

"According to James, no."

"Then where's my new book?" she demands, her tone light-hearted and playful, trying to be heard over the Kirov Opera's rendition of 'War and Peace' blasting through the room's integrated speakers.

"*Your* new book?" I try to sound annoyed, my eyes barely rising from the computer screen as my well-manicured nails pause on the keyboard, the next thought already flying out of my head thanks to Samantha's sudden appearance.

I stretch my suit-clad body, willing the tension in my shoulders to abate, but all I can feel is the protest from muscles being bunched too long and the mental fog created from not getting enough sleep. For the moment, I refuse to explore the reason.

"And do you have to listen to this music so early? How can you get anything productive done to this racket? Opera has got to be the most depressing thing I've ever listened to." She rolls her eyes. The New Jersey accent hints right around the edges of her words, no matter how much she works at trying to get a neutral tone to her voice. It's not enough to notice, but I love teasing her about it.

"First you are demanding the completion of a new book and now you are complaining about my music?" I hit the volume button on the remote and the music becomes part of the ambient noise around us, fading into the background.

"How do you expect me to get anything done when you interrupt me?" A smile tugs at the edge of my mouth. I work to furrow my brows to show my utter dismay.

She looks up from her coffee, places her hand on her forehead, then dramatically acts as if a significant burden has come upon her, and she can take no more.

"*My* publisher is demanding *my* new book. The fans are beating down the gates! Whatever am I going to do? How can I disappoint my adoring public?" she exclaims in a forced, exasperated tone.

I shake my head and sigh.

"No, technically *my* publisher is demanding it. The one I was just working on when you so rudely interrupted the artistic process —again."

I walk over to the coffee bar and fill a black coffee cup with the words, *Define naughty*. The cream creates spirals and swirls, catching my attention as the two meld together.

"Earth to Devereaux." Samantha waves her hand in front of my face. "If you weren't burning the candle at both ends and in the middle, the *book* would be done and I would be back on tour with those hunky guitar players. It'll be *months* before we can set a tour schedule at this rate, and a girl has needs!" she whines, trying to look disgusted, but the expression doesn't hold.

"If you hadn't kidnapped me the other day, I would be closer to finishing," I shoot back, taking a deep breath and forcing a smile. "I'll get the book done."

My voice sounds tired, but the smile doesn't waver. I'm used to looking like the person everyone expects to see, no matter the situation, and when I can't—I recruit friends. My mind wanders as I settle my body onto the bar stool.

Samantha and I have been friends for what feels like forever. We went to grad school at Boston University. I lived on campus while Samantha commuted daily. It was only by a chance meeting we even met. I was studying business, and she was working on a master's in public relations.

To relieve stress, I wrote edgy erotic fiction. There was something freeing about playing with taboos and living out fantasies on paper with no risk. On a lark, I sent a sample in to a publisher during our last semester under the nom de plum of Sam McKenzie. From there it was a roller coaster like none other. Th publisher accepted it, and within months it had hit the New York Times Bestseller list. Subsequent books followed. Everyone was demanding interviews and book tours. People wanted pictures and autographs, but everyone has secrets, and I wanted to keep mine.

I'll never forget Samantha bemoaning that the success over-whelmed me. Whining about how much fun it would be to do book tours and interviews, with that dreamy look in her eye.

"Fine, why don't you do it then if you think it would be so great?" I shot back angrily during one of our many disagreements about how I should handle the sudden spotlight.

That was the birth of the persona of Sam McKenzie. I wrote the books and Samantha Kingston toured as if she were a one-woman show, living out the books with every rock-and-roll guitar player on nearly every continent.

They splashed Sam McKenzie across every tabloid news rag on the planet. Her exploits damaged everything I'd worked to create. The only suitable answer was to clean the mess, and we created McKenzie Kingston, Ltd. The success of that clean-up had garnered the firm more high-profile business than we could usually handle.

I pull myself out of the memory.

"What time is it?"

Samantha picks up her phone and looks at the screen.

"Eight thirty-two. Why?"

"Shit!" I jump up from the bar stool, knocking it to the ground as my coffee spills all over the counter. "I'm going to be late!"

I scramble over to the small desk in the corner of the apartment and pile up all of my writing papers, then turn and stuff the papers for work into my briefcase.

"What about the book? The deadline is looming." Samantha looks unsympathetic to my current plight.

"It's a new client appointment. He told Melody it was of a rather urgent nature when he called yesterday."

"Reschedule the client. Tell them you're out sick. You're the managing partner, for goodness sake. Hell, I can take on the client." Her voice is hopeful, but her face looks defeated.

"Not that you ever take time off," she mumbles under her breath, "or delegate."

"You are the one who took him on! And I'll get the damn book done," I snap. "Have I ever missed a deadline?"

I glare at her from across the room, grabbing the keys from the island.

"No, ma'am," she answers meekly. "You've never missed a deadline, but I've also never seen you so driven and trying to keep up such an insane pace for no reason."

I take a deep breath and soften my stance.

"I'll be fine. Stop with the guilt-inducing drama. I'm already late."

"Fine! Have a marvelous day at work, sweetie," she calls out to my back as I head down the stairs, her tone dripping in sarcasm.

On my way out of the front door, I nearly collide with our receptionist on the stairs.

"Good morning, Miss Devereaux," she says and steps to the side in an attempt not to be steam-rolled.

"Morning," I say, trying to keep my voice pleasant. "Can you please tell Samantha to chill out this morning?" I toss over my shoulder, continuing to walk to my car.

Melody turns. "I've been trying, but she's worried about Miss McKenzie's upcoming book deadline. She goes on and on about how it can't be missed." She looks nervous, like she's telling me a secret, but she's worried that her boss will get mad because she confided in me.

"Oh good grief, does her guilt and manipulation know no bounds?" I mutter under my breath, sliding into my silver Mercedes.

"Have a great day, Melody," I yell over the roar of the engine, closing the door harder than intended. Hitting the volume, I'm engulfed in the sounds of Lorde proclaiming, "Everybody wants to rule the world."

"Yeah, until they try it," I say to no one.

I glance up in the rearview mirror as the large estate fades away. The headquarters of Kingston & McKenzie seems dwarfed beside it.

I maneuver the car down the long drive. In front of me, the iron gates open, their intricate scrollwork gleaming in the morning sun, the brass work so polished it looks like weather never touches it. Taking a deep breath, I press on the accelerator, leaving my world behind and entering one I find far more challenging to understand.

"MR. GABRIEL, YOUR NINE-THIRTY IS HERE," THE TALL THIN brunette who looks like she's walked off the glossy cover of a fashion magazine announces. Her hair's pulled back in a perfect chignon, not one strand out of place.

She turns back, smiling.

"This way please, Miss Devereaux."

Following her, I get the first glimpse of our newest client's corner office with floor-to-ceiling glass windows overlooking downtown DC. The modern office is furnished with an eclectic mix of antique wooden pieces and modern soft goods. It creates a look that is at once beautiful and jarring. On the far wall, a haphazard arrangement of small individually framed photographs creates the form of a maze at a distance in an odd and breathtaking design.

"Miss Devereaux." His smooth, deep voice pronounces my name like a caress.

I freeze mid-step.

One side of his mouth lifts in a slight smile. "I'm so glad you could grace me with your presence, Cinderella."

He rises from his chair and my gaze travels up to meet those calculating gray eyes which are dancing with the delight of a boy who's been found in the cookie jar and proud of it. I'm suddenly thankful I met him as Alexandra, or this situation would be even more nerve-wracking. Every fiber in my being seems to call for this man. I want his arms to wrap around my waist as his hands fist in my hair...

"Mr. Gabriel, I presume." My voice barely holds firm against the images in my head while my eyes try to return a cold appraising look. I'm doing everything I can to stand my ground, but my hold is tenuous.

"Please take a seat, Miss Devereaux." He motions to the two chairs in front of me.

The room is crackling, once again, with an indescribable tension.

Making his way around the large executive style desk, he walks toward me. The throbbing in my ears works in time with my rising pulse. My eyes fall to those lips, and the quick pace of my breath makes me light-headed.

My mind works to wrap around the fact that this man kissed me three nights ago. His scent, voice and feel have haunted almost every waking and sleeping moment, and now I'm supposed to conduct a civilized business meeting.

"Please, Miss Devereaux." He motions again to the chair, slowly lowering his own body into the one next to it.

Straightening my shoulders, I give a slight nod and take my seat.

"Let's get started, shall we?" He smiles, leaning forward as he grabs a pad of paper and a pen from his desk.

"Yes, Sir," I reply. His head swings in my direction. "First you can tell me why I'm here. Your requirements were very vague, but you specifically asked for me."

My demand for information sets me on more familiar ground.

"I've heard impressive things about your firm's ability to keep certain information out of the public spotlight. I've met your partner in a few unusual circumstances since Saturday evening, and we discussed my basic requirements. She assured me you were a perfect match for me, especially in being able to avoid media attention."

"I see. So you need help keeping your image flawless?"

"Yes and no. My sister announced the other day she was running for another term in Congress, and some of my more private activities could cause her issues if they were to come to light since I've recently moved back to the area." He leans back in his chair and his eyes narrow as he steeples his fingers in front of his mouth. "Your firm advertises lifestyle activities as your specialty, and that the exploits of Sam McKenzie seem to disappear almost as fast as they pop up in the media, it seemed like an excellent match based on some of my personal desires."

Smiling, I think of all the trouble *Miss McKenzie* has gotten into over the last year and shake my head.

"Yes, Miss Kingston and our associates are excellent at social and media relations. We can get as much, or as little, press as desired. In today's instant media environment it can be more challenging to control, but not impossible."

"I'm sure." He nods, looking thoughtful. "How do you handle it?"

"Being in control of all things," I reply.

His eyebrows shoot up, and I'm reminded of my meeting with him yesterday.

"That is very interesting, Miss Devereaux. It seems to be the third time I've heard a similar statement in as many days."

"Being in control is a very important thing in my business, Mr. Gabriel." An edge of a challenge hits my voice. The last thing I need is an outsider connecting dots that shouldn't be connected because I've gotten discombobulated and careless.

"*You will never have a greater or lesser dominion than over yourself... The height of a man's success is gauged by his self-mastery; the depth of his failure by his self-abandonment... He who cannot establish dominion over himself will have no dominion over others* — Leonardo da Vinci," he quips. "I'm sure in your line of work you understand having dominion over others."

I stare at him. My next moves could be some of the most crucial ones I've ever made in my dual life. I calculate each thought.

"My dominion is the reputation of others, the height of our success obvious in our own self-mastery of it."

The amusement of the situation pulls on the edge of his mouth as his gray eyes twinkling with mischievousness.

"That's too bad. Self-abandonment is so much more enjoyable to watch. Just because something yields doesn't make it weak, Miss Devereaux."

Air sticks in my throat, and I feel claustrophobic in the spacious office.

"I'll send over the information we'll need for the proposal and we can write up a contract from there, with all the expectations outlined for both parties."

"Excellent. I know you're a busy man," I blurt out, standing and gathering my briefcase. I paste on a smile and look into his eyes, willing myself to be impassive.

He rises from his chair and steps into my space. His hypnotic gaze holds me like a snake charmer willing the snake to follow his lead. His lips hover just above mine. Internally, I curse when my tongue as it swipes across my bottom lip.

"You've controlled my every waking thought since the gala, Miss Devereaux," he says, his breath raking across my ear. "Maybe it's time to give up a little control."

"Control isn't a commodity I can afford to lose, Mr. Gabriel." My tone hardens as I try to gain the exact thing I said I couldn't afford to lose.

He takes a deep breath of the air between us. "You smell divine."

His lips return to hover just over mine.

"Oh, Miss Devereaux, I can't wait to see you begging me to take control as your body dances under my touch, your lips willing to do anything for another taste."

"Never..." I say.

He threads his hand through my hair, pulling my head back and presenting my lips seconds before his come crashing against them.

The kiss lacks finesse. It is raw, pure, built-up animalistic need and desire. Sensations run through my body and I moan into his mouth.

He takes a sudden step back and my body feels the loss. My legs go weak. I grab the back of the chair to steady myself.

"How's your control now, Miss Devereaux?" His voice sounds

unaffected by what just happened, but the front of his pants tell a different story before he reaches down to correct it.

The ferocity of his gaze both calms me and makes me want to run at the same time.

"I look forward to the finished contract." His voice is firm and full of unspoken meaning.

The turn of phrase makes me struggle to grasp which contract he's talking about—the one he came to the firm for help on or the indecent one his double entendres seemed to demand right before the kiss stole my control.

"Would you like me to get the paperwork pulled together and sent over?" His lips lift in a half smile.

"I'll let you know what we need for your sister's situation," I say, rubbing the seams of my skirt with my fingers, trying to soothe my frayed nerves and shaking the confusion from my head.

I gather my things and turn to walk toward the door.

He places his hand on my lower back, walking with me. "I'll send over your personal contract, Miss Devereaux. Your body won't let you say no," he says, and his whispered words register in my brain.

"Nancy, please send in my next appointment," he calls out to his secretary.

"Have a wonderful day, Miss Devereaux, I look forward to our mutually beneficial and pleasurable arrangements."

I turn to reply, but he's already back in his office. Taking a deep breath, I reprimand myself all the way back to my car.

CHAPTER NINE

I pick up my Bluetooth headphones, place them over my ears, and hit the music button. The first notes of Annie Lennox ring out, soothing my mental irritation when it's interrupted by the sudden ringing of my phone.

Closing my eyes, I take a deep breath. The 'Do It with a Rock Star' ringtone tells me that Samantha is getting ready to demand my time.

"Devereaux," I say flatly into air, the headphones around my neck already connecting to the phone.

"Atlas, darling," Samantha coos from the other side in a chipper voice that tells me she's getting ready to ruin the rest of my day.

"Samantha," I acknowledge coolly.

"How did it go with Mr. Gabriel?" she says, the edge in her voice telling me she's up to mischief.

"Fine. You set me up, and we'll talk about that later. He needs help making sure nothing in his world causes his sister issues. Seems she's running for reelection and his rather colorful pastimes could cause issues if they became known. He's sending over the general information sometime today. This has a tight turnaround so let the assistants know to forward anything that comes in from him to my house," I say with exasperation. "I'm headed back into the office for a couple of hours and then my plans are to take work home."

"This evening all I want is wine, a soaking tub, and a view of DC from my balcony, while enjoying one of the many piano concertos currently cued up on the audio system I rarely get to use lately." My voice holds firm, but I stop walking, waiting for the next disaster she will plant in my already long day.

"So you're coming back into the office? Cool, I'll see you in, say forty-five minutes or so." She cuts the line without further conversation.

I rub my right temple absentmindedly. She knew it was the same guy from the gala and... The image of Kade, Samantha and Mr. Gabriel sitting at the club's bar flashes through my head. I'm going to kill her.

With a click of the key fob, the lights on the Merc blink and the locks release. With a defeated sigh, I slip onto the leather seat and lean back to allow its softness to mold around me.

I press the start button and the engine rumbles to life under my fingertips. The stereo lights up with Avicii's 'Liar, Liar' filling the cabin, and I throw the gearshift into reverse.

Reaching over, I hit the button to release the top. It disengages from its locked position and begins the dance of raising the trunk to stow the roof neatly inside and rolling the windows back. I maneuver the roadster through the twist and turns of the garage as the trunk lid clicks in place at the same time the wheels cross the edge of the garage.

I take a deep breath and press the accelerator down. The car responds as the sheer power of the engine comes alive under my hands. Turning off my phone, I throw it into the passenger seat and turn up the music, the steady beat helping to free me from the feeling of an impending disaster.

Forty-five minutes later, I step into the reception area of McKenzie Kingston's headquarters and brace myself for the chaos that always seems to surround Samantha. Her heart is always in a good place, but it's often her methods that cause me extra work to ensure things remains in place after she's torn a path through the situation.

With a quiet sigh, I try to prepare for whatever new scheme Samantha has concocted now. The office is quiet. Samantha's assistant is out to lunch. There have been no immediate emails for action or urgent voicemails, and I groan thinking about this morning's conversation, hoping this won't be an instant replay.

A few minutes later, Samantha breezes into the office, a wide grin plastered across her perfectly made face, and I know I'm in trouble. I brace myself for whatever is getting ready to come out of her mouth, knowing it will not be pleasant for me, but she will think it's the most amazing thing ever.

"Atlas, I've had the most glorious day," she croons, waltzing to her desk opposite mine. The large wooden surface is cluttered with stacks of papers in well organized chaos.

"Dare I even ask his name?" I say, trying to sound annoyed, but her energy is almost infectious.

Samantha flips through her daily diary and makes a face.

"Oh, darling, you have to do something with that minor book thing. My publisher has called me three times wanting to know when it will be ready. I have to keep pushing them off with promises of tour dates with the other two books."

I roll my eyes at her references, unaffected by them and growing annoyed at the lack of substance to explain why I just endured an hour of DC traffic to sit at yet another desk, getting the same lecture she attempted this morning.

"By the way, if Kade calls, I didn't do it. I swear it's a total misunderstanding."

The last sentence makes my head shoot straight up, and I glare at her from across the room.

"What have you done now, you imp?"

She grins but ignores the question.

"I have a full appointment set this afternoon. I've told your assistant to forward anything from Reece Gabriel to your home address, since you're working there for the rest of the day."

The whirling dervish of activities while she rattles on is like watching chaos in motion.

"Why would you send it to my home address? You know work is work and I keep things separate."

"Relax. It's by courier and you use your cell phone for business, with a forward from the office. You worry too much," she says in a flippant tone.

"Speaking of Mr. Gabriel, you knew he was the man from the gala and still you set the appointment?" I call to the back of her head.

Her stuttered steps tell me everything I need to know, but she doesn't stop.

"If you need me, I'll be on my cell," she yells over her shoulder as she heads out the door. "Live in the moment, Atlas!"

The door shuts with a resounding bang to punctuate her dramatic exit.

CHAPTER TEN

The day wears on into the early evening hours. A soft knock pulls me from my deep concentration, and I look up to see my personal assistant standing in the doorway.

She's young, ambitious and beautiful, but her demeanor gives her an air of naïveté. I smile as I remember when the world still allowed me to be so soft, open, and almost vulnerable.

"I'm about to head out, Ms. Devereaux. Is there anything else you need?" she asks, her face begging me to say no.

"No." I shake my head. "Have a good evening, Melody."

"Thank you." She nods and turns on her heels.

I look down at the clock on my computer. It reads six o'clock and I exhale. So much for heading out of work early and working from home.

The muscles in my shoulders are screaming as usual from the tension bunched in them. I lean back in my chair and debate my next move, but piles of paperwork still beckon my attention.

My cell phone vibrates insistently on my desk, and I look down to see who is calling me at this hour.

I smile slightly at the number. It's been forwarded from my other *job*. Reaching down, I click accept, suddenly feeling restless.

"Speak," I say into the phone.

"Good evening, Ma'am." The confident voice on the other end of the call pauses, waiting for my acknowledgment.

"And a good evening to you," I say. My voice is clipped and arrogant, the Southern drawl giving it a slight aggressively sweet tone. My body relaxes as I allow the new persona to weave its way through my veins.

"I was wondering if I could see you this evening, Ma'am. This week has been very stressful." The male voice continues, "If it pleases you, of course, Ma'am."

I suppress a laugh at the intentional gaff.

"Is that so, boy?"

"Yes, Ma'am, very much." His voice is the picture of control, with only the hint of desperation under the surface. I wouldn't have noticed if we hadn't done this so many times before.

"You are being very presumptuous in thinking my calendar could have even the remotest possibility of a moment to spend on you when you call me so late." My tone sounds annoyed and I wait for his next move. His reaction will tell me all that I need to know.

"Yes, Ma'am, I understand, Ma'am. I am so sorry for calling late. Work hasn't allowed me many moments to breathe recently," he says, sounding defeated.

"Is that so? Your work has you so stacked that you can't spare the slightest moment to call me, but you believe me to be so open as to accept you at a moment's notice." I push him.

The dance is just beginning. I know his cock is already hard and the stress begins to fall out of his body from just this phone call.

"What tribute are you prepared to offer for your insolence?"

"Triple the normal tribute, Ma'am, and I've bought you a gift from my last trip to Paris."

Hope returns to his voice.

I allow the silence to stretch long and listen to his breathing. It increases in anticipation, unknowing which way I will decide.

As the seconds tick by, I think over my day and the plans for the evening. What plans? I laugh to myself. Tonight I had no bookings and would only continue to work here, for some insane reason, trying to beat the ghost of *never being enough*, knowing it will always just be out of reach.

'To take command, one must first create the illusion that command is already yours.' The Denise Domning quote flows through my thoughts and I smile.

Finally, I allow my breath to be audible on the phone.

"You will be ready and waiting for me upon my arrival at seven-thirty pm. I've had a long day and my tolerance is low."

"Yes, Ma'am. Thank you so very much for accommodating me this evening." His breath comes out in a whoosh.

"Don't make me regret this, boy," I say, my tone brokering no argument.

"I will see you at seven-thirty this evening, Ma'am. Thank you."

I click off the phone and stare at the ceiling.

Power... the simple act of taking authority and having someone else believe they owe it to you. Not all power is cruel and ruthless, even if sometimes it looks that way on the surface. Actions, reactions, and the results are not always what you think you see.

The thought strikes a cognitive dissonance. An image of gray piercing eyes comes unbidden as my finger rubs my lips in an unconscious reminder. I pick up the phone and hit speed dial and refocus my errant thoughts.

The phone rings twice before the call connects.

"Yes, Ma'am. How can I assist you this evening?" a pleasant voice on the other end answers.

"Good evening. I have a client coming in at seven-thirty. Please have my room ready," I say with a smile as if my request were as easy as making hotel reservations.

"Of course, Ma'am. Anything in particular you will need for this evening?" The keyboard clicks as she inputs my requested information.

"File two seven-nine. You should find everything you need in the records," I reply. My mind works over a plan while I wait for the information to be confirmed.

"Yes, Ma'am. We have everything on file. I look forward to seeing you soon."

"Thank you for all of your assistance."

"Glad to be of service, Ma'am," the voice replies, and the phones clicks off.

I look down at the clock—six thirty-two pm. There is less than an hour before the appointment.

After tidying up my desk, I walk to the back of the office. Each step allows the internal mask to shift and change, altering between my corporate image and my much less conservative one. The move is a physical manifestation in mindset from vying for power to owning power with completion. It should relax me, but it doesn't. I've worked for the illusion of power on all fronts for most of my life. Power is always an illusion.

Now there's a lesson I wish I would learn at someone else's hand. The unwanted thought hijacks my mind and I stop mid-stride.

Taking a deep breath, I think of the man who will kneel in front of me. Ready to obey my every whim. Once my mind settles, I take the next step, moving my thoughts in a more desired direction.

I watch the second hand tick by, letting the anticipation build. My fingers skim the books with my manicured nails scraping against the binds until it lands on *The Art of War*. I nod to it in recognition, like an old friend who has helped you out of the deepest depths, as my finger hooks into the top of the book. I pull it toward me and take a breath. With each step into the dim tunnel, I let my mind shift from Atlas to Alexandra and prepare for tonight's entertainment.

MORE THAN AN HOUR LATER, I PUSH OPEN THE DOOR TO THE private play room, revealing a man in a well-tailored suit kneeling in the middle of the floor. A small silver tray balances in his hands. On it sits a small white card and a wine glass, a third full of a deep red liquid.

Picking up the card, I walk over and swipe it across the top of the room's touch-screen. The room automatically adjusts the settings. Around the room the lights lower and music plays in the background. Beside me, the door to the studio lock clicks into place as the status to the security room lists the name of the client, length, and type of session.

Once everything settles into place, I step over to the man and remove the glass from the tray. With practiced controlled movements, I bring the glass to my nose, inhale its bouquet, and take a long sip. The red liquid caresses my tongue as the aromas and flavors seem to hover right on my palate with a sweet, perfumed intensity. I savor the wine as I sashay over to the large throne-like chair dominating one end of the room.

The baroque chair's jewel-encrusted sapphire velvet fabric calls to me. My hand glides across the hand-carved wood. Its size gives a sense of grandeur to the room, and I feel a surge of inner power.

I can feel his eyes gazing on my backside. The anticipation is palpable.

"Eyes down, boy. You know the rules," I say without turning around.

"Yes, Domina. Please forgive my insolence. I hope you are enjoying the Domaine de la Romanee-Conti La Tache two thousand ten, my Lady," he comments in a quiet voice.

I watch his eyes fall when I turn to sit. His arms shake as he works to hold the tray level.

His call has cost him, but then again, that's why he waited to the last minute to set up this appointment. The outcome for him was positive, no matter how it went.

If I had rejected him, then he would have smiled all the way home. When I accepted the appointment, he knew that it would relieve the physical manifestation of his internal burdens. Either way, it was a win/win for him and a good exchange for the club.

"It is exquisite," I reply without emotion, again tipping the glass back to allow another small sip of the pinot noir to slip along my lips, watching him over the rim. "Calling me at the last minute is rude."

I lower the glass, my eyes hardening as I focus on his struggling arms.

"Yes, Ma'am. My deepest apologies, Ma'am. My sincerest appreciation to you for making your valuable time available for someone like me." His voice is robust; even in this position there is no weakness in it.

He looks up and catches my hard gaze. His body goes rigid, and he doesn't take his eyes off mine. I stand up, smiling, swirling the wine in my glass. Closing my eyes, I savor one more sip and walk over to put the wineglass on the trembling tray.

I lean over and whisper against his ear, "Don't you dare drop that glass and spill red wine on my white carpet."

His body quivers. A drop of sweat beads on his brow. Focused concentration etches his face, willing the muscles in his arms not to fail.

"The wine is exquisite. Not only would it be a stain, but what a waste of something so spectacular because you could no longer hold the tray steady." My voice slides silkily through the air with a haughty undertone, each word placed carefully into his mind.

"Yes, Ma'am. That would be a tragedy on all fronts."

"I'm sure your legs are suffering. As the circulation is restricted by your kneeling position," I say, circling his body, my hand brushing against the jacket that's pulled taut across his shoulders. "The muscles are aching. I love watching you push yourself to the limit for me. All of those hours at the gym, pushing your muscles to failure, seem to pay off."

I step back toward my chair and bend over, running my hand up the outside of my boot. Behind me, the whoosh of air escaping from his lungs is audible.

When I turn around to sit, the muscles in his arms begin to fail.

"Go place the tray on the sideboard," I say, my tone flat.

In front of me, he struggles to gain control over his body, willing his arms to give him a little more before they fail. He rises to his feet, each movement planned to allow for the circulation to return before taking his first step. He knows that if he stumbles, there will be no way to catch the glass before it crashes to the floor. I allow no hands on top of the silver salver.

"Tonight your punishment for the disrespect of calling me at such a late hour, and thus telling me my time isn't worth enough to ensure advance notice, will be to stand while I tell you all the things we could have been doing, if I had your respect." The sweet Southern tone sits in opposition to the words. They are without feeling, emotion, or care as they hang in the air.

His steps falter and his head whips toward me, but in the same moment he realizes that the sudden action has imbalanced his tray. He adjusts, the wine glass settling at the last second. His breathing is rapid, pushing his shoulders, which strains the fabric of the jacket, while he works to get himself back under control.

My eyes turn hard, my lips pulling into a straight line. It has nothing to do with how I feel, but it is the expected reaction in this situation, and I know the part I play.

Edmund places the tray on the white sideboard table that's been created in the same style as the chair from which I watch each movement. Once the tray is in its proper position, he adjusts it multiple times, turning it this way or that, before he pivots and steps into a full attention position. His eyes look straight ahead and every muscle tenses in anticipation for my next command.

He'll be waiting long moments for it. I watch his face, his mind churning in anticipation as his muscles scream for him to move.

This version of the game is so often underrated, yet it is one I enjoy the most as I am watching the mind do all the work for me. His thoughts will oscillate between the fear of my next word and the love of control he gives me.

I sit, watching his body twitch from the tension. A smile turns the corner of my mouth upward. With a flick of my wrist, I send a silent command across the room.

His eyes light up and in milliseconds he moves, turning with precision on his heels, filling the wineglass back to its appropriate level and moving at full attention across the room toward me. He holds the glass across the flat of his hand, the edge of his thumb touching it just enough to balance it in its travels towards me. Each movement requires attention and precision to create the flowing artistry before me.

"I'm glad to see you were paying attention, boy. The tray would have been rather inconvenient had you allowed your mind to wander from your sole focus."

Reaching out, I take hold of the wineglass proffered. As soon as he's fulfilled the task, he returns to full attention.

My eyes gaze across his body. He's beautiful in the well-cut tailored suit. It is something which aligns with his position as a CEO for his Fortune 500 company. It amuses me when I receive his call. This is a place where he celebrates impressive victories and faces the agony of defeat. After most of our sessions, there's a news story about his company, both positive and negative, the next day. I always know he needs these moments to destress from the rigors of constant heavy decisions and impossible deadlines, the weight of which keeps him up at night.

This is his sheltered moment. There are no thoughts for him to think here, except for the rampant anticipation of the most subtle movement of my body, giving him the next task. No big gestures or harsh words. No, these are elegant moments, a game of cat and mouse. He tries to focus on the interminable stretches of silence while I use his body against him, pushing his mind to observe the smallest details.

For the next hour he stands, squats, and kneels in front of me.

Each movement is based solely on the movement of my finger, the positioning of my hands, or the pattern of my breath. It's been a challenge to keep my movements subtle and yet noticeable. The game has kept us both on our toes.

"Come here, boy," I whisper across the quietness of the room.

He lowers himself to all fours and crawls toward my chair. When he arrives, he lets his lips hover just above my crossed ankles. His breath skims across my skin. He works to maintain control.

"Not tonight." My tone brokers no argument. "You will afford me the respect I have earned, or I will not allow you the moment you desire."

"Yes, Domina." A defeated breath falls from his mouth. Edmund rocks back on his heels and lowers his forehead to the ground.

I look at him for a long minute, sighing to myself. Rising from my chair, I walk over to the control pad and flip settings to end the session. The soft click of the lock from the automated system, is the only stark sound in the room. I place the white card on the silver tray and turn to exit through the door to leave Edmund kneeling in front of my chair.

"Domina, please wait a moment. I beg that you will give one such as me but a moment more of your precious time." His voice cuts through the stillness.

I turn to see him kneeling up, looking at me.

"Go ahead, boy. You have already interrupted my movements, but make it quick. I have no patience for further insolence this evening."

"Yes, Ma'am."

His breath catches as a mix of emotions crosses his face.

"For the past few years I have served you faithfully. In that time, I have shared you with the world, but I have been so envious of that world, wanting you more to myself. I want to give you everything you desire, to never have you lift a finger. I can give you the biggest house you've ever dreamed of living, the finest clothes and the most glorious shoes." The dreamy look in his eyes confirms that it was not only my feet he craved.

"Ma'am, you will want for nothing. I will be there to feel your lash at night, to ensure you have the most perfect world. You can punish me in whatever way you desire."

He pauses.

Reaching into his suit pocket, he pulls out a large solitary diamond. The brilliant cut shines in the dim light. In the sunlight, it must look like it's on fire.

"Alexandra, will you please marry me?"

I stare at him dumbfounded. The man before me controls a multi-national corporation, is known to be a hard-as-nails negotiator, and he's proposing to his Professional Dominant. This day cannot be happening.

"Edmund, I am flattered. Truly," I start, watching his face and edging toward the panic button just in case.

He's been my client for years. In that time he's been a gentleman in every conceivable way, but emotions after a scene are edgy. "You are one of the sweetest people I have the privilege to know, but I'm not good in a 'caged' situation. No matter the gild on the cage, you are asking me to give up my life to be your Mistress."

I watch the wheel in his head spin.

"What a glorious life we'll have too. You can spend all day thinking up the most glorious tortures and punishments for me. When I am naughty, you can set me straight. Without these other distractions, it will be even better than it already is for us."

Smiling, I turn to the keypad and type in a secondary distress code. The lights dim and the music rises.

"That sounds very nice for the right Mistress," I say, turning to find him standing only a couple of feet away.

"Alexandra, please don't tell me no. You are the most perfect Mistress any man could be lucky enough to have, and I want you all to myself. I want to be that lucky man you always dominate."

The loud knock on the door draws both of our attentions at once. Kade rushes in and looks straight at me.

"Alexandra, I'm so sorry to bother you, but we have a 1D 10 T situation." His firm voice confirms the graveness of his assessment.

"Edmund, I'm so sorry, I have to go. My answer has to be no. I hope you find that special person. She will be a very lucky Mistress."

I smile and turn to follow Kade out of the door.

CHAPTER ELEVEN

I sink into the steaming water as my fingers glide along the edges of the large soaking tub, giving me enough purchase to stay above the surface. Mounds of bubbles fill every area as I settle into a comfortable position and exhale.

My muscles try to relax, and I groan as the tension races out of my shoulders. I watch the large hills of bubbles dance through the air when my breath pushes against them. The melodic sounds of The Piano Guys play, *The Cello Song* creating the comfortable background. I try to let the strange craziness of the day float away.

Closing my eyes, I allow myself to enjoy the long, lingering moments of a well-deserved soak. The wineglass and my current book, perched on the side of the tub, beg for my attention, but my arms refuse to work their way out of the sudden weight of the water.

I turn the hot water tap with my toes to keep the ideal temperature as I sit up and scrub the loofah across my skin. Picking up the wineglass, I let the mellow liquid engulf my tongue, and I breathe in the heady perfume.

The mounds of bubbles become a fading memory of white foam on the surface of the water as I wash my hair.

Fingers well pruned and muscles far more relaxed, I step from the bath, watching the water spin down the drain, willing it to take away the day with it. I turn and slip into my oversized robe, then wind a towel around my damp hair.

I glance up at the mirror and shake my head. It still looks like the weight of the world is firmly planted on my shoulders. Thoughts of giving up everything and lying on a beach in the middle of nowhere flit across my mind, followed by images of all of my current responsibilities. I nod to myself in resignation and turn to step out of the bathroom.

"James," I call out to the house.

"Yes, Ma'am. How can I be of service?" the computerized voice asks from the speakers.

"Schedule a massage at the club tomorrow night."

"Done," he replies promptly.

"Lights—evening."

The lights throughout the penthouse dim to eighty percent of their normal levels, other areas turn off, and the shades on the large bank of windows close as I make my way to bed.

"You have an incoming text message," James informs me.

"Read message."

"Message from unknown sender: There is a carrier at your door with my proposal. You have forty-eight hours to reply."

Before the reply is complete, there are three sharp raps against the front door making me jump in shock and surprise.

"I have a package for Miss Devereaux." A deep male voice carries through the thick steel door.

I look down in frustration, realizing I am clothed only in a robe with a towel wound around my head. Avoiding the hallway mirror, I pad over to the front door, looking through the peephole to see a courier waiting with a large envelope.

Unlocking the front door, I meet the young man's gaze head on.

"Um, Miss Devereaux?" he stammers.

"Yes." I try to sound polite, but all I want is for him to leave so this day can end.

"This package is for you. Could you please sign here?" He holds out the electronic form and stylus, balancing it across the palm of his hand.

I snatch the stylus from his fingers and scan the signature page. Clenching the pen, so as not to betray my shaking hand, I scribble my name across the LED screen, then push it back toward him.

"Have a wonderful night, miss." Nodding, he hands me the package, then turns to leave.

I stand in the doorway for a moment, amused at the interaction before I realize my front door is wide open, it is late, and I am standing in a robe. Turning, I force the door closed too hard, and the slam reverberates around the foyer, making me wince.

"Ma'am, slamming the door is neither productive to your mood nor is it good for my structure."

I roll my eyes at the ceiling and rip open the envelope. I stare at the words running across the top: 'D/S Contract.'

I take the paper no further out of the envelope than the heading.

"You have an incoming text message, ma'am."

"Read message," I say, staring at the papers in my hand and making my way back toward my bedroom.

"Message from unknown sender: Your decision will change your life. I hope you are prepared for the consequences. Sleep well."

I shake my head at the audacity of the message playing throughout the penthouse.

"Many men have tried and failed, and you'll be no different. *Show no weakness, show no vulnerability.*" I mutter the motto my dad has pounded into my head since I was small.

"What is it with indecent proposals today!" I scream to the air.

"I'm sorry, Ma'am, but I do not understand indecent proposals."

"Neither do I, James, neither do I."

I sigh. Maybe a good night's sleep will find me. At least I can depend on James for being reliable and always doing what I ask of him the first time, every time.

I smile to myself, comforted by the thought.

"Goodnight, James."

"Goodnight, ma'am," the computer replies as the lights slowly dim and fade to darkness in my walk toward bed.

CHAPTER TWELVE

After a full morning of client meetings and contract negotiations, my mind is numb from constantly trying to figure out how to help people who have done stupid things. The pile of paperwork on my desk screams that I still have mountains of work to do. People are stupid. Well, I guess they aren't stupid, just more apt to do stupid things to *live on the edge*—a concept I try to understand but come up short each time.

I stare at my computer, willing for the things in front of me to fall in line. Looking up at the clock on my computer, I note it is only three thirty-seven in the afternoon. My eyes are blurry from my deep concentration. I'm spent. At this rate, I'll never make my deadline. There are too many chaotic emotions tumbling through my mind, and none of them are helping me focus.

Standing up, I turn and put papers into my briefcase, then head for the front door, stopping by Melody's desk.

"I'm about to head out, Melody. Is there anything else you need before I go?" I say, my face begging her to say no.

"Um, Miss Devereaux, you have a five o'clock appointment with Mr. Gabriel," she says, watching my face with a wary expression.

"Cancel it and reschedule it for tomorrow," I say, trying to sound pleasant. It's not her fault my day is a challenge. "If he can't wait, put him with Samantha. I know he has a tight turnaround on a couple of things, but she can handle him." I nod and turn toward the door.

The last couple of times we were together were full of electric tension. He is the last distraction I need right now.

"Yes, ma'am." She nods as she dials the number.

"Mr. Gabriel." She starts full of authority but as each word falls from her mouth, I can hear her backing up from the man on the other end. "I apologize but Miss Devereaux... Yes, Sir, I realize your time is important... I can place you with another... Then I need to reschedule your... Um, yes, Sir, but... Yes, Sir... I understand, Sir. First thing on her schedule, Sir..."

Part of me wants to be entertained by the number of *Sirs* at the end of the conversation, knowing I will have to deal with an unreasonable man tomorrow.

We don't always get what we want, when we want it, Mr. Gabriel, I think to myself, trying to ignore the conversation as her voice grows fainter with each step.

Making my way outside, I see Steven already holding open the driver's side door. I nod and smile.

I grow concerned as I think about the one-sided conversation with Mr. Gabriel. Melody never backs down to a client, and reschedules often happen but rarely cause an issue. I shake my head, ignoring the nagging feeling her conversation has created in my stomach.

WALKING BAREFOOT THROUGH THE PENTHOUSE, I TRY TO JUMP start my mind from the real world to the fantasy one sitting on my writing desk.

How am I ever going to reconcile two characters with such extreme backgrounds? Can they fall in love and live happily ever after? If only the real world would work out so nicely, I scoff.

"Maybe he tells her he wants her, she gives in, they have great kinky sex and ride off into the sunset." I chuckle at my musing. I look across the counter of the kitchen in search of the corkscrew, when my gaze lands on the paperwork from Mr. Gabriel. I have to admire his boldness for going after what he thinks he wants, but I'm shocked that he thinks I'd jump right into such an arrangement.

"Ma'am." James interrupts me from my reverie. "Incoming call from Mr. Kinkaid."

"Accept," I call out. "Afternoon, Kade. Is this a social call or are you crashing my afternoon with business?"

"Hello to you too." The smile in his voice is obvious. "Consider this a mixed call. I wanted to see how you were doing after the 1 D 10 T incident."

I pause for a moment, the smile falls from my face, and I attempt to even out my tone before answering.

"I'm fine. It was just an unexpected shock after a long day."

"Everything okay, Atlas?" he asks, his voice laced with concern.

"Yes it is, Thomas." I cringe when I hear his first name slip across my lips, my subconscious mind overriding my outward desire to keep the turmoil to myself.

Kade hates it when anyone calls him by his first name.

I met Thomas Kinkaid when I was still in graduate school. Samantha and I were doing non-profit work with the local returning veterans group. Growing up, everyone picked on him in Catholic school when he'd played the opposite side of an argument, and called him a doubting Thomas. His first name was a source of irritation, and a signal when something was off.

"I'll be over in twenty minutes." His firm voice tells me he's in no mood to argue.

"Kade, I'm fine... really. It just slipped. If everyone keeps interrupting me, I will never get this—"

The line goes dead before I can complete the sentence.

I sit back down at my desk and stare at my computer, willing my fingers to type something in a vain attempt to stop the cursor from continuing to eat the words off the page. Not even the aggressive writing program meant to motivate me to continuously write is helping me focus on the work at hand. The entire thing adds to my frustration, and I watch in numb resignation as the page once again goes blank.

"Good afternoon, Atlas." Kade leans on the door frame, his eyes watching my every move.

I jump at the sound of my name. James has failed to alert me to Kade's presence. He must have overridden the program. As my chief security officer, and often personal bodyguard, Kade has some of the most intimate access into my life. I keep little from him, except my emotions, but I keep them from everyone, and besides, he doesn't need those to protect me from outside threats.

Looking up, I paste on a smile.

"Afternoon. You didn't have to drive all the way over here, you know."

"Have to? No, but I thought it was important to do so."

The intensity of his gaze unnerves me. I stand up to get an equal footing, but at six foot two inches, he's still taller than I am when I'm barefoot, a fact I forget because I'm most often in tall heels.

"So is this a social call?" I walk toward him. "I was just about to get something to drink, would you like anything?"

He moves to the side, letting me pass, then follows me back toward the kitchen.

"How are things at the club?" I ask nonchalantly.

Business conversations are always so much easier than dealing with personal matters, and if I can ease the concern that is rolling off him in waves, then I'll have less need for my life to intrude on his.

"There have been a few security violations, more than the run-of-the-mill stuff, but nothing my team can't handle." While the answer is straightforward, the edge in his voice sends a shiver down my spine.

"Keep me apprised if they become too serious, and we'll figure out how to address them in a more stringent way."

"The more concerning fact is the incident we had after your session with Edmund."

I pause, my fingers fumbling with the wineglass. Twice before I've had a client proposal, and the rejection set off a nasty chain of events. It's not unusual for a paying submissive to get wrapped up about the relationship they have with their Pro-Dominant. Lines get blurry in their head about how far things can go.

The club was established and designed to keep those situations safer. Cameras, the payment systems, the private rooms all allow for the creation of a fantastic fantasy environment in a secure location, but the work is emotionally and physically taxing. To always be on with perfection, to ensure we meet their desires without crossing the line. Eventually, it becomes too much.

So I opened the club to the alternative lifestyle communities to give them a protected, fun place to live out their fantasies in luxurious surroundings. The handful of clients I continue to see have been with me a long time, and I have become comfortable, if not slightly complacent, in handling them.

"Edmund just got overzealous, Kade." I say with a sigh. "He's been under more pressure, the board of his company has been pushing him harder because of the economy... the faltering price in the market and such."

"You can't just blow this off, Atlas," Kade warns. "We need to monitor him over the next few days."

"Don't harass the clientele, Kade," I say, ignoring his eyes.

"I'm just trying to be prepared. You don't need another incident; besides, it would affect the members this time."

"True," I reply with a nod.

"How are you doing?"

"Eh, I'm fine. Stressed, but it's to be expected based on the schedule I've been keeping as of late," I mumble, turning to pour white wine into my glass. "Would you like some?"

"No. I'm on duty tonight, and the rope group is having a party," he says, walking up to the long bar and planting himself on a stool.

"Wonderful group. Should be a quiet night, all things considered."

"Yes."

A lengthy silence stretches between us. I ignore his gaze and act like I'm focused on sipping my wine and caught up in the thoughts in my head. In reality, Kade was right. The turn of events with Edmund was startling and unnerving. His monetary and political power is immense, and while he might be submissive in a session, there is nothing submissive about the iron fist with which he runs his company. He is a man who's rarely told *no*.

"I want extra security on you for the next couple of months. There's no reason to unnecessarily risk your safety." Kade's voice breaks the silence.

"No. I don't need extra security, Kade. For goodness sake, I don't need the security I've got now. *Alexandra's* driver is security, the doorman downstairs is part of my security team, not to mention the valet at the club. The only time I don't have *security* is when I'm me, running errands for the PR firm. Even here, James the computer provides a certain level. I'm covered in it."

"Don't press me on this one, Atlas. You hired me to keep you safe, but outside of that, I take your safety very personally. I've seen what happens when it all blows apart, and I never want to see you like that again."

"I'm not her." My eyes harden and I turn toward him. "I'm not the young doe-eyed girl who thought it was all just a simple game, neither is it some dark horrible world. That was a long time ago. The world has changed. *I* have changed. The club is beautiful, there are cameras everywhere, and there's not a safer place anyone could be. Just drop it, Kade. There's nothing to worry about on this one."

At the beginning of my Pro-Dominant career there were a few harsh situations. I'd missed two safe calls when Kade was my submissive. Both times he came to my rescue. He put one in the hospital when he found the guy looming over me with a knife at my throat, telling me how all dominant women just wanted a man to force her to submit. Another time, he found me only moments from being raped. A man had turned on me when I had rejected his bid to be my live-in submissive. The moment had gone from sweet to sinister in seconds. I shake my head to clear the memories.

"This discussion isn't over, Atlas," he growls, causing me to take a slight step back and mentally change tactics.

"How well do you know Reece Gabriel?"

"Reece and I were in the Rangers together. Why?" His face lightens up with a curious sideways smile.

"Mr. Gabriel has asked us to take on a PR case for him to ensure that his *chosen proclivities* don't become public knowledge, since his sister is running for Congress." I try to keep my face neutral, but the unbidden images of his masked kiss make me blush along with an unidentified feeling.

"That's all well and good. What are you not telling me?"

"He came by the other day to see *Alexandra*. It seems you talk about her quite a bit." I quirk my eyebrow to stress the unspoken question.

"We were talking about the club. You know I have nothing but outstanding things to say about you—well, outside the fact you are a controlling, stubborn woman who would look good... Anyway, I said nothing but good things, I assure you. Besides, I tried to tell you he was coming by at lunch the other day."

A devious smile dances in his eyes, and his lips turn up on one side.

"I'd look good how, boy?" My persona's Southern drawl fills the air.

Kade's eyes light up like huge saucers, and I smile.

"We all have our secrets, my dear boy, and I know yours as much as you know mine."

"Reece already knows I like to submit to beautiful women, so you can't hold that one over me. But the way you say boy..." The smile makes his blue eyes dance, then cloud. "I miss the way we used to connect when we were in session. The way I always felt cleansed and forgiven afterwards. The weight of the world lifting from my shoulders."

"Me too, but you know it's better this way. Simpler. It's better not to mix business and pleasure. I need you to be objective, and I worry you'd be anything but if we still had sessions." I finish the last bit of my wine. "Now, if there's nothing else for you to worry on, I need to get back to writing."

"Atlas, when it comes to you I'm rarely objective. I still want to up your security detail," he says firmly, rising from his seat.

"No, Kade," I say, standing my ground. "The thing about being the boss is that I get to make the ultimate decisions and pay for them if I get it wrong."

"For now." He walks over, looking down into my eyes, bracing his finger under my chin, raising my face until I'm looking into his intense blue eyes. "If anything changes, you are to let me know. Am I clear, Miss Devereaux?"

"You are, Mr. Kinkaid. Now you need to get back to my club and make sure the rope group is safe tonight. I have story characters to get back to before their yammering drives my brain over the edge."

I force a smile so he won't worry about my own concerns of the situation.

"You know that makes you sound..." His hand gestures that I might be off a bit.

"Get out before I have my security team throw you out," I kid.

Kade chuckles. "Have a good night Atlas."

Leaning down, he plants a kiss on each cheek before he saunters out of the door.

The front door clicks closed. My eyes drag across the counter. The large envelope catches my attention. I exhale, pulling the pages out as I slide my eyes across the contract. I refill my wineglass and read it.

D/s CONTRACT

The Code:

1) The Dominant may not harm the submissive, or, through inaction, allow the submissive to come to harm.

2) The submissive may not harm the Dominant, or, through inaction, allow the Dominant to come to harm.

3) The submissive must obey the orders given to her by Dominant, except where such orders would conflict with number 1. It is the desire of the Dominant that obedience will come from submission rather than rule.

4) The Dominant must protect his own existence. In doing so he ensures no undo stress on his submissive partner's life.

5) The submissive must protect her own existence.

The Rules:

Self-Care: The submissive will ensure that she maintains a full level of health at all times.

Sleep: The correct amount of sleep necessary to create health will be observed by the submissive at all times. When she is alone, she will maintain approximately 5-7 hours but no more than 9 hours of sleep per day/night. The dominant will prescribe the amount of sleep when they are together in an overnight situation.

Clothing: The submissive will approve all clothing choices through the Dominant. When so desired by the Dominant, the submissive will wear the clothes prescribed by the Dominant for his pleasure.

Diet/Exercise: Proper physical health will be maintained through proper diet and daily exercises. Both shall be logged. The submissive is accountable for missed times or improper food choices.

Personal Safety: The submissive will not put herself in any situation which may cause unnecessary conflict or danger.

Personal Qualities: The submissive will not enter any scene-based relationships with another person, unless so ordered by the

Dominant. The submissive will ensure her conduct is above reproach and will not cause harm to her own character or that of the Dominant.

Obedience: Orders and instructions are to be immediately obeyed, without hesitation. Failure to comply will result in discipline or punishment.

Discipline & Punishments:

The submissive will ensure that she follows the code and rules at all times.

The Dominant will ensure that all instruction is understood, and the rules are consistently observed. He will ensure behavior is controlled through the use of disciplinary training to create a measure of control to enforce compliance and order.

These measures will help the submissive learn to obey rules or accept authority, thus producing a satisfying situation to both the Dominant and submissive through the improvement of moral, physical or mental status.

Consent through this agreement gives permission to use the authority given to the Dominant to punish, correct, train, or enforce obedience.

The submissive needs the discipline and control in her life to obey - she needs to know the rules, learn the behavior, and accept that there will be consequences if she is disobedient.

These consequences will be based solely on the effectiveness for the submissive.

'THIS IS YOUR LAST CHANCE. AFTER THIS, THERE IS NO TURNING back. You take the blue pill - the story ends, you wake up in your bed and believe whatever you want to believe. You take the red pill - you stay in Wonderland and I show you how deep the rabbit-hole goes.' (The Matrix is such an interesting movie, don't you think?)

Blue Pill: Text my number with 'Blue Pill'

Red Pill: Text my number with 'Red Pill'

If you are reading this, and your eyes are rolling, it means you know exactly what this contract implies and aren't willing to 'jump' into such things without thinking. Based on my belief in what I've seen, I believe this to be true and will almost be disappointed if I've received a text from you at this point.

However, make no mistake, it is the dynamic of which I prefer in my relationships. I look forward to having dinner with you soon, Miss Devereaux. Please have your personal assistant set up a time if you would like to continue our little game. I look forward to seeing you under my control. ~ RG

CHAPTER THIRTEEN

I continue to clean the counter where I've spat out wine, twice, while reading the contract. Once I've completed it, I'm not sure if I want to laugh, smack the man, or text him with *Blue Pill* for his presumptions.

Why in the world would he believe that I'd know anything about the D/s lifestyle? Nothing in my entire personal world says anything to point him in that direction, and not one thing points to any desire to be submissive.

My thoughts drift to Reece Gabriel and the three times I've encountered him. There is no doubt there's a powerful connection between us — almost hypnotic. In those seconds I felt both safe and nervous; not the kind that causes fear, more like the nervousness when you know you are stepping into a different level of the world. Safe, but pushed. Grounded, yet flying. A place of comfortable oxymorons taking me out of my comfort zone.

The last time I showed interest in the concept of a submissive relationship was back in grad school. Samantha thought it would give my erotic writing a better perspective and bring the characters to life on the page. I secretly adored those moments for the first few months, though I openly railed against them. I never could wrap my mind around the difference between true strength and weakness, but those moments took me away from the cares of the world.

Samantha introduced me to Dominick, a Dominant who took me through several months of training as a submissive. When he offered me more, I'd signed a contract far more invasive than this one, and thus began a five-year path which gave me the skills I use today as a Dominant.

I adored Dominick. Every order or command I obeyed with absolution, but I could never submit to him. There was never a reason to give in to the emotions. There were skills to learn and knowledge to gain. My service and unwavering obedience was the payment.

Personal safety, growth, and security were paramount to him. His authority in my life was absolute, guiding me both personally and professionally. It was an amazing experience in the grand scheme of things, even when it dipped into the darkest realms of life.

He gave me a secure hold when the storm of success raged around me, but the whole experience left a seed of craving I've never understood nor nurtured.

I read back through the contract again, this time relaxing, realizing that if such a contract were in place, I'd be breaking at least half the rules. Not getting enough sleep, not eating well, and I haven't seen the topside of my treadmill for at least a month, not to mention my back is a mess of tension. At least I've scheduled an appointment for a massage soon. I mentally pat myself on the back. The one line that catches me is personal safety. Kade's words run through my head, and I work hard to shake them away.

A seed long ago abandoned suddenly flairs to life. The desire to submit rather than just obey. Few understood the difference. Even my clients rarely submitted. There were exceptions who would do anything for me because of their respect and love for me, but most of them simply enjoy the moments of reacting to a command. Pretending to feel as if they had little choice to reject or oppose my authority. If they'd only experienced it for real, they'd see it in a different light.

Even then I wondered what it would be like to want to follow. To have a place where I knew the other person had me so completely I could just let go and yield as their power washed over me. To live a moment where being on my knees, yielding, wasn't seen as a weakness but rather a place of respect and adoration.

Dark thoughts rumble into the moment. Trust no one, do it all on your own. Only then is it success.

I sigh. The seed of desire recedes into the dark recesses once again. Taking a sip of wine, I put the amusing D/s contract aside and flip through the rest of the pages. Walking back through the penthouse, I once again abandon my characters and sit down to review the file with the required information for the PR firm to work on the setup to protect his sister.

The simple contract is easy compared to the life I once lived. Still, I've made a home with an independent life, and I refuse to give it up for anyone.

CHAPTER FOURTEEN

"Melody," I call through the office. "Could you bring me the current bill accounts for the last thirty days and the current correspondence on that young race car driver... What was his name?"

"You mean Nick Norris?" she calls back when the main number rings. "Good afternoon, McKenzie Kingston. How may I direct your call?" She pauses and allows the other party to speak. "Yes, Mr. Gabriel, Miss Devereaux is in. Please hold while I connect you."

The phone on my desk lights up, and I look at it with trepidation.

"Pick it up already, Atlas. Live a little for God's sake." Samantha looks up from her desk, a cheeky smile growing across her face.

I pick up the phone and glare at her.

"Good afternoon, this is Atlas Devereaux."

"Atlas."

The sound of my name falling off his tongue makes me melt. I can't understand how a man's voice can sound that sexy.

"Mr. Gabriel, to what do I owe this unexpected call?"

"I wanted to make sure you received all the paperwork I sent over the other night."

"I did," I confirm lightly, keeping my tone all business. "It appears everything is in order. I've reached out to your sister's campaign manager to make sure we are working in tandem with their publicist. There is one question that seems to be unclear in your file."

"What can I clarify, Miss Devereaux?"

"Does your sister know of your particular interests?"

The question hangs in the air for a few seconds.

"Yes, but she prefers the position of plausible deniability. Her perception of my personal affairs are not always in line with mine."

"I see. Then I will tread lightly with her campaign team," I confirm, making notes across my blotter pad.

"Unless you have further questions, my sister is not the reason I'm calling."

"Oh? Do tell the reason you rang my phone then, Mr. Gabriel." The smirk on my face causes my tone to take on a slightly sarcastic nature.

"Since you have confirmed that *all* the paperwork was received, and in proper order, I was wondering why I had yet to hear from your assistant regarding dinner."

His bold move startles me but then again, the *paperwork* was bold, understated intensity in actions. Nothing forceful or domineering but leaving little question to the outcome he desired.

"Um, yes. My schedule has been rather busy. I'm sure Melody will fit you in over the next couple weeks—"

"Tonight," he interrupts my disregarding ramble. "I will pick you up at six-thirty this evening from your office. Do you like sushi?"

"Yes," I reply automatically.

"Excellent. Until then, have a wonderful afternoon, Miss Devereaux."

I sit with the phone up to my ear, listening to the quick tones of the fast busy signal, telling me he has ended the call. Placing the phone back into the cradle, I stare at it like it has grown tentacles and is the most abhorrent thing I've ever seen in my life.

A paper ball flies across the room, smacking me in the center of the forehead.

"Ow!"

"That did not hurt." Samantha rolls her eyes and stares at me from her desk. "What was that all about?"

"He asked me to dinner. Well, not exactly asked, he told me I was having dinner with him tonight and that he'd pick me up at six-thirty from here."

"Excellent! You should totally raid *you know who's* closet. She'd want you to," she replies, grinning ear to ear, like a young schoolgirl.

"I will not raid *you know who's* closet," I say through clenched teeth in a loud whisper.

The front office door chimes, drawing our attention. The tall, lanky courier struts into the office before placing a long thick box on the counter in front of Melody's desk as he leans in toward her.

"I've got a package for a Miss Devereaux," he says, looking at Melody, "Could you sign here for it please?"

Taking the stylus from the young man, she scrawls her name across the screen. "Thank you, miss, have a good one," he calls out, stepping back across the threshold into the bright sun.

Samantha is on her feet, around her desk and standing in front of Melody. Her lightning fast movements mean there will be no end to the teasing I will endure if this package is not from a client.

Standing up from my desk, I walk across the mahogany parquet floor and watch Samantha's gaze grow impatient when she doesn't think I'm moving fast enough.

Grabbing the box, she nods toward the white leather couch in the reception area.

"Get over here, Atlas, so we can open it." Her eyes dance like a kid's on a holiday morning.

I walk over to the couch and sit. The cushions of the overstuffed couch conform to my body as I sink into them. Joining me, Samantha immediately plops the enormous box across my lap. With trembling fingers, I grasp the smooth white cardboard lid and lift.

A small linen card lies across the layers of gleaming white tissue paper.

'When so desired by the Dominant, the submissive will wear the clothes prescribed by the Dominant for his pleasure.'

I desire to see you in this outfit this evening. I am looking forward to our dinner. ∼ RG

SETTING THE CARD ASIDE AS I IGNORE MY RISING DESIRES AND thoughts, I turn my attention to the contents. I unfold the layers of tissue to reveal a silk twill dragon print dress. The dark ebony is embroidered with a rich tapestry of oriental-inspired flowers. A red silk bow is tied around the under-bust and a simple satin trim outlines the neckline. The elegant lines of the dress are breathtaking. Placing the box on the couch, I stand, lifting the nineteen-forties-inspired dress to my shoulders, its cutaway tulip hem falling just below my knees.

Samantha gasps at the sight. Reaching back into the box, she pulls out a pair of four and a half inch red suede platform stiletto sandals. The open link design embraces the foot while binding it with a concealed zipper.

"Wow, does he have excellent taste," she says, letting out a low whistle. "Looks like you won't need to go visit you know who's closet."

Her mischievous grin tells me she's loving every minute of my uncomfortable silence.

"What time did he say he was picking you up?"

"Six-thirty pm," I reply, letting a sigh escape.

My stomach churns at the thought of those arms wrapping around my waist, his soft lips leaning down to kiss me senseless. It's been far too long since I've felt the tenderness of desire from a man, especially one that affects me this way. Leashing the wayward thoughts, I look up at Samantha's dancing eyes, her giddiness erasing any traces of stress from her face.

"Excellent." Samantha jumps up from the couch. "You have just enough time to get ready. It's three pm now. Go finish up what you feel you must, then shut down your computer and go upstairs."

Her firm hands guide my shoulder, forcing my feet to make a path back through the office.

CHAPTER FIFTEEN

For the next hour, I attempt to clear the pile of paperwork, though most of the time spent on the work is in vain. My mind runs from the note, to the contract, to the dress and back again. Each turn causes a fresh burst of anxiety and insecurity. I want to know what it's like to feel someone else's control like a shelter in a storm. A moment to breathe, even if it is short-lived.

I give up on work, grab the box, and make my way up to the writer's studio apartment on the second floor of the office. The unique space is a place of solace when I need to get away while being in the middle of everything with one job or the other.

Today it is an escape from Samantha's constant grin and quips about my *having a man* or the fact I am going out or how shocking the concept is for a hermit like me. The final straw comes when she no longer contains herself and breaks down to a fit of giggles at my irritation when she announces that it might come as a shock, but some people get laid on a date. While I ignore most of her comments, the last one sends me sailing over the mental edge, and I retreat from the battle.

Walking back downstairs forty-five minutes later, both Samantha and Melody gasp as I enter the office.

"What?"

"Atlas, I don't know what to say... it's... it's incredible," Samantha stutters.

"Well, well, Miss Kingston, I can't believe a situation has left you speechless."

"Pshaw." She rolls her eyes and swipes at the air. "I'm just saying it is so incredible that you are letting a man take a light lead, and you aren't kicking or screaming about it."

"Whatever," I huff, letting my body take over a well-practiced sensual walk across the floor, my arms swinging only from the elbows while my hips sway with each crossover step.

"Ah, there she is," Samantha snickers behind me. "I knew she wouldn't let you go on a date without her."

Shaking my head, I smile to myself. I developed the walk I use as Alexandra to entice and to show an extreme level of independent confidence while shielding me from those who attempted to intimidate. It keeps me in the right mind frame, as it shows Alexandra's command presence, even when I don't feel it.

"You know it will be a great evening, Atlas," Samantha whispers. "He seems like a great guy, and you deserve someone who's absolutely taken by you."

"How do you know? You've never..."

"Lunch," she replies. "Alexandra had just sent him off with her assistant for a tour."

The image of Reece looking straight into the camera before turning to the table with Samantha and Kade rushes through my mind, my face blushing at the thoughts of that day and all the ones since. Nothing is balanced anymore, and it is driving me crazy.

"I'm about to head out, Ms. Devereaux. I hope you have a wonderful evening. That dress and those heels are a knockout on you," Melody says, her animated face full of envy.

Looking up, I paste on a smile.

"Thank you so much. Have a wonderful evening, Melody."

"Thank you, ma'am." She nods and turns toward the front door, her heel clicks echoing in the quiet office.

The clock on my desk reads six-fifteen pm. Butterflies take flight en masse around my stomach. So much for being calm, cool, collected, and totally in charge of myself. I scowl at the thought.

"Careful now, your face will freeze that way," Samantha quips, walking past my desk. "Though Melody is right, that dress looks amazing on you, like it was made to measure. It's astounding how well it fits. I wonder how in the world he got your measurements so close."

Samantha smirks, and I glare at her with suspicion.

The front door chimes, causing both of our heads to swivel toward it as it opens. Reece Gabriel is dressed in a dark gray bespoke suit, and I try to school my stare as it rakes from the floor all the way to the smile he flashes when he catches my appraisal.

"Good evening, ladies," he calls across the office, striding toward us with a bouquet of dark blue roses.

"It is good to see you again, Mr. Gabriel." I stand upon his approach and smile.

"Reece, please. I believe we've passed the point of such formality."

Reaching my desk, he smiles and hands me the bouquet.

"I understand you have a penchant for an unusual color of rose. I hope sapphire is to your taste."

"They are lovely, Reece," I say accepting the bouquet and pulling them to my nose, inhaling their fragrance.

I look up to see Samantha's mischievous grin lighting the room, and I know she had something to do with this piece of intelligence.

Reece turns away and walks over to Samantha's desk, reaching out for her hand. When she extends it, he brings it up to his lips and places a light kiss across her knuckles.

"Lovely to see you also, Miss Kingston," he says conspiratorially.

"And you, Mr. Gabriel. The dress you sent over for Atlas is stunning."

She nods in my direction, and both of them stand there

appraising me from across the room, making comments in inaudible whispers.

"That's enough," I say, feeling far too much tension from being the sudden center of attention. My discomfort is entertaining as both faces blossom into broad grins.

"Are you ready to join me for dinner, Atlas?" His smooth voice sends shivers down my body.

"That was a high-handed demand telling me we were dining tonight, rather than waiting for my assistant to contact you."

"And yet you are dressed in the outfit I sent over for such an occasion." He nods in my direction.

I open my mouth for a full retort and think better of it, knowing Samantha will take advantage of any open opportunity. My love life, or lack thereof, seems to fascinate her to no end. Mainly because hers is so active, I'm sure.

"Shall we?" He smiles knowingly, offering his arm to escort me through the small office.

Walking around my desk, I cautiously place my hand on his proffered arm. His closeness causes my body to ramp into overdrive, and every long dormant need surfaces and plays havoc on my attempt for a calm, no-nonsense exterior.

"Have fun, kids," Samantha calls out as we walk toward the door.

"Have a wonderful evening, Miss Kingston," he says with a wink in her direction.

Once outside, he hands me into the open door of the town car and slides in next to me. His driver shuts the door carefully, walks to his seat, and eases the large car down the driveway.

"I AM GLAD YOU CHOSE TO JOIN ME FOR DINNER." REECE SMILES, his face changing from focused man to an amused boy.

The silence hangs in the air between us as my mind swirls with more questions than I could supply answers to. I work to keep a casual, friendly smile on my face while my thumb worries across the crystal on the nail of my little finger in a juxtaposition to how I attempt to appear.

"Why did you put on the dress?" he asks, his face an expression full of intensity and focus. "There was no doubt of the path the dress would lead after I sent the *contract* over followed by a specific time—not to mention the note in the box."

"Yes, the breadcrumbs were most definitely new and entertaining," I reply with caution, unsure where he was going with the questions or what he wanted me to say.

"So then, why did you put on the dress?"

"Curiosity," I reply.

"Curiosity?" he asks, his face a mask of confusion.

"Yes, curiosity. The same curiosity which drove Alice to follow a white rabbit who was running late down a hole that led to a cake that said *eat me*, and a bottle that said *drink me*, which led to a whole new world that changed her reality," I reply, meeting his gaze. "Or the same reason Neo chose the red pill."

His soft chuckle bounces around the back of the car.

"Welcome to Wonderland, Cinderella. It looks like this will be quite the interesting fairy tale. Although I get the strangest feeling this isn't your first trip down the rabbit hole."

The car comes to a stop, and I startle when the door opens, thankful for a slight reprieve in the conversation.

"Looks like we have arrived at our destination," I say as I look up through the open door.

"I wonder," he says, his face turning back toward me as he leans into my personal space. "If you found a little sign that said *eat me* or *drink me* would you follow the directions just to see what would happen?" he asks, his face hovering just above mine.

The smell of his subtle cologne fills the space as warmth radiates from his body.

Kiss me, I want to scream but hold still.

"I guess we shall find out, Mr. Rabbit, but I hope you are never late, for I have little tolerance for such."

"And I hope you are never *late* either, but I'm sure we'll get to those arrangements later." He smirks, turning his body away and stepping out of the car.

I roll my eyes at his back. *Good grief, all men must be boys,* I think to myself, taking his proffered hand when it appears through the door.

CHAPTER SIXTEEN

R eece is the perfect gentleman. Every door we encounter, he opens. He pulls the chair from the table, turns to the waiter, and orders in fluent Japanese. His style both impresses and unnerves me.

Lulling Japanese music sets the perfect tone in the background of the elegant restaurant. A small forest of bamboo grows in graduating stalks behind the kitchen's picture window, and fine pieces of pottery elevate the stylish surroundings.

"I hope you don't mind, I've ordered for both of us." He tests the waters for my reaction with his no-nonsense tone.

"As I thought you might, Monsieur Rabbit."

He laughs. "Mixing languages, I see."

"Unlike you, I'm not fluent in Japanese."

"I know enough to be dangerous and to get around when necessary."

The waiter, dressed in a black tunic style uniform, pours a clear liquid into small etched-crystal glasses.

"Plum-wine," Reece remarks when the waiter steps away. Both of us tip the glass to our lips. The sweet, slightly thick liquid is the perfect sip. The apéritif gives me a moment to settle into the situation.

"Tonight, I've ordered an Omakase meal for us," Reece explains as they deliver the first course to our table. "We've handed over control of our dining experience to the chef, who will choose the flow. Each progression will be an interesting mixture of textures and flavors. This sushi chef is well-known for his quality of ingredients and skillful preparation."

I'm thankful he's taken the lead over dinner. Trying not to think about the last time I went out on a date with a man brings up all the reasons I normally don't.

"See how nice it is to give over small moments to someone else?" Reece says as the waiter places a grouping of small bowls filled with a minced vegetable salad coated in seasoned mashed tofu.

"It can be so freeing just to follow. Much like we are with the chef this evening. Allowing him to lead us down a path of his choosing for our pleasure." He takes a bite, watching me with an intensity that makes me squirm. "There may be things we don't like on the journey because we find it's not to our taste, but we fearlessly brave a more interesting dining experience. Letting us find things we never knew we enjoyed had we not followed his lead."

I'm not sure how to respond. Normally I don't date, or as Samantha would say, I'm a horrible workaholic who doesn't step out of my comfort zone. On some level she's right, which makes me wonder if that nervous feeling running through my entire body is because of the nearness of the man sitting across from me, who exudes sensuality and is watching my every move. My body isn't immune to the attraction jumping between us, and the fear of messing up the entire situation keeps me far more tight-lipped than normal.

"Why did you send the contract over?" I blurt out, trying to sound calm and nonchalant, but internally cringing at how brash the question sounds. "It was either a bold or a very arrogant move."

"It is too bad you lack opinions, Atlas," he said, chuckling slightly, causing me to cringe at my obvious faux pas. "Samantha warned me you don't suffer fools well."

The waiter returns, pausing our conversation once again to relieve the table of our salad bowls and present us with an elegant platter of sashimi, each fish unique.

"It's so fresh you can taste the sea on each morsel," he tells us.

When the waiter steps away, Reece turns his gaze back to me.

"There's something different about you. There's a look in your eye, like you are holding yourself back somehow," he says, picking up a slice of sashimi and savoring it. "An unexplainable intensity behind your very reserved veneer."

I smile. "Some would say it's not a veneer, but rather me all the way through."

"Tell me about yourself." The bland statement rolls off his tongue, but his eyes dance in the dim light.

"I have a straightforward life," I reply with caution. "You know, get up, eat, work, go to bed. Rinse. Repeat."

"What are your interests outside of work?"

"My tastes are multi-faceted. I find my work" — I pause for the word that would sum it all up with ease — "to be mentally stimulating, emotionally intriguing at times, and periodically — physically demanding."

"I didn't realize that PR work could be physically demanding," he comments, one eyebrow cocked.

The meal once again grows silent as each of us seems to size the other one up. My mind flashes to the feel of his hand on my body, and my breath stutters. Visions of being on my knees in front of him run unbidden through my mind and I work to tamp down rising needs that should have long ago been eradicated.

I know better than to get involved. Every relationship has ended in tragedy of some type. I'm better off with superficial encounters where I maintain full control. No matter what they say about the submissive having *all the power* in a power exchange, both people have it or there is no exchange. It is a silent dance, one to find out who will lead and who will follow.

His eyes bore into mine as if he can read my soul.

"How long has it been since you've submitted to another?"

"Who says I've ever done so?" My voice is full of challenge, the question causing my heart to race and my palms to grow clammy.

"Your body says it, the subtle movements of your eyes and head say it—almost scream it."

"Ah, arrogant then, or possibly just cocky," I shove back, easy enough not to be rude, but enough to let him know I'm not easy prey.

Reece raises an eyebrow but doesn't comment.

I size men up for a living. From bigger, better, badder attitudes to the soft, sweet, shy types. Watching each movement, word, and tone to find their most precious secrets. Getting inside their heads before they know what's hit them, but Reece feels — unreadable. Almost as if he can block each move, stepping aside, only to find my weak spot when I move past. It is unnerving, and yet it calls to me, wanting me to step closer to figure out the puzzle.

"Do all of your first dates start this way?"

"No," Reece replies, his eyes never wavering from mine, daring me to look away.

"Why this time?"

"There's something about you that's indescribably beautiful and enigmatic, and I so enjoy a delightful challenge." A smile tugs on the edge of his lips when he asks, "Do you know the difference between cocky and arrogant?"

"No. I didn't realize there was a difference," I reply, enjoying the verbal spar.

"Yes, quite a difference. Cocky means you can talk the talk, arrogant means you can more than back it up."

"Well, can you?" My voice challenges him as much as my words.

"Jump down the rabbit hole and find out, Atlas." His soft words entice me to engage, pushing and pulling in the same breath.

"Why did you hold the door for me? Send me flowers when I ran?"

"I'm a dominant sadist, Atlas. I'm also a gentleman and a hopeless romantic. These traits aren't mutually exclusive."

"I've not always found that to be true," I reply.

"Which part goes away?"

"The wrong one."

"I'm sorry that's been your experience," he says, cupping his hand under my chin.

"No different from the belief that a woman who submits is weak. Besides, you've no reason to be sorry; you aren't part of my past." I let the ending hang in the air, wanting to put a *yet* on the end, but everything in me screams to give this a chance. Something in these moments makes me feel alive, like I'm breathing after holding my breath too long, and I want to believe it is possible.

"Shall we adjourn to a more comfortable location?"

"How about we adjourn to my place?" I offer, knowing James can help me if things were to go wrong, if I have somehow miscalculated — I shove the negative thoughts to the side.

"If it will make you feel more comfortable, then I think it is an excellent idea," he says, rising from his seat and walking around to pull my chair back for me.

"But before we go" — his breath brushes against my ear — "I want you to go to the ladies' room, remove your sexy panties, then slip them into my suit pocket when you return."

Everything in me trembles. My breath hitches, becoming ragged. I nod my compliance.

"Soon, the proper response will be *Yes, Sir*."

His breath caresses my skin, his sensual tone full of promises. Then I'm lost, moving toward the restroom on legs that seem to progress on their own. Desire threatens to overwhelm me on so many levels at once. I hear Samantha's words run through my head, *Live a little.*

I'm so turned on that I can feel the moisture collect between my thighs. My entire body buzzes with excitement. Walking into the ladies' room, I spy an empty stall at the end and step into it.

Calming my breathing, I slip the sliver of the white fabric they sell as a thong, down my legs, and step out of it. My arousal is clear. Thoughts run through my mind. I've been down a similar road before with someone who methodically laid out the path he wanted to explore, but it never created this kind of reaction.

From here I can see each of Reece's carefully planned steps and smile. Desire snakes through me while my mind demands caution to a situation that could get out of control in short order.

With the confidence of my position in the world, I walk back into the restaurant and step next to Reece. Leaning in, I lift the fabric and tuck my panties behind the handkerchief in his pocket. His eyes follow each movement until I step back and challenge him with a smile as it sneaks across my face. He turns his head, and he inhales over his breast pocket.

"You smell delicious," he whispers, the hungry look in his eyes telling me his exact thoughts. "It is so beautiful to see such a confident, sexy woman submit."

He turns me toward the door, pressing his hard length against my ass.

"Now look what you've done, my dear," he says, his voice low enough that his words barely register as we make our way back to his car.

Once we settle into the town car, Reece adjusts his body to turn toward me.

"It's unusual for a woman to invite a man to her apartment after the first date," he comments, watching my face.

"I'm an unusual woman."

"That you are, Miss Devereaux."

We cover the next thirty minutes in calm conversation. The topics stay in a nice neutral territory as we work through social commentary, followed by an awkward silence when they get too personal. The cycle continues, both of us dancing around the other, sizing up the situation and making our own internal decisions.

My door opens. I look out at the open gap and realize we've arrived at our destination. Pulling myself together, I turn and lift my hand.

"Good evening, Miss Devereaux," the doorman says as he hands me out of the car.

"Good evening, Henry," I acknowledge the doorman with a warm smile.

He turns, opening the lobby door.

"Have a wonderful evening, ma'am."

We walk in companionable silence toward the elevator. The chemistry between us is palpable, but I've never been one to rush into a hook-up situation.

CHAPTER SEVENTEEN

"Good evening, Miss Devereaux." The computerized voice resonates from the speakers throughout the penthouse, and Reece startles.

The emergency lights rise in soft increments to create paths in all directions.

"Status—Evening," I call back.

"House transitioning to evening mode," James replies.

The drapes across the patio doors move to the sides, revealing the skyline, the lights twinkling in the fading twilight. Around us, the house lights illuminate to seventy-five percent as soft orchestral music plays in the background and the emergency path lights dim.

"Miss Devereaux, I sense an unknown presence in your abode. Would you like your visitor to have access to the systems or statuses?"

"James, this is Reece Gabriel, status—Guest," I reply to James.

The status sends a message back to the security monitoring room, alerting Kade to the unfamiliar presence in the house. I know that I will hear about it when I break down and talk to him, but at least he'll be grateful that I've used a level of reasonable precautions for my safety, even if no genuine threat exists. Besides, Kade's confident reference of Reece helped to ease my wariness in our initial interactions, giving me the freedom to enjoy our interesting dinner.

"It is nice to meet you, Mr. Gabriel. Your current status is Guest. If you reply, then I will take a voice print to begin the process of voice recognition."

I turn around to see a slightly wide-eyed man standing in my kitchen, and I smile. James is such a normal part of my life, I often forget that he can overwhelm someone when they first meet the disembodied voice who runs my house with quiet efficiency. Part butler, part virtual assistant, and part security, the system helps keep me on top of so many things, I'm unsure how I'd ever live without him.

James' counterpart runs the club in a similar manner, though I have disabled the voice module to reduce the unnecessary computing power. While I love the quiet feel of McKenzie Kingston, I miss having James or his counterpart there to do the most menial things. One of these days I need to upgrade the office systems. I make a mental note to distract me from my awkwardness.

"Hello, James," Reece finally calls back into the penthouse.

"I was thinking you did not wish to speak. Ma'am, would you like me to continue the voice recognition compilation based on ambient conversation?"

"Execute voice recognition."

"Done."

The room falls silent, and I watch Reece's cautious face.

"Would you like a quick tour?" I offer as he nods.

"Well, this is the kitchen, obviously."

"Obviously," he replies dryly.

"You've met James. He is my automated butler, home automation, personal assistant, and security system."

"You mean like JARVIS," Reece replies, recognition filling his eyes.

"Mr. Gabriel, JARVIS is a fictional comic book character brought to life through the use of special effects. While I am special and far more useful."

"I think you offended him, Reece," I say with a laugh.

"How can you offend a talking box?" Reece asks, following me through the large open living area. The patio doors line one full wall. Hidden technology and appliances give it a clean minimalist feel while being high tech.

"This is the living area," I remark quickly, overriding James' rather sarcastic interface as we walk through the open floor plan. Turning to the right, I push open the glass-enclosed fitness room.

"This is fitness room." I point, shoving the glass door forward into the room.

"Welcome back to the gym, ma'am. It has been forty-two days since you last visited — " James starts, and I pull the door shut.

"All reports off, messaging on," I call out.

"Now that is interesting." Reece leans his hand on the gym door. "Forty-two days since you've visited such an amazingly equipped facility—why on Earth have you not visited this poor corner of your home in so long?"

I stand there staring into a pair of gray eyes as they try to bore into me.

"Um, I've been busy as of late."

"You've been too busy to take care of this sexy body? Then maybe you should let me do it for you," he says with a wolfish grin.

His hand runs down my hip, leaving a trail of heat wherever it rubs across my dress, causing my muscles to clench in response as I push my hip harder into his hand. He continues to languidly explore my body and pushes me against the glass enclosure.

Leaning to me, his lips graze my temple as they work their way to run down my neck. My head tips to the side and gives him more access to the soft, vulnerable skin.

"Yes, I think you should give me control of this beautiful body. Let me show you how I can make it feel. Give your mind time off. What do you say, Miss Devereaux?"

His palms cup my breasts as he runs the tip of his thumb across my hardening nipple. My skin heats along the trail blazing across my body. My breath catches as a moan escapes my lips.

"I want you to show me this beautiful body without all of this fabric covering it," he moans against my skin, continuing his explorations.

My head falls forward, bracing against his firm shoulder, each touch making my simmering body catch fire, building into an inferno of need.

"Yes, please," I moan against his shoulder.

My body stiffens, the thought both arousing and terrifying. What am I doing? I'm not one who just falls into a man's arms.

"You're thinking too much," he murmurs, tangling fingers in my hair. "Enjoy the moment. It's for mutual pleasure, mutual benefit and to take care of this gorgeous body. Trust me."

I tilt my head back and his tongue licks across my mouth a second before he closes the distance. Each move is slow and tender as if he has all the time in the world to taste every inch. He moves us to the couch, small steps I barely notice. His mouth doesn't leave mine until he steps back, leaving me breathless in his wake. My lips tingle as if they can still feel his touch.

His gray eyes darken as his mouth turns up in a half-tipped smile. Spinning my body around to face the couch, he bends me forward, placing my hands across the back ledge.

"You will stay still, leaving your hands where I put them," he says in between kissing his way down my spine. His hands float to my body, lifting my skirt and leaving me bare from the waist down.

"I'm so glad you removed those panties at the restaurant. This is so much nicer. You have such a lovely ass. It is absolute perfection."

His hands press against my lower back, bracing and pushing it level. A finger slides down the crack of my ass. I jerk and try to stand, but his hand holds me firm. The finger continues its exploration through my folds as my breath comes in gasps.

"Mmm. You're already wet for me," he growls.

As he slides his finger over my slit and buries it into me, my hips push involuntarily back toward him. I squirm with each movement, struggling to keep my hands in position.

Pushing his hard cock against my leg, he murmurs, "I'm looking forward to burying myself into your slick, soaking pussy. Feeling you wrap around me like a warm velvet glove."

My mind spins at his admission, the heat building between my legs, his fingers punctuating each statement as they work in and out of me, inflaming my desire.

"Giving you pleasure has haunted my every moment," he says as his thumb rubs against my sensitive nub.

I groan in reply.

"But I don't want to simply control you, Atlas, I want to possess you, all of you. To know you so well, I can sense your thoughts, moods and needs."

His fingers pause. In an excruciatingly slow pace, he moves them in the same pattern once again. My entire body screams in protest at the loss of friction.

"Of course, there is the matter of an agreement between us. I know you are a woman of business, insisting that every *i* is dotted and every *t* crossed."

His thumb grazes across my clit, causing me to buck with need as my entire core burns with molten desire.

"Please." The word escapes my lips. I need him to touch me more as my entire body throbs for him.

In and out, the fingers continue, soft stoke then hard, fast then slow, until every nerve ending rebels, craving the next touch.

"Pleasure is an interesting thing, Miss Devereaux." His fingers move in and out of my slick folds, in quick succession, with each word. "One never understands how much they miss something pleasurable — until it stops."

On the word *stop*, his fingers pull out of my pussy, and he stands as his own need presses hard against my thigh.

I moan, suppressing a scream of frustration.

"This-this-this," I stutter, "this is duress."

My breath comes in stops and gasps, my mind unable to finish the sentence.

"Duress? Duress would imply that I'm doing something against your will or under a threat of violence or constraint. Does this feel violent or constrained?" His voice is even and firm with only a hint of need found in each controlled breath.

I nod, then shake my head, then nod again, proving my mind's struggle to override my body's burning desire.

He chuckles.

"Too bad it won't hold up in court. So I don't think the duress angle will work for you on this one."

His hand slaps hard against my upturned ass, a guttural moan ripping from my throat unbidden.

"You like that, do you? Why do I get the picture there are many such pleasures you deny yourself, Atlas?" His voice caresses my ear.

The pain of the next slap melds with the pleasure of his returning fingers, my mind melting into the next sensation.

"Tell me you agree, and I'll thoroughly satisfy both of us."

Agreeing makes no sense, the last vestige of my sane mind screams.

"Agreeing makes perfect sense," he retorts, removing his fingers. "You are in this position because you want to be here, you crave to know what it will be like to be under another's command, to desire it. If you refuse to move forward, you will always wonder what it would have been like. You can feel what is between us, can't you?"

My hips involuntarily push against the air. Every fiber of my being burns with an awakened hunger. I crave to hear his next command, feel his next touch, or experience his next pleasurable *torture.*

"Yes," I moan. "Please."

"You are so exquisite," he murmurs in my ear. "Confident, strong, sexy as hell. Your body is driving me mad."

His hands move to pull my dress down over my upturned ass, and I reel in confusion.

"Turn around and have a seat, beautiful."

For long seconds I don't move. What did I do wrong? What in the world has caused this sudden change? Confusion winds through me as it turns to anger in my mind while passionate desire still courses through my veins.

I turn around to sit on the couch. He walks across the room and sits in a chair.

"You did nothing wrong, so wipe that look off your face," he whispers, his arousal still clear.

"Then why did you stop?" My voice is far more forceful and demanding. "What did I do wrong or did you just want to see if I would fall quickly?"

"Atlas," his voice rumbles in a low growl, "you did nothing wrong. You are an amazing woman."

"Then why the hell did you stop?" I hiss.

"Feisty." He grins. "How do you feel right now?"

"Other than furious and thinking you are an irritating ass rather than the gentleman you proclaim?"

"The burning need between your legs will consume your body for me. Everything in you screams for my touch, and your mind is almost in agreement." He pauses, letting the words hang in the air between us. "I want to possess you, master you, and dominant you, but I'm not a domineering prick. What I want is for you to willingly do it, to submit out of deep desire and enjoy the game. When you are ready to sign the contract I sent over, then we'll move on from there."

"It's great in theory." I stare down at the carpet. "The practicum doesn't always weigh the same."

"How can I convince you otherwise?"

"You can't," I sigh, shaking my head. "I've played this game before, and it only ended in pain."

"Then you've been playing the wrong game."

He unfolds his sizable frame from the chair and walks over to the couch before bending and tucking his finger under my chin. "And I am so looking forward to playing with you."

Leaning down, he captures my mouth with his. His tongue explores mine without hurry as he possesses me with tenderness.

"Why did you take your panties off when I asked?"

My mind babbles a series of quiet pleas.

"Because it felt interesting, daring, sexy."

"Good. I love it when a woman feels those things, and I so look forward to making you feel that way more often. Good night, Miss Devereaux," he murmurs.

I sit stunned, watching him saunter across the penthouse and out the front door.

"James," I call out to the room.

"Yes, ma'am."

"Set house to sleep. Start shower." I might as well take care of the ache between my legs since this evening has gone into some strange places.

"Ma'am, you have an incoming message from Mr. Gabriel," James announces as I make my way toward the shower.

"Read message."

"I had a wonderful evening, Miss Devereaux, and quite look forward to seeing you again soon. Please do not take things in hand tonight. I want you to enjoy our game."

"He's got to be kidding," I call out to the empty house.

Need aches between my legs as desire licks through my core, and now he wants me to do nothing about it.

"New message," James announces. "Sweet dreams, Atlas."

I come to a halt, not knowing whether to laugh or cry. He knows that it is all my decision. Taking care of myself in the shower would ease the ache between my legs, but holding off may lead to a path that eases the ache much deeper. Good Lord, he's good.

"Shower off," I call out to James, sighing as I walk toward my bed and try to think of anything that will help me sleep.

CHAPTER EIGHTEEN

"So?" Samantha demands as I walk into the studio kitchen above the office.

"So what?" I reply, pouring myself a cup of coffee.

"Atlas, you can't leave a girl hanging! How was your date?"

I sit down next to her on a stool at the kitchen island and fill her in on the details of the dinner date. I even include how he got me all worked up and left me there.

"He's persistent," Samantha says over the top of her coffee cup. "I'll give him that, but that doesn't surprise me. What surprises me is that he walked away."

"I'm not sure how to feel about that one," I comment, staring down into the mocha-colored liquid. "I feel like I'm playing a game of risk and control, and I'm losing to him but it in a way that just feels so right and wrong all at the same time. One minute I want to push the point I am a free, independent woman, and the next I want to fall to my knees and see where jumping down the rabbit hole takes me."

"Atlas, life has been rough lately. With the businesses doing well and the death of your father, you have a lot on your plate. It's obvious you're attracted to each other. Why not live a little?"

"Living a little is what got me into this situation, Samantha," I reply, letting out a sigh. "He wants a contract."

"What type of contract?"

"A basic D/s contract. It's light in comparison to most of the ones I've entered into in the past, and somewhat vague, but it's put together in the right aspects."

"Is that your professional opinion, Alexandra, or your personal one, Atlas?" Samantha chuckles.

"Both. I've dealt with my fair share of written agreements for dynamic relationships."

"Yes, but you were always on top. You were always in control, deciding on what path to take next or turn to make. This time you're the one waiting on the next turn or path."

"Not always," I mutter, then nod without looking up.

"I know what it's like to be truly out of control, but not like this. It's like jumping over the edge without a net, where you must trust and just let go. If I screw this up —" I shrug.

Under normal circumstances, I could juggle a casual relationship with running two businesses and all my other miscellaneous *side hustles*, as Samantha refers to them. Unfortunately, this isn't one of those moments.

My hiatus after the death of my father left the companies vulnerable, and though I love Samantha, she constantly needs to be reined in. She hates to be responsible for making things happen, preferring to be more of an instigator. With no one actively leading the PR firm or the club, things quickly headed toward disaster.

It was a wake-up call, and I worked tirelessly to put things into place to help the companies continue to run in case I ever got hit by a bus. And right now, Reece Gabriel is trying to be the one that could derail everything. Things are still not steady enough to ensure they'd all balance without my daily input. The safest thing to do is to stay focused and in control or risk letting everything slide like it did before.

"Besides, he's a client, and that's not a line that should be crossed," I say with finality.

"Atlas, really? I can take on his case if you're so worried about a direct conflict of interest. Do you think he won't respect you if you enter a D/s relationship with him? You're long overdue for something great like this in your life."

"Perhaps. I don't think it's a chance I should take."

It's been years since I've even contemplated submitting to another person. And here it is, placed before me on a silver salver by a drop-dead gorgeous, devastatingly charming gentleman. He challenges me in every way and could make my life far too complicated.

"What will it hurt? Those contracts are only as binding as the people in the relationship. If you don't like it, then you know how to walk away. In the meantime, enjoy the amazing kinky sex and fun unexpected moments. I think you've earned a fun, sexy time in your life."

"Says the girl who recently whined that I'm not writing fast enough for her to go back out on a book tour so she can have a fling with a guitar player." I stare at her pointedly. "In all seriousness, Samantha, I have to keep my mind in the game for the businesses. Those couple months after I lost Dad put us in desperate shape in some places, and we're just now recovering."

"You're overthinking this one, Atlas. It's heated fun with a smoking hot guy who showers you with gifts and desires you greatly."

"Well, when you put it that way, I have to say it is amazing to be wanted the way he seems to want me."

We both grin at each other.

My phone vibrates, causing me to jump, and I reach into my bag to retrieve it.

Good morning, Beautiful. Hope you slept well. RG

I grin down at my phone, my stomach doing flip-flops at seeing his name and feeling young and stupid with a grin plastered across my face.

"Must be good." Samantha smirks.

"It's simple," I whisper.

Good morning, Mr. Gabriel.

I type the reply, feeling like a teenage girl back in high school, but smarter—at least I hope so.

"Don't tell me you two will start sexting or something. I mean good grief, Miss Devereaux, how will you ever cope with actual sex in your life?" Samantha's Manhattan accent sounds far more elitist than usual.

"Jealous much?" I remark sarcastically.

"If you got time to text, you got time to write, girlfriend, and I need me some action."

Her face lights up at the thought and I shake my head and laugh.

I hope your sleep was pleasant. Though I wouldn't feel guilty if you stroked my ego and told me you couldn't sleep because every time you closed your eyes you thought of me.

"Good lord, men have such egos." I roll my eyes at my phone, causing Samantha to grab the phone out of my hands and laugh.

"Well, someone is full of himself." She pauses. "I wonder if it is arrogance or cockiness."

"For some strange reason, I think this one can back it up. But I do so look forward to seeing if it is true."

"What? You won't just fall to your knees and tell him what a wonderful Master he is because he rescued you from... wait, damn, girl, you don't make it easy, do you? What's this man going to rescue you from, anyway? You know white knights don't like standing idly by while the woman cleans up her own issues and keeps on moving without him."

"Not my issue." I smirk.

"Oh, I see." Samantha grins across her coffee cup. "Do you ever make it easy for them or do you make it hard because you can?"

I shrug, trying to shove off the feeling of frustration.

"I prefer the control to be in my hands."

"You know," Samantha starts, "it's okay to hand it over periodically. There really are some amazing male Dominants out there."

"I suppose."

"Give him a chance, Atlas. I have a good feeling about this one. He's doing all the right things and putting all the right pieces in place."

"Yeah, that's the part that worries me. He seems almost *too perfect*."

"Maybe he's just trying to impress the most amazing woman I know, and you are hard to impress."

She stares at me, daring me to contradict her words. "Atlas, you can't burn the candle at every end and expect perfection. Take a moment to breathe. Take *this* moment to breathe."

"We nearly lost the firm the last time I needed to *breathe*. There's no way we'd survive another round of *Atlas living in the moment*. I need to make sure that everything is secure."

Samantha's hand covers mine, and she gives me a soft smile. "And we're still standing. Lots of things have changed since then. Besides, it's not like you're leaving for a month with little contact. You're right here and stronger than ever."

My phone pings with an incoming text, and Samantha lets my hand go.

"Well? What does hot and sexy have to say?"

I look down to see the message:

Dinner this evening. 7pm. I'll pick you up at your office. Please wear a little black dress and strappy heels.

"It says he wants to dictate my outfit and go to dinner." I roll my eyes.

Part of me truly wants to rebel and wear something different, and the other part wants to see what he has in store if I play along.

"That's so hot." Samantha swoons. "What time is he picking you up?"

"Looks like seven o'clock."

"You go, girl." Samantha's grin is infectious, and I allow the giddy feelings to rush over me. "I've got a client meeting tonight at five-thirty. Don't forget the scarf on the front door."

She laughs, turning back to her desk.

For the rest of the afternoon, I pretend to work on my stack of client cases. Internally, I count down each excruciating minute, as I debate the pros and cons of jumping in with both feet and having some sexy fun time as Samantha would call it.

Still humming with unfulfilled need, I sit wondering at both the frustration and intense sexual desire coursing through my body. While it has made focusing on work more challenging, the anticipation of seeing Reece again makes me realize how much I crave his touch. The delicious tension between us makes each text and thought so much more delicious.

CHAPTER NINETEEN

At four-thirty, Samantha packs up and heads out for the evening, followed by Melody. Turning up the music, I try to concentrate on work for the next hour and a half, while my eyes constantly look at the clock. Finally, I slap my laptop shut and head upstairs to the studio apartment to shower and find the perfect outfit.

The clock ticks down to seven o'clock as I slip into a sexy cocktail dress. The black fabric forms to my curves. I feel emboldened and alive. My feet slide into a daring pair of five-inch strappy black patent heels with a back zip closure. I walk to the jewelry case across the small bedroom and picking up the long pear dangle silver earring, holding it up to my left ear, and a multi-teared drop earring ending with a sapphire on the end, holding up it to my right one. Moving my head back and forth, I try to decide which one is perfect before choosing the sapphire one and pushing it into my ear.

"You look stunning," Reece says in a low, strained whisper.

I whip around as I press the other earring into place.

Reece leans on the door frame, hands in his pockets. The dark gray collared shirt and light gray suit hugs his body in all the right places. He's flawless, sexy, and even a little intimidating, but not enough to be considered arrogant. It's much more subtle.

My fingers push the earring back home and I tuck an errant strand of hair behind my ear. The tension between us sparks around the room.

"The front door was open," he replies to my unasked question. "You should lock it when you're here alone."

"These grounds are the safest place I could be." I turn and bend over to pick up my clutch. "So where are we off to this evening?"

When I turn back, I step forward right into his expansive chest, my left hand splayed against his hard pectoral to catch my balance.

Before I can think, his hand is in my hair, pulling my head back and bringing my face up. His lips crash against mine. A moan escapes me, giving him more access to explore my open mouth. With a slight hesitation, my tongue joins his in a passionate kiss.

With his other hand, he grabs my wrist and moves it behind my back. The sudden movement pulls me forward against his hard body. I'm helpless against the onslaught of feelings adding to my already inflamed senses.

"My God, you're beautiful," he murmurs against my lips before deepening the kiss.

He holds me in place as my body begs to feel more of his touch.

His head pulls back and eases the kiss without breaking our contact. The tip of his tongue grazes across my lips, taunting me with teasing licks, his hand still fisted in my hair.

My heart races from the way he holds me in place, possessing my body like he owns it. His grip is firm, like he has every right to keep me there for as long as he chooses. A minor part of me wants to protest his boldness, but the desire coursing through my body clouds all rational thought.

His hand untangles from deep in my hair while the one on my wrist releases its grip. When he's sure I have my balance, he takes a step back. His breath is ragged as he stands staring at me.

"So—" I try my voice, pushing through the breathlessness of the unexpected kiss. "Where are we headed for dinner?"

"Maybe I'll have you for dinner, since you look good enough to eat." A sly grin plays on his lips. "And as much as I would love to be the envy of every man in the room, I'm suddenly in the mood for delivery."

We walk out of the bedroom into the living space.

His eyes rove across my body.

"How about a cheese board and charcuterie plate instead?" I ask, blushing at his open desire.

"That sounds perfect," Reece says, walking off toward the kitchen.

"There's a bottle of Pecchenino Dolcetto di Dogliani San Luigi two thousand twelve over in the wine refrigerator, if you'd like to pour two glasses while I pull together the board."

I motion to the dual-zone bottle refrigerator at the end of the kitchen island.

"This studio is well-equipped for something above a PR firm," he says, moving toward the beverage cooler.

I hand him a wooden box with the tools to de-cork the bottle and reach under the counter to grab the decanter and wineglasses. Once everything is settled for Reece, I turn to pull out the wooden board and prepare the cheese and meats.

"The apartment is a place for anyone in the firm to crash. We work long hours and it's nice to have a sense of home just steps from the office. When the owner of the club offered us this place, this space was unfinished. So we renovated it to make this studio, walling off the bedroom for a bit of separation."

We continue to make small talk throughout the process, though lengthy periods of silence often fall when Reece's focus and attention are directed toward my body rather than the conversation. On multiple occasions, I catch him staring at my ass as I bend over to pull something from the refrigerator or cabinet.

The laden board sits in the middle of the island counter. The fresh La Tur cheese from cow's, goat's, and sheep's milk sits in the top right corner. Beside it is a small cut of Weinkase Lagrein. The Italian semi-soft, soaked in herbs and wine is a perfect complement to the sweet, creamy Gorgonzola Cremificato. Ribbons of sopressata, smoked pancetta and prosciutto run between each cheese serving. Clumps of white grapes sit on the edge, while ramekins of olives, pickles, and a small honeycomb sit interspersed on the large wood platter.

"That's quite a spread," Reece says from across the island. "Shall we take this feast to the couch?"

He picks up the board and takes it to the sitting area, setting it down on the large wooden coffee table next to the wineglasses and decanter. I follow behind with a small plate of various flatbreads and crackers.

We both settle next to each other on the couch, facing the bank of windows along the outside wall, just in time to see the setting sun.

"Now that's what I call a view," he says, pouring wine into the two glasses.

We both take a sip, and I sigh with contentment.

"That's a well-balanced very fruit forward wine," Reece compliments.

After placing various items from the platter on a small plate, I lean back on the couch to enjoy both the view out of the window and the one beside me. The silence between us crackles in sexual tension without creating an awkwardness.

"Are you always persistent in your pursuit of things?" I ask, breaking the stillness.

"Only when it is something I truly desire."

"Oh, I see," I reply, smiling.

He watches me, almost with caution.

"You're different. There's a depth about you that is subtle, but unmistakable."

A frown creases between my eyes.

"Okay."

I sit pondering his statement.

"Is it difficult when you're not in control?"

I pause, absorbing the question both in meaning and implication.

"I have to exercise control in all things, Mr. Gabriel. It ensures that everything continues to run smoothly for everyone else. I know what happens when I let up."

"How's that going for you? The constant need to control every-thing, never catching your breath. It must be exhausting."

"It's not always easy, but it's what's required and I'm happy to do it." I try to keep my voice light, but a sadness creeps into my tone. "Do you not exercise control in all parts of your world?"

"Me? No. I learned a long time ago to be very selective in the areas where I exercise absolute control. Something or someone has to hold my attention well in order for me to want to take on that level of responsibility."

"What about your businesses or your hobbies?"

"Delegation and a talented team. A balance difficult to achieve."

I laugh, snorting my wine in a most unladylike fashion. Reece's face creases with concern. Once I recover, I reply, "I guess I'm just one of those leaders in the trenches with everyone else."

He nods.

"And most likely in need of help saying *no*."

My mouth opens to reply with a cutting remark, only to shut in the statement's indignant truth.

"Don't you think it would be nice to take a break from such a heavy load? To let someone else take responsibility for a while?"

I nod, finishing the cheese on my plate while watching the last rays of sun disappear across the horizon.

"Just let go, Atlas. I'll take control. Let me take care of you." His soft voice calls to a need long buried.

"Yes," I whisper in the air.

"Pardon?" he quips. "I don't believe I heard your reply."

"Yes — I agree." My breath comes in hard pants and the words barely form.

"Yes what?" His dark, rich voice makes my stomach quiver.

"Yes, Sir," I force out.

"This feels different, doesn't it? It feels right," he whispers next to my ear.

My head nods in reply.

"Let's begin, shall we?" He turns to face me. "Stand." The command is firm and quiet, and I have to strain to hear it, but I know exactly what he's doing.

Unfolding from the couch, I pull on my dress and straighten my form to its full, confident height.

"Strip and come here," he whispers.

Everything in me goes still. My body reacts with a flood of need while my mind screams against the decision to hand over control at an intimate level.

He says nothing, just sits there watching me. There are no emotions playing across his face, no change to his now steady breath.

I know the thoughts I would have sitting in that chair when you don't know if the person in front of you will follow through on your command. Everything hinges on that first decision to depart from control. Suddenly I'm standing on the other side again. The one deciding. We stare at each other while I try to find it in me to move.

I'll sign the contract and accept the challenge just to feel this alive again. I know the game like my very breath. Hell, I'm a Mistress of the game, and yet here I am, scared for unknown reasons, frozen stock-still like an innocent virgin, trying to calm every nerve in my body, demanding one of the warring internal parties to win. Either I strip or I call it off, but something has to move.

"I'm not in the habit of giving a command twice, Atlas." He cocks his head to the side. His soft, smooth tone is no less authoritative.

Bracing for the internal storm, I work my hands down to the hem of my dress, and with all the bravado I can muster, pull it over my head, leaving only a demi-cup bra, black full panties and strappy black patent heels adorning my feet.

My body trembles, not from fear but from the disbelief of the situation. So many times I've dreamt of doing this all again, each time pulling back in fear of it ending the same way it did with Dominick. I look up to see Reece's eyes boring holes through me, and I know he's appraising each move and pause.

"Take off your bra."

I reach between my breasts and unclip the clasp, my eyes never wavering from his intense gaze. Everything in me refuses to back down. Handing over control will be on my terms, and I want him to know each move is a choice. A personal desire from a place of strength, not weakness.

"Relax, Atlas. Take a deep breath." His deep voice is husky with need. "I know you've done this before based on how you've reacted at every step along the way."

He walks across the room and stands behind me. His fingers stroke down across my shoulders and my back, massaging slow circles at the base.

"What are your safe words?" he murmurs against my ear.

"Yellow when something is off, but I don't want it to stop, and red when I need it to stop."

"Good girl."

His hands brush across my breasts, pulling my body against his chest. My nipples respond, hardening under his touch as I arch into him. Stepping back, I hear the fabric of his tie rip through the collar of his shirt.

The fabric slides across my eyes. He ties it behind my head, blindfolding me. I wait in the darkness with bated breath. His teeth graze across my nipples as he licks and nips the skin. Losing sight only heightens the sensation. I push my body forward and he releases me. I moan at the loss of his touch.

"Kneel." His quiet firm command sounds loud in the darkness.

I bend my knees, lowering my body to the floor while his hands steady me. The sound of wood scraping against wood echoes in my head.

"Lie across the coffee table." He moves with me until I am stretched across the expanse of wood, my ass upturned and exposed.

"I want you to count the strokes for me."

"Yes, Sir," I whisper. Every nerve tingles.

His hand strokes my naked ass, squeezing and fondling every inch. There is no hurry in his movement. His fingers explore my skin. Then his hand lifts and comes down across my ass. Pain and pleasure mix in the firm but gentle impact. My body shudders in release and my emotions grow still as I focus on his touch.

"One," I groan as my need liquefies between my legs.

He caresses me, and I savor the change, knowing the next blow will come. On the heels of the thought, his hand smacks across my skin in a series of quick successive solid blows, and I count, my breath coming in pants when he stops. I wiggle when his hand scrapes across the sensitized skin.

"I'm glad to see your body approves," he says, dipping two fingers inside me. "You will make a fine dessert."

His fingers methodically pump in and out.

"Like any sweet dessert, I think it best if we whip you into a frenzy."

The smack is hard. I cry out, pushing off the table. His large hand lands between my shoulder blades and forces me back into position. He continues to rhythmically pepper my ass. The blows alternate between hard, taking my breath away and allowing the pain to spread deep into my body, and soft ones, which give me enough time to breathe.

I try to keep count, but I'm awash in the adrenaline coursing through my veins and I stumble over the words. The blows stop. It arouses me as the endorphins give my brain an ethereal feeling of floating.

Somewhere between the physical connection to the activity and the mental feeling of floating away. Every part of me is super-sensitive to stimuli for both pain and pleasure. I wait for Reece to stop and pull me into his arms.

"You don't think we're done, do you? We are just getting started."

Soft fabric brushes against my warm flesh.

"When you face something hard, it is best to change to something soft. It keeps one on their toes."

His grin is clear, even if I can't see it.

Reece's silk-wrapped hand moves across my form. Lips press gentle kisses across my back and move down the responsive skin. I jump at the slightest touch as the anticipation of the next blow keeps me on edge.

"Stand up."

Firm hands wrap around my waist, and I work to balance on wobbly legs. When I am upright, Reece gathers me in his arms and walks us across the studio.

The rough fabric of the bedspread abrades against my warm bottom, and I inhale.

"Lie back." His hands push on my shoulders.

The soft velvet tip of his tongue flicks across my clit, causing me to jump.

"Don't you dare come without permission," he murmurs against my skin.

His precise expert skill ebbs and flows across the wet skin. Each flick floods my sensitive nerve endings with a renewed sensation as his lips curl around my stiff clit, sucking and taunting it with promises of relief.

"Oh my God," I moan. The walls of my pussy clench as he holds me on the precipice of release.

I suck in a sharp breath.

"Please. I need to come, Reece."

He moans against my clit, sucks hard, and moves back.

"No. I'm not ready for you to come yet."

He pulls back, smacking the inside of my leg. The pain causes my body to shift, pushing the orgasm from the edge.

Once my body settles, he again takes up his place between my legs. His tongue works me over until I again beg for release, only to hear him deny it.

I feel him move from between my legs, his body pressing against me. The fabric of his suit sets off a bundle of sensations.

Reece grabs a handful of my hair and pushes two fingers deep into my drenched opening, working them in and out in a rapid pace.

"Don't you dare come without permission," he growls into my neck, his teeth grazing across skin.

My body clenches around him.

"Please," I moan.

"Please what?"

"Please, may I come, Sir?" I struggle to hold the tide of orgasm at bay.

All movement stops, and he pulls his fingers out. He takes my hard nipple between his teeth and bites down, intensifying everything. I cry out, but he doesn't loosen. My body pulls taut at the pain and I pant softly.

"No."

I struggle to breathe as a moan escapes. The edge of orgasm once again recedes.

He slides his hand down, grazing my clit as he dips his fingers back into my pussy. Once again they travel in and out until my body tightens on the edge of release. Everything in me flares with desire. The slightest touch drives me toward the edge, and I thrash with need.

Powerful hands flip me over, and his hand strikes hard against my ass. It is that wonderfully strange combination of pleasurable pain. I revel in the moment and the distant memories it stirs.

I push my bottom into his hand as the strokes rain down over my hot skin. My mind skitters in wild patterns of thought until it empties and focuses only on the sensation. I need him to fill me.

Reece rolls me back over. I hear the unmistakable sound of a condom wrapper tearing above me. The bed dips. My ragged breath comes in soft pants, and I arch upward in a silent plea. The thick muscles of his legs press against my thighs, urging me to open, and I wrap my legs around his waist, as he enters me with excruciating slowness. Above me, he groans as my muscles clench around his hard cock, but he refuses to change his pace.

Each movement is a study in perfect control.

"Please. Please just fuck me. Put us both out of our misery," I plead. My hyper-aroused state holds me on the brink of orgasm.

His hands grab my hips, stilling my efforts to push him deeper as he pulls his hips back. The head of his cock teases the entrance with light strokes as he just moves the head in before retreating.

"Reece. I need to come. Please, Sir."

"When I am ready to allow you to come, then it will happen." His voice is strained, but his motion does not change. "When I fuck you, it won't end until you come uncontrollably and beg me to stop."

I sit on the edge of oblivion as the head of his cock pushes in and out of my drenched pussy, bobbing in a precise rhythm.

"Who's in control, Atlas?"

"You are, Sir. You are in control."

He leans down to find my mouth. Our tongues tangle. Pushing his cock deep, he holds his body perfectly still as he deepens the kiss.

I struggle to move. His hands grasp my wrists, lifting them above my head, pinning them to the mattress. A cry escapes as I delight in the swirl of sensation, my body stretching to accommodate his hard length.

"Perfect," he says, pulling back then thrusting hard into me.

Each stroke is deliberate, filling me before he pulls back in long controlled pauses. The measured moves broker promises of release, but the rhythm only teases me back to the edge.

"Reece, I can't take it anymore," I plead in a hoarse voice.

The lengthy pause drives me to the edge of frustration.

"Don't move your arms."

He releases my wrists. His fingers press into my hips as he drives his cock into me with deep, punishing strokes. His pace quickens as he claims the depths of my body.

"Please, Sir, I need to..."

"Come for me, Atlas."

The words send a shudder through my body as the wave of orgasm crashes over me, and I shatter in ecstasy.

"Give me all of them."

Everything in me responds like I am starved. Continuous waves of orgasms roll over me, crashing through my fragmented thoughts. Reece continues his relentless rhythm as he feverishly drives toward his own release.

With a loud groan, his erratic thrusts continue until he pushes deep. His cock pulsates inside me as he collapses onto his elbows. His head lands on my shoulder as his ragged breath caresses my neck.

My legs fall limp from his hips. I lie in the darkness and mentally float away. For the first time in far too long, I am content and well satisfied.

Soft lips brush against my neck.

"Where have you been all my life?"

His voice sounds disconnected, like a dream somewhere in the untouchable area of my mind.

Above me, Reece shifts, separating our bodies. The mattress moves at the absence of his weight. I barely register the sound of water echoing on the walls.

A warm damp cloth wipes across my inner thighs. I gasp when it brushes against my hyper-sensitive clit.

He climbs into bed next to me. This time I can only feel the softness of his skin as he pulls my head to his chest, the heavy feeling in my limbs making it impossible to move.

"You're so beautiful," he whispers against my hair, his fingers brushing through it. "So strong and sexy."

My mind wants to stay here listening to his soothing voice, but my body refuses to stay above the surface. I feel the pull of darkness as the world fades away.

CHAPTER TWENTY

The smell of brewing coffee demands my attention as my disoriented mind works to recognize my surroundings. Sore muscles scream their complaint when I stretch.

"Good morning, James," I call out to the air without opening my eyes.

"Good morning, beautiful."

Even though his voice is quiet, I start at the sound. My eyes fly open, and my head snaps around until I am staring into his eyes. His body lies in a relaxed incline next to me, as he drags a hand up my body and palms my breast.

"Um, oh my God, I'm..." I stutter. "What time is it?"

"Nearly seven o'clock," he replies.

In one fluid motion, he's above me. The fog in my mind tries to process the move as my head lulls back and I stare up at him. Moisture forms between my legs in anticipation as he rolls on a condom. His hands come down on either side of my head, and he levels me with an intense, determined look. Everything in me lights with desire. Insatiable need courses through me when the tip of his hard cock presses against my opening.

"Spread your legs wide."

Leaning down, he captures my nipple in his mouth, sucking it hard.

I moan and open my legs for him.

"Good girl."

He teases me with his cock while his mouth devours each nipple.

"God, you smell amazing." His raspy voice screams his internal fight against his own needs.

In one smooth motion, he pushes deep and pins me to the bed with his hips. He lifts his head before he bends to claim my mouth with a scorching kiss as his hips stroke back and forth in rhythm, mimicking his tongue.

I struggle against the tide of sensation and groan into his mouth as he fills me completely. His slow drive pushes me toward the peak. Each time I get close to falling over the edge, his rhythm slows or pauses, pulling me back from the precipice. When I think I can take no more of his delicious torture, he grabs my hips, thrusting hard with punishing strokes which claim and possess me.

"That's it. Give it to me, beautiful," he says, straining against his own release.

The climax rips me apart, pulsating through me as my body clenches and shudders around him. Above me, his face contorts, then relaxes in release. His body goes rigid as his breath comes in ragged gasps. He falls onto his forearms, kisses my forehead, then rolls his body next to mine.

For a few minutes we lie in silence. Only the short pants of our breath break the stillness. The smell of coffee wafts into the room again.

"Did you make coffee?" I say, my lazy mind trying to make sense of the smell.

"No." His wolfish grin tells me he knows something. "I heard someone moving around in the kitchen earlier."

"Shit." I try to bolt upright, but his arm holds me down.

"Too late now. You might as well enjoy the afterglow."

"Reece, I work with these people."

"Atlas, you work on the grounds of an alternative lifestyle club. There's no doubt they know you have sex."

I glare at him, and he returns it, ratcheting up the intensity. I'm the first to look away.

"My private life is private," I reply just above a whisper.

"And it still is. Just because people want to jump to conclusions doesn't mean you have to give in to them."

He brushes his fingers through my hair. "Now go get into the shower. I'm not done with you yet."

I get up, walk into the en suite, and turn the shower to the perfect temperature. Behind me, Reece strides into the bathroom wonderfully nude. He exudes a confident grace as his muscles flex in the mirror's reflection. I drop my gaze to the semi-hard package between his legs. My nipples harden in response, and goosebumps race across my skin.

"Like what you see?" A knowing smile crosses his face.

"Yes." I return it with a mischievous grin of my own.

We step into the shower. The warm water sluices off us, and I run a soapy hand over his demigod body, then sink to my knees before him.

My lips wrap around his hard length. Above me, Reece gasps, and his hands slam against the tile to steady him, as I lick the tip of his cock. With a deliberate motion, I wrap my lips around the head and plunge him deep into my mouth.

"God, Atlas." Reece groans and sucks in a deep breath when his cock hits the back of my throat.

I pull back, and his cock leaves my mouth with a pop.

"That's Goddess Atlas to you."

He answers by digging his hands into my hair as he pushes me back onto his cock and fucks my mouth in a slow constant pace.

I moan against him. Seconds later, he pulls my head back and his body goes rigid in release.

Untangling his hands from my hair, he reaches down and lifts me until I stand before him. In the next instant, my body is pinned against the shower. Between my legs, his fingers tease my clit in retaliation until an orgasm wrenches from me, and a scream rips from my throat.

When he's sure I have my balance, he runs soapy hands in trails across my body and rinses me with the hand shower. As he steps out of the shower, he leans in until his breath grazes my ear.

"I'm sure the entire office heard that one," he whispers, then turns to step out of the shower.

I watch as his fine, firm, naked ass disappears through the bathroom door. A rush of heat flushes through me. For the next thirty minutes, I work through the rest of my morning routine and step into the bedroom.

Across the room, Reece stands immaculately dressed in a navy blue suit, the white collared shirt finished with gleaming silver cuff links.

My head cocks in confusion.

"When..." I start.

"My driver picked up my dry cleaning."

He hands me a cup of coffee and gives me a look that promises a range of wicked ideas. It is a controlled, civilized look in deep contrast to the frenzy of insatiable moments only minutes before. The thoughts make my heart quicken, and my sore muscle clench in response.

"Miss Devereaux, that look could have you tied up for days," he warns over his coffee cup as he leans against the wall.

"I could lose my job over the stunt you pulled," I hiss.

He barks out a laugh.

"You're the managing partner. I'm sure it will not be an issue."

I lift the dress off the bed.

"Are you trying to dictate what I wear, Reece?"

"I enjoy seeing you in beautiful, sexy but tasteful clothes. The paperwork is rather clear on this issue."

"Paperwork I've yet to sign," I say as I finger the fabric of the dress. "It's beautiful."

"What's wrong, Atlas?"

I shake my head and turn to open the closet and pull out a dark black pinstripe pantsuit. For too long I've been independent. One night of passion won't be my undoing. It was wonderful to let go of control in the heat of it all, but I need to maintain a grip in the rest of my world.

Reece watches me dress as a strangled silence descends over the room.

"I want to see you tonight and wrap you up in rope like a gorgeous package."

"My schedule is packed today. I won't be done until early evening."

"Don't make excuses, Atlas." His features harden.

"Since when is working an excuse?" An angry tone creeps into my voice as guilt crawls across my psyche in not explaining my double life.

He sighs with a frustrated exhale.

"Let me in, Atlas. This only works when we both learn to trust each other."

I nod, swallowing hard.

"It's complicated, Reece." A breath leaves my chest in a heavy sigh. "I'd love to spend the evening with you."

"Before we go, I was hoping you'd wear this for me." He hands me a velvet jewelry box.

I cock my head to the side.

"Don't you think jewelry is rushed at this stage?"

"I wanted to give you a reminder of last night so you'll have a wonderful thought in your day. Something to anchor you when the helm of your ship is battered by a squall."

Opening the box, I spy a small padlock charm with a singular diamond across the body. It shimmers in the light. My mouth goes dry as I stare at the necklace and its implications.

"May I?" he asks, plucking the necklace from the box.

I nod, too stunned to trust my words.

Reece steps behind me, pulling the charm to the hollow of my throat. Once he's satisfied with its placement, he fastens the chain and lets it drop to the top of my spine, sending a shiver down my body.

"You are the most amazing and stunning woman I've ever met. The diamond pales in comparison." He plants a soft kiss at the nape of my neck.

"Ready?" I mutter, taking a step toward the bedroom door.

He settles his hand on the small of my back. The heat of his touch sends a ripple through me, and I work against the vulnerable thoughts as he steers me out of the room.

CHAPTER TWENTY-ONE

Samantha sits at the kitchen island, tapping away on her tablet computer when we enter the studio kitchen.

"Good morning, Miss Kingston, lovely to see you again," Reece says.

"And you, Mr. Gabriel," she says as her eyes lift, staring at me.

Reece turns toward me.

"Trust," he whispers. His smile fades as he runs his thumb against the curve of my cheekbone. The ache in my chest at his tenderness makes me wonder how far I should open to him. He bends down and gives me a chaste kiss before pulling away.

"Until this evening, Miss Devereaux," he says, then turns to Samantha. "Have a wonderful day, Miss Kingston."

Both of us stare for a long minute at Reece Gabriel's backside descending the stairs. When the front door dings, Samantha's animated face turns toward me.

"Oh my God, Atlas, if that scream was any indication, your evening was amazing, and it doesn't look like you even left the office."

A mass of emotions surge through me — lust, exhilaration of the memory, and utter embarrassment.

"Samantha," my tone warns, "if you say anything about seminal emission, submission, control, sex, or any of the hundreds of other thoughts racing through your mind, I will not be held responsible for my actions."

She smiles.

"I'm enjoying thinking about the tightly controlled Miss Devereaux in the heat of passion, losing her mind to the point she forgets herself. I can't believe you are dating."

A frown creases my face.

"I don't date, you know that. Fucking differs a great deal from dating."

My phone dings and I pull it out of my pocket, glancing at the screen to see R. Gabriel displayed across it.

The evening was full of wonderful revelations. I look forward to peeling back your multi-layered facade. RG

"Well, at least you're scratching that itch for once." Samantha watches my faces as she tries to continue the conversation against my distraction.

"I suppose," I answer without commitment. "There's work I need to do here this morning, then I'll be at the club for the rest of the day. I've let far too much slip over there as of late."

Without waiting for a reply, I turn and head down the stairs to the office level while texting back a quick reply.

———

It was enjoyable, Mr. Gabriel. I hope we can continue forward in an adult manner. AD

———

I WALK OVER TO MY DESK AND FLIP ON MY COMPUTER.

"He's definitely into you," Samantha says, her heels clicking across the floor. "This one might be able to warm that ice-cold heart of yours."

My phone dings again as if agreeing with Samantha's observations.

An adult manner is exactly the way I'd like to continue, Miss Devereaux. RG

"THAT'S ENOUGH," I GROWL BOTH TO THE PHONE AND TO Samantha. I scowl, focusing on the computer screen, scrolling through emails.

"Finally, someone who might be able to bring the infamous Atlas Devereaux to her knees and add a little balance," Samantha quips.

"I don't believe in happily ever after, and my life is full as it is. I don't need a complication and Mr. Gabriel's heady combination of subtle arrogance crossed with a chivalrous nature means he's hiding something somewhere."

"And you should know."

I don't look up from my phone, trying to find the best way to push back.

I'm sure you would, Mr. Gabriel, but my schedule is packed today. We should postpone until another evening. AD

I LOOK UP, GLARING AT SAMANTHA.

"Hence my point. Do you think he'll stick around when he realizes I'm a pro Dominant and own the club next door? Men like him want to be in total control; they barely give it up unless it suits their purposes. I know. They've knelt before me. Besides, it doesn't end well when people try see all of me, or want more than I can give."

"Atlas, you can't cloud your present with your past. That's not fair."

"I'm not clouding the present, rather I'm finally being realistic. It is a fun situation, but it can't develop into anything serious."

"Jaded much?" Samantha says as she quirks an eyebrow.

"Please don't start."

"Okay," she replies, not ready to let go of the subject.

"Where are we with the Nick Norris case?"

Samantha pauses, staring at me hard for a long moment.

"We are working up his publicity campaign. He's done well in the last couple of races. I've got calls out to two dozen sponsors. We should hear something this week."

"Excellent," I reply absently. "Is there anything on Mr. Gabriel's background that should concern us going forward?"

"Is that a personal or professional question?"

I close my eyes, struggling to control the flare of exasperation.

"Professional." I reply through clenched teeth.

"Other than his consistent attempts to hide his preferences for an alternative lifestyle, there are no other skeletons in his closet. There have been a couple of anomalies in his background, but nothing to be overly concerned about."

"Anomalies? What type of anomalies are we talking about here?"

"Nothing major. I'm trying to track down their sources to give you a better answer, but I'm not worried. I've reached out to Ian Brecken-ridge, his sister's campaign manager, to see if they have anything on their radar."

"Okay," I reply with a deep sigh. "Just keep me posted on any changes."

Samantha nods, hitting the remote for the audio system. Sofia

Karlberg's voice croons, *Let it Go*, and I look down at my vibrating phone.

***

What I wouldn't give to be the distraction that relieves you of your packed schedule. ~ RG

***

I SHAKE MY HEAD AND SMILE AT THE EVENTS OF THE PREVIOUS evening as I set the phone on my desk before turning to work through my emails.

My body zings with excitement and contentment. The flirty texts add a new element to my world. I feel carefree and giddy as I walk through the club. The recent stress is excised from every corner of my mind, and I'm light on my feet. I've changed into one of my favorite *Alexandra* outfits, a dark blue corset and pencil skirt with a suit blazer. It is the perfect combination of sexy and corporate. The dichotomy makes me smile as I walk toward my office.

"Alexandra," Kade calls from down the hall.

Turning on my heel, I greet him with a smile.

"Good afternoon, my dear boy. How is life treating you?"

"Um," he stutters, stopping in front of me. "Good?"

His eyebrow quirks.

"Most excellent. What can I do you for?"

"Well. Is everything okay?"

"Never better. Tippy tappy and top o' the world."

"Are you on something?" Kade looks concerned.

"No. Can't I be happy for once?" I laugh.

"Of course, but it's so..."

"Unusual, odd, weird, frightening, worrisome? Which word were you going to end on?"

A smile pulls at the edge of his lips. "My God, did you get laid?"

The race of blood flushes under my skin. It's just sad, for someone who owns a sex club, who can walk through it watching a large amount of sordid activities, to be embarrassed when someone brings up their private life.

"That's what people do sometimes, Kade. You should try it."

Kade throws his head back in laughter.

"I do. Often. The same can't be said about you though." His eyes survey me again, as if it doesn't quite add up. "So who's the lucky guy?"

"Really, Kade? I don't kiss and tell."

"Cool. I'll torture it out of Samantha. We'll both enjoy it, and she'll give up your secret."

"Brat," I say, punching him in the arm.

"Why, Miss Alexandra, how very unladylike."

I roll my eyes.

"I believe you interrupted my day by yelling my name from down the hall rather than approaching me like a properly trained civilized submissive."

On cue, Kade's eyes fall to the floor, and I smile at his response.

"Yes, Ma'am." His reverent tone does nothing to mask the grin plastered across his face.

"Come on then, let's find out what's so important."

We walk back toward my office in jovial silence. Kade throws me sideways glances as he shakes his head.

"Katie, hold my calls," I say, rounding my assistant's desk.

I saunter over to my desk, clear a space, and hop onto it. My fingers curl around the edge. I smile up at Kade as I swing my legs.

"Okay, hit me, big boy. What have you got for me today? Sex in the swimming pool causing us to drain it or do we have unusually high chlorine count that turned a blonde's hair green? I know, blood on the carpet in studio B. That would be too bad, the ivory carpet really is beautiful. Wait, I know, someone's written with lipstick on their submissive's back and pushed them against the freshly painted wall in Corridor C." I shake my head. "No, that can't be right. They did that last year, causing us to paint again."

When I look up from my funny tirade, Kade is standing in the middle of my office, mouth agape.

"Like what you see?" I jump down off my desk, lifting my skirt slightly and wagging my eyebrows.

He blinks twice, the effort not to laugh obvious as he slams his mouth shut. The telling bulge in his pants amuses me. Our banter is hitting all the right buttons, and I smile at our easy relationship.

"Wow. Whoever he is, he must be damn good in bed. I'll pay him my entire bonus to keep you like this." The words rush from his mouth.

I grin.

"Have a seat, Kade. Let's see what you've got."

Leaning back against my desk, fingers curling back around the edges, I wait until he settles his large muscular frame into the chair.

"I almost hate to discuss this with you. It's been so long since you've been this relaxed."

"Kade, this place is my responsibility. No matter how stupid, frantic, or odd things get, the buck stops here. You know that. If I can take it on and save everyone else the headache, then that's why I get the big bucks and you all keep me around longer."

"You don't know how happy I am to see you this way. If anyone deserves it, you do."

"Okay, enough with buttering up the boss with flattery. It's bad if you're stalling this much."

Kade pulls a report from his folder.

"We've had several reports of what we think are reporters or paparazzi. The guards haven't been able to catch the suspects, but we've seen evidence on the security feeds. We're not sure exactly what it all means, but the heightened unusual activity is cause for concern."

"What has you the most concerned?"

"The membership's privacy; however, the locations of the various breaches have the team concerned in other areas."

"Spill it, unless the next words out of your mouth will be something about increasing my personal security."

Kade blows out a hard breath. My shoulders fall. I walk around my desk and settle into my chair.

"I will say this once more... There is no reason to raise my security level."

"Alexandra, we've seen them outside your office here, and on the McKenzie Kingston grounds. There's only one thing that ties those things together."

"Yes, I am well aware of the tie. It's all supposition at this point. When you have something solid, then bring it to me." The smile falls from my face. "I understand your concern for my safety, especially considering the recent proposal, but I haven't heard a peep out of Edmund since. You can't think every client who steps out of line is a repeat."

Kade's blue eyes stare at me with intent. "It was too close the last time..."

"And that was a lifetime ago," I interrupt. "I've grown up since then. I'm not the wide-eyed innocent who walked into a world that was vastly different than what I expected."

"No, but you're still vulnerable."

"That's enough, Kade." My sharp tone pierces the air. With a deep breath to settle my rising emotions, I work to regain my composure.

My thoughts turn to Reece and where he fits into my maddening world. There's no way I can keep up my normal charade and have the kind of intense relationship he offers. Kade's concern collides with my reality.

I close my eyes, as a myriad of emotions washing through me. When I reopen them, my expression is determined and bleak.

"I know that look." Kade's voice is full of concern. "Stop that train of thought right now. You can't just let him go because your world is a little more complicated with a relationship. Open up to whoever it is and share yourself. If anyone deserves happiness, it's you."

"No, you were right earlier. In my opinion, this security concern is nothing, but it's not fair to drag an unsuspecting person into my weird life. I chose this life, and all the decisions which led to it. We both know I'm ultimately not good for him or his sister, and it's better to end it early before we get in any deeper."

"Ah. So Mr. Gabriel is the one who's gotten under your skin," he says with an understanding smile. "There's always a choice, Ma'am. Trust, and take a leap that it will be okay."

"No." I shake my head. The world dissolves, leaving a wide yawning abyss before me. "I don't want to let him go, but I have to. It's for the greater good."

Tears swim in my eyes, and I blink them away.

"You are falling in love with him. It's obvious. Don't throw it away out of fear; just give it some time."

"No." I work to force down the emotions.

"Don't be stupid!"

I glower at Kade, grabbing the anger at his insistence. Anger is better than falling into a tearful puddle.

"I'm not being stupid. I'm being sensible. Finally. It is stupid to think I could have it all. Stopping at good — no, great sex is the intelligent path."

"You've been looking for balance for so long, you can't just quit when there's a slight bump in the road," he challenges.

"A bump? You call this a bump? There will always be security concerns, or other problems. This is my life. It's my home."

"Yes, this is only a bump. You need to get a grip, figure out how to settle this situation, and get on with your relationship."

I stare at Kade. My mouth is dry, my anger boiling just under the surface. More than anything else, I am furious at myself for not being able to handle Edmund, whose money makes him dangerous. Everything in me prays the security concern and his threats aren't linked. I am disgusted at myself for creating this entire situation.

Regardless of my good intentions, I am obviously not good for Reece.

"Don't fucking tell me how to run my life!" I scream in frustration as my emotions fray out of control.

Kade stares at me impassively. The long silence stretches between us. I wrap my hand around the glass of water on my desk, taking a welcoming sip. I inhale a deep breath as I try to control my frayed nerves.

"Ma'am, yes, Ma'am. I read you five by five." His tone is harsh but controlled. "Will there be anything else, Ma'am?"

Our eyes lock in a hard gaze, neither of us backing down, but he knows that I have only the slightest of upper hands based on my position and responsibilities.

"No," I calmly reply as a steel edge pervades my tone. "There's nothing else. You are dismissed."

"Ma'am." He glares at me, his eyes warning me that this is far from over. "Yes, Ma'am."

His flat tone sends shivers up my spine. For a long moment we stare at each other over my desk.

With suddenness, Kade gives me a slight bow, turns on his heel with military precision, and walks out of the door. Its meaning sends shivers up my spine.

CHAPTER TWENTY-TWO

"Ma'am?" Katie knocks on the door, peering inside.

"Come."

"Ma'am, Edmund is here to see you. He doesn't have an appointment."

I nod, hoping that things will once again return to the way they were just a few days ago, the whole incident forgotten and past.

"Send him in, Katie."

Her voice lowers to a whisper as she quickly approaches my desk, "Should I alert security, Ma'am?"

The sincere question makes me realize that Kade paid her a visit and explained his concerns. The only reason she's asking me instead of following the orders I know Kade left is because of her recent mistake in handling Mr. Gabriel's unannounced visit.

"No need. It will be fine. Show Edmund in." I look up and give her a soft smile but not believing a word coming out of my mouth. Admonishing myself for allowing history to bias my current situation, I look back down to the page on my desk as a way of dismissal. When she turns to leave, I lift my eyes slightly to watch her disappear through the door.

"Alexandra will see you now," her soft voice lilts, and she once again appears with Edmund in tow.

Keeping my head down, I pretend to write and focus on the task I was working on before the announcement of Edmund's arrival. It's all an act. Power to make sure that Edmund believes nothing has changed because of his proposal. The power still lies with me, without question or concern.

His tall, fit form stands gracefully in his well-tailored bespoke suit. He holds a dozen blue roses, tied elegantly in a long velvet ribbon. His long graceful fingers put just enough pressure on the stems to balance them but not enough to show tension in the situation.

I look up from my desk, placing the top on the carbon fiber fountain pen and setting it into the mahogany box with a myriad of others. Each move is slow, elegant and precise, refusing to show any level of tension or concern.

"Please do come in, Edmund. Have a seat."

In measured steps, he approaches my desk, laying the bouquet in front of me before unbuttoning his jacket and gliding down into the seat.

"They are beautiful, thank you," I acknowledge in a slow Southern drawl. "To what do I owe this most unusual visit?"

Edmund has only ever graced my office once in the nearly ten years of our professional interaction. It was the day he applied for membership, our professional association starting shortly after. In all that time he's been nothing but a gentleman. He is intense but soft-spoken. Every movement is done to perfection, and when perfection is not obtained, the need for true, harsh punishment is always obvious. Our sessions give him the time to tangibly feel all the comments, thoughts, and emotions he can't afford to acknowledge throughout the day.

His stilted business posture makes the hairs on the back of my neck stand on end. While we have a formal ritualistic relationship, there has never been a hard undertone or power struggle in our interactions. I watch his eyes narrow and realize that for all my trying to remain relaxed, he must notice my tension.

His face softens. "I feel I owed you an apology, Mistress. My proposal caught you off-guard. It is my only desire to make your life wonderful and allow our relationship to intensify in a way that our current constraints do not allow."

"Thank you, Edmund." I force a smile. "I hope we can return to the way things were and put this little incident past us."

For a moment he sits and stares at me. "With all due respect, Alexandra, I am not rescinding my proposal. Nothing could be further from the truth. I want give you space to come to its acceptance." The lines on his face harden before he relaxes, but it is the tone of his voice that has my hand on the edge of my desk, searching for the silent alarm button.

"Now, now, Alexandra. There's no need to call the cavalry to rescue you. We are only having a polite, civilized conversation. Besides, we both know that the minute I walked in, Katie alerted the security desk but told poor Kade to stand down. I'm sure he'll be disappointed when I take you away from here."

I relax a little at his words. Kade isn't one to back down once he's aware of a situation, and Katie's call means he's on his way, or at least I hope it does.

"Just imagine how wonderful it will be, my dear. We'll vacation in a tropical paradise, go on tours of Europe. Your every whim and desire will be catered to. With me as your submissive, you'll be able to do darkly delicious things to me. When I come home after a long, arduous day at work, you'll be there waiting with your whip. Those luscious legs encased in tall black shiny patent leather, while you demand I crawl to you and kiss your feet. With no reason to work outside the home, you'll have so much time to think on novel ways to punish this wicked boy."

I stare blankly across my desk. Fear licks through me.

"Won't it be wonderful, Alexandra?" He says my name like it is the sweetest song he can intone. "You can give up making sure these commoners have their little fantasy playground."

When he pauses, the silence in the room becomes deafening. Every possible mental alert goes off in my head. The smile drops from my face.

"I... I can't accept your proposal, Edmund." The words are far less confident than I desire, but I'm glad my vocal cords are still in the game. "It is an extremely generous offer, but I quite enjoy owning this club and the work I do here."

"You can't be serious. You can't tell me you enjoy the fact that people here pretend to provide deference when in reality it is a microcosm of irrelevant power games of small-minded plebeians."

An incredulous look etched across his face turns his features into a distorted strain.

"Edmund, people come here to enjoy their fantasies, to live out an escape from the rest of the world. The same as we did each session." My even tone is strained.

"No, Alexandra. What we have is elevated above the common masses. I do not desire to share you with them when there is no reason I can't have you all to myself."

I take a deep breath and steady my thoughts, my finger brushing across the panic button. Standing up quickly so that my actions aren't noticed in the distraction, I push hard on the alarm button. My fingers curl firmly around the desk, holding me steady.

"I think you should go, Edmund." My firm voice doesn't waver, but a nervous shiver runs through my body as it moves from imperceptable to noticeable. I need to get him out of the room before he realizes exactly how much he's unnerved me.

Edmund rises fluidly, never taking his eyes off mine. In an unprecedented move, he steps up to the desk and leans over.

"Oh, Alexandra, darling," he says, his voice barely a whisper, "I had the silent alarm disabled from your office yesterday. There's no reason for this tension between us. When you finally say *yes*, you will see how wonderful life will truly be for you." His voice is soft, kind, and gentle.

Edmund leans in further and places a soft kiss on my cheek. Then lifts his head.

"And if you so much as think about declining my offer, you will find your club, your friends, and everyone around you in ruins so quickly and so irrevocably they will never forgive you. The words alone, exiled, unlovable, and loathed will have a new meaning for you," he hisses in a whisper.

When he straightens, he's once again smiling. His eyes flit over the small diamond encrusted padlock sitting in the hollow of my throat.

"Interesting necklace. When did you get it?"

"Recently," I reply noncommittally.

He nods without taking his eyes off the padlock. Finally, he looks up, smiling.

"You should tell Kade that I just came by to apologize and that you are re-thinking your initial shocked reaction to my proposal." His eyes lift and smiles at the camera in the corner of the ceiling.

Then, grabbing my hand, he lifts the knuckles to his lips, planting a kiss lightly across the skin. "I'll see you soon, my darling." His voice is once again soft and gentle. Quietly turning, he takes measured steps out of the door.

For a long moment I stand there, staring at my open office door. Any minute now, I know Kade will come walking through it, demanding to know if I'm okay. Then he'll interrogate me for every little detail of the interaction. I know he means well, and he wants to keep me safe, but Edmund's threat runs through my head. The thought of ruining everyone dear to me nearly brings me crumpling to my knees.

The need to be around people pushes through my foggy brain. I need to be in a crowd. Kade won't interrogate me there and no one will approach me—safety in numbers and such.

Glancing in the mirror, I make sure my ebony wig is still perfect, knowing that by making it look like I'm touching up my makeup, Kade will be slower to rush in. Pulling out my lipstick, I drag the color across my lips. I make each movement sensual, enticing and elegant. The move forces me to focus in an attempt to calm my shaking hand.

After taking one last look, I turn on my heels and glide across my office. The footfalls click in a staccato echo off the tile as I walk to the bar on the other side of the mansion.

CHAPTER TWENTY-THREE

Three sets of double doors open out to the pool deck. The area is bustling with cocktail waitresses and members. A cool spring breeze creates havoc on napkins and paper products every time someone picks up a glass. The crowd is soothing, and its rhythm settles my shaky nerves, and I relax into my favorite sport of people watching. Taking in the entire scene, I zero in on certain people as I focus on interactions and body language, finding context with each moment.

My hand flicks the straw in my glass of iced latte. Condensation drips down the side in testament to the length of my idle avoidance. Inhaling a deep breath, I look around the room, but my mind refuses to let me savor the moment. The tumultuous thoughts threaten to take me under while I battle to stay afloat above them.

"Good afternoon, Alexandra."

The voice pulls me from my internal darkness. I blink twice, startled, and raise my head to look into Cassandra Clark's emerald green eyes. Her short, white cropped hair glowing in the bright sunlight stands in stark contrast to her golden skin. "I was wondering if I might have a word with you."

"Of course, Cassandra." I nod my consent toward the chair across from me.

Her long, lithe body liquefies into it.

She came to the club about a month ago, telling me she was trying to find herself. I reviewed her application, amusing at the 'undecided' mark of particular proclivities and desired positions. She wrote that she didn't know what she was other than fascinated. Her background check came back clean. Once she completed the orientation classes, the club granted her full membership. Like many members, I rarely interacted on an individual level, but she seemed like a sweet girl.

"Is there something on your mind or is this a social chat?" My tone comes out harsher than I mean, but I have no desire to hear another member tell me how something should be done or field another complaint about some perceived power they have in the club, especially when I'm trying to figure out how to handle the current mess with Edmund.

"Um." She smiles, and I notice her mauling a napkin as she twists it in her hand. "I was wondering if I could ask you a question."

"You just did," I reply with no inflection.

"Oh." She giggles and glances at the floor. "Um, that's not what I, um, meant..."

"It's usually polite to look at someone when you are talking with them," I reply as my curiosity piques at her nervousness.

"I was wondering, um, Domina, I mean, Miss, I mean, Alexandra." Her uneven breath causes her voice to waver.

"My eyes are up here, girl," I command.

Her fidgeting stops and her eyes rise to meet mine.

"Yes, Ma'am, I'm sorry."

I nod my acknowledgment. "What was your question?"

"I was wondering why you're a Dominatrix," she blurts out all at once.

The question catches me off-guard as it sends me reeling. I don't flinch, but it is only through a colossal amount of effort.

Normally, I would quip about how much I love to see a man on his knees, or at my feet. Maybe I'd talk about holding control in those moments or say something about holding another person's trust and life in my hand. Right now I can't say any of those things without feeling like a fraud.

I don't feel in control at all. Quite the opposite. Fear and dread aren't coming from a place of fun, trust, or play, but from an exertion of non-consensual power. Everyone in my life, those who touch it from afar and those who are close, are now in unknown peril based on the decisions I will make in a brief period.

My answer forms in my mind. I am a pro Dominant because I desired to give others the feelings that I could not give myself permission to experience. The thoughts roll over me as I ponder my best answer to her.

"Dominatrix drags up such poor imagery. I quite prefer pro Dominant or Dominant if I am not paid for the service or it's part of a relationship."

"My apologies, Ma'am, I meant no offense," she says, her voice now quavering a bit.

Reaching out my hand, I capture hers, stopping her fidget.

"None taken. I am simply giving you new vocabulary. Nothing more."

She slowly nods.

"Why did you choose a dominant position? What made it better than being a submissive or even top or bottom?" The words spill from her curious mouth.

I can almost smell the new to the lifestyle smell wafting from her.

"First, I am a person. One who has the most interesting of inclinations. Just like any person, they don't make up all of me, nor are they always the most interesting parts."

I smile, knowing full well I'm evading the question.

The long silence flows between us as she shifts in her chair. I let her experience the unspoken power that comes completely from her own mind, though I skillfully use it to my advantage.

"Power and control are an illusion. These surroundings allow people to escape the harsh realities of the day and give them a place where they are safe enough to face their fears, desires, fantasies, and pleasures. It is a heady feeling to be instrumental in that process, but it is the connectedness to another which is unexplainable," I reply. "I am in this role because I enjoy leading in the dance as I take someone into a transcendent world where angels fear to tread."

A mix of confusion and frustration dances across Casandra's face until she frowns.

"Were you expecting me to say because I love the power of seeing someone on their knees following my every command?" The sarcastic edge of my words cause her eyes to shoot up.

"Yes, Ma'am."

"Ah. You've read too many fantasy books and have little personal experience. It is the difference between theory and practical reality."

"How did you learn to be a Dominant?" She is focused as she tries another tack for the answer she thinks she wants.

"You mean the skill set?"

"Yes, Ma'am. How did you learn to throw a whip or a flogger? I mean, you do know how, don't you? They say you are a skilled — one of the best in the club." Her face is once again hopeful.

The images of Dominick pushing me to do a skill again, the welts marking my body when I lost control of the whip, the time spent in my room working to understand the perfect execution of a skill or concept, floods my mind. The punishments for getting it wrong, or when I accidentally hurt a bottom. Reading books on psychology and human anatomy between classes. The training was almost as rigorous, if not more, than the grad program I was taking at the time.

"I had an amazing trainer. He pushed me to learn and grow in every skill, and when I didn't execute them to his satisfaction, I was punished." The matter-of-fact tone settles my inner turmoil.

"Does everyone learn through a trainer?"

I shake my head. "No. The world is changing. Information is accessible. Most people learn by trial and error with a willing partner.

Often finding a specific skill they both enjoy and exploring it as they get better over time."

"How did you end up with a trainer? They say you have a wide range of skills." Her curiosity is now clearly piqued, and she leans forward to the table.

"Luck." I don't elaborate on if I thought it was good or bad. "I had a friend who introduced me to someone who took me under his wing. He was exceedingly demanding and took my success in each skill very personally."

My words sink into her mind, and her hands lay flat on the table as her breath comes in rapid, uneven pants. Cassandra's eyes dilate a little as the words rush to a deep-seated part and her clear desire grows with each passing minute.

Looking up, I lean back in my chair and let my gaze fall across the crowded bar. Groups are gather as they whisper and glance in our direction. It is rare for someone to approach my table so informally.

When they say it's lonely at the top, they fail to tell you it is because most people stay away. They are intimidated by your confidence or judge you on their biases. Over time you become the mask of the person they create, conforming to their labels and assumptions.

The gentle breeze falls across my neck, and a shiver races down my spine. Kade strides toward my table from the other side of the bar, coming up short when he sees Cassandra sitting across from me. For several minutes, the weight of his gaze surrounds us while I avoid looking at him. He wants to talk, but I'll struggle to pretend that everything is fine, so I ignore him.

Edmund's threats run through my mind and I shove them away. Taking a deep breath, I turn back to Cassandra.

"Will you train me? Teach me how to be a good Dominant?" Her words come in a rush.

"No one can teach you to be a good Dominant, Cassandra. That is a path you have to learn on your own. Someone can only teach you to be competent in certain skills or how to wield our chosen... tools."

"I see." Her eyes fall to the table.

There's so much of me, so long ago, in her. The open eagerness, the slight bit of innocence not yet clouded by the jading of reality.

"Will you train me in those skills, Ma'am?"

A thousand reasons to say no rush to my mind. The time commitment alone can overwhelm, and with all the current situations in my world, I have more than enough reasons to decline her request.

"I want you to write an essay on what you desire to learn and why. What you see in this lifestyle, and why that draws you. Then I will decide," I hear myself say. "Do not rush the process. I do not want to see it unless you have spent a full month or more on the assignment. When it is complete, I will give you my answer."

Excitement gleams in her eyes, and her body vibrates as it sits straighter in her chair.

"I don't know what to say. I will not disappoint you, Alexandra, I mean Ma'am, I mean thank you. You will not regret it. I promise." She twitters on, her face reflecting the rush of thoughts in her head. "Thank you. Thank you so very much."

She pops up from her chair.

"Sit," I order.

The look on her face is priceless. She stands stock still before once again liquefying into her chair.

"'Self-control is strength. Right thought is mastery. Calmness is power.' — James Allen." My calm, even tone gives me the air of aloof authority. "I did not dismiss you. It is rude to leave a conversation when you have gained your desired outcome but contributed nothing in return."

My eyes don't meet hers, but I can see her mouth sag open. Closing it quickly, she casts her eyes down.

"I'm sorry."

"You are forgiven. That was but a taste of your request. Mastery of self is paramount to the journey you are seeking to travel." I smile. "You're dismissed, Cassandra. I look forward to your essay."

She sits there for a moment, then gracefully moves her body upward.

"Thank you so much for speaking with me."

"My pleasure. I hope your day is pleasant and you are able to fully enjoy such beautiful weather."

With a slight nod, she turns and walks off toward the pool. Once she feels she's far enough from the table, I see her pumping her fist in the air as she runs to a group of her friends as they chat excitedly.

I look around to see if Kade is still lurking in the corners, already preparing for his onslaught, when the waitress walks up to my table.

"Ma'am, pardon my interruption, but Mr. Kinkaid asked that I deliver this to you as soon as you were available."

She places the handwritten note on my table and turns to walk back toward the bar. I take one last glance over the crowd and brace myself as I glance down.

SAW EDMUND'S VISIT ON THE MONITORS. HE SEEMED OVERLY *friendly. Let me know when you can discuss. Kade*

I TWIRL THE NOTE IN MY HAND, AND I'M SUDDENLY ALL TOO aware of the cameras, almost feeling Kade's team watching my every move for signs of distress to his note. Slipping from my chair, I smile and wave to the bartender as I make my way back to the office.

Several members stop me along the way to discuss their compliments or concerns about the club. Each time I smile and chit-chat, making polite conversation as I work to appear relaxed while Edmund's threats are now a constant internal beat.

Finally, reaching the sanctuary of my office, I send a quick note to the security room and flip the switch to turn off the camera. I think about my upcoming massage appointment in hopes it will help take away some of the day's tension.

Walking around the edge of my desk, I pick up the appointment calendar and read through the appointments. I'm glad for a light schedule and smile to myself until I see a gleam of metallic paper. Looking down, there's an envelope perfectly centered on my blotter. My gaze travels across the rest of my desk—each item is rearranged to an exacting order. Cold tendrils of fear run through my body, clenching my nerve endings as I stand there in stunned silence.

Hesitantly, I lift the envelope. *Alexandra* is written in beautiful calligraphy across the front. Turning it over, I nervously slide the card out of its confines.

It was so nice to see you today. I've missed you, and wanted to ensure we understood each other, knowing my proposal simply waits on you to accept it. In case you thought my words were hollow — I know who you are, Atlas. I meant every word I said. Tell anyone of our more intimate conversation and I will destroy you. I can't wait until you are all mine. ♡

THE CARD ISN'T SIGNED, BUT THERE'S NO DOUBT WHO SENT IT.

The paper shakes in my hand as my eyes fall on the bouquet of blue roses Katie arranged in a vase.

This can't be happening. He's been in my office, but there was no security detail when I arrived. If he'd walked in, then the cameras would have alerted the Command Center to his presence, and Kade would have rushed a team to my office. My eyes glance off the bouquet of blue roses. For a moment, I stop and wonder if that is true. Did she place them there or...?

I admonish myself for thinking the worst and realize I must be reading the situation wrong. He has an infatuation. After a few days it will all calm down. My ragged breath makes me light-headed. I land in my seat without grace or elegance. With shaky hands, I press the intercom for Katie's extension.

"Yes, ma'am?" Her voice crackles across the speaker.

"Please cancel my appointments for the rest of the day. Have Adam meet me out front with the car in five minutes."

"Yes, Ma'am." Her voice is edged with concern. "Is everything okay?"

"I'm fine, Katie. I have a headache," I reply, straining to hold on to the Southern drawl and make the words seem far less urgent than they feel.

"Adam will be around with the car immediately, Ma'am, and your schedule is being cleared," she confirms, though I barely pay attention. I know she is efficient.

"Did anyone come by while I was out?" I say, keeping my tone light.

"A woman came by and handed me a gold envelope. I put it on your desk and tidied your office a bit. Those roses are beautiful."

"Yes, they are," I reply without thinking. "Thank you, Katie."

Kade's number appears on the caller ID as the cell phone vibrates across my desk. I smash the reject button as I rise from my chair and make my way to the front door. I wish there was something to distract me from the entire situation. Rubbing my temple, I walk out of the club with purposeful strides and avoid the security cameras along my path.

In the driveway, Adam stands beside the open door of the midnight blue Audi LW12. I slip into the back seat just in time to hear Adam's cell phone ring. He walks around the car and slides into the driver's seat.

"Yes, sir. I have her. No, sir. I will let you know as soon as I have a destination," he confirms before flipping the phone closed.

I take notice. Kade will be relentless until I find a way to calm his intuition.

Sighing, I sit back as the large estate fades as we move down the driveway. The wig feels heavy. I pull it off and toss it across the gray leather seat. It's time for Atlas to face the world. Alexandra's issues weigh too heavily.

I punch the button for the rear seat massage and heat. The soothing sounds of Adagio in G Minor for Strings and Organ fills the cabin through the Bang & Olufen audio system as The London Phil-harmonic carries me away from the day's turn of events. Reaching into the console, I grab a small pack of makeup remover and rub the towelette over my face as I wipe away the last traces of Alexandra's mask.

CHAPTER TWENTY-FOUR

"I ordered dinner. It sounded like you had quite a bit on your plate today," Reece says as we walk through the front door of the penthouse. "By the way, that's a very hot outfit, not quite the pantsuit you dressed in this morning and more daring than the dress I asked you to wear."

I set my wineglass on the counter as he follows me into the kitchen. My hands run over the steel metal stays of the tight corset under my suit jacket. I internally groan at my oversight. In my haste to leave the club after Edmund's visit, I failed to change clothes. Normally this is not an issue. Since I live alone, there's never a reason to be overly conscious of my attire.

"Want a glass of wine?"

Reece nods as the doorbell sounds once again.

"Looks like dinner arrived just in time," he says as he walks to the front door.

The aroma of rich spices fills the space between us when he returns with a plastic carry-out bag. He moves gracefully through the kitchen.

"I hope you like Thai food—pumpkin curry and spicy duck fried rice," he says, raising the bag as he gives me a smile.

"It smells amazing. Let me go change and I'll join you for dinner."

"No. I think you look perfect." His eyes roam over my body. "I'm not sure why you changed in the middle of the day, but you look sexy as hell."

He steps behind me, setting the bag on the counter and rubbing his hands across my tense shoulders. "Let me take care of you. You look like you had a long day."

He plants a light kiss on the nape of my neck as his fingers work through the tension.

A masked smile pulls across my face and I nod.

"Several unexpected situations..." I start.

He pulls me around, placing a finger over my lips.

"It's not important. What *is* important is this minute. Not what came before it. Now, go kneel comfortably before the chair in your living area." His tone is soft, yet firm.

I nod and walk across the room, folding my frame down onto the couch rather than the floor and watching his face as he sits across from me.

"Why are you here, Reece?" I ask as he removes the takeout containers from the bag.

"I mentioned it this morning, but I really did just want to see you again."

"But why are you *here*, specifically?"

He hands me a pair of chopsticks as he places the pumpkin curry and spicy duck fried rice on the glass coffee table.

"I thought I'd surprise you with dinner. When I came up and you didn't answer the door, I headed back downstairs. Worst-case scenario, I'd leave dinner at the concierge desk when it arrived. Imagine my delight when you ran into me in the elevator."

His casual tone sets me on edge, but it is his confidence that causes me to pause and stare at him.

"So you thought you'd just drop by?"

The chopsticks pause in his mouth and he nods. "I enjoy your company and it was better than my plans."

"And what exactly were your plans?"

"Working. We have an upcoming acquisition."

"Don't tell me, your *staff* has it covered."

His eyes light up in delight. "Actually, my staff kicked me out as a detriment. It seems my mind was wandering too much today."

"I don't even know what that's like."

"Eat."

His chopsticks point toward the coffee table.

"A bit high-handed, aren't you?"

"No. Actually the opposite. You've probably run through you day with little thought of food or drink. I'm banking you skipped lunch between meetings. Feeding you is about caring enough to lift something off your shoulders." He looks down and picks up some duck.

I dip my chopsticks into the pumpkin curry. The rich spices and coconut milk blend in my mouth. The mix of soft, tender, crispy and crunchy textures of the pumpkin, potatoes, and carrot are layered with the multidimensional flavors carried by the combination of coconut milk and spices in a red curry sauce.

"This is good," I say, dipping my chopsticks in for another bite.

He smiles, watching me as I consume dinner at an ever-increasing pace.

I pause, taking a sip of my wine when I realize how hungry I was. The dry wine hints of a fruit undertone, the complexity cutting with ease through the rich curry sauce.

"So it would seem. I'm glad it hit the mark."

He lifts his glass in a silent salute.

I nod and lean forward, propping my elbows on my knees to relieve the pressure of the corset against my stomach.

Reece stands, picking up the containers before walking them back to the kitchen. His tight ass moves with animalistic grace. He holds my gaze when he returns to the living room.

"Shall we enjoy time out on the balcony?" Reece asks.

He holds out his hand. I place my hand in his, and he pulls me into his arms, kissing me lightly. Taken by surprise, I clutch his firm biceps. He runs his hand down my side, across the corset stays, and turns me around to walk out onto the balcony.

The cool air blows across my skin, raising goosebumps and sending a shiver down my spine. Our bodies face out toward the city, standing at the waist-high concrete wall surrounding the open-air patio. The round steel handrail gleams as Reece stands behind me, watching the rapidly fading sun. The lights twinkle as the city slips into the elegance of evening.

"I can't wait to get you naked," he whispers against my temple, "and wrap you up in my web of rope."

"You want me for my body then?" I ask, internally bracing.

"Oh, Miss Devereaux, I want all of you. Your body is just the most accessible part."

Heat radiates off his body, taking the edge off the cool breeze. He pulls me hard against him as his erection presses into my lower back. I should push him away, nothing in my world is good for him, but there's something about the connection between us. A comfortable companionship. On some strange level, I'm drawn to him. In his arms, I feel safe.

We stand looking at the city in silence, his hands slowly roaming my body. There's no urgency, no forcefulness, but his touch is firm and confident.

"The corset under your jacket is interesting. It's like armor and makes me wonder why you are wearing it." I tense against his touch. "Do you push away anyone who cares about you?"

His question startles me, but his hands don't stop.

"I shut everyone out," I reply softly. "Don't take it personally. We're both adults. There's no reason to get in too deep."

"Maybe I want to get in deep with you, Miss Devereaux. You're a fascinating woman."

I laugh. "And how did you put it—aggravating and frustrating?"

"Don't forget passionate. So very passionate."

His fingers float across my skin, sending shivers down my spine. Every nerve ending comes alert to his touch as his musky cologne engulfs me. He slides my hair over my shoulder, grasping a handful at my nape, pulling my head to the side, and exposing the delicate skin. The muscles in my stomach clench as a wave of desire sweeps away my hesitance. What is it about this man? He barely touches me and I'm as weak-kneed as a naïve schoolgirl.

"You smell delicious," he whispers against my neck. "Just hand me control, Atlas."

"We have negotiated nothing yet. You sent me a contract and thought I'd fall in line."

"Quite the opposite. I baited the hook to see if you'd bite." His teeth graze across the skin.

"I haven't agreed to it."

"Yet... You missed the word *yet*. You want to step away from control. I saw it last night in how your body responds. The wonderful way it opened to me. Everything about you screams it. Why do you deny it?"

He hooks his hands into the laces of my corset.

"Turn off the lights in the penthouse, Atlas," he whispers.

"James. All lights off, pathway lights only."

"Lights off," James replies as the lights around us fade and plunge us into darkness. The only light comes from the streetlamps below, making us mere shadows in the dark.

"Good girl," he murmurs against my hair, loosening my corset and unbuttoning the bodice.

It falls away, and he pulls the undershirt over my head, leaving me fully exposed from the waist up. My nipples harden in the breeze. Reece covers them with his palms, then moves his hand until he rolls the pert nubs between his thumbs and fingers.

"Mmm... lovely," he whispers. "Place your hand on the rail."

With a brief hesitation, I reach out, wrapping my hands around the cool metal.

"Relax. No one can see us. We are just two shadows in the night."

He unzips my skirt. With unhurried movements, he pushes the fabric down until it pools around my ankles, then turns his attention to my panties and lets them skim across my skin. The light tap on my leg tells me to step from the now pooled fabric. I oblige the request, shifting my weight, lifting each leg.

The darkness does nothing to help my exposure. The sounds of the city surround us, the long pull of sirens rushing to an emergency while horns blare the consternation of the drivers. Yet here above the streets, I stand almost naked. Only the stiletto heels covering the smallest amount of flesh. A breath of air from the light breeze sends a tremor through my body when it passes across the dampness between my legs.

"Beautiful. I've never seen a sexier woman," he says as his hand slips between my thighs. "Even in this open state you exude confidence, though the tremble may tell a different story."

I gasp when his finger rubs across my clit.

"Let me wrap you up in rope. Take away your ability to escape." His silky voice lulls me into acceptance. "Leave your shoes here and come inside."

I nod and he leads us back into the penthouse.

"Stand in the middle of the room, Atlas," Reece directs.

I step to the position where he points and wait.

His hand grazes my arm. My shoulders flex as I try to control the light shudders running down my body. Lips rest against the back of my neck, vibrating against my skin.

"What are you afraid of, Atlas?"

When I don't answer, his tongue glides down the nape of my neck. I arch back toward him in response to its long, hot, smooth stroke.

"Let's dance." His voice is soft as it soothes across my nerves.

"But there's no music." I sigh as his hand moves around me to cup my breast.

"That's okay. I can fix that problem." His teeth graze across my shoulder. "James, playlist Rope."

I scowl at his command to James as the music lilts across the penthouse and Lana Delray declares her Burning Desire.

Reece pulls a length of rope across my skin, the rough hemp abrading it while it fills the room with the soft scent of sweet cut grass. The fragrance carries my mind from the worries of the day. It is the perfect juxtaposition of harshness and softness.

He runs the rope through his hands, the movement causing his body to visibly relax. His deft fingers fold it until the center point lies against his palm.

The folded rope wraps below my breasts, the double wrap hugging my rib cage. He threads the long length through the naturally formed loop across my spine. Slowly he works the rope back around in the opposite direction. After a couple of turns, he repeats the same movements over the top. My breath is uneven. The energy between us grows with each connection of the rope as he tightens it. The long end lies across my left shoulder, and he weaves it under the bottom line before crossing back over the right one. He gives the harness a firm, decisive tug before tying off the ends. I gasp. Desire surges through me as my breasts swell and my nipples harden.

Stepping in front of me, he drops his head and slowly drags his tongue across my pert nipples.

"Very nice," he whispers appreciatively against my skin.

I moan and he continues his ministrations. The soft flick of his tongue is followed by slight nips of his teeth as his breath blows against the sensitive skin and his thumb strokes across my other nipple. Reece lavishes attention on each one as his hands massage the entire breasts before returning his focus to the edge of each nipple.

My body is alight with desire. I reach up, running my fingers through his hair to pull his mouth closer.

"Put your hands behind your back. Your palms touching your opposite arm," he commands softly, trailing a kiss down my shoulder.

My arms move to obey, and he coils the ropes around them until they are securely bound behind my back. Each wrap binds my arms to the chest harness.

My pussy throbs with need. His large hands run down my arms, and I relax into his touch. Reece tosses the rope hard over the exposed beam. In the next instant, he tugs it and I'm forced onto my toes for balance.

"What are you afraid of, Atlas?" His voice is firmer this time.

"Everyone fears many things, mine are of no consequence," I say, not wanting to talk. Everything in me just wants his hands to explore my body.

"They are to me."

His mouth closes around my nipple as he sucks the tender bud, then sinks his teeth into my skin until I gasp in pain and jerk back. The ropes hold me firm, my movements making the nip deeper than intended. His mouth releases me. Those gray eyes lift and stare into mine.

"Fighting me only leads to pain, Atlas. Follow my lead, and we both find pleasure."

Without taking his eyes off mine, he winds his hand down to my core.

"Mmm. Beautifully responsive." His voice rolls over me like a trance.

A finger pushes against my soaking folds, teasing the entrance, keeping up a slow tortuous rhythm. I push my hips forward in need, and he quickly withdraws his finger.

"It's not that easy, Miss Devereaux. You still haven't told me what you're so afraid of." His lips nuzzle against my ear.

Picking up another piece of rope, he runs it through his hand. His eyes still don't leave mine. With practiced movements, he folds it in half before reaching around me to pull the rope snug against my waist, then hitching it and letting the two lengths run down my stomach.

"This should ensure I have your undivided attention."

He knots the rope just above my pelvic mound, pulling the ends between my legs and wrapping it over the waist rope. Separating the line, he threads each one through the ropes running down my stomach and then pulls the ropes in opposite directions to form a diamond. When he's finished, he ties the ends off to the back of the waist rope. Reece pulls on the knot just above my pelvis, drawing the two course lines in a path through the folds of my dripping entrance. Flames of lust shoot through my body. His fingers move in slow circles around the edge of my clit and push the two lines apart as his fingers slip inside. He stretches and teases me, then pulls out once more.

Fisting his hand in my hair, he pulls my head back as his mouth crashes on mine in a desperate, passionate kiss, forcing my lips apart. Fingers pinch my nipples hard, making my body convulse in the heady mix of pain and pleasure as I writhe in his hands on the edge of orgasm.

"I don't think I'll let you come," he says against my lips.

His fingers stroke down the front of my stomach toward my pulsating clit as he thrusts two inside, pushing me higher onto my toes, my legs throbbing from the exertion.

"Your body is soaking wet. Its need sitting right on the edge." His hoarse voice punctuates the movements.

Fingers work in quick succession and my mind empties, only open to the intense sensations. My ragged breath sounds loud in my ears, his movements causing me to dance on my toes. In the next instance his fingers are gone, leaving me to balance precariously. My body screams at the sudden loss of friction.

The rope pulling me upward slackens, his arm wraps around my waist the moment it no longer holds my weight. I sag against the hemp lines binding my limbs.

Scooping me up into his arms, he carries my bound body to the bed before setting me down on the edge. My mind floats, but my body screams from the edge of need. Reaching back, he runs his hands down my arms to check for temperature changes. He works the ropes to release the waist harness, sliding the coarse line against my tender pussy. I gasp as it runs across the small sensitive nub of my clit.

"How are your arms?" He looks up as he sinks down, kneeling in front of me.

"Good."

"No numbness?" His tongue laps at the wetness between my legs, causing a loud gasp.

I shake my head.

"No circulation issues?" he murmurs against my skin.

His tongue swirls around the edge of my throbbing clit, then returns to lap up the moisture gathering on my inner thighs.

"Do you know how wonderful you taste?"

His tongue barely ceases its movement as he looks up toward my face. I glance down to see those penetrating eyes driving home his thoughts.

"Look at me, Atlas. I want to see your face when the world lifts and you explode into a thousand pieces."

My body begs for relief as each movement hangs me off the precipice as two fingers push inside and rub along my G-spot. The movement is my undoing. The orgasm rips through me with the ferociousness of a tsunami. I try to stay focused on his eyes, but the overpowering force of the orgasm renders my efforts useless as they slam shut. I pant, vaguely aware of my surroundings as I ride the wave of pleasure.

"Please," I incoherently beg.

His tongue redoubles its efforts on my overly sensitive clit as his fingers fuck me with a soft ferocity. I pant and squirm against the unforgiving bonds of rope as they bite into my skin. The pain pushes me over the edge, and I shout my release as the second orgasmic wave consumes me.

My breath is ragged as I come down from two powerful orgasms. He stands and grabs me by the waist harness, flipping my body until it is bent helplessly over the bed. The sound of a foil wrapper brushes against my empty mind.

Reece's powerful hands grab my hips and pull me backwards. He lifts his left hand and wraps it around the chest harness. My face presses into the mattress as he slides a finger over the pucker of my ass before positioning himself behind me. The thick tip of his cock presses into me without a rush. My stomach clenches in anticipation.

His hand clenches tighter around the harness and thrusts into me until he's buried to the hilt. He pauses and backs out before repeating the move with more force.

Moaning into the mattress, I tilt my hips higher as my body screams in pleasure at the friction. I clench around him. He curses, plunging inside again. Each movement makes my moans grow louder, only to be dampened by the mattress. Wiggling my hips against him, I sob as I feel the orgasm race across my nerve endings, threatening to overwhelm my senses. I pull against my bonds and growl in frustration as he plunges into me fast and deep, only to move back too slowly to maintain the continuous friction.

Just when I think I can't take another second of the delicious torture, he hammers into me and pushes me into the abyss. I am consumed by the whirlwind ripping through my body as I explode into a thousand glorious pieces, every muscle tensing in unison.

Above me, he groans. His breath comes in ragged pants. Every forceful stab of his cock prolongs my blissful agony. The hand on my chest harness pulls back with force as he slams his hard cock deep. His thrusts are erratic as his body goes rigid with jerks and shudders when he finds his release.

After a long moment, he pulls out and tosses the spent condom in the trash bin. His warm body curls up next to mine as I struggle to breathe normally. Behind me, he works the knots loose from my arms. Unwinding the ropes, he massages the muscles to help the circulation return. Once he is satisfied, he slides the rope from my chest. The delicious friction pulls a moan from me. My body is covered with rope marks and abrasions. He toys with each impression along my skin.

We lie together, basking in the afterglow and connection between us. My arms and wrists ache, but I'm beyond caring. His eyes drink me in as they caress down the length of my body before returning his intense gaze to my face.

"What exactly are you afraid of Atlas?" he murmurs in my ear as my eyes close.

I lose the fight to stay in the world of consciousness and my head lulls against his broad chest as I fall asleep.

CHAPTER TWENTY-FIVE

"Good morning, James," I call to the ceiling and stretch in search of Reece's body.

An eerie silence greets me.

"Good morning, James," I call out again.

"Gooooddd Mmmmooornnning, mmmmammamm," a deep, slow Lurch type voice resounds through the speakers. "Iiiiii aaamm nnot ffeeling ssssoo gggggoood thisssssss mmmorrrning."

"What the hell?" I scream.

Fear and panic seizes me. I rely on James for so many things, the obvious change causes the blood in my veins to turn cold.

"Awake mode," I demand, hoping against all hope that this is a simple glitch in his morning program.

"Oooonnneee mmmmommmmmennt," James attempts. "Command does not, does not, does not compute."

I reach over to the bedside table in a desperate search for my phone. Finding it on the other side of the nightstand, just barely in reach, I pull it toward me. Once in hand, I punch in Kade's number. On the other end it rings four times before succumbing to voicemail.

'This is Kade, you know what to do,' it proclaims. Once the beep sounds, I let out a heavy breath.

"Kade, it's Atlas. Something's wrong with James. Please call Tanner and tell him to get over here as soon as he can. Thanks." I punch the disconnect button and sit up.

A thousand thoughts swirl in my head in light of Edmund's recent threats. Mentally going through several scenarios, I throw off the covers in an effort not to swirl into panic.

The house is eerily quiet. There are none of the usual sounds of clicks and whirls I now take for granted, as James's program adjusts the penthouse to fit my morning routine. He's such an integrated part of my life, I don't think about it until he's gone.

I pull on the designer jeans and T-shirt Samantha forced me to buy on our spa day. With a deft hand, I put the basic touches on my appearance and head to McKenzie Kingston.

STEPPING INTO THE OFFICE, I BREATHE A SLIGHT SIGH OF relief. There's something about the grounds of the Empyrean Club. Here I feel safe and secure. Walking across the office to my desk, I spy a gigantic bouquet of light blue roses arranged perfectly in a vase on my desk.

A smile creeps across my face, thinking of Reece. Images of his face light up my mind, my body responding to the memory of his hands and mouth.

I miss you. I know who you are, Atlas. I know where you work. I meant every word I said — Tell anyone of our more intimate conversations and I will destroy you.
I can't wait until you are all mine.♡

My breath stops in my chest. This can't be happening. I rail against both the fear and the internal conflict. When Edmund threatened me in my office, I felt safe behind my Alexandra persona, confident it was strong enough to protect me from his infatuated obsession. How did I miss all the clues? How did these get to my desk in a locked office on secure grounds?

The front door rings and Samantha's heels click across the wood floors. I shove the card into my pocket and pull my hands behind my back to hide their nervous shaking.

"Well, well, well. Look who got flowers," she beams, walking over and bending down to inhale their fragrance. "From Mr. Gabriel, I presume."

I smile noncommittally, letting her draw her own conclusions.

"What's wrong, Atlas?" Samantha's eyes narrow.

"Terrible morning. Something's wrong with James."

The mischievous grin crossing Samantha's face makes me raise an eyebrow.

"What?" I demand.

"Did he sound like Lurch?" Her grin broadens. "Yyyyooouuuu rrraaannnggg?" she mimics in a deep, low drawn-out voice.

"How did you know?" My surprise is obvious.

Her laugh carries through the room.

"Easy, I hacked him. April Fool's!"

"You what!" I scream.

"I hacked him. The other day I was bored and found a code glitch in one of the late system patches. I thought it would be funny if your computerized butler sounded like Lurch rather than a prim, proper English gentleman."

"This is going too far, Samantha. You had me crawling out of my skin. I called Kade, and had him contact Tanner, in a near panic."

"Oh." Her face falls. "I'm sorry for scaring you. It was just a little clean fun, no actual harm to the system. Besides, James is a hard-working computer, he was feeling a little under the weather today."

I glare at her when she finally notices my attire.

"Why aren't you dressed for the office?"

"Because, when James went offline I headed here, rather than staying home to get ready. It unnerved me, that's all. He didn't respond to my commands, but maybe it was because I sounded off," I reasoned and try to sound more casual now that I know it was all just a harmless prank.

"Why would you panic, Atlas? The system was just offline. Technology does that periodically."

I shrug.

"Chalk it up to stress. I woke up with my world off-kilter and then his voice was wrong. He didn't do what I commanded... it got to me."

"It was just a bit of fun. No harm, no foul." Samantha's penetrating gaze locks stubbornly on me. "There's something you aren't telling me."

"I think you're pretty much in the loop on everything," I say, sitting down in my desk chair, the flood of relief counteracting the fear which has held me hostage all morning.

"So what did the card say?" Samantha's head nods toward the bouquet of blue flowers between us.

"Nothing much."

"He must really have connections. I've never seen flowers delivered before eight in the morning around here."

"I guess he wanted to surprise me when I got into the office and didn't know when I'd be here."

"Interesting. Mr. Gabriel seems to be quite the man."

I nod silently, turning to my computer as a signal that the conversation is over.

For the rest of the morning, I pretend to work, but the uncomfortable silence looms between us punctuated only by periodic phone calls or comments on a client.

"I need to take care of some things at the club," I mutter, walking around my desk.

"Tell Alexandra I said hi." Samantha smirks. "And if she can remove the stick that is suddenly planted up your ass, that'd be great too."

I open my mouth with a scathing retort but close it immediately. It's not Samantha's fault. My mood is foul because I refuse to rely on others as I try to protect everyone close to me the only way I know how — by keeping my own secrets.

"You know, Atlas."

I pause mid-step, waiting for her to finish her sentence.

"You have friends who care about you and will do anything for you. Whatever is eating at you doesn't have to be something you deal with alone."

Taking a deep breath to settle my nerves, I turn and plaster a smile on my face.

"I'm okay. Things are complicated at the club. You know how people can be. I know you're going stir crazy being stuck here and not out in the spotlight. Worst-case scenario, I'll hire a ghostwriter to get the book complete."

"I'm not worried about the goddamn book, I'm worried about you. The entire world doesn't have to sit on your shoulders."

"With a name like Atlas — really?" I raise an eyebrow, daring her to challenge me.

"Touché. Your dad, rest his soul, was cruel when he gave you that name."

"Not really. When he lost Mom during childbirth, I became his universe."

I turn on my heels and head toward the bookcase. "Besides, I'm used to carrying the world. Just look up the story."

"You don't have to just endure, Atlas. There is a life out there, and you deserve to have a wonderful one."

My fingers stroke across the necklace, and I think about the similar words from Reece.

"Thank you, Samantha."

"Cheer up, sunshine, it'll be okay."

"I'm sure you're right." I fake a smile as I turn to the darkened passage of the club.

CHAPTER TWENTY-SIX

The ebony leather corset skirt wraps tightly around my body as the short single tail whip swings loosely at my side. I take a deep breath. I don't understand why Kade insists on these sessions. He's such a wonderful submissive. My every wish materializes with so little thought. Rarely do I find he's stepped out of line with our negotiated contract, and when he does, the reasoning is sound and most often to protect us.

I watch him kneel before me. His bare back tenses and releases with each breath. His enormous hands wrap around the dowels on either side of the whipping post. There is no reason to bind him. This session isn't about fun, nor is it because he's full of sexual frustration. Kade is a man in need of emotional release, and the only way he can find it is to endure enough physical pain to blot out the world until his emotions no longer haunt him.

The roughness of the braids contrasts with the softness of the leather as it slides across my skin. The whip curls in my hand before a single flick of my wrist makes it sail toward my target. He doesn't flinch when the tail bites into his skin as it leaves an angry kiss in its *wake. With the slightest movement of my arm, I bring the signal whip back and prepare for the next strike.*

His breath is even and his head bows in utter resignation. The next strike does little more than soften his body. Each one creates a welt on his scarred skin. Not like the sting of a lover. No, this is his atonement. It is his chosen punishment for wrongs he perceives he's added to the world. So he comes to me—knowing I won't judge, I won't preach, I won't comment or condemn. Instead, I'll offer a place for him to find his version of solace. These are his demons, and he deals with them as he needs. I simply supply a way for him to exorcise them.

Each strike is timed for absorption as I prepare for the next. The flick of my wrist creates a reaction in his body—he can't stay stoic and numb to the sting of his punishment for long. Beads of sweat form across his shoulders as his muscles flex and relax after each strike.

Samson Francois's fingers caress the piano keys in the background, the surround sound speakers cocooning the reverence of this scene in Prelude No. 4 as it falls into Nocturne No. 1 with barely a noticeable silence. Kade isn't even registering the music. I can tell by the way his breath undulates between ragged and even. No, the music is solely for my benefit. It calms me and allows me to focus on the job I'm paid to do.

I let loose the next strike and a hiss of air escapes from between his teeth. The whip bites the skin already angry with a scattering of red welts. I ensure each one is well-placed, not straying too high or too low. Pinpoint accuracy is the only acceptable outcome. I touch the whip to his skin only where I desire.

His back bows sharply as the leather slices his flesh. I don't give him time to collect himself. The next several blows land in quick succession. There is no time to process or breathe through the onslaught. Each whip kiss is seconds apart as the leather places a wicked mark everywhere it touches. Behind him, I appear impassive as his body contorts and his breath comes in sharp hisses or periodic grunts.

A particularly harsh one makes him pull his body toward the bar like a tortured chin-up. The muscles twitch across his back, and I wait for him to settle. When his knees touch the floor, the next one makes immediate contact.

"Six more, Kade." My voice is soft but firm.

"Please, ten more. Please, Domina."

His voice is gravelly and rough. Even in this state there is a self-assured confidence exuding from his form.

"Six, Kade," I say with a firmness that brokers no argument.

My wrist flicks and the crack of the whip explodes in the quiet room without making contact. The sudden sound makes Kade jump with a start, and he bows his head.

"Yes, Domina."

I can't take any more of this self-assured man punishing himself for his perceived sins when he's saved me countless times. Kade will push himself over the brink, suffering for days, if I don't remain in control of the situation.

Taking a deep breath, I clear my own thoughts and focus only on the kneeling form in front of me. With calculated slowness, I curl the whip into the fingers of my left hand, allowing the tail to slip through them. My right wrist flicks the handle again, sending the tail racing toward Kade's abused back. I do not make the strikes lighter or more tender. No matter my feelings, I will not rob him of his need.

I regulate my breath and send the whip to impact his back five more times. When I am done, I walk over and place the whip into the bin marked 'Implements to be Cleaned' and return to the dais at the other end of the room. In one smooth motion I step up, turn, and lower myself onto the throne style chair and cross my ankles as I try to relax.

Kade works to absorb the pain and emotions wracking through his body. For all outward appearances I am impervious to his suffering, but internally all I want to do is comfort him and tell him he couldn't possibly deserve this kind of punishment. But I am a friend and will give him whatever he needs. In this moment, he needs this torture and pays me handsomely for services rendered. This is why I rarely cross the line between friends and business.

The piano lilts in the background as I gaze at the heaving form in front of me. Kade's breath falls back into deeper inhales as his hands move off the bar of the whipping post. I let out a quiet sigh of relief. With a slow, concerted effort, he pulls his body onto his hands and knees, then crawls across the floor toward me. The only sign of pain is the occasional hiss of breath through his teeth, but he never stops his forward progress.

When he reaches my chair, he curls up at my feet and waits. His back rises and falls with each breath. The moment stretches out in an interminable silence.

"Go ahead," I say, my voice emotionless, almost harsh. I haven't earned the right to my own feelings. This is about Kade and his needs.

His body lifts with a labored breath as he plants a soft kiss across the top of each foot in between the straps of my black stilettos.

"I deserved more."

His breath caresses my skin as his lips hover above my foot.

"Not your call, Kade. I know you, and you know the rules. It is always my call unless you use your safe words. My job is to provide you what is needed and keep you safe, even if it is from yourself."

My tone is clear, there is no room for argument or discussion.

"Yes, of course, Domina," he whispers as he lifts his head until his gaze meets mine. There is a hard, intense look in his sea-blue eyes. It speaks of a protective ferocity, and it's impossible for me to look away.

"You would do well to remember the same applies to you outside of this room, Alexandra."

His tone brokers no room for argument. It is stated as fact. I will myself not to give him the satisfaction of knowing the effect he has on me or that he is correct.

"Head down, Kade," I command to give me time to regain control of myself and the situation.

"As you wish, Domina." The tone in his voice does not change, but he nods as he lowers his head to the floor and his body visibly relaxes.

I SHUDDER AT THE MEMORY AS THE INTENSE LOOK IN KADE'S eyes fade from my vision.

Our current disagreement makes me long for a time when I thought power exchange relationships were more about the physical rather than the multifaceted layers I've come to appreciate.

For all my experiences, it feels like I'm missing a part of me. Under Dominick's tutelage, I became proficient in the mental arts and skilled at wielding every implement on his vast wall, but I failed to learn about the connection in an exchange.

The psychology of it all seems easy on the surface, at least the 'what' and 'how' part. It is the 'why' I never evaluated. If I had, maybe I would understand why it feels so good when I hand over control to Reece. Why do I feel so relaxed and calm when my time in a dynamic situation kept me on edge as I searched for perfection? Why is everything in juxtaposition to everything I thought I knew? Why is everything down, up and everything up, down?

I slam my fist on Alexandra's desk. The tremor causes everything to bounce as the crack echoes off the walls.

My mind paces like a caged panther.

Emotions have no place in this line of work. The concept was hammered into me from every direction from the most important men in my life. Otherwise, I would be vulnerable and weak, something I could not afford. I scold myself for the outburst.

A text pings across my phone.

Call me when you are available.

Samantha's name lights up across the header.

I pick up the desk phone at the club and dial her number at McKenzie Kingston, just across the length of the driveway.

"Kingston." Her distracted voice answers the phone in an automatic response.

"How can I help you today, Miss Kingston?" I ask in a slow drawl.

"Ah, Alexandra, it's so good to speak with you. How are you this fine day?"

The obvious grin on her face causes me to shake my head. She's mocking me and enjoying her little joke.

"I'm doing well, and yourself?"

"Well, I'm out of sorts. It seems my managing partner, a Miss Atlas Devereaux, hasn't been in for the past few days because of other, more interesting things I suppose. However, there have been some developments, and I'd really love for her to show up to work. Do you think you can reach out to her and help me out?"

I roll my eyes.

"Do you have to always be so dramatic, Miss Kingston?"

"Do you always have to be so closed off, Alexandra?"

"Samantha," I start, a steel edge in my tone.

"Don't you dare Samantha me. You are running away, hiding in your damn hole, and I will not stand for it. I get that things are getting done, but this is ridiculous."

I sigh into the phone. "Miss Kingston, I'll ensure that Miss Devereaux graces you with her presence tomorrow. Will that be acceptable?"

"Sure. And could you tell her that whatever stick she has firmly planted up her ass needs to be removed before she gets here?"

"Understood." I barely get the word out before the line goes dead.

CHAPTER TWENTY-SEVEN

Picking up the phone, I call for Alexandra's car as I try to focus on all the right words and accents when all I want to do is go home and curl up in my bed. Hiding out in the club and pretending Atlas is on a business trip is a welcome respite, but the persona is tiring.

A few minutes later, I step out onto the drive as Adam hands me into the car. The drive home is a swirl of light outside my window. In every part of my life there's something urgent pulling on me. There's an unspoken fear Edmund has me under surveillance when I'm Alexandra. As Atlas, I'm trying to make everything run smoothly while McKenzie is behind on her latest book. I'm on the edge of a breakdown and everything in me wants it to all go away.

Adam pulls the limo up to the penthouse curb. In the next minute he's at my door, ready to hand me out of the car. I nod as I step out onto the sidewalk.

"Thank you, Adam. You can go home."

"I am on security duty for you tonight, ma'am." He turns without waiting for my reply and walks to the driver's seat of the car. I watch in frustration as the Town Car disappears into the underground garage. Kade and I will have to have a chat about this. I've told him repeatedly that I don't need extra security, and he's obviously not listening. While I'm grateful for his protectiveness, there are days it is stifling in a world which is already constrictive. Besides, I hate feeling guilty when things impact everyone else's life, like Adam not going home to his family.

The doorman holds the door open for my entrance, and I smile as I turn around.

"Good evening, Miss Devereaux."

Acknowledging no one else, I rush through the lobby, then slam the elevator button to whisk me to the safety of my penthouse.

Once inside, I walk over to the wet bar in the living room and fill a crystal cut low ball glass to the brim with the clear liquid. I take a long pull, as I demand it to take away my worries and thoughts of failure. If I can't run away from the world, then I can make the world run away from me. At least for a little while.

"Evening mode," I call out to James.

"Evening mode initiated, Ma'am."

"Ah, it's good to have you back to normal, James."

Relief floods through me at his response as the dramatic orchestral music fills the room. A breeze billows the curtains as the patio doors open, and I let out a sigh before throwing back three more shots in quick succession.

A subtle numbness snakes through me, taking the edge off the troubles blasting across my thoughts. Filling the rock glass once more, I pick it up and move out to the balcony. The cool steel railing braces me as I stare unseeing out across the DC skyline.

The world tilts as the alcohol takes hold, and I move to the chaise lounge. Pressing the cool crystal against my forehead, I force away the image of a tumbling house of cards falling around me as I search to find a way to stop various situations from exploding the whole things into a million tiny shreds. I take another

healthy gulp from my glass to hasten the journey to a more carefree existence.

"Ma'am, Mr. Gabriel is on his way up." James's voice cuts through the penthouse as he lowers the music.

"Deny access." The command is thick in my mouth.

"I'm sorry, Miss Devereaux, but an override code was used. I cannot deny access to Mr. Gabriel."

No sooner does James finish his explanation than the front door opens.

"Good evening, Mr. Gabriel."

"Location," he commands.

"Miss Devereaux is currently located on the balcony."

"Traitor," I growl under my breath.

Reece steps out onto the patio. His face is a swirling mixture of concern, anger, and an emotion I can't quite interpret as I rise from the lounger and stumble on my way toward the living area.

"Good effening, Mr. Dabriel."

I incline my head as he approaches, and raise my glass in salute.

"You're drunk, Atlas." He spits out the words.

"And you're observant."

I take a long gulp of vodka and look up at him with a smile as I bask in the mindless feeling.

"For someone so in control, you look pretty out of it at the moment."

"Quite," I acknowledge. My tongue twists on the word, feeling heavy in my mouth. "At least I have the sense enough to do it alone and in the safety of my own, ever so humble, abode." I giggle at myself, realizing the words I've spoken. "Abode is such a funny word. It means to wait."

I giggle, then frown and glare up at him.

"Speaking of waiting, how the hell did you get across my threshold? Never mind, I'll ask the box," I say as my focus blurs and my brain buzzes from the excess alcohol. "Thames, status. No... James, personnel status."

"Ma'am, System Status: Evening Mode. Personnel Status: Atlas, Owner. Reece: Security Access."

"Who changed Mr. Dabriel, grr... Gabriel's status?" I demand as I make my way to the living room couch.

"Security Status granted to Mr. Gabriel, per Mr. Kinkaid's last input," James reports.

My emotions are a mix of confusion and irritation. I stare at Reece, willing the situation to compute, but it refuses to pass through my muddled brain. I remember Kade's last visit. We discussed... the thought falters.

"Fucking traitor," I say out loud, thinking of all the ways I'll deal with Kade later. He knows I have a threshold issue, and to add Mr. Reece Gabriel to my list without my knowledge is crossing a hard line.

"Why are you here, Mr. Mabriel, Fierce... Reece?" I scream as my words to fight through the crashing thoughts and the fuzzy waves spin my world.

"It seems others are worried about you but aren't sure how to take you in hand. They'd have come but thought I could handle the job with more... efficiency." His voice is firm, but it's laced with an odd amusement.

"Thhhhere'ssss nothing here to sssssee, this is not the ssssubmissive you are looking for, move along." My tongue's heaviness grows with each passing minute, but I'm so close to the state of not caring that I take another sip of my vodka.

"Go home, Monsieur Gabrielle, let God be your strong man," I mock and wave my hand dismissively in the air.

"Atlas, what are you running from?"

His question strikes a sudden chord, and I pause in my personal reverie, staring at the mouth which is attempting to sidetrack my evening.

"You are quite the suave debonair."

I push off the couch and stumble toward the kitchen. His powerful arms are around my waist, catching the full weight of my body before I sprawl to the floor. I flail against his hold and turn to face him. His face is composed. No emotions flash across it except for immediate concern for my well-being.

"Do you drink to excess often?"

My eyes meet his, challenging his presumptive manner.

"If you are asking, am I Washington DC self-medicated? Probably. Do I get drunk for the hell of it? No — I like control too much."

"Why?" His simple question stops my spinning mind.

"Pardon?"

"Why are you drinking alone to excess this evening?"

The question hangs in the air as his eyes search my face for the unspoken answers.

"You know it violates our agreement. When you're sober, we'll discuss your actions. Nothing productive comes from this course," he says as he releases me.

I take a step away from him and pause.

"We don't have an agreement. Besides, it's the only way I can find a moment of clarity and pureness of existence. The only place where the universe is still, and I can breathe its unadulterated essence. Where I can be present and live in the moment like everyone keeps telling me I need to do. A place where the past doesn't haunt me, and I don't fear the present or future."

The vulnerability and clarity of my words stuns me. Vodka always makes my mind and mouth work with no filters, which was why I was alone. It is the vice that opens my emotional soul like truth serum. I stare at him for a long minute. My mouth didn't even stumble over the words. It was like it wanted to tell him the exact answer it longed for so many before him to ask. I want him to care, but I can't afford for it to be true.

"Then I'm doing something wrong," he whispers.

"You can move along now, Mr. Gabriel, there's nothing here for you."

I sigh and turn my back to him as I focus on each step, debating the pros and cons of more vodka versus water. Tears cloud my eyes, and I blink in an attempt to hold back the undesired emotions. Unruly memories flood my mind. I grasp the counter, helpless to fight the onslaught as tears stream down my cheeks. Angrily, I swipe them with the back of my hand. I pull the refrigerator door open and grab a bottle of water before slamming it shut.

"I'm sorry," he says against my ear.

"For what?" My harsh tone is full of nothing but venom.

"For the pain he caused." His hands wrap around my waist, pulling me into his warm embrace. "For the pain you've suffered. For whatever has caused this callus to form around your soft, vulnerable heart."

"It's fine." My voice stutters. The echoing motto rings through my mind- no weakness, no vulnerability. "It's no big deal."

I twist in his arms, but he holds me fast as my drunken state works against my sensibilities.

"Here, take these," he breathes, holding the pills out in his palm.

I swallow them without protest. Reece maneuvers us to the couch and pulls me into his lap. I go willingly, suddenly wanting to be close to him. His hands stroke my hair in a protective and possessive manner as he murmurs to me.

When the tension leaves my body, he wraps his arms around me, enveloping me against his chest until my tears run out and I fall asleep.

CHAPTER TWENTY-EIGHT

L ight from the morning sun streams in through the small seam in the heavy curtains. It cuts through the darkness with a single ray of light as I blink my eyes and brace for the raging headache that wasn't there.

"Good morning, beautiful." Reece's voice vibrates across my skin as he kisses my temple. "You were in quite the mood last night."

He wraps a cuff around my right wrist and pulls it over my head. "How are you feeling this morning?"

"Better than I probably should. Your proactive measures seem to have held off the worst-case scenario."

"Good. Then I won't feel bad that your body is doing my job."

He continues to the other side and places the cuff around my left wrist, pulling it tight. The cool, supple leather holds me firm while the soft lambskin lining encases them to prevent irritation.

I pull on the restraints.

"Why?"

"Punishment. Something is off with you, and I aim to find out because I can't imagine a woman so impeccable in her control would let herself get so dangerously out of it," he replies as his lips travel up my stomach.

His teeth graze across my naked skin and his fingers skim my hips and trace the edges of my breasts. Underneath him, my breath comes in soft ragged bursts. My hands wrap around the bars of the cuffs as his teeth continue their assault on my body, scraping over my taut skin before traveling down toward the apex of my legs. Quivering, I want to beg him to move faster, but I know Reece, and he will take his torturous time.

He lifts my hips as he parts my tender flesh with a flick of his tongue. My pants come in a staccato rhythm as the harsh breaths echo off the bedroom walls. A finger adds to the torment as he strokes it down my soaking slit. His fiery breath blows across my hard clit, and I gasp for air.

"Please, Reece," I whisper.

"Please what, Atlas? Give you a break so you can tell me what's wrong?"

His lips land across my throbbing core, and his hot tongue circles the edge of my clit. When I can't take another sensation, he pushes an intruding finger through my folds and paints the liquid across my quivering thighs. My body quakes, tensing and releasing under his attentions.

Reece doesn't pause. The slow, soft movements of pleasure continue. I arch and push against him as I beg for deeper penetration or more friction. Anything but the constant push to the edge only to force it to recede.

"Please." I force the word across my lips.

"Please what?"

"Please, Sir? Please." I moan.

He chuckles softly, but he continues his delicious torture.

Reece's fingers move past my drenched entrance, and I push my hips toward him in a silent demand.

"You're not in control here. A lesson which you obviously need to learn," he reprimands gently as he pulls his finger back to tease me. "This is mine to take pleasure at the pace I desire."

To punctuate his statement, Reece inserts several fingers into my needy pussy. His knuckles rub across my G-spot. Fluid runs freely from my soaking entrance. I descend into a mindless state. My entire focus centers on the movement of his mouth and fingers. His excruciating pleasure is all that remains. Then he halts.

I cry out in pure frustration, still riding the wave he built as it recedes once again. His knee slides between my legs and my breath catches as his hard length presses against my thigh. Placing kisses on my neck, he smooths my hair from my face and moves his lips back up along my ear, nipping the outer edge of my lobe.

"God, you're sexy," he breathes into my hair, pulling back to look down from his looming position.

I stare up into his hungry intense gray eyes. His knees force my legs apart as he slides his hard cock deep into me with one stroke. My breath stutters, my back arching upward. The cuffs on my wrists pull against the headboard as he pushes into me, picking up the speed with each stroke until he pounds into me.

"Mine." His hoarse voice forces into the air. "Completely mine."

He twists and pulls hard on my nipples. The combination of pain and pleasure shoves me over the edge. I thrash and writhe against the leather cuffs and ride the wave of pleasure.

I float back toward Earth. Reece watches every move and reaction as he adjusts his weight on his arms. Inside me, he still hard.

He runs a thumb across my bottom lip, then lowers his head and traces the same path with his tongue as he slips from me. I raise my hips in silent supplication to his still obvious need. The fire in his eyes tells me I'm not wrong.

"He who controls others may be powerful, but he who has mastered himself is mightier still — Lao Tzu," Reece quotes.

He smiles as he rises from the bed. My eyes graze his hard, taut body.

"You haven't taught James how to get drinks," he explains as he walks out of the room. His footfalls grow fainter as he moves through the penthouse.

My body settles into the amazing afterglow, but my thoughts focus on one word. *Mine.* Said in a moment of passion, it doesn't count for anything, my brain taunts while the jumble of oxymoronic emotions send me down a different path. *You're not in control. Completely mine.* Fear runs along the edge of the mixture of thoughts and emotions.

"You're thinking too hard," he says as he walks back into the room. His deep sultry voice halts further internal discussions.

He holds my head up, lifting the cool water to my lips.

"Drink."

The icy liquid slips over my tongue, and I sip the water in grateful gulps.

"Good girl," he murmurs, setting the glass on the side table. "When I came in, I could swear there was smoke coming out of your ears. The look on your face screamed that the gears of your brain were grinding and already re-engaged. Do you know what an ego-blow that can be?" His face looks wounded, but the upturn edge of his mouth tells me he's teasing. "I guess I'll just have to cool off your body to get to your mind."

Reaching over to the glass, he pops an ice cube into his mouth and a mischievous look dances in his eyes as he bends down. Reece draws it across my neck and down my breasts, encircling my nipples. I moan. The chilly water streams across my body as he creates a winding path down my stomach and back again. Each move makes me shiver and squirm. His mouth captures my hard nipple. The ice is in juxtaposition to his warm breath. I shiver as his renewed attentions push me back into the swirling waters of desire and need.

His mouth trails across my skin in a lazy random pattern, over-sensitizing it with each pass. I struggle and pull against the restraints.

"What do you want, girl?" His head barely lifts from my body. The ice splashes against my stomach, and I jerk under him.

"Please."

"You keep begging, but I don't understand what you're begging for, my dear. Maybe you are begging me to continue." His mouth hovers an inch from my body while his arms push him further south. In seconds, his tongue laps across my clit and I scream.

"Maybe you are begging me to stop."

He pulls himself back up the bed until his face is floating right above mine. My ragged breath tries to force air into lungs screaming for oxygen.

"Please don't."

"Please don't continue? How very sad. I was having such an enjoyable time."

His tongue traces just around the edge of my lips. My head lifts to capture his mouth, but he moves just out of reach.

"Oh, Atlas, you *do* have a stubborn streak." His mouth dips and pulls away as he pushes the tip of his cock right to the edge of my entrance, mimicking the same movements. Reece alternates back and forth, teasing and denying until I squirm without control under him.

"What do you want?" he says, continuing to torture me with his soft taunting movements.

"Fuck me, please."

"Fuck you please? You want me to fuck you. No strings attached. Just for our mutual enjoyment. Is that what you really want?" He doesn't stop as my mind tries to comprehend what he's asking. "I don't just want a fuck, Atlas. I want to possess you. All of you. Make love to you."

He sighs. "But the girl just wants a fuck. It's so sad when she could have so much more, but this is just about fucking. So today I want it to consume you. To know you are burning for my next touch. Until every thought centers on how it will feel when I finally choose to acquiesce and fuck you," he says as he strokes my clit.

My hips push against his fingers, and I moan in desperation.

"I thought you made love," I challenge in a breathless reply.

"I do that too. Slowly and completely. There's room in life for both. The hard and the soft," he says, working his fingers in and out of me, pushing them deeper with each word.

I close my eyes and hold my breath to keep from crying out. Everything in me works to grab the crest of the building orgasm. Without warning, his fingers halt. My eyes fly open in shock as the orgasm recedes.

"You can't leave me like this," I say, my desperate plea more forceful than I intend.

"Can and will. Punishment is used to teach a lesson. Maybe you'll find a way to open and let me in, so to speak," he says.

Reece leans back and gathers his erection in his fist. He strokes himself. His intense gaze never leaves mine. He holds me mesmerized as he pumps his cock. The hard look on his face sends shivers down my spine. I moan as my need escalates with his. Above me, his breath comes in ragged pants until his body shudders and convulses in release as his cum splatters across my skin.

"If I just wanted a fuck, Atlas, I'll take it in hand myself," he snarls as his cock rests limp in his fist.

Rising from the bed, he walks into the bathroom.

"Start shower — one hundred and one degrees," he calls out to James, and I'm left bound, needy, wishing it were my hands caressing his body.

When he is ready to face the day, he unbinds me and leaves for work without another word.

CHAPTER TWENTY-NINE

Reece walked out of my penthouse a week ago.

The memory of our last time together kicks against an odd mix of pleasure and offense. The feminist in me screams about his arrogant, egotistical attitude. While the submissive swoons at being shoved backward as he removed the world from my shoulders.

This is why I turned dominant. It was easier to shove all of those needs down into the pit of my soul and throw away the key.

Before Reece walked into my life, my general mood was outwardly emotionless. Well, that's not true, I emoted flat, frustrated, sullen, aggravated and angry with ease. There were always infinitesimal moments of joy, but it was like only part of me was fed. The rest of my soul sat emaciated in my cultivated existence.

The days were a continuum of work activities, checking off the next client, the next meeting, the next club activity, or the next book chapter. Weekends blended into weekdays with little more than the commentary on the radio, reminding me there was a distinction between them. I am restless, and now all I can think about is how wonderful it felt to be in the grips of Reece's control.

He doesn't demand I give up my life or myself, though he's

missing knowledge of a large section of it. Still, in those moments, where he demands full control, I can breathe. My body relaxes, my soul wants to give him everything he asks, but my mind screams in protest as it lists off reasons that a real woman shouldn't give in to him. My inner feminist and submissive each take a stance as they internally war. One argues that a lack of control or kneeling for a man is a weakness, while the other pronounces it a strength to be vulnerable, which only leads to further exasperating thoughts.

In the time we've been apart, I've tried to use my home gym to work out my internal frustrations. I even pulled out my vibrator, hoping that personal intimate time would give me the balance I need. Not even the kickboxing class here at the club helped. Instead, my trainer growled that my lackadaisical attitude toward training made me end up on my ass more than my feet.

Everyone is a bundle of contradictions, but my internal desires are at war. I wish I could be more like Samantha, even if her constant attempt to balance her desire to be present conflicts with the focus needs of our business. So often her outward actions mimic my internal thoughts as she flits with whatever emotion takes her with her *live in the moment* style.

"Ma'am." Katie's voice crackles over the intercom speaker on my desk, startling me out of my unproductive thoughts.

"Yes?"

"I have a Miss Cassandra Clark here to see you."

I glance down at my calendar and note I have fifteen minutes until my next meeting with the general and restaurant managers.

"Send her in."

The door opens tentatively as Cassandra walks into the room. Her eyes dart around, taking in every aspect of my office.

I rise from my chair when she enters the room.

"Nice to see you again, Miss Clark. Please have a seat." I motion to one of the chairs in front of my desk. "To what do I owe this unexpected visit?"

She fidgets as she sits before me, and I lower myself back behind my desk.

"You asked me to complete an essay on the lifestyle and return it to you. I've completed the assignment as requested."

With trembling hands, she picks up the tan envelope from her lap and places it on my desk. "I hope you will find it an acceptable answer. I really want to train with you, Ma'am." Her words fall from her mouth in a rush.

I smile.

"It's not my question you were supposed to answer."

"But, you said," she stutters.

"What did I say, Cassandra?"

"You said to write an essay on what I wanted to learn and why." She frowns in confusion.

"Yes. Note the *you* in that statement. It is irrelevant to me, but you have to understand your own desires first."

I carefully study her. Under my gaze she shifts her weight on the chair. Her eyebrows clench, and her mouth pulls back a millimeter. The expression is gone before it can truly register. It's followed by another similar expression of surprise.

"Why are you surprised at my statement, Cassandra?"

"They say you're tough. You read people by watching them. I didn't think it was true." Her face is a mixture of emotions, moving from one to another ever so slightly as thoughts rush through her head.

"Understanding other people is what makes a great Dominant or submissive. Learning another person so intimately that you can anticipate their next thought, understand their reactions or know why they do what they do. Understanding what inspires them to rise to a challenge, how to balance positive and negative reactions. Each decision is based on learning the smallest detail about a person, nurturing the positive parts of their personality to draw them out more fully, and disciplining the negative traits to make them recede."

"Who decides what is positive and what is negative?"

"If they are submissive, then I do."

"So you do it because you don't like being wrong. You're just another domineering person who gets off making others work for them," she says haughtily as her body language shifts. "It is the fine line between the desire to control one's own destiny and realizing that such a thing means doing as you please to follow your inward bliss."

"Quite the opposite, actually," I state. "It is more intelligent to surround yourself with people who know more, or have better skills. That way everyone rises when challenges occur. Thus, providing growth for everyone."

"Then wouldn't that make you submissive to your team?"

"No."

"Why not?"

"Because the ultimate decision lies with me. It doesn't matter if it is popular, it does not matter if it isn't perfect. What matters is that I decide and others live by it. Then we move forward collectively."

She processes my statement.

"Okay. In a club this size that makes sense, but what about in a one-on-one situation? Why would someone give up control to another person?"

My fingers tap against the envelope. I want to open it, but I also want to feel Cassandra out, to understand what makes her tick.

"Think of it like a car." I hear Dominick's voice in my head, and internally laugh as I'm about to use his line. "How many people can drive a car?"

"One."

"Can the person driving the car also navigate?"

"Well, they could."

"And if they had a passenger in the car who do you think should navigate?"

"The passenger. It keeps them both safer. The driver can focus on driving, and the passenger makes sure they miss no turns." Her face is full of confusion.

"In that example, either could be dominant and either could be submissive. Who is in control?"

"It's obvious that the driver is in control."

"Oh really? Why?"

"Because they steer the car. They are deciding on the direction."

"I think the passenger is in control. They provide the navigation and if they provide dangerous directions, then both are equally lost," I counter.

Cassandra opens her mouth and then snaps it shut.

"Now if the driver tried to both drive and navigate without ever asking the passenger for help or an opinion, then it would put them both in a very unsafe situation. That is neither a good Dominant nor a good submissive, but paramount to domineering abuse. The need for control and not a power exchange."

"So in the car with two people and both are providing input, where is the power exchange?"

"It is in the actions as they work together. The driver needs to give up a level of control to the passenger, trusting them to give accurate directions or corrections as needed to keep them on course. On the other hand, the passenger places their life in the hands of the driver, who holds power over the car. That way they both arrive at their destination safely, changing direction when necessary based on the input from both parties due to road conditions, weather, directions and a whole host of other realities."

"I never thought about it that way. Everything I read is about one person controlling another. About rules, contracts, behavior modification and service. It always sounds like it's for the benefit of the Dominant. Getting what they want, how they want it, all the time."

"When done well, Cassandra, it is nowhere close to one-sided."

"So what does the submissive get following the rules and whims of another person?"

"Depends on the submissive. It also depends on the Dominant. Everyone has a unique flavor of what they want in a power exchange."

Her eyebrows wrinkle once more. This time the expression isn't fleeting, but an obvious look of frustration.

"If this were all straightforward and easy, then everyone would live happily ever after. It's all about people and psychology. Learning those things will serve you well if you go down this path."

She sits quietly for a minute but shifts and fidgets in her seat. After a few long seconds, she pulls herself together, sitting up straighter.

"Does this mean you'll train me?" she finally asks.

"I'll look over your paper to see what you've discovered about yourself in the scant time you've been here. In the meantime, I suggest you read these."

I hand her a postcard with the website to the 'Ekman Micro Expression Training Tool 3.0' and place *The Art of Choosing* and *The Honest Truth About Dishonesty: How We Lie to Everyone (Especially Ourselves)* books on my desk.

"Regardless of my decision, those are a suitable place to start on your path."

"Um. Thank you, Ma'am."

"I'll be in touch, Cassandra. Good luck with your reading," I say, my dismissive tone clear as I rise from the chair.

Cassandra rises and scowls, obviously unsatisfied with the results of the meeting.

"Thank you for your time," she mumbles as she hurries out the door.

CHAPTER THIRTY

"Good lord, the eye candy around this place is fine today," Samantha says, picking up a French fry.

"Bless your little heart, you can't seem to find what you're lookin' for 'round here, now can ya? Cuz' you say that every time you look out over the pool over yonder. The eye candy is no different today than it was the last time we had lunch here, sweetheart."

I know I sound exasperated, but there are too many things on my mind to care. Edmund has been blessedly quiet for more than a week, and I am hopeful it is a good sign. On the other hand, writer's block, too many issues at the club, and the PR firm hold my attention.

"What's eating you?"

"Just another day in paradise, darlin'."

"With an extra helping of Southern girl attitude," she mocks in her best Brooklyn accent.

I lay my hand across my forehead like I can't go on.

"Well, frankly, my dear Scarlett..." She pauses and smiles.

"You and the rest of the world."

She laughs lightheartedly, and I'm glad to see she's calmed down after her frantic last few weeks. I know the book deadline has her bugged, but she's always sweating the little details, while letting the big ones blow in the breeze. Ultimately it's why we get along so well, opposites attract and all.

"Anything amazing planned this weekend?"

I look up to the ceiling as if I'm thinking through my schedule.

"Yeah, work."

"Mr. Gabriel hasn't made plans with you yet?"

"He's been away on business, and making a couple of campaign stops with his sister."

My phone vibrates across the table, and Samantha scoops it up to see who's calling.

"Speak of the devil."

"Just let it go to voicemail, I'll call him soon."

"Such a nonchalant attitude. Everything going okay?"

I nod. "I don't want to jump into anything too fast. Just trying to keep it casual but..."

I stop mid-sentence as my thoughts turn to kneeling for Reece. There, I wait in silence for his next command as the cares of the world slip from my shoulders.

"But?" Samantha repeats as her eyebrows lift in interest.

I pick up my burger and take a bite, then look at Samantha with an apologetic face.

Samantha glares, but quickly lets her gaze fall across the pool.

"What I wouldn't give for some solid play. You know the kind when you're on your knees and he bends down, then whispers in your ear that he will cane you until you cry. You know it will hurt so good, but oh, the emotional release when that's done just right. Or when you get tied down to the table and the Top's voice is a soft mixture of compliments, telling you that you're beautiful and how wonderful you look with his cane marks across your ass."

I nearly choke on my lunch, and Samantha grins.

"Wouldn't that be nice, Alexandra?" she says, watching my reaction.

Taking a large drink of water, I clear my mouth.

"That sounds like quite the lovely time — for you."

She snickers.

"That's a given, I'm a slut and proud of it. Though it's been so long since I found a new conquest, I'm thinking the Slut guild will revoke my membership card."

"Sweetheart, I think you're in the hall of fame."

I smile conspiratorially.

"I can't just rest on my laurels! I have a reputation to uphold."

"And quite the reputation it is, too."

"Why, thank you." Samantha beams.

"Cassandra came by my office today."

I change the subject, knowing it will come back around to Reece and the plans I don't have for the weekend.

"Have you decided if you will take on the extra project of training a pro Dominant?"

"I'm debating it. Maybe what I need is a distraction, but I'm not sure she'll be into my style of training. Most of the people who approach me want me to teach them how to throw a whip and tie people up. They think the training is just about getting off."

"You know for most, it's just about sex, right?"

"I guess, but it can be so much more," I say wistfully. "It's just so much better when you can get inside each other's head, or when the power exchange is real. There's nothing else like it."

"What's wrong with just having enjoyable kinky sex?"

"Nothing," I reply carefully. "I just want more. There was a time I was so close to having it all."

I slide off my stool and give Samantha a smile. "I need to get back to work."

"It's hard to make a connection if you never come up for air," she says with a scowl.

I nod and turn toward the club.

With the transformation from Alexandra to Atlas once again complete, I head back through the tunnel between the club and my office at McKenzie Kingston. My phone pings, and I pause.

I miss you. Are you avoiding me? RG

Why yes, yes I am, Mr. Gabriel, but not for the reasons you think.

I've just been very busy. AD

I stumble, dropping my phone, glad for the hundredth time Samantha insisted on the protective case. The smell of the damp tunnel overwhelms my senses, and I feel claustrophobic. Normally I'm not afraid of small spaces, especially since sensory deprivation is one of my favorite types of play. The feeling of the blindfold or my body wrapped mummy style in plastic while white noise plays in my ears is often a relaxing diversion. I shake the thoughts from my head and pick up the phone. I once again head toward the PR firm's hidden entrance.

You can't be too busy. I'm standing in your office, sitting at your desk as a matter of fact and you aren't here. RG

THE TEXT STOPS ME DEAD IN MY TRACKS AND I STAND IN THE dimly lit tunnel trying to figure out my next step.

Client appointments. AD

I HOLD MY BREATH, HOPING HE'LL TELL ME WE CAN GET together later.

Interesting. Melody says your calendar is clear this afternoon. You should give her a raise, she's really quite helpful. RG

YES SHE IS AND VERY EFFICIENT, WHICH IS A WONDERFUL THING, *but right now she's a detriment to my mental and emotional state.*

I'll have HR look into it, and see what we can do. Thank you for the business advice. Is there something specific you needed on your case, or was this a personal visit?

Excitement runs through me as my heart pounds. I feel like a spy in some action movie. It's not quite the pace of my normal life, but heart-racing moments are good for the soul. The pep talk does little to calm my nerves, and even less to actually help me find a way out of my predicament.

I want to kidnap you and take you to Paris. :)

MY BREATH CATCHES IN MY THROAT. HE CAN'T BE SERIOUS.

My calendar is a little too booked for Paris at the moment.

I TURN AROUND AND HEAD BACK TOWARD THE CLUB.

My finger slides across the screen, bringing up the contacts list. Punching Kade's number in, I pray for him to answer.

"Kade."

"It's Alexandra. Atlas is in a bind. Mr. Gabriel is sitting at her desk."

Kade laughs.

"That's quite the challenge you have there, little lady," he teases.

"This isn't funny."

"Actually, it's hilarious. This is what you get for trying to be all coy. Why don't you tell that man about your dual identity?"

"Because the fewer people who know, the safer things stay. And too many people already know. Loose lips, sinking ships, and all that rubbish."

"What are you afraid of?"

"Right now? Being stuck between the PR firm and the club. Can you tell me if the path out of Alexandra's room is clear?"

"You know, if I had extended security surveillance into McKenzie Kingston, I'd be able to tell you the best escape out of you little deceit. But since I only have visibility into the club..."

"Kade, now is not the time to discuss your need to voyeur the entire grounds."

"I'm not a voyeur, I'm a security professional."

"Yeah, that's what the vanillas tell themselves so they can sleep at night. We know better. Now are you going to help me or not?"

Kade chuckles.

"Too true. Okay, looks like you can come out of Alexandra's room and take the service entrance down to the valet garage. I'll have Adam at the entrance with the keys to the AMG. Does that work?"

"Yeah. I'll head there now."

"Are you trying to avoid Reece, or are you just worried he'll see you coming out of the tunnel and start asking questions?"

"The tunnel is my concern," I say absently.

"Good to know," Kade says, his tone lighthearted. "Adam is on his way down to the entrance now."

"Thanks, Kade, I owe you one."

"Yeah, you do."

I can hear the grin in his voice, but my entire focus is on the escape route. My body shakes. Adrenaline pulses through my veins as I walk back through *Alexandra's wardrobe*, and turn the knob to the corridor door, peaking out to ensure I'm actually alone.

With a sigh of relief, I turn to my right and walk down the service hall. Adam waits at the entrance of the shared valet garage door. While I rarely need to come down here to get my car, today I am glad both the PR firm and the club share the same area.

"Ma'am," he acknowledges with a smile, handing me keys. "She's in bay 9."

"Thank you, Adam."

Taking the keys, I move through the underground garage. The click of my heels echo off the black concrete walls and create an eerie soundtrack to my grand escape. Reece's words run through my head. I can't help smiling at the concept of being kidnapped and whisked off to a foreign country on a whim.

The fantasy plays in my head as I round the corner and spot the car in Bay 9. With shaky fingers, I punch the unlock button, but nothing happens. Frantically, I press it again and again. Stepping up to the car, I bang my hands on the roof and lay my forehead against the cool metal.

Someone shifts behind as they gather both wrists in one hand while the other one wraps around my mouth. Every nerve ending goes on alert. I want to scream, but all my self-defense training reminds me to stay in control. Terror laps at the edge of my senses.

"I believe those are my keys. Drop them in my hand."

Reese's husky tone reverberates through the garage, and I relax a little as I inhale his cologne. Overhead, the security cameras whirl as they pan and tilt. Kade is a dead man when I get back to the club, but I relax into the situation. Reece is safe. The pure panic of other scenarios drains away. Soft lips graze down the side of my neck as hands capture my wrists, pinning them behind my back.

"It's not very nice to lie about your whereabouts, my dear," Reece croons in my ear. "I'm so glad my dear friend Kade gave me some pointers when I texted him in frustration."

My body shakes, but it's no longer due to fear.

Kade will pay for this, one way or the other.

A mix of anticipation and desire slithers through me as his hands leave my wrists and skim across my arms.

"Don't move," he commands.

I revel in the sensation of his touch and comply. His hands move up the back of my thigh, pushing under my skirt as his fingernails rake against my skin.

A finger slides between the firm cheeks of my ass. Reece growls against my ear as he squeezes and pulls them apart. He steps closer and presses his hard bulge, still locked behind the confines of his pants, into me. A moan slips from me, and I arch toward him.

"I want to feel your mouth on my cock," he murmurs against my skin. "I want you on your knees, looking up at me as I push it into that warm, beautiful mouth."

His hands drop to my shoulders, pushing until my knees buckle, and I slowly sink in front of him. The hard bulge tents his pants, but he quickly slides the zipper down and pulls his hard cock free of its confines.

I dart my tongue and swipe the pre-cum from the tip. A sharp intake of breath tells me my move is well received. His need becomes my own. I lean forward and take him deeper into my mouth. I suck and flick my tongue up and down his shaft. He groans in response. My body shudders and emboldens me.

I reach up and wrap a hand around the base of his shaft while the other caresses his tender ball sac. My tongue glides along the length of the base, bobs around the tip, then my mouth engulfs his length.

His hips jerk as his hand fists my hair and pulls my head back. The head of his cock pushes deeper as it scrapes against the back of my throat. I struggle to control the pace as I work his cock and balls softly in my hands, but my efforts quickly become useless. The fist in my hair silently demands more depth and a faster rhythm. I release the base of his cock to oblige his wishes.

My free hand works down my body. Then caresses my thigh on its way to my pussy. His thrusts grow more frenzied as I gag and choke. I moan against his cock when my fingers scrape against my clit.

"Are you touching yourself?" he grinds out. "I didn't give you permission."

My hand halts. A shudder rushes through me at the sudden loss. The head of his cock moves across my lips, letting them swirl over the tip before he shoves it to the back of my throat.

His fingers dig into my scalp, forcing my mouth to work his cock in a frenzied pace. Each stroke pushes my body's need closer to an edge. I desperately need to touch myself.

Reece moans and pulls my head back as his cock jerks from my mouth with a sudden pop. He wraps his hand around the shaft, working it up and down as his cock bobs in front of my face. The hand in my hair pulls my head back as his moan echoes around the garage. Cum streams in long ropes across my face as he draws out every ounce of pleasure from his climax.

His breath comes in short gasps above me. I rock in an attempt to cool the heavy need between my thighs. A soft cloth wipes against my cheek as he cleans me with his handkerchief.

"Stand up and bend over the hood."

His voice is steady, but his breath is labored.

On shaky legs, I stand and slowly bend over the hood of the car. He steps behind me and zips his pants while the cool air blows between my thighs.

His fingers rub along my soaked slit as they coax the orgasm back to life. Waves of pleasure roll through me, and I push against his fingers. Two of them sink into my sopping core as his thumb grazes my clit.

He nips at my shoulder. The pain only increases my need as my hips pump of their own volition.

"Please." The word barely forms on the edge of the next breath.

"Please what?" The edge of his voice across my ear sends shivers down my spine. "What is it you want, girl?"

I can barely form words as the pleasure soaks my brain.

"Please," I say with more urgency.

His fingers stop and my hips push back against air. My moan resounds in the garage.

"If you don't know what you want, how could I possibly get you there?"

A whimper rides my exhale. I can't comprehend what is happening, my need is so great it is driving me to the edge, but the tidal wave slowly recedes.

The smile in his voice is obvious, even though I can't see his face. He once again leaves me on the edge, knowing it will be torture until I am satisfied.

"When I said mine, I meant mine. Now get in the car, it's time to go."

My body feels the sudden loss of warmth. The world moves in slow motion as I discreetly work to sort myself.

When I look up, his eyes watch me intently as I move toward the passenger door and slide in. Leaning back against the seat, I let out the breath I didn't realize I was holding.

CHAPTER THIRTY-ONE

Black fabric covers my eyes and the world goes dark.

"Place your hands together in front of you."

Plastic zip ties bind my wrists, and he pulls the seatbelt across my body.

"Everyone has a level of incentive which propels them forward. When you find those things, then persuasion and influence are more readily controlled," he says against my ear.

A breeze blows through the garage, sending a shiver up my spine. Goosebumps break out along my arms as his words fill me with trepidation and excitement.

"Senses are a privilege. Removing them is my prerogative. Giving them back is my discretion. The only thing you need to acknowledge is that you feel safe."

"Yes, Sir. I feel safe," I say. My voice is confident, though I'm full of anxious anticipation.

"Good girl."

He places headphones over my ears, filling my world with soft, lulling music. Next to me, the driver door opens, and he slides into the seat. Reece's musky scent mixes with his cologne and embraces my senses as I settle in the darkness.

Within moments, the car roars to life. The abrupt motion is disorienting as we back out of the bay and down the garage ramp. Once we're on the road, I drift off to sleep like a baby in a cradle.

"WAKE UP, SLEEPYHEAD," HE CALLS AS HE LIFTS MY HEAD FROM the passenger door window.

I startle. The car has stopped and I wonder how I've missed the end of our ride.

Reece removes the headphones but leaves the blindfold in place. When the driver's side door slams, I jump at the noise. There's no way for me to know where I am or how long I've been asleep. I can't believe I'm so stupid for drifting off, but there's something that makes me trust this man. Everything feels so natural with him, so easy and right.

The passenger door opens. The wind catches the bottom of my skirt. Reece runs a hand along my inner thighs and a shudder races through me as I moan.

"Open your legs." His voice is full of need.

For a moment I hesitate, and his hand slaps my thigh. In response, I push my legs wide.

"Much better."

His fingers inch up my thigh, stoking the fire he'd left smoldering in the garage, coaxing my orgasm back to the edge. Desire courses through me, and my hips move in a rhythm all their own, trying to find friction with the light brush of his hand.

"I love that your passion runs so deep."

The wind flutters across the bottom of my skirt.

"Bring your arms straight up and hold still."

I raise my hands. My breath goes shallow. The dull side of a knife blade runs across my skin as the sharp edge slices through the plastic.

He rubs each wrist and plants a soft kiss where the zip tie sat moments before.

Unbuckling my seatbelt, he places a hand under my right elbow.

"Stand," he orders as he helps me from my seat.

We move forward. He guides me by the elbow. The uneven ground causes me to stumble twice, but his firm grip catches me before I crash ungracefully to terra firma. The smell of brackish water fills the air along with the sound of waves lapping against a hard surface.

"Stop," Reece commands. "Sit."

The words make sense, but the lack of sight makes me nervous. Cautiously, I bend my knees, easing my body downward. My hands fly out when I lose my balance, but he catches me around the waist. Something soft brushes against my leg when I settle into place and I realize I'm on a blanket.

"Close your eyes."

I nod and close my eyes. The blindfold falls away.

In slow increments, I let the bright sunlight creep into the non-impervious darkness. Once my eyes adjust, I'm stunned by my surroundings. A few yards from us, the Potomac River laps across the rocky shore lining her banks. In the distance, there's a large cardboard replica of the Eiffel Tower. Around us, a lavish picnic is spreads out on the blanket. Reece smiles as I take in the sight.

"I told you I would kidnap you and take you away to Paris. If I tried much more than this, you would have found a thousand work excuses. I really owe Kade for his help."

His cocky grin tells me he's obviously pleased with himself.

"Did you have to kidnap me to get me here?"

"Obviously. The direct method wasn't working."

"True."

"We've quite the feast. Some pain aux céréales, not up to par with Eric Kayser, but we can have that when we make it to Paris. It is the best bread in the world. Here we have some Brie de Melun. Over there, grape and bocconcini summer salad. Cherry jam, some crackers and a small sample of charcuterie. And, finally, a lovely bottle of Sauternes," he says with a flare, pulling two wineglasses from the picnic basket.

"While the view is not the Seine, I thought the Potomac might stand in for now. We can even see the Eiffel Tower in the distance and let's not forget the pièce de résistance..." He slides his finger across his smart phone. From behind two well-placed rocks, traditional Parisian accordion music surrounds us.

"Wow."

Reece smiles at me with an arrogant confidence.

"I told you I was a sadistic Dominant with a hopeless romantic side."

"Yes, I believe you've proven that combination yet again."

"I hope you are finding it to your tastes." He smiles down at me.

It is a perfect clear spring day as the pale blue sky stretches above us. The weather is comfortable, neither so cool to need a jacket nor so hot to be miserable. The shade of the tall oak tree creates a shadow over our blanket, the sun slowly invading the space. I gaze out toward the Eiffel Tower cutout and back over the Potomac 'Seine' and laugh to myself. The afternoon sun caresses my skin as the slight breeze off the water adds a delightful contrast. For the first time in far too long, I relax in the moment.

It is then that I realize how much I've changed around Reece since I met him. He drives me to a frisson of excitement much of the time, but his calm, controlled manner allows me to let go. Though I've yet to be comfortable enough to express it. It has always felt so hard to explain to others how even a powerful person needs someone just as strong, or stronger, to lean on.

I savor the moment whilst feeling a little guilty for enjoying the afternoon in the middle of a work week. As soon as the thought takes hold, Reece offers various things for me to taste as he explains their significance in his Parisian extravaganza.

If only life could always be this wonderful and comfortable with just that hint of a dangerous edge. My mind drifts to the journey here. From Reece's text threat of kidnapping to its execution with his more than willing victim.

After Reece regales me with his array of foods, we enjoy our late afternoon snack in quiet contemplation, both lost in our own thoughts, enjoying each exquisite morsel. When we're done, Reece packs everything back into the picnic basket, and we watch the world go by together.

"What is bringing that devious smile to your face?" he asks.

My smile grows wider. "I was just thinking about how ridiculously romantic this whole situation turned out to be."

"What can I say, I'm like a rose."

"A rose?" Confusion laces my voice.

"Of course. The rose is a tarot symbol of balance. A red rose, a symbol of romantic love. A white one is about purity and innocence while blue roses signify the unattainable or the impossible. Regardless of the color, it is most associated with its thorns. The pleasure of the soft petals and its beautiful fragrance accompanied by the threat, and often delivery, of pain to obtain the desired bloom. Ultimately, it is all about balance — where pleasure and pain combine to create the wonderful ebbs and flows."

"Well said," I say with a nod as I think about his words. Beside me, Reece stretches out on the blanket and stares up at the sky.

"How did you find me in the garage?"

He rolls over to his side, propping his head on his hand.

"I told you. Kade advised me of your location. Originally I was going to surprise you in the office."

"Then why in the world was your car in the valet?"

"It wasn't. That's Kade's Black Escalade. He gave his keys to Adam. His texts reference something about being a voyeur and I wanted you all to myself. When Kade told me you were trying to escape and elude me yet again, his team provided an assist. He hoped the excitement would get you out of your head."

"The rat!"

Reece chuckles.

"So what's the history with you and Kade? He talks about you all the time but not intimately, more like a girlfriend who became a close friend."

I startle at the question and sit for a moment debating how much to reveal.

"We met when I was in graduate school. He'd just gotten back from his last tour in the Middle East, and I was working with a vet group. From there we sort of just bonded."

"Were you two play partners?"

"Yes. He was the first man I ever trained. The first time I watched someone submit, but I think he taught me far more than I dominated him, though I taught him how to dress. Goodness knows the military didn't do it for him.

"We found a balance of give and take in our needs. I wanted to learn skills, and he gave great feedback. So we worked through some of his emotional guilt from some of the things they had ordered him to do while he was in the Rangers, and I learned to handle stress in stride."

"You two don't play now?"

"No. He works security on the grounds my PR firm shares with the BDSM club next door. I've always had a rule about business and pleasure relationships. Being on the same grounds is close enough, so I don't cross that line. You seem to be the exception, and it's been quite the conflict."

Reece chuckles, his eyes lighting up like a mischievous boy.

"Am I now?"

"Yes. When it ends, I'll see if it was worth the high." I smile, looking down at my toes curling around the edge of the picnic blanket.

"When it ends? You don't think this is destined for happily ever after?"

"We're both adults who live in the real world. Even a hopeless romantic knows the realities of life."

"It doesn't mean we have to accept them."

"I think we should focus on happy for now." I turn my head and meet his gaze. "Don't you?"

"Yes, Miss Devereaux. I'm good with starting there. I'm curious, based on your background. Are you normally the dominant partner in your relationships?" he asks as his body tenses.

"Depends on the innate dynamic. If you're asking how often I submit or bottom, the answer would be — rarely. The reason I got into kink, originally, was to research ideas for a book I was writing. Samantha introduced me to a friend of hers who was a Dominant and professor at the university. Things progressed from there. For me it was about the techniques more than the emotions."

He sits up, leaning into my personal space. "Is this about technique or emotion?"

The hunger in his eyes devours me, and my breath catches.

"Hard to tell."

"Is it now? How's my technique so far?" Reece moves to invade my personal space.

My breath becomes shallow, a shiver runs across my skin, and I work to make my voice even. "So far so good."

"Just good? I think I will up my game if this is considered good to you."

Our mouths are inches apart. His breath grazes my lips.

"Yes. I'd like to see you up your game, Mr. Gabriel."

"Would you now, Miss Devereaux? And would it be upping my game if I took you right here on the bank of the 'Seine' Potomac?"

I hold my breath. While our picnic spot is out of the way, it is not hidden. In the last hour, we've seen four kayaks, two canoes, and one fishing boat. The chances of getting caught in the act seem relatively high, and my skin flushes with a combination of excitement and anxiety.

"You wouldn't."

My words are barely out when he moves forward, possessing my mouth. I groan against his lips as he seals his over mine. The soft, firm kiss exerts a possessive gentle pressure, and I return his exploration with eagerness, dipping my tongue inside his mouth, tasting him in leisurely laps. My kiss is confident and slightly aggressive when he returns the favor, grabbing my hair, pulling my head back to gain more control.

Deepening the kiss, he growls against my mouth. My heart pounds and my body's frenzy matches his desire. His hands are everywhere at once. They push up my dress. Fingers scrape across my clit, igniting the earlier tease and denial like a match to dry kindling.

"I want you, Atlas. All of you."

His muscles strain, his face a mixture of need and desire. I push toward him, wanting to touch his body, needing to feel him and not be denied again. I slide my hands into his hair, pulling him back into the deep kiss. He savagely answers my silent plea.

My legs fall open to accommodate his body. He shoves me onto my back and shifts above me as he grinds his erection against my clit. The friction of his pants against my lace panties sends a thrill of exhilaration through my body. I lift toward him to force a harder friction between us.

"Savor," he growls in a reminder to himself. "God knows all I want to do is fuck you hard and fast."

Reece rips my delicate underwear to shreds, tossing them onto the blanket. His hands move over my body with urgency, caging my wrists above my head.

"Don't move."

My hands remain still, and I arch toward him, demanding to feel him inside me again. My muscles strain to hasten the contact between us, desperate to explore the connection.

He trails nips and kisses down my neck as growls in frustration as his fingers work frantically to unbutton my dress. Finally, he gives up, pulling the fabric apart. Buttons fly off in every direction.

Bringing his face to mine, he once again lowers his mouth. His kiss bruises my lips on the razor edge of violence. I slide my hands back through his hair, pulling him closer to me and returning the hard kiss.

His hands roughly palm my breasts, pushing the thin fabric shreds of my blouse aside. He pushes the bra out of the way and his mouth catches my nipple. Each action fuels the growing fire between my legs.

"You are the sexiest woman alive." His lips vibrate against me.

"Please, Reece," I moan into the air. "I can't take this torture."

"Torture?" he growls in response. "Let me show you my brand of torture, my dear."

Reece's hands glide down my body, and then he lifts my legs higher around him. He reaches between us and pulls his cock from the confines of his slacks. Rocking forward, he teases my soaking entrance with his hard length. Each movement sends a quiver through my body. I arch toward him, trying to push my body onto his, but he pulls back.

"Now, now," he says, his voice barely maintaining the edge of control. "Savor the moment. Savor each move. Let it build."

I settle beneath him while he rolls on a condom. Then he repositions his body until his cock is once again resting at my entrance. A moan escapes as my hips lift to meet him, and he pulls back.

"Please, Reece. I need this now."

"I want you too. Right here where the world can see your wantonness as you lie open before me."

The words startle me, and I pull my hands to cover me, but he pins my wrists above my head, his hips forcing mine against the blanket. My shallow breaths barely lift my chest as I wait for his next move.

Reece reaches above me, wraps a line rope around both wrists, then pulls it snug. Moving down my body, he pulls each leg to the corners of the blanket. My mind reels trying to understand how the ropes appeared so quickly.

"Staking out a blanket to make sure it didn't move around the ground for our picnic creates so many possibilities." Reece grins at me from above as if he could read my mind.

The blade of a steel knife runs along the straps of my bra and cuts it free. He works it along the front of my dress and along the seam of the skirt. My eyes are wide and I feel vulnerable as he continues to reduce my clothes to rags.

"Looks like I need to take you shopping, my dear. Now that your clothes have somehow been reduced... pieces."

A devious grin plays on his lips as watches me as he moves his fingers through my wet folds and curls them against my sensitive G-spot while he kneads the hard knot of my clit with his thumb. Each move brings me to the edge of release, only to have him back off right when the orgasm is about to consume me. Working his tongue down my body, he leaves wet trails along the edge of my thigh and moves to replace his thumb.

"Oh my God, please, Reece, I need you in me."

"And I want to have my dessert first," he replies, pumping his fingers as his tongue circles and flicks across my clit.

Each move spurs my craving. He is merciless in the way he takes me to the edge without allowing the wave to consume me. Every nerve ending is alert to the slightest touch and movement. Teeth graze across my most sensitive spots as he nips and bites.

The building pleasure between my legs makes me want to beg, but his slow brand of torture only fuels my desperate need and desire to see what he has in store. A surge of emotions swamps me. The combination of his caring touch in juxtaposition with the binds and naked exposure combines to tear down my emotional walls.

The weight of my world presses against my heart, making my chest heavy. I need to let go and accept this excruciatingly wonderful tangled moment. I shift beneath Reece, trying to force more friction to shove my body into oblivion.

He drives his fingers hard and deep into me. Pleasure over-whelms my senses as his tongue dances between hard strokes across my clit and feather-light kisses.

"Please, Reece."

His name is a mere whisper when the orgasmic wave crashes and I release a scream of pleasure. Every thought shatters into a million fragments as the overwhelming pleasure explodes through my body. The world is a mix of distant sounds and silence as I shudder through the aftershocks of the orgasm.

I barely register the tears sliding down my face until he kisses them away.

"I'm sorry," I murmur, trying to turn away from him.

"You're beautiful. Your tears are beautiful. I'm honored you trust me with them," he whispers between kisses.

I tug against my bonds as I float back down to Earth.

"We're not done yet, gorgeous. I love watching you come for me. I love it even more when you clench in pleasure around me."

Reece adjusts his body. I open my eyes, drinking in the sight of his hard muscular body looming above me. Deftly, he rolls the condom on to his sizeable erection. Bending down, he takes a nipple into his mouth. His tongue flicks against the tip. I jerk against the ropes.

He cages my head with his hand, lifting his face to mine, his eyes boring into me. Nothing else exists around us. With slow movements, he pushes against my soaked entrance and buries himself inside.

I struggle against the rope as my body begs to have all of him. His hips lift slightly, the stroke of his cock overwhelming my most sensitive skin. His mouth captures mine as he pushes hard inside, and I utter a small cry against his soft lips. I stretch around him. Everything in begs to feel him drive into me, feeding the growing orgasm he has once again brought under his control.

Each sensation is powerfully pronounced in the wake of the powerful orgasm. For a long second he barely moves. His hips make only minor adjustments to his position. He fills me completely. Everything in this moment is perfect, and I delight in the sensations. Time stands still around us.

"I want to hear you scream my name. I want your body clinging to mine." His voice sounds hoarse in my ear.

My body stutters at his words. Something deep in me stirs. I want to know what it is like to be owned by this man. To be possessed, cared for, loved... My heart stumbles on the last word.

Reece moves slowly out of me, changing his angle slightly before re-entering hard and fast. I gasp at the power of his stroke, struggling against the bonds, wanting to wrap my body around him.

"More," I cry out, overwhelmed by each thrust as each sensation pushes me fast toward the precipice of another orgasm but needing more.

"My pleasure," he grinds out, his body responding with punishing strokes.

He picks up the pace, the friction of his strokes driving me toward my release. I moan, and he responds by mercilessly pounding into me in a relentless rhythm.

"Reece," I scream, my body pulsating around him, my hands wrapping around the rope to find an anchor as the pleasure explodes through me.

Above me, Reece finds his own release, hammering himself deep into me, emptying himself with a loud groan. His body jerks and thrusts into me as his breath comes in pants. When he finally stills, he bends down, kissing me gently.

His hips pull back, and I sigh softly at the feeling of loss. Quickly he disposes of the condom, then works to loosen the ropes. Reece plants soft kisses across each rope mark, massaging my hands and wrists along the way. When he's done, he trails kisses down my body until he reaches my ankles. He releases each one and massages the rope bites.

He helps me to sit and then stands to adjust his clothes. I scowl when he tucks his cock back into his pants.

"What's wrong, my dear?" he asks, a smirk gracing his face as he looks down at me.

I pull my knees to my chest, wrapping my arms underneath, suddenly very aware of my nakedness.

"You cut my clothes to rags."

I comment without emotion, but the blush creeping across my skin betrays me.

"So it seems. I like you naked. If I could, I would always have you this way."

"How impractical."

"Depends on the situation."

"And in this case, it seems you've created a difficult one."

Reece kneels down, his eyes level with mine.

"Atlas, I will never put you in a place in which I can't protect you," he says before kissing my forehead.

Part of me wants to be enraged for his patronizing tone, and another part wants to feel challenged and cared for in the same moment.

He walks over to the basket and pulls out a short kimono. The semi-sheer textured fabric hangs open at the front with long-dropped sleeves as he holds it out for my inspection.

"Seriously?"

"Quite."

"It barely covers anything. You tore or cut all of my undergarments off."

"I did." A smile hints around his mouth. "And I can't wait to do it again. Now let's get you home," he says holding up the kimono, "I'm not done with you yet. Of course, I'm okay if you want to refuse my generous gift."

An arrogant grin pulls across his mouth.

Reluctantly, I stand and slip my arms in the sleeves. Once I'm dressed, Reece helps me into my shoes, and we head back to the car.

CHAPTER THIRTY-TWO

Forty minutes later, we are barreling through the door of the condo, a tangle of arms, legs and mouths, touching and grabbing one another. He'd used my state of dress to his advantage for the entire drive, and I'm once again in a frenzy of need.

I fumble to remove his shirt, licking and nipping at his skin, tugging at his pants to free him. His hands push open the kimono, fingers teasing my nipples. In minutes both of us stand in the foyer nearly naked, his white shirt the last vestige of our haste.

Mouths and fingers roam over fevered skin, trying to get enough of each other. His hands are everywhere, massaging my bare breast with one while he fingers my clit with the other.

Reece hitches my leg over his hips and presses me against the wall. I gasp when he grinds against me. My hand slides through his hair, tugging him down to my mouth.

He returns the passionate kiss as he dissolves the fevered frenzy into something deeper and slower. He teases and tantalizes me with his tongue, while his hard cock presses against my thigh.

I reach between us and grasp his erection.

"If you tease it — you cover it so I can do something about it," he growls in response.

I look up at him in confusion.

"Check my shirt pocket," he says, stepping back.

I dip my fingers into his front pocket and find the condom sitting there waiting in anticipation.

"Quite the boy scout." I smirk.

"It pays to be prepared, Miss Devereaux."

I smile back, staring into his eyes as I rip open the package and place the condom between my lips.

In a smooth motion, I slide down the wall, my eyes never leaving his. I catch his cock in my hand, grasping it and coming to the top, to tease just the tip.

A heavy sigh above tells me I've hit my mark.

I bend forward, positioning my condom-filled mouth just above his hard cock and swallow him inch by inch with my lips. I lick and flick my tongue against the material as it covers him and work my mouth across it to smooth it all the way down. Reece groans above me when his cock hits the back of my throat.

"Up here, now," he says, reaching down and lifting me back to my feet.

He circles my waist with his hands, lifting me up and coaxing my legs around him. The sudden move forces me to let go, grabbing his shoulders for balance. He rocks into me, a promise of what's next.

My nerves are a raw bundle, his commanding attention spurring on my insatiable craving for him. He settles me onto his hard cock, pinning me against the wall.

"Take me, Reece. I need to feel you."

Without a word, he pulls his hips back, slamming me into the wall as he pounds into my pussy, driving hard and deep, again and again. I'm consumed with desire.

"Oh my God, Reece," I scream.

"That's it, come for me, baby."

The words shoot through me, pushing me over the edge. I grasp his shoulders, my fingernails sinking deep into his skin as the orgasm erupts through me.

"Don't stop," I moan against his damp skin.

"You want more?"

"Yes, I need more, so much more," I mumble, my body desiring something my voice can't communicate. Everything in this moment is insatiable. I need his commanding voice, his unapologizing touch in this mindless need.

Reece halts and then pushes deep into me.

I moan in frustrated confusion.

"Wrap your legs around me," he commands, his voice laced with a slight desperation.

I do as he commands.

He pushes off the wall, walking us over to the couch in the living area. Setting me onto the floor, he pulls from me before turning me over and pulling me on to my knees.

I push my hips push back against him in confusion and desperate need. His hand fists my hair as he slaps me hard across my ass. The pain courses through me as I react with a strangled scream. Three more hard smacks follow before I register what is happening, and he rams his cock back inside.

The punishing thrusts combine with the pain to drive me to the singular focus of connection between us.

"More," I cry.

"More what?" he growls, pounding into me.

"Yes."

"Don't move."

The palm of his hand once again makes a sharp crack across my ass, the sting of the pain mixing with the rising pleasure of my building orgasm. Reece pumps into me with steady strokes, and the emotional walls disintegrate. Everything is perfect. I am an oxymoron of roiling emotions, and I embrace them as they course through me.

He continues his hard slaps, pausing his driving rhythm to add more. My body sits on the precipice, emotions swirling through me without attached thoughts. His hand connects hard against my ass, and I scream as the orgasm rips through me in response. My fingers curl around the back of the couch, trying to steady myself on legs that feel like jelly. After two more hard strokes, Reece joins me as his body shudders against me.

Together, he takes us down to the couch in a tangle of arms and legs as I ride on waves of bliss. My fingers caress his chest, making slow, lazy trails down his body.

Physically, I'm spent. My body feels glorious, glowing in the aftermath of losing control to his firm command. The swirling thoughts in my mind wind slowly and uncomprehendingly across the fog.

My eyes meet his reverent gaze as he leans down, pressing soft kisses across my swollen lips and forehead.

"Atlas, you are so amazing." He shifts slightly, moving across me, then stands.

I whimper my objection at feeling the loss of his body against mine.

"Hush," he whispers, lifting me into his arms.

"James," he calls out to the room. "Goodnight."

The lights dim around us, and the whirl of blinds and curtains closing echo across the quietness.

"Goodnight, Mr. Gabriel," James replies from the speakers as the pathway lights toward my bedroom illuminates.

Reece pulls me tight into his arms, whispering adorations against my temple, carrying me back to the bedroom. I can't remember the last time I felt so spent that thoughts ceased, leaving only quiet contentment in their wake.

He lays me down on the bed, then bends down to pull the covers over me before slipping in beside me. His possessive arms wrap around my waist and tuck me against his broad, hard chest.

"This is where you belong, beautiful. Right here next to me," he whispers before lifting to kiss my temple.

"Sweet dreams, my love."

He continues his soft murmurs, and I slip into the bliss of exhausted sleep.

CHAPTER THIRTY-THREE

The sun peeks through the curtains. I roll over to find myself alone in my bed, and I stare at the ceiling when the smell of bacon registers.

"Good morning, James."

"Good morning, Miss Devereaux. It is good to see your sleep length has improved recently."

"Time."

"It is eight zero two am."

"What!" I exclaim, scrambling out of bed. "Shower on."

The sound of water streams from the bathroom and I rush into the shower, trying to clear the fog from my sleepy brain. There's nothing I would love more than to stay in bed with the gorgeous man who seems to take my normally ordered life into a tailspin of bliss, but my plate is full as usual. Yesterday afternoon's picnic will mean today's extra workload.

"Yeah, it was worth it," I say out loud, smiling to myself.

"What, pray tell, was worth it?" Reece's deep voice resonates throughout the tiled room.

"Why did you let me sleep so late?" I try to sound angry. "James, shower off."

The water stops and I open the door to step out. My breath catches at the sight of Reece neatly dressed in a navy blue suit, light blue shirt, and coppery red tie.

"Now this is how things should be."

Reece grins as he hands me an enormous bath sheet.

"What? You dressed and me naked?"

"You, girl, follow me, man. Do as I say!" he says in a halted staccato.

"Yeah, right? Okay, Mister Caveman. You've made me late."

A broad grin blossoms across Reece's face, causing an infectious reaction, and I work to suppress a laugh.

I pull the bath sheet around my body, trying to look serious.

"I'd apologize, but you looked so peaceful sleeping," he says, bending down and brushing a kiss across my lips. "And watching you shower is a simple pleasure all on its own."

"And now you're unapologetic about making me late!"

"Maybe I should take you into the bedroom, turn you over my knee and adjust your attitude a bit, so you understand the simple pleasures of life."

His face is a mixture of amusement and seriousness.

"You wouldn't dare," I say, staring back.

"If I didn't feel so guilty about making you late, that's exactly what I'd do." He steps into my personal space and dips his head until his breath caresses my ear. "I look forward to turning your ass bright pink again. But for now, I must leave you to get ready. I will be gone for a couple days on business, but I look forward to seeing you again."

Reece pops the front of my towel, sending it to a puddle around my feet. His fingers wrap in my hair, his lips descending on mine in a searing kiss. Desire shoots through me as I moan against his lips.

When his head lifts, his breath is as ragged as mine.

"I should go before I carry out my promise here and now," he growls. "I'll see you in a couple of days. I made you breakfast. It's sitting on the counter."

"Thank you. Be safe."

I smile. All I want is for him to take me back to bed. Instead, I watch him turn and walk out the door.

THE MORNING IS IMPOSSIBLY BUSY. MY DELAYED ARRIVAL AT the PR firm, accompanied by taking the prior afternoon unexpectedly off, has caused a rush of activity. More of it is caused by my feelings of guilt over not working rather than any actual emergency, but the swirl of activity helps to lower increased distraction, going by the name of Reece Gabriel.

My cell phone dings, and I hit the button to see the incoming message.

Your pink ass, along with the rest of you, has been on my mind all morning. I believe you are driving me to an extreme distraction, Miss Devereaux. Whatever am I going to do with you? RG

A SMILE SPREADS ACROSS MY FACE AS I READ THE MESSAGE. AT least he's suffering in the same way I am.

Mr. Gabriel, I quite believe that it is you that is driving me to distraction. Was it not you who kidnapped me in the middle of the work day? AD

"Well there's a sight rarely seen," Kade says, startling me out of my reverie.

My head jerks up to meet the smirk on his face.

"Oh?"

"You look like a woman in love, Atlas," he states matter-of-factly.

"It's all fun. A distraction, I'm sure." I try to keep my voice light-hearted, but his words echo the ones in my mind over the past few days. "Though I hear I have a score to settle with you."

I try to harden my tone but fail when I see the proud look cross his face.

"Oh? Do you now? What score could you possibly have to settle with me, Ma'am?"

"The matter of the key switch in the garage yesterday," I reply pointedly.

"Did Adam pick up the wrong keys, Ma'am? I am so sorry. Be assured the matter will be handled appropriately."

"What, with a high five, atta boy and a fist bump?"

"I did say appropriately." He smirks. "You look hot on your knees."

I look at him confused when the memory of the camera motor in the garage hits me full force.

"Oh my God, your team didn't..." I stutter, unable to fully come to terms with the level of humiliation possible if the security team saw my performance in the garage.

"One day you'll learn to trust me." Kade's protective tone asserts itself rapidly.

"So they didn't watch?"

"No." His reply is slightly hesitant.

"But you did," I reply, rolling my eyes.

He smiles and nods. "Best porn on television. It was hot."

"Was it?"

"Yes, Ma'am."

He grins like an unapologetic schoolboy.

"I should tan your hide over this situation, you know."

"Probably, but we're well past that stage in our relationship, which is unfortunate. I always liked it when you whipped me into shape."

"I'm sure gloating over your help to Mr. Gabriel's scheme is not the reason you dropped by."

"It really is an excellent reason, but alas, it's not." Kade watches me. "There have been more security reports. I am upping the membership security levels, but that's still not the reason."

"Let's take this up to the studio," I mumble.

I join Kade, and we walk across the room. The echo of our footfalls bounces off the walls.

"Melody, please hold all my calls," I call out when we reach the bottom of the stairs.

"Yes, Ma'am."

My phone dings as we climb toward the studio.

I'm thinking how good you look all tied up. Helpless to my ministrations, feeding you by hand and turning you over my knee to make that ass hot to my touch. Playing your body like a fine instrument. Watching your reactions as I play with you. What a fine dinner that would be. RG

I stumble on the stairs, Kade's hand catching my elbow.

"Are you okay?"

I nod, my face blushing as I shove the phone in my pocket.

Kade watches me expectantly. Once he's sure I've regained my footing, he releases me, but the knowing smile curling across his lips makes me shake my head.

We reach the top of the stairs, and Kade settles on a barstool in the studio kitchen.

"Want something to drink?" I ask, pulling on the refrigerator handle.

"Do you have a beer?"

"Yes. IPA or stout?"

"Stout," Kade replies, running his hand through his hair.

"Well, something has Mr. Kinkaid rattled."

I turn, handing Kade a beer, then set my glass water bottle on the island.

Kade pops the top on the island's bottle opener and kicks the beer back. After a long swallow, he sets it gingerly on the countertop.

"Interesting," I comment calmly, settling on the stool next to him. "What has you all atwitter, Thomas?"

"Atwitter? That's the word you're going with here?" he asks, rolling his eyes.

I snicker and wait for him to collect his thoughts.

"Have you decided on Cassandra yet?"

"A decision?"

"On training her to be a pro Dominant? I know she spoke to you about it. I also know that you are very selective about your trainees. Your plate is currently full with many other endeavors."

"Her essay is well written. She seems sincere, though I admit there's something bugging me about her. Why?"

"I'd like to take her on as an apprentice," he replies, running his hand through his hair.

"Really?" My brows crease in confusion as I try to figure out Kade's angle, other than he's obviously into her.

"Yes, really. The last two I trained turned out nicely, according to your personal evaluation. It's been a while since I took on a personal project."

"Do you think this is really an appropriate fit?"

"I do."

"You realize she's not submissive. She's a follower by day, but I can't imagine behind closed doors she'll submit too much."

"I hope not." His voice is tense. "Besides, I don't want her submission. I want her obedience. I want her dedication to the craft."

"Why?"

"There's something about her, and I think it's the best way to keep a close eye on her."

"Something about her in what way? It's obvious you're attracted to her, but you know I don't allow that in a training pair."

"Honestly, I'm not sure. Don't get me wrong. I find her attractive, but something is off and it's bothering me."

My hand covers his, and he looks up.

"Maybe you need a vacation."

"What I need is obedient control. Action and reaction, cause and effect. Something straightforward."

I chuckle lightly.

"You know it's not that simple. There are always curve balls in training. Maybe she'll turn out to be submissive. Fall all doe-eyed for the great Thomas Kinkaid, Master of all he surveys."

Kade gives me a wry smile.

"Stop that. You know women fawn all over you when you smile like that."

I playfully punch him in the arm. The solid muscle doesn't even flinch, but a light pain shoots through my hand.

"Yep, got me out of many a punishment when we first met," he replies, turning up the wattage on his smile.

"I learned fast."

"That you did, Miss Devereaux. To the point few would guess the independent woman sitting before me wants to submit."

"Don't." I shake my head.

"What? Make you admit your own needs, wants, desires?"

"I cut those off some time ago." I smile softly.

"Yes, and a certain Mr. Gabriel has found the key to ignite them to a brilliant flame."

"It's been fun." I nod as my fingers caress the padlock charm resting in the hollow of my neck.

"Why do I feel a *but* coming?"

"Because you know me well," I reply and flash him a smile.

"Don't sabotage this, Atlas. It's the happiest I've seen you in so long. You may present as a wonderfully independent woman, and you can run circles around most people I know, but give yourself a place to unwind. It's okay to let someone else control the helm, you know. Let your submissive side out. Enjoy it."

I sit for a moment, letting his words mull around my own thoughts.

"Perhaps."

"You are truly the most stubborn woman I know."

"It's because I had this training partner who became my stubborn, challenging submissive, and I learned my lessons well."

"You can't pin this on me. You were already pigheaded before we met."

"Possibly. Though I prefer focused, assertive, and tenacious."

I grin at him proudly, and Kade chuckles.

"Do you want to submit to Cassandra?"

"No. I want to get close enough to figure out what she's up to. She seems too perfect but doesn't really interact with people."

"Maybe she's just shy."

"Possibly. I'd know if I was interacting with her. Think of it as a win-win. If she's good, you'll get a new house Dominant that will help the business."

"And if your gut is right?"

"I'll resolve a problem before it becomes one. That is what you pay me to do. Besides, maybe she's a lost soul, and she'll find her way like someone else I know."

"True. Okay. I'll let Cassandra know that Alexandra has placed her with a House Trainer."

A confused look passes over Kade's face. "Did you say okay?"

"Yes. Is there a problem?"

"It's just that you never okay something on the first round."

"Maybe I'm growing," I say, rolling my eyes. "Everyone has been harping on me for some time about growing the business and delegating responsibilities. If there is one thing I've learned recently, it's that I have an amazing team and I need to let them grow when the opportunity presents itself."

"That's quite the life lesson," Kade replies, grabbing my shoulder and pulling me in for a bear hug.

"It's something. At least, it makes me less of a controlling bitch and more of an effective leader."

"You were never a controlling bitch, and you still aren't." His quiet tone gives reverence to his statement. "You think you need to hold on too tight out of fear."

I nod. "Fear makes people do strange things they wouldn't normally do."

"Yep. That's why it can be so much fun," he says, rubbing his hands together.

"Now don't scare her off, but make her well-rounded."

"I know your standards. She'll live up to them. My reputation is on the line," Kade says as he picks up the bottle, tips it toward me in a silent salute, then finishes off its contents. Putting the empty beer bottle back on the counter, he appraises me silently. "There's some-thing different about you."

"Good different or bad different?"

"Good different. More balanced, perhaps."

I smile noncommittally.

"I'd better get back to SecOps," he says, rising from his seat.

"I look forward to your training reports. Alexandra will have her assistant notify you and Cassandra. You know the drill after that point. Report in once a week with her progress."

"Of course, Ma'am." He bows slightly, turns, then makes his way down the stairs.

I sit for a long moment staring after Kade as I breathe out a sigh of relief. Cassandra is a perfect distraction for him. While I feel guilty about not being open with him on the Edmund issue, I also know that keeping him from focusing on it will help ensure he stays out of harm's way. Besides, relieving pressure and ignoring Edmund's attempts to gain power through fear will probably deescalate the whole situation faster than feeding into it, since he's been so quiet.

I pull my phone out and stare at the last message from my distraction and smile.

Bring it—cause you will need it. AD

FOR A MOMENT I HESITATE, RE-READING THE MESSAGE. THEN with gusto, I press send. Within seconds, my phone dings with a reply.

Oh — Miss Devereaux — will I ever. RG

A SHIVER OF EXHILARATION RUNS THROUGH ME.

Share with the rest of the class, Mr. Gabriel.

A COCKY SMILE CREEPS ACROSS MY FACE. THIS IS A GAME IN which I'm well honed.

You spread-eagle on the bed. Wait, we did that on the bank of the river. Your upturned ass splayed over a spanking bench. No, we did that over the couch. You tied up so tight you can't move. Hmm... did that too. Perhaps you cuffed to a St. Andrew's cross while I flog your cares away. Or we go deeper into the rabbit hole and you finally sign the contract.

———

I SHAKE MY HEAD HARD AND GATHER MY WITS. MY HEART RACES at a furious pace and a heavy blush sweeps through my body. What is wrong with me? I admonish myself to get the wayward thoughts and reactions under control.

———

Well played Mr. Gabriel.

———

PICKING UP THE BEER BOTTLE, I STAND AND WALK OVER TO THE trash can. The phone dings with an incoming message as I head back down the stairs.

———

We haven't even played yet Miss Devereaux. This is just the titillating warm up.

———

I FUMBLE THE PHONE AND LISTEN TO IT BOUNCE DOWN THE stairs, glad once again that my phone is life-proof.

CHAPTER THIRTY-FOUR

The cell phone vibrates across my desk and I shake my head. Reece has been persistent in his messages for the past few days. There are times he's driven me to salacious distraction while accusing me of the same.

In an effort to calm the building anticipation, I've turned the PR firm and club into a flurry of activity. I've written five chapters in my book, and I know Samantha will be thrilled. Melody has organized all seven file drawers in the PR office, Katie has organized the club's files and I've driven everyone to the edge with my exuberance to get things done. There doesn't seem to be a surface that hasn't been polished, buffed, or shined.

More than once my staff, in all areas of my life, has taken time to ask if I'm feeling okay. Each time I smile and nod, explaining that I'm feeling much more balanced after the past few months and making sure things are being caught up. Then, more often than not, I apologize for the extra work. I know I've made mistakes over the last few months as I've tried to get the businesses back on their feet, but now that they are stable again, I want to do everything in my power to keep them this way.

"When's he due back?" Kade's voice resonates behind me.

"Whatev'a do you mean, Mr. Kinkaid?" My accent is thick as I turn to face him in the club corridor.

"You're driving the staff insane."

He chuckles.

"A li'l bit of work and elbow grease is good for all of us. A few too many months of trying to get my head together has given everyone time off. Now it's time to get back to work. I'm pulling my weight in the ditches with them."

"As you always do, Alexandra. You are most definitely the hands-on type of leader."

"There's another way to be?"

"Yes. Tied up so we can all breathe," he says with a twinkle in his eye.

I roll my eyes and shake my head.

"When are you going to tell him about all of this?" Kade asks, cocking his head to the side and raising one eyebrow.

I sigh, my lips pulling in a thin line.

"Listen, Jiminy Cricket, I'll tell him when the opportunity presents itself. No reason to ruin moments of perfection," I say, my voice lilting in a sing-song manner to lighten the heavy statement.

"Better earlier than later."

"He has his secrets and I have mine. It is part and parcel to a relationship, my dear boy."

"Yes, Ma'am, I'm aware. I'm also aware all of this can even be hard for open-minded people when they realize what it entails," he says, his hands spreading to indicate the club.

"Which makes my point succinctly. The proper opportunity will present—"

The ping of my phone interrupts me, and I look down to see the message. Kade snickers in the background.

Meet me in front of Saks Fifth Avenue in an hour. RG

I grin like a little girl.

"Finally." Kade lets out an exasperated sigh.

"Finally, what?"

"Well, with the phone in your hand and the grin on your face, it can only mean one thing."

"And what's that?"

"That you can get distracted, and we can all breathe a sigh of reprieve. Please thank Mr. Gabriel on behalf of the entire staff."

"Fine," I say, rolling my eyes. "Go be the good cop and tell the troops to stand down. The boss lady has flown the coop."

"Yes, Ma'am." He pops to attention, snapping a salute. "Good to see you smiling from the inside and not because you put on a mask. Reece seems to be good for you."

"Thank you for everything, Kade." I give him a quick hug. Then turn to walk down the hall towards the corridor leading to my dressing room and ultimately back to the PR firm.

An hour later, I'm sitting in the club's Audi, waiting on Reece. As I sit in front of Saks Fifth Avenue, my mind races at his directive. The thrill of seeing Reece again mixes with anticipation and trepidation at the odd meeting place. On the outside I work to appear calm, controlled and collected. However, the reality is anything but the presentation.

A black Suburban pulls up beside me and parks. The driver gets out and opens the backseat door as Reece steps out. Then he turns, smiles when he sees me, and walks over to the car. He opens my door and appraises me without saying a word as he looks me up and down. The look in his eye causes a shiver to run up my spine.

We spend the shared moment assessing each other. For the last few days, we've been pushing each other with double entendres, light conversation, and general flirting. Now that we are in the same physical space, we are both on high alert to see where the game will take us next, but right now Reece has the upper hand. He summoned me here, and I willingly came to see what he had planned.

Looking down, he smiles at me before dropping a light kiss on my forehead.

"Good afternoon, Miss Devereaux. I am so glad you could join me for a jaunt out."

"Of course, Mr. Gabriel. You lace your messages with such succinct sincerity, how could one decline your request for an adventure?" The sarcastic tone drips from my words.

"Shall we go inside?" he asks with a mischievous smile.

A wave of self-conscious concern falls across me. I hate shopping. Once I had enough staff working for me, I delegated the responsibility. For the last several years, a personal shopper has met with me quarterly to update my wardrobe. The bills have come in, and I've paid them. A neat, clean transaction. Having someone else pay for a shopping spree, however, didn't sit well. It was one of the many areas of dichotomy I could never resolve between being taken care of and not losing my independence.

Reece winds his way through the store as I follow behind him. Periodically he pauses at a rack, slipping his hands across fabric or picking up a dress I would deem far too short. Other times, he browses racks of skirts that are so long the fabric would brush against the floor. Every piece he selects works with the previous ones. The personal shopper follows along with us.

At the back of the store, Reece peruses the shoes with precision.

Without turning toward me, he points to a nearby chair. "Sit."

I look at him in confusion but know better than to argue. Gracefully, I lower my body into the chair and watch the hustle of the staff.

He continues through the department when a young woman approaches.

"Can I help you, Sir?"

Smiling, he turns and nods.

"Yes, I would like to see several shoes on this lovely woman's feet."

"Do you have anything specific in mind? A color? Or a height?" she asks, never taking her eyes off his face while ignoring me.

He glances over, and his hungry gaze rakes over my body.

"Heel height at a minimum of four inches. Color does not matter.

Style must be fashionable and I prefer a stiletto," he replies. "And she's a size nine, before you need to ask."

The woman nods, turns toward the storeroom, then disappears.

Reece turns to me.

"From this moment on, you will have no say in the decisions. You are to give an opinion on size and fit only. There will be no discussions. Are we clear?" he says with a smile.

"Yes, Sir."

For the next hour, various shoes come in a continuous parade from the storeroom. I comment on the fit and comfort, but when I try to give an opinion, Reece gives me a look that stops the words in my mouth. Internally, I'm not sure if I want to revel in the lack of need to decide or feel violated by his sudden control.

After what seems to be a hundred pairs of shoes, Reece tells the saleswoman he's decided and points to half a dozen pairs. He picks up a blue pair of strappy five-inch stiletto platform heels.

"She'll be wearing these home," he says, his megawatt smile making her preen.

I place the shoes on my feet and follow his directions to walk around the floor, his eyes following the sway of my body, making sure the new shoes create the desired motion without causing missteps or issues.

When he's satisfied, he signals to me, almost imperceptibly, and we walk toward the lingerie department.

Once again, he discusses the situation with the clerk. She measures my chest, looking me up and down. In moments, she returns with a black satin garter, smooth black Cuban heel stockings, and a black lace bra with satin inserts to match. Full of confidence, he picks up the items without a further fitting. I watch as Reece and the clerk converse just out of ear shot. He nods, smiles, then turns and takes my hand as he leads me to another part of the store.

"Now we've got all the foundations covered," he says, smiling down at me before kissing me on the forehead and leading us into the women's dress department. He hands me into a high-back chair. Once I'm settled, he disappears among the racks.

Engrossing myself with people watching, I attempt not to think about the unusual shopping trip and its implications.

He walks up behind me. His hands land on my shoulders and massages the tension.

"Relax, Atlas."

I bend my head back to look at him. His intense gaze bores through me.

"Katherine will assist you in trying on the outfits we've picked out. You'll try on the ten outfits we've chosen. With each one you will come out and show it to me. Am I clear?"

"Yes, Sir, crystal clear."

"I have arranged for you to change in a nearby dressing room." His voice is calm and soft, brokering no question or comments.

Discreetly, I rise and follow the clerk into the dressing room.

"Let me know if you need any help."

She smiles politely, pulling the door closed, leaving me with the selection of clothes.

I pull out a short blue dress with an illusion and lace bateau and long lace sleeves. Its form looks shapeless on the hanger. I step into the dress and turn to face the mirror. It hugs every curve of my body. The image looking back at me is perfect in its sensual sophistication and I know there is no reason to try on any other outfit.

My hand tentatively wraps around the dressing room doorknob and I step out toward Reece.

He's talking on the phone. When he looks up, his mouth hangs agape before slamming shut.

"I'll call you back," he says into the phone, pressing the end button without looking down.

"That dress looks incredible on you," the saleswoman gushes, joining Reece in his stare.

"I'll take the dress. Please place the other purchases in the dressing room for her, Katherine."

"Yes, sir, Mr. Gabriel," she replies, then moves with haste to do his bidding.

"Atlas, please add this to your outfit." He holds up a bag, letting it dangle from his forefinger. "I want you to wear everything, including what is in this bag. There will be no hesitation on your part while you dress."

"Yes, Sir, as you wish," I say, a smirk crossing my face as I lift the bag and wiggle my hips to tease him.

In the dressing room, they've removed the other outfits and replaced them with the shoes and lingerie. A set of diamond earrings lies on top, the fire of the stones sparkling and dancing in the light.

I place the bag on the bench, wondering at the contents as I remove the dress and sit down on the edge of the bench.

Without hurry, I remove my bra and panties, replacing them with the ones Reece has purchased, and run my fingers through the silk stockings, working them up my legs, attaching them to the garter belt.

My eyes fall to the bag, and I reach inside, pulling out two small boxes with notecards inserted across the tops.

INSERT ME.

OPENING THE TOP, I GASP WHEN MY EYES FALL ON THE CRYSTAL ended butt plug. My body flushes and I set it aside to look at the other box.

ENCIRCLE THEM.

Inside there are two non-piercing nipple shields.

I take a deep breath, cringing at the thought of the butt plug. Anal insertion has always made me feel calm and vulnerable, but it is no longer a normal activity in my world. Moving to the easier item, I pinch my nipples and place the shield around each one. Arranging my bra, I take a deep breath and settle my rising nerves.

The war in my head quiets with each step of the process as my submissive side wins out, allowing me to relax in the anticipation of the unknown. I step into the dress, smoothing it down with my hands.

Next come the shoes. My feet slip into them and I rise.

Looking down, I stare at the silver plug and shiver. I pull the skirt around my waist and bend over, jumping at every sound in the fitting room.

I look at the small packet of lube and tear it open. Picking up the plug, I smooth it across the top. Reaching back, I push the plug against the tight pucker of my ass, pressing it past the initial resistance as I force myself to relax. Taking a deep breath, I slide it home as the muscles pull it into place.

Goosebumps run across my body. The exhilaration of the situation rushes through me and I close my eyes, forcing my breathing to slow. The deep breaths help clear my mind, and I straighten, arranging the dress back into place, once again smoothing it down. Last, I pick up the earrings and insert them into each lobe.

I take one last glance in the mirror and stride with confidence out of the dressing room, the plug reminding me of its presence with each step.

Reece looks up at my approach and smiles.

"Lovely, my dear."

"Thank you, Sir," I say with a curtsy, suddenly aware of every movement under his wicked gaze.

He holds out his elbow and I lay my hand on his arm. Reece leads us through the store to my waiting car.

"You know, you could dismiss your driver, and we could take the Audi," I say as I tilt my head towards the R8.

Beside it, his driver stands by the open car door of the large black Suburban.

Upon our approach, Reece's head pivots between the Audi and the Suburban.

"Beautiful R8."

"Yes, but sadly it's not mine. It belongs to a client who owed me a favor. I thought it would be fun to take it out today."

Reece nods in response.

"Want to drive her?" I ask as he stares at the car.

"I shouldn't."

"Come on. You only live once, and she's a blast to drive."

Reece walks over to his driver, and they have a brief conversation before he returns to the car. His driver returns to his seat up front and maneuvers the SUV through the parking garage and out into traffic.

"You look stunning," Reece says, lifting my fingers to his lips. "I quite enjoyed our public private play."

"Thank you, Sir," I reply with a slight nod.

I hand Reece the keys and walk around to the passenger's side as he slides behind the wheel. We pull out of the parking lot. Reece opens up the engine as we pull into traffic.

"And how is everything settling, above and below, so to speak?"

I cock my head and gave him a quizzical look.

"How are you doing mentally and physically?"

Realization of his reference dawns on me and I laugh.

"A rather loaded question, Mr. Gabriel."

"Quite," he acknowledges. "Since we don't yet have a signed contract between us, and we've not discussed the edges and boundaries, I'm going about this by feel."

"And quite the path you've chosen too," I return his verbal play.

"You know how to make things change direction should they become too much for you. It is a presumption, but one I feel safe in it since I know you have experience in such a path."

"I do, and I've felt no need to use it."

"There is no harm or fowl in it if you felt the need to do so at any point. While we live life when we step outside of our comfort zone, I don't want you so far out it is harmful."

"Understood."

I muse at my experiences compared to this soft sensual approach and smile.

"Good, because tonight will continue to challenge you."

"In what way?" I focus on my breathing, exuding a continuous air of confidence, even while the plug in my ass makes my mind focus on its taboo presence.

"We'll be mixing business and pleasure. My sister is having a campaign fundraiser tonight, and I promised I'd make an appearance."

"Did you say we are going to a political fundraiser for Congresswoman Elizabeth Davies?"

"Don't make it sound so huge."

"Is it a party fundraiser or a single candidate?"

"Party," he replies.

I let out a deep sigh as my stomach clenches with nerves.

"Is there an issue, Atlas?"

For a long moment I let the fear course through me. Normally political fundraisers were easy to do. You bring the checkbook, do the necessary networking, steer the conversation toward the topics you want to discuss and get out. However, I have a butt plug stretching my ass, reminding me I chose to follow his commands to place it there. Nerves race through me as I brace for my worlds to collide.

"No issue, Sir," I whisper.

"Superb. I know you comfortably move in these circles. The added challenge to your focus should be as entertaining to you as it is to me."

"As you say," I comment absently, watching the DC cityscape rise around us.

CHAPTER THIRTY-FIVE

W hen it comes to political fundraising, Congress doesn't travel very far. Most take place within a three city block radius of the U.S. Capitol. As the Audi winds its way up Independence Avenue, I muse at this.

A small line of expensive cars waits outside the hundred-year-old building which houses the Sonoma Restaurant and Wine Bar. The line moves forward, and my door opens.

"Ma'am," the valet says as he reaches in, helping me from the passenger seat, while another valet holds Reece's door.

Stepping onto the sidewalk, I gain my balance and wait for Reece to join me. Photographers call out to the guests as they make their way through the front door and into the reception line to pose for pictures with the congresswoman.

"Reece!" the Congresswoman exclaims over the light din as we enter the restaurant.

He leans down and gives her a kiss on the cheek. Over my left shoulder, the photographer calls to her and Reece pulls me in close for a quick photo with his sister.

"Please play nice. I need this to be successful," she says to him through a gritted smile.

"Of course, my dear sister. You know how I love these evening receptions."

"Free food, free drinks. What's not to love?" she whispers beside him.

"Before we fade into the crowd to do your bidding, may I introduce my plus one, Miss Atlas Devereaux."

Turning toward me, he continues, "Miss Devereaux, may I introduce Representative Elizabeth Davies."

"A pleasure to meet you, Congresswoman Davies," I say, holding out my hand.

Her hand is soft with a firm grip when she returns my handshake.

"The pleasure is all mine, Miss Devereaux. My apologies for not being able to take the time to chat, but I look forward to getting to know you," she says, smiling, her eyes turning toward Reece in a silent statement suggesting I'll be the topic for discussion soon.

"I look forward to it." I give her a polite nod, then turn toward Reece as he makes a path through the crowd.

We make our way up to the second floor into The Pennsylvania Avenue Lounge above the main dining room. The intimate bar and open floor plan are perfect for the number of donors, handlers, assistants, and all other forms of the staff milling around. In some areas the nine-foot ceiling gives the illusion of intimacy, while in others, the sixteen-foot ceiling soars above us, creating the juxtaposition of open exposure. The thoughts are not lost on me as we walk through the gathering crowd.

Reece leads us to the Avenue Lounge's fireplace. The raised semi-private space within the lounge shows off its three panoramic windows overlooking the Library of Congress.

I make my way toward the windows, trying to find a place to get out of the shifting crowds and settle my nerves.

"Beautiful, isn't it?" Reece says behind me.

"It reminds me of my brief time on the Hill."

"I didn't know you worked up there."

"Briefly, as a congressional intern then aide. The work didn't suit me, but it led to some very lucrative client contacts."

"Is that how you and Samantha grew the PR firm?"

A man clears his throat behind us, and we both turn at once.

"Senator Smith, it's so good to see you," Reece says to the tall, handsome man who is easily in his mid-sixties. He holds out his hand and they shake.

The air in the room stills around me when recognition assaults my senses. His pony play harness manifests across his face in my mind. He was one of Alexandra's first clients when I moved to DC. The Senator loved pony play, and we'd use his small family farm in Middleburg when he wanted to let go of the DC stress.

We talked frequently afterward about his needs and desires. He explained, for him, it was the balance of an internal release of personal control, structured grace, athleticism, and reaction to commands, both verbally and more subtly through the reins. Being able to roleplay as a horse freed him from the guilt of indulging his need as a man.

I learned so much from our association and was thrilled when he met his wife, Janice. For a time, I worked with them both as they transitioned into their own brand of play. My admiration for their balance, in being able to maintain a public life with a taboo private life, left me in awe. As I look at the Senator's face, I realize how much of my life has been consumed with fulfilling the fantasies, images and desires of others, while sacrificing my own.

I uncomfortably shift beside Reece, the plug adding to my sudden vulnerability, and I smile at the reminder of how life is changing once again.

"May I present my companion, Miss Atlas Devereaux."

He turns toward me.

"Miss Devereaux, may I introduce Senator Smith," Reece says with a proud smile.

There is a slight pause in the senator's movement, a micro-expression of fear and recognition which shadows his face before the smile returns. Since he was such an early client for me, I had not learned all the techniques of close-up disguise that I now use. For a long moment, we both stand in the same internal place, our worlds colliding in an unexpected and unenviable way. I watch the senator's face but give a slight shake of my head and reach out my hand.

"It is good to meet you, Senator," I say, full of confidence I don't feel.

Both of us know what is at stake as we stand in a mutually destructive moment.

"Miss Devereaux is the managing partner of the McKenzie Kingston's PR firm," Reece says to shore up our association. Then, more quietly, he leans into the senator and says in an indistinct voice, "She's trying to keep my bad boy image out of the spotlight, so Elizabeth doesn't kill me during the campaign."

The irony of the moment isn't lost on me as I see a twinkle light up the senator's eyes.

A white suited server moves effortlessly through the crowd. Reece grabs two glasses from the tray before handing me one.

"How is Janice?" Reece asks.

"Doing well, thank you for asking. She's over in Europe at a symposium on horse handling. She's a consummate trainer for our Arabians."

"On horse handling?" Reece asks before taking a sip of his wine.

I choke on the liquid already moving through my mouth and both men turn toward me.

"Are you okay, my dear?" the senator asks, his voice full of concern, his eyes full of warning.

I nod and work to catch my breath.

"One should not attempt to breathe and drink at the same time. My apologies. If you'll excuse me, gentlemen."

I back away from the conversation and turn to make my way toward the ladies' room, trying to catch my breath as I push open door. Setting the drink on the counter, I thrust my hands into the sink. The cool water from the motion sensor taps runs across my skin and soothes my nerves.

"Are you okay, Miss Devereaux?"

The soft voice startles me, and I look up to see Elizabeth Davies standing behind me, an expression of concern written across her face.

"Yes. I attempted to breathe and drink at the same time," I say lightly, coughing again to clear my throat.

"How long have you and Reece been seeing each other?" Her voice is soft, but the tone is more forceful, in complete juxtaposition to the relaxed expression on her face.

"A few months," I reply without commitment.

In my world, less is often more in the knowledge department. More than once I've learned the correlation between power and knowledge isn't a joke.

"Do be careful, Miss Devereaux. My brother may appear very charming, but his tastes are very... unusual. You seem like a very nice young lady and I don't want to see you get hurt. He's far darker than he seems."

I turn to face her. The ribbons of the garter belt pull across my leg as my lace panties bunch into the creases and crevices, forcing the edge of the plug to move inside me. Reece's control over my body is as clear standing here alone with his sister as it is when we are in the bedroom. I revel in the thought. The connection I never understood during my experiences suddenly becomes clear. For the first time I glimmer an understanding of how the senator and my other clients feel, while fighting against it from a purely societal idea.

"Thank you, Congresswoman Davies. I appreciate your concern. Your brother has been nothing but a genuine gentleman around me."

"Then maybe you are the exact influence he needs in his life. He seems to be quite taken by you, and you seem adept at moving in these social circles."

"Yes. I spent time on the Hill early in my career," I comment without further elaboration. "I hope tonight's fundraiser is a rousing success for you, Congresswoman. If you'll excuse me, I should return so that Mr. Gabriel doesn't cause an unnecessary ruckus."

Elizabeth smiles at me with a mixture of admiration and confusion.

I turn with care and walk out of the door. Sauntering back into the Lounge, I return to Reece's side, who's still standing in front of the bank of windows. Upon my approach, I notice a prior client of my PR firm and a couple of staffers who have joined the growing conversation and just shake my head.

Upon my approach, Reece smiles, snakes his arm around my waist, and pulls me to his side.

"Gentlemen, may I introduce Miss Atlas Devereaux. Atlas, may I introduce Ian Breckenridge, my sister's campaign manager."

"Ah, Miss Devereaux, lovely to see you again."

Ian smiles, kissing my hand.

"Likewise, Mr. Breckenridge," I reply, returning his smile.

"We met at the autism gala," I say to Reece, by way of an explanation to the question on his face.

"Parker Chase," Reece continues around the circle, "is an artist who causes quite a stir when his gallery events open."

"How are things in your world, Parker?" I ask as I give him a nod and smile with warm affection.

Parker bends ever so slightly at the waist in a slight bow.

"Very good, Miss Devereaux, and yourself?"

"Doing well," I say and turn toward the one female in the group. "Mrs. Richardson, I hope things are well with you."

I'm so glad to see Rebecca Richardson smiling again. The McKenzie Kingston firm stepped in to help during a very messy divorce in which the media attempted to crucify her based on the popularity of her husband. It took months of work to rebuild her reputation, but when it finally paid off, she found herself in a much more lucrative position.

"Much better, thank you." Her warm smile lights up the room.

I look up at Reece and give him a soft smile.

"Should I do the last two?" he jokingly says, but the look in his eye tells me we will discuss my background at some length.

For the next hour we work our way through the crowd. Reece is in his element, introducing me to prominent businessmen, lobbyists, high-ranking military personnel, and a couple of actors. It is an interesting mix, and one rarely seen during a fundraiser, but it seems to have worked out well for the congresswoman.

Reece leads me to a quiet corner. "You've been driving me mad all evening thinking about what is under this dress."

"Mr. Gabriel, it is you who dressed me in this outfit," I whisper with a conspiratorial lilt. With a smile, I take a sip of wine and give a nod to a group walking past.

"And I can't wait to get you out of it," he growls against my ear as his hand caresses my ass.

I wiggle my hips in reply and push back against his hand.

"Miss Devereaux, I am shocked at your behavior."

"Then maybe you should turn me over your knee for some corrective action, Mr. Gabriel."

He shifts behind me, pressing his erection into my hip.

"I believe it is time to get out of here. Enough work," he says, grinning. "Now it's time to play."

With a playful swat of my ass, he turns and heads to the front door.

CHAPTER THIRTY-SIX

Two days later, Adam hands me out of the Audi Q7. We are ladened with the latest haul from Reece's enjoyment of shopping like I am his favorite doll. In front of us, the doorman holds open the door, and we walk through in a riot of laughter from his latest 'threat.'

"Good evening, Paul," I say absently as we walk past the concierge desk.

From the corner of my eye, I see Paul hastily push to his feet to tell me something, but I shake my head, not wanting to deal with anything after such an amazing day.

"Miss Devereaux!" he calls out.

Reece stops in the middle of the lobby and turns toward Paul, looking past me.

"Go ahead, I'll just be a minute," I say to Reece, smiling, confident the interruption is a building notice or a message about something I've asked them to check.

Reece nods and heads to the elevator, and it slides open as I approach Paul.

"Good evening, Paul. What is so urgent?" I ask. My tone is light, but I frown at the obvious interruption.

"Ma'am, I'm sorry, but this came for you this afternoon. The person who dropped it off said it was important that you receive it as soon as possible."

He hands me a gold envelope, no bigger than a business card, my name embossed on the outside.

"And I was told to give you these," he says, reaching under the desk to produce a half dozen dark blue roses.

Nausea hits me in a relentless wave, and I fight the urge to heave on the concierge desk. My bags drop to the floor. The envelope trembles in my hand. For a long moment I stare at it in disbelief. I can hear Paul asking if I'm okay, but his voice sounds like it's coming from the bottom of a deep well.

I pull my finger across the ridge of the envelope and remove the small card inside.

I know where you live—
It is unfortunate you've chosen another over me.
He will pay for your decision.

FEAR PARALYZES ME. MY MIND CLAWS FOR CONTROL. I REFUSE to allow this person to rule my life. My head spins as my stomach convulses. Blinking away the tears from my eyes, I work to focus.

The fear is in your mind, control the fear and you control the moment, my self-defense trainer's words give me the hold I need, and a deep shudder runs through my body.

"Miss Devereaux. Miss Devereaux."

I hear Paul's voice punctuate the air around me. With a blank stare, I snap back to reality.

"Ma'am, are you okay?" His voice is full of concern.

I nod, afraid if I speak the torrent of overwhelming emotions will take over the light grip I have on them. Pasting on a smile, I give Paul a nod and straighten as I turn and walk to the elevator. This situation has to stop, but I'm at a loss on how to make it end. The elevator door slides open and I step in with haste, repeatedly slamming my finger on the button, willing it to get me home. I watch Paul pick up the bags I left neglected in front of his desk.

When the elevator opens on my floor, I shove my front door open and race inside.

"Ah, there you are," Reece's smiling voice says as I dart past him toward the bathroom.

The contents of my stomach give up their location, spilling into the toilet. Terror races through me as my body continues to react with the violence of unspent emotions. Water runs in the sink. A cold cloth presses against my forehead. Fingers work the straps of my shoes, then move to the zipper of my dress.

My body collapses, spent, on the floor. Without a word, Reece continues to work me out of my outfit, refreshing the cloth every few minutes. Once I'm down to my bra and panties, he pulls me into his lap. He whispers soothing words and cradles me until my body settles.

When I have control over my body once again, I wiggle off his lap and settle against the wall.

"Are you okay?" he asks, the rhetorical question filling the space.

"I'll be fine. Must have been something I ate, or possibly because I didn't eat enough. All the fun excitement of the day and such." I attempt to force a smile, but my head lags in mental and physical exhaustion.

"I'm sorry I pushed you so much. We should have eased you into a higher level of play," Reece replies, his eyes full of sorrow, in a tone of guilt.

A thousand memories assault me at once, and I let out a hard sigh. There's so much I'm holding back, but I don't know where to start. With Edmund's threats looming over me, it is safer to stay walled away.

"You have nothing to be sorry about," I say, taking a deep breath to push down the internal terror still circling my mind. "Truly. I'll be fine. I'm sorry our fun sexy time is getting cut short because I didn't take care of myself."

"Just means I must double down next time," he says, a ghost of a smile crossing his lips.

"Yes, please," I whisper.

"Let me get you showered, then I'm putting you to bed."

"Thank you, Reece, but I can get myself sorted."

He watches me closely. The war on his face between pushing for control and allowing me take care of myself is obvious.

"Okay. Let me make you some ginger tea to settle your stomach," he says. "I saw the Korean ginger and honey in a jar the last time I was in your refrigerator."

I think about protesting, but it's nice to have someone lift the world, and I nod.

"Thank you."

He helps me to my feet and kisses my forehead.

"James, shower on, one hundred one degrees," he calls out to the air as he turns and leaves the bathroom.

Thoughts of Edmund move through me. My stomach clenches and I work to keep myself steady. I ease the plug out and drop my bra and panties to the floor. Steam fills the room. I look at the bathtub with longing, but I know if I curl up in it, I'll fall asleep.

As I step into the shower, water sluices in large runs off my body. The day was so wonderful. Scenes replay across my mind. Reece's domination gave me a chance to relax and opened me in ways which pushed me to mentally balance my internal and external feelings. The game's edge was a soothing balm to so much of what I'd pushed down years ago.

"James, shower off," I call out, and the flow of water ceases.

Reece opens the shower door and wraps me in an oversized

towel. He works his hands across my body, drying off each limb with great care. Once he's satisfied, he lifts me into his arms and carries me to bed as he settles me against a mound of pillows.

"Drink this," he says, handing me a cup of hot ginger tea.

I take the offered cup and sip the hot liquid.

"What did the concierge desk want?"

"Standard notifications of some maintenance."

"Is that so? Must be a major level of maintenance to make you turn pale and walk away without your shopping bags."

With intense focus, I blow across the fiery liquid as I watch the ripples. Reece's hard gaze bores through me as he tries to understand what is going on. It's best this way. The less he knows, the better.

"Not really. I'm sure all of this fuss is just my body catching up with me."

"I see," Reece mumbles, and the edge of his tone makes my nerves stand on end. "We have to be honest with each other, Atlas. If you feel you have to hold a part of you back, this will never work."

"We all have our secrets, Reece."

"Yes. That's true, but in this kind of relationship, we can't."

"We haven't decided on what kind of relationship this is yet."

Reece runs his hand through his hair, sighing in exasperation.

"We'll discuss this later," he says with finality.

He tucks the comforter around me, picks up the cup from my hand, then sets it on the nightstand.

"Let's get you tucked into bed."

I slide down as the covers cocoon me and Reece slowly runs his hand through my hair.

CHAPTER THIRTY-SEVEN

The last few weeks have been quiet. After Edmund's last threat, I'd feared the worst, but even he seems to have backed off again. Maybe I'm being naïve in thinking everything will work out, and he will get over his infatuation, but for now I guess it is a matter of more time and distance for him to accept the rejection of his proposal.

I turn away from my desk, staring out over the vast paddocks of the estate. I miss Samantha, her straightforward way of handling all the various issues in our clients' lives and my own. Even how she allows me to talk through the problems, feelings or simple ideas. No matter what, she's always supportive and helpful.

"Ma'am." Katie knocks on my door.

I turn in my chair and meet a pair of haunted eyes.

"What's wrong?"

"You need to see this," she says, laying the paper across my desk, "and the email I sent you."

I look down at the newspaper, unfolding it across my desk. On the front page, the large headline proclaims, *Congressional Candidate Elizabeth Davies - Family with Dark Secrets.*

Elizabeth Davies has been a shock to many, including the establishment of the Republican Party, with her rise to become the front runner of her district. A mother of an autistic daughter and local community organizer, the former family lawyer's rocket to the top took Washington, D.C. by storm.

Today that spectacular rise to the top came to a halt when it was discovered that her brother and financial supporter, was caught with a Dominatrix at an exclusive sex club in Potomac, Maryland.

I stop reading as bile comes up into my throat. I swallow hard. Shock races through me at the blatant lies and half-truths in the article.

They took the picture on the day of our shopping trip, as Reece and I exited the car that evening for dinner at a local restaurant. I told him I'd borrowed it because a client owed me a favor, when in reality Kade's intuition had been pinged so high he'd demanded I take security along. Anyone who saw the plates could trace them back to the club's fleet. I presume they jumped to the conclusion the woman was Alexandra as the owner of the club from there.

While the large sunglasses hid my face in the image as I'm being handed into the car, Reece looks straight into the camera. I wrack my mind trying to remember any traces of paparazzi that day but come up empty.

"Thank you, Katie," I say, my dismissive tone clear of my intention.

"Let me know if you need anything, Ma'am," she says, the soft click of the door telling me I'm once again alone.

Minutes later my phone rings and I glance down to see Kade's name across the caller ID. Punching the screen harder than necessary, I answer, my tone clipped, "Speak."

"Did you see the front page of the Post?"

"Katie just laid it across my desk."

"Well, that would be the easy version. It is already viral on the Internet. I presume you already know."

"No." My voice shakes, wishing Samantha wasn't out on tour as McKenzie right now. She usually runs fast interference when we have an issue. Her cyber background comes in handy in the social media realms, along with her search bots, analytic programs, and white hat hacking.

"Has he called yet?"

"No."

"How could this have happened? Do you have any idea who would want to hurt either of you?"

I hear his tone. There's no doubt we've just stepped from caring friend into investigative security personnel.

A deep breath fills my lungs, and it still feels like I'm drowning. The illusion of a stable world is shifting like unexpected quicksand under my feet. Just when I'd finally found someone to open and trust, I failed to do the one job he'd placed into my hands. His sister's campaign is now in jeopardy, while a bastardized version of his personal life is splashed across every news rag in DC and the Internet is burning up with speculation on the impact to the campaign.

"Alexandra?"

Kade's voice seems distant in my ever-swirling thoughts.

"Yes, Kade?"

"What are you not telling me?"

"You know everything I do at this point. Katie just gave me a copy of the Post, and I'm as shocked as you are about the picture on the front."

He sighs heavily into the phone.

"I can't help if you don't tell me all the angles."

"Kade, my job in public relations is to get ahead of all issues, which is itself an oxymoron at the mach speed of today's media. All I can do is try to figure out how to contain the situation to the best of our ability."

"You have an amazing team surrounding you, but we can't back your play if we don't know the details. It's neither weak nor vulnerable to ask for help." Kade sighs into the phone. He knows something is up, but I refuse to let anyone else get hurt.

"Thanks for your concern, but this situation is getting out of hand too fast for me not to be the lead on it."

"When you decide to let us help, let me know. It's easier to take you out when you stand alone. I thought you'd already learned that one."

"I did too," I whisper.

Nothing in my mind is helping me keep it together.

"We're here if you need us."

"Thanks, Kade."

I place the receiver back into the cradle. The cell phone on my desk vibrates, and I swipe the accept button without looking down.

"Devereaux."

"What the fuck is going on, Atlas? I hired your firm to protect my sister from me, not make the fucking front page of the Post and the Times. Not to mention being a viral online joke with a supposed sex scandal instead of a serious congressional representative. How the hell did they make a jump from dating a PR rep to a Dominatrix?"

His voice is so loud I take the phone away from my ear and cringe. My lack of trust has brought me to this exact situation.

"Well? Atlas?" he demands.

"Reece, I can explain everything."

"Then you'd damn well better start. My patience is thin on this one."

"Why don't you come by the office?"

"Are you serious? I have reporters crawling up my ass and your office is on the property of a known sex club. How the hell do you think that will look on the front page of tomorrow's paper?"

"I'll send a car over. My security team will take care of the rest. Can you be ready to bug out in thirty minutes?"

"Wait. Your security team? Your driver? What are you talking about?"

"I don't deserve your trust, Reece, but in this situation I need you to do what I ask. Please. I can have you away from the paparazzi in under an hour."

"My sister's campaign manager is going nuts over this. He's already called and screamed at me twice."

"Let me see what I can do about Ian. Right now, you are my priority as a client. Your sister has her own PR management. We'll be glad to work with them, but I can only solve one issue at a time."

"There better be a damn good explanation for all of this," he screams into the phone.

"Yes."

My noncommittal answer doesn't garner any encouragement.

"Since you know Thomas Kinkaid, he'll be in touch shortly to let you know how they will handle the extraction. Just let him know where you are, and he'll take it from there. I'll see you soon."

Reece hangs up without another word. Every part of me wants to scream. This screw-up could professionally ruin the firm, and when Reece realizes that I've kept something this large from him, I'm sure it will end our relationship too. I shake the devastating thoughts from my head.

My desk phone rings.

"Yes?"

"Alexandra." Katie's calm voice comes across the receiver. "Miss Kingston is on line one."

"Thanks, Katie."

I hesitate for a second before pressing the blinking line.

"Good morning, Samantha, how's the book tour?" I try for professional calm.

"Atlas, I don't know what the hell is going on down there in DC, but the entire interwebs are alight with their version of a sex scandal and you are all over front pages, social media, Twitter, blogs—you get the idea. What the hell is going on?"

"Well, since I found out this information less than twenty minutes ago, I'm not sure."

"Let's start at the top then. Why does the press think Atlas Devereaux is a professional dominant?"

"I don't know," I lie. "But my name isn't coming up with it in the stories."

"Okay. Why are you a target?"

"Looks like Reece's sister is the target."

"Stop it. You've been doing this long enough to know that's a bull-shit answer, and you wouldn't accept it from a client. Don't even try it with me. Now why are *you* a target?"

"I don't know. Everything is pointing to Reece and Elizabeth as the targets. Right now my job is to figure out how to spin this, which is near impossible in this frenzy, or get them contained so the media and social media will turn the press in on itself."

"Yes, I agree with that strategy, but I'm talking about root cause analysis. Not spin. Not containment. Cause. We don't know if he should apologize, lie low or disappear for a while without knowing the cause. Is he good in front of a camera? This can't be fixed if we don't know why it is happening."

"We've never used disappearing target strategy before. How does that work?" I ask, thinking it might be helpful if the situation continues to escalate.

"The target is removed from public access. Everything goes dark. All social media accounts, public appearances, and finances if they can raise enough cash fast. Then they go into hiding until the whole situation cools down, several news cycles rotate, and they can come home," Samantha answers my question like it might be a possible solution. "With Elizabeth in the middle of a campaign, I don't think it would work unless we said Reece is in rehab, which opens other issues. Now, why is this happening to them?"

"It's happening because someone doesn't want Elizabeth to be in Congress."

"Bullshit. Elizabeth and Reece are collateral damage and you know it! How can I battle this if I don't know what I'm battling? How the hell can I clean up a mess if I don't know how big it is? We are janitors in the media world, Atlas, and you can't tell me if I'm dealing with a soda spill or a nuclear meltdown?"

"Samantha, you're supposed to be touring as McKenzie right now. Thomas has his security force covering the client. This will be fine in a couple news cycles."

"You are evading every question I ask," she huffs into the phone. "Glad to hear *Thomas* is on it, which would explain why he called me with a ticket home, but you're hiding something, Devereaux. I don't know what, but I aim to find out. I am wheels down in an hour. Between now and then, I'll work on cleaning up this mess, but when I get there, we will sit down and have a serious talk."

"Good God, why does everyone think this is about me?"

"Because we know you, and something is hinky."

"Can you get in touch with Ian Breckenridge? You seem to have a beneficial relationship with him, and he's freaking out about the campaign. I believe you two are on good terms."

"On it," Samantha acknowledges.

"Safe travels, Samantha."

My breath comes in heavy pants, and I work to get myself under control, but I feel it all slipping away fast. For the past couple of months I've tried to keep Edmund at bay, believing that time and a lack of attention would end his infatuation, but each time his threats have escalated. Never did I think he'd go to such lengths. His civilized demeanor during our session made me believe he would chase me until he knew I would not change my mind, but never did I think he would try to actually destroy me. While his threats felt real, I knew he struggled to connect and ultimately took them as poor judgment in his often awkward social interactions. Now, the hope I've held on to for dear life vaporizes as I face the reality of my situations.

With shaking hands, I pick up the phone and call Katie.

"Yes, Ma'am?"

"I need you to coordinate our security team on behalf of McKenzie Kingston. They have a client in trouble and in need of an evacuation in the middle of a press mob. Tell Kade the name of the client is Reece Gabriel. He should have all the information he needs, but Melody can give him anything missing from the dossier. I need them at the client's house in twenty minutes."

"Yes, Ma'am. Anything else?"

"No, this is your highest priority."

"Yes, Ma'am," Katie replies, then ends the call without further questions.

I sit staring at nothing for the next few minutes, my entire body shaking. The next hour is critical both to understand how big this will explode. First step is getting Reece safe and away from the press. None of these things are out of the normal realm of my job. It is what happens once he's on property. Will he accept the truth or walk away? The fact the papers are all reporting facts, even if they are only half-truths in relation to the situation in the article, and that he is the one in the dark, is an entire issue I don't even want to comprehend.

The cell phone on my desk vibrates, and I glance down, expecting to see a text from Samantha. Instead, it shows No Caller ID. I push the screen to view the message.

If I can't have you — no one can. I warned you.

An icy shiver slithers down my spine as I stare at the message. The full realization that I'm not playing the right game pushes me to the edge of a mental abyss.

CHAPTER THIRTY-EIGHT

From the time the news landed on my desk, I've worked every angle in the media, from contacting media outlets to sending them on wild goose chases to spinning the use of Alexandra's car. Each time I contact social media conglomerates to post opposing news in an effort to move the fiasco vortex in another direction.

My entire focus is to keep it all to a simple farce rather than a crisis, but the sheer volume, velocity and venom of the social media makes each recent move, thought or idea look like we are moving backward rather than forward. In the end, I realize that without Samantha's network and white hat hacking skills, it will be a long seventy-two-hour news cycle at best, and the destruction of Elizabeth's campaign at worst.

A knock on the door startles me from the focused thoughts. My head jerks up as my eyes meet the hard, impassive gaze of Reece Gabriel.

I rise from my chair. His soft gray eyes are like shards of black glass as anger comes off of him in waves. To add fuel to the fire, Kade steps into the office behind him, looking just as angry. A tremor runs down my body as I grasp the edge of my desk.

"Where the hell is Atlas Devereaux?" he roars.

"Please don't be angry with me," I whisper, dropping Alexandra's accent and letting her confident body posture slouch forward.

Reece runs his hand through his unruly hair. He looks frustrated, angry, and confused.

"Explain," he commands.

"Please have a seat, Mr. Gabriel," I say firmly to exude confidence I do not possess.

"Just tell me what the hell is going on, Alexandra, or whoever the hell you are!"

Kade lays a hand on his shoulder.

"Try to calm down, Reece. I know it's been a trying day, but it would be best if you have a seat as she requested."

He nods, cautiously folding his frame into the leather chair.

I take a deep breath and pull the wig from my head, revealing the blond hair Reece is used to seeing on Atlas. Next I grab a makeup towelette from my drawer and remove the heavy makeup from my face.

Reece's eyes never leave me. He sits stock still, watching each action with riveted attention. When I'm done, I toss the towelette in the trash, lower myself into my office chair and look over Alexandra's desk as Atlas.

"Alexandra and Atlas are the same person," I mumble, internally demanding my voice to remain even. I close my eyes and take a deep breath when it quivers. "I believe the reason for the connection is that the car we used during the shopping trip is registered to a larger company under Alexandra's ID. While I don't know where the breach happened, our security team is working to find the leak."

I nod my head toward Kade.

"What you may or may not have concluded," I continue carefully, "is that Alexandra runs the club and is also a professional Dominant with a limited clientele."

"Why the fuck didn't you tell me?" he growls.

I squirm uncomfortably. The greatest relationship in my life is about to end. It has all come down to a self-fulfilling prophecy: if they don't leave on their own then I will give them a reason. I try to meet his gaze, but my eyes fall to the blotter on my desk.

"Tell me," he commands.

When I remain silent, he continues, "There are throngs of reporters staking out my home, my sister's home, her campaign head-quarters, and any other place they think they may get a glimpse of us in this humiliating state and you're telling me it's true?"

I nod, not trusting my voice. He closes his eyes and takes a deep breath. When he opens them, his anger seems to multiply.

"You are a professional Dominant," he spits. "A fucking whore? You know trust is paramount. We had to be open and honest with each other for any of this to work. They aren't just words, or do you ignore the needs of your limited private clientele the same way?"

I close my eyes, rubbing my forehead, my long fingernails scraping lightly across the skin when his words and accusations suddenly hit home. It is the exact thing I need to pull me out of the mentally submissive shift.

"Mr. Gabriel." The formal tone returns to my voice. "I understand that you're personally angry at me for not informing you completely of my proclivities and work habits. There are reasons for my deci-sions, which are private. All I can do is apologize for the situation and work to correct it. It was never my intention to involve you in this part of my life. Quite the opposite, in fact. However, if you think I do not take every one of my PR, club, or private clients seriously, you've got another think coming."

"Miss Devereaux, if that is even your actual name, someone needs to take you down several pegs. The punishments that come to mind would keep you sore for days and not a funishment." He punctuates each word with a slow rise from his chair until our faces are inches away from one another.

"Well, Mr. Gabriel, you are obviously not the man to do it."

I swallow to steady my breath, never breaking eye contact.

"Obviously." His voice is ominous and soft, as if he's resigned to an inalienable truth.

My heart sinks, but I refuse to let the emotions play across my face. I had finally opened up to an amazing man and in one day I destroy him because I can't protect him, while I underestimated someone I thought was a friend.

He turns stiffly and shoves past Kade. Reece walks out of my office without looking back. The door slams behind him. For a long minute I stare across my office.

Scalding tears spill down my cheeks and I shove them away with the back of my hand. How could I have been so idiotic?

"Atlas." Kade's voice breaks through my internal turmoil. I have no idea how long he's been calling my name. "Atlas, calm down. Think about the situation. Understand it, but don't overanalyze it. You need a plan to move many pieces forward at once. Make him work as much as you are to get through the relationship piece of it. He will either give you the necessary feedback or deal with his choice to walk away."

"You sound like Dominick," I throw back at him.

"Good, at least you listened to him," he throws back at me. "Dominick may have created you, molded you, given you an unusual path, but he meant for you to grow past him. We all have our fuck-ups, quirks, and idiosyncrasies. When Reece forgives you, you'll realize how much better things can be with emotions. That was Dominick's mistake with you. He taught you that you must sacrifice yourself completely. At every turn you were told you weren't allowed to express emotions because of your path."

"Reece is so perfect. A balance between romantic and dominant, the push-pull that everyone dreams of having in this type of relation-ship. And I've fucked the entire thing up." I shake my head.

"Stop it. You know none of that's true. The more perfect they look on the surface, the more skeletons they have in their closet—and his closet isn't empty either."

"I'm sure I've fucked this one up beyond repair."

My body falls into the desk chair, the force propelling me backwards.

"He needs time to cool off. You two are good for each other. You challenge each other and push each other to be better than you were before. Think about it, he found out his perfectly imperfect submissive is a professional Dominant. That's got to be a confidence shaker, not to mention his life is blowing apart in a publicly spectacular way."

"Speaking of which, Samantha should be landing about now," I start.

"I've already got a team at the airport to pick her up," Kade finishes.

I nod at his efficiency. "You're an amazing submissive, Kade."

"Don't, Atlas. Just don't. We both know what it took for us to get here."

All I want to do is curl up and cry, but there is an entire world out there that wants to politically hang Reece's sister for him being near me.

"I'll let you get to work. Reach out if you need me."

"Okay," I say, my voice just above a whisper.

"That wasn't a request, Atlas." His firm voice soothes my nerves.

"Thanks for being a friend, even when you think I'm being a stupid ass."

"Just returning the favor." Kade smiles then turns to walk out the door.

CHAPTER THIRTY-NINE

I'm sitting at my desk when the front door of Kingston pings.

"She said what?" Samantha shouts into the phone, slamming the front door behind her. "Ian, if you don't calm down there's no way in hell we'll be able to work together on this one... I don't give a damn what you think or what your media relationship guys say. Containment and a lack of exposure is the best way to keep this a fiasco and not a crisis. You're still over five months out from the polls, and if you play this right, no one in America will even remember this incident...." There is a long pause in her conversation, but it is obvious the person on the other end of the phone is livid. "If you want to be an ass, that's fine, you'll be to blame for her going from the top to going down in flames." Samantha's voice gets tenser the longer she's on the phone, and I cringe.

"Listen, Mr. Breckenridge," she hisses. "When you get your head out of your ass, feel free to call me, but if you go out there in this firestorm with an apology, you will fry your own candidate. You've got as many skeletons in your closet.... Who's threatening, sunshine? I'm making a promise," she snaps, sliding her finger across the screen of her phone.

"You know, if people would bring their team in on situations, so they can understand the true nature and cause, then it would be so much easier to clean up shit before it gets out of hand," Samantha says as if the room were empty.

On cue, Kade walks through the door, and I roll my eyes.

"I know exactly what you mean, Samantha. Some people know more than they are saying, but their tight-lipped attitude has us spinning in circles. We're trying to keep the property secure, but we don't know what we're up against or why. You'd think, based on past lessons learned, we'd be wiser, but nnnoooo."

"Yes, Kade, I know exactly what you mean. Here I am after flying back from the most amazing tour. And let me tell you that guitar player, oh, ho, ho, was his ass luscious, and good in bed." She kisses her fingers like she's complimenting the best chef in the world. "That man is fine."

"So it would seem," Kade says casually, shaking his head at her obvious loss. "Need a cold shower to get back to business, Sam?"

Samantha laughs.

"No, what I need is for someone to tell me what in the hell is going on and why I am here and not on tour. I thought I'd left everything in the extremely controlled and capable hands of one Miss Atlas Devereaux. Then I'm summoned back home because the sky is falling on one of our clients."

"At this rate, you can consider me a former client, Miss Kingston," Reece says as he walks through the door. "If this is how your firm handles this type of case, I'm positive I don't need your help. I could have caused this scandal all by myself."

A scowl mars his face, and every muscle in his body ripples with tension. If I were a punching bag, I know exactly what my current fate would be. We've spent so much time together over the last few months, I can see the sadness in his eyes before he blinks and the rage returns. My thoughts are a jumble of mixed messages bouncing around inside of my head. In the middle of this brilliant crowd, I am isolated and alone.

I sit stock–still as the drama plays out in front of me. I hate that this entire situation has me in the spotlight, and that my entire world is so angry they are having a full discussion about me as if I'm not even in the same room. Everyone is challenging every decision and every move, as they try to figure out exactly what is going on. How do I even explain that I am taking a beating to keep them all safe?

The thought is distracting and irrelevant. All that matters is the crisis we all trying to avert. Once this situation is handled, I must figure out how to remove other variables from the equation of their lives.

"Mr. Gabriel, from a professional point of view, I can assure you that we are doing everything in our power to contain this story," Samantha confirms.

"Contain it? How the hell did you let it happen? I will presume you both knew of the split personality of Atlas/Alexandra or whoever the hell she is," he seethes.

"Reece, Atlas has reasons for her dichotomy." Kade's tone is full of warning.

"So you knew, you son of a bitch, and you never told me? You never let on that there might be more than meets the eye?"

"It wasn't my secret to tell, like your secrets aren't mine to broadcast to others. Now, if you'll calm down and let them handle it—"

"*Secrets!*" he explodes. "This isn't a secret. She gets paid to be kinky with people! How the hell do you not tell your best friend he's dating a professional sex worker?" Reece snarls.

I shiver in fear. This is an atrocious combination. Reece is irrational and angry whilst Kade is protective and will steamroll anyone who threatens me.

The muscles in Kade's body ripple, his stance changing from relaxed and calm to angry and defensive. His face darkens, and his mouth presses into a thin, hard line as he clenches his jaw. It's been years since I've seen him act this way, barely holding on to his self-control.

If I don't take charge of the situation, all I am trying to protect will be for naught. I can't let Kade's friendship with Reece become another casualty of Edmund's attack. Nor will I sit here powerless, letting the drama play out in front of me as it rolls over me like a small doll tossed on the waves of a storm.

I shoot up with such force that the chair slams into the wall.

"If you all are done talking about me in the third person, maybe we can make headway," I roar. "Gentlemen, turn down your testosterone or I'll turn it down for you."

My body is rigid as I glare at both men.

Kade intelligently backs down, staying ready in case things get out of hand. Reece returns my glare.

"Mr. Gabriel, either you find a civil tone or security will find it for you."

My words are crisp and measured, and I turn to Samantha.

"As for you, if you'd given me more time to work around your goddamn book tour and the needs of your libido, we would have had the staff while you were gone," I huff.

Samantha's mouth opens to defend herself before she clamps it shut. "I didn't think. I'm sorry, but right now we have a client issue," she finally says.

I ignore her and storm over to face Reece.

"Don't think that because you labeled me as a sex worker that I am less than you. If you want to get self-righteous, go right ahead, but it will only prove that you are a close-minded, insignificant man, which until this moment was not my experience. You have no right to judge me for some conclusion you've jumped to based on a societal stereotype, and unless you can tell me you've slept with less than five women or men, you have *zero* things to say about my work."

He stares at me, but I refuse to let him speak.

"Yes, I am a professional Dominant and I'm damn good at my job, but I am not somehow less of an intelligent person because of it. I'm a very successful businesswoman who can run rings around your ass in the board room any day, so don't you think for a second that because you saw me on my knees in an intimate situation, you ever had power or control over me."

Out of the corner of my eye, I see Kade's astonished face. Across the room Samantha inhales an audible gasp.

"Now if you are all quite done blaming me without engaging me, then maybe we can, in fact, find a strategy to solve this situation, incident or whatever the hell we want to call it before it really gets out of hand."

My labored breath echoes in the forced silence. My heart slams in erratic beats. I work to calm the disarray of thoughts and emotions running through me as I glance up at Reece.

Everything between us was so wonderful. The perfect balance of romance, dynamic and play, but now it is just shards of tortuous memories. The seconds stretch out like an eternity as I realize all is lost. I can see it in his eyes. He hates me, I know it. Everything about me is repulsive. The hideous feelings are overwhelming, but I force them down. Spinning on my heels, I storm back toward my desk. I refuse to fold or look weak, but I'm crushed. Right now I want to run away and tell the world to go pound sand, but too many people depend on the decisions I make in the next twenty-four hours.

Taking a deep breath, I put on my professional façade. Authority isn't requested, it's earned, and I refuse to apologize for using it. I can get through this debacle, and I can get my team through it, I tell myself.

Mustering as much calm as I can project, I walk to the conference room at the back of the office and take a seat at the head of the table.

"Now, Miss Kingston, what did Mrs. Davies' campaign manager have to say?" I say with a confident calmness and turn my head to watch three sets of eyes stare at me in stunned silence.

Samantha walks across the room to join me through the deafening silence.

"Ian is obviously livid. He's all threat, no bite, and I think he'll come around once he calms down from being blindsided." Samantha pulls herself together and slides into her professional mode.

"Good. You conveyed that we were blindsided by this situation too, I hope," I say to acknowledge her concerns.

"Well, I did to a degree. I wanted to wait and address it with you before I put on a full court press to our innocent involvement. Ian has been to the club and to these offices, so his concern of cross-contamination is valid."

"It's been valid and irrelevant since the day we opened. What's the next area to address?"

"How can you say it's irrelevant?" Reece's fist hits the table, and I work to contain my startled reaction.

"It is irrelevant because our PR firm deals with non-traditional clients who don't care about the club next door, are in the industry, are in entertainment, or take part in non-traditional lifestyles. The same reason you came to us with your particular proclivities and activities, Mr. Gabriel." I glare at him. "If you cannot control your personal outburst, then I will have you removed from this meeting. Do we have an understanding?"

Reece runs his hand through his hair, pacing beside the table. His normal control slips another notch, and I watch him under hooded eyes. My breath is shallow while I wait for his next move.

His body tenses, and he looks like he wants to argue, but decides against it.

"As you wish," he sighs, pulling out a chair. "Please proceed, Miss Devereaux. Your point is well taken."

The words are civil, but his tone is no less irate.

Nervously, I tuck my loosened hair behind my ear, hoping to hide my shaking hands, and let out a deep breath, glad a confrontation has been avoided for now.

"Thank you, Mr. Gabriel. Kade, can you give me a rundown of the security concerns you mentioned earlier?"

I look at Kade, who's still standing across the room, surveying the scene unfolding before him.

The front door pings and all heads turn toward Melody as she rounds the front of the reception desk and halts, her face going pale.

"Melody, could you please set the conference table with drinks and such? We'll be here for a while. There's been a slight hiccup with Mr. Gabriel's sister." I force a smile and nod, turning my head toward Kade. "Mr. Kinkaid, I believe you were enlightening us about your concerns."

The words kick-start his brain, and he's in motion toward the table.

"Yes, Ma'am. We've had several breaches over the last two months. There are no patterns or correlations with events at either McKenzie Kingston or Empyrean, but both locations have experienced heightened paparazzi activity and other security concerns." He pauses, clearly thinking about his next comment. "The only common thread seems to be the fact you work in both locations under separate personas. It is possible that there's been a leak, you've made a mistake that is being exploited, or you are under threat, as I have mentioned in my reports previously. The last one is of particular concern based on the recent hack of James in your penthouse."

Before his report is complete, all eyes are back on me.

Melody works in the background while Kade gives his report. Without intrusion, she moves through the room, placing glasses of water in front of each participant and setting a small snack tray in the center of the table before withdrawing.

"I have addressed the penthouse hack. Miss Kingston's propensity for practical jokes has been noted and that event can be taken off the board as a root cause. The idea that I am under threat for any reason is similarly dismissed. The threats I receive in my line of work are generally of the stalking variety. An overzealous client or a reporter who wants to exploit the perceived taboo of Alexandra's line of work. There was a client incident, as Mr. Kinkaid can attest, but there's been only a couple of points of contact since. Thus, we can also take that possibility off the board," I lie, picking up my glass from the table.

Instinctively licking my lips, I glance down and take a quick sip of water before returning to the expectant faces around the table. Inside I cringe, hoping Kade has missed the micro expression which skimmed across my face. He's the only person who's better at reading people's body language than I am, and right now I'm praying he missed it. Kade has suspected Edmund since the night of the proposal, but what Kade doesn't seem to appreciate is the power and influence he wields.

On the other hand, I can't believe how stupid I was to miss all the signs that Edmund's threats were so real. Everything in me always believed they were a simple plea for attention after I'd turned down his proposal. The lies and denials simply piled up over time until they led me here.

"So it looks like we need to concentrate on either Mr. Gabriel or his sister as the target." I turn to face Reece. "The hardest but best action would be to let the story and speculation run. It will be a very bumpy couple of weeks and while I am not a campaign analyst, I think they should be far enough away from elections to make the necessary course corrections. Unless there is something else in your background we are missing?"

"No, Miss Devereaux, I'm quite the open book." His firm voice reverberates in the room, but his eyebrows raise and pull together as his eyes tense while his lips pull back in the slightest expression of fear.

It is so fast I'm sure I've misread him. I shake the thought from my head. For goodness' sake, I misread Edmund so completely I can't trust my abilities anymore.

"Very good, Mr. Gabriel," I say and press my lips into a tight smile.

CHAPTER FORTY

"I will contact Ian again in a few hours and see if he's calmed down. Ultimately, this is sensationalized yellow journalism, but the social media side can be as damaging with misconceptions as it can with the truth. I've already started multiple search bots and keyword listening programs. We'll see what insight that analysis will provide in about four hours. Is there anything else you want me to do?" Samantha looks up from her tablet.

"No. Keep monitoring things online. If we need to sway social media outlets, then prepare the offshore campaign teams."

"Got it," she says, standing up and making her way back to her desk.

"Kade." I look him in the eye. "Please take care of the club members. Bring in extra staff because I know there we will be mobbed with questions and while no-comment sounds great on the TV, it will not work here."

"Yes, Ma'am. Anything else?"

I know he wants me to tell him what's going on. The expectant look in his eyes has been there for days, except now he looks like he wants to beat it out of me.

"Be reachable and clear those cameras off my front gate. The membership should not have to worry about their own privacy from those piranhas. There's already enough of my blood in the water for them to feast for days if they get the right angle."

"Yes, Ma'am, my apologies for not focusing on it earlier."

"It's been a trying day. Thank you for dropping everything and helping with this situation."

My tight-lipped smile conveys the gravity of the situation. I grab Kade's arm as he walks past, and he pauses.

"Please stop worrying about me," I mumble.

"No, Ma'am. That is not an order I'll follow. It would be insincere to say otherwise." His eyes search my face. "I pledged my loyalty in another life for a lifetime. It held there, and it holds here."

I close my eyes and take a deep breath. Everything in me tries to recover my equilibrium, but to no avail.

"For all we've been through, Atlas, I can't believe you are hiding something from me. Please let us help you," he whispers in my ear.

He straightens his tall frame when I open my eyes. I let my gaze move across the T-shirt pulls taut over his shoulders, straining across his tan biceps. Finally, I reach his face and find a dark look staring back at me.

I lightly squeeze his arm.

"It'll be okay."

He takes one last look at me and nods. With an abrupt turn, he walks toward the front door.

When I look back toward Reece, who hasn't moved from his seat at the conference table, he's watching me. His evaluative gaze draws across his mouth in a hard, impassive line. The look on his face is cold and distant with a hint of confusion.

"You two seem close," he says in a clipped tone.

"Yes," I acknowledge.

"A client of yours?"

"Kade has never been a client."

"Not that you'd tell me." Reece's tone rings with accusation.

"Mr. Gabriel, I am sought after for my extreme level of discretion, among many other talents."

"I'm sure," he sneers.

"Nothing has to change between us. I'm still the same person, Reece. The only difference is that you are now privy to more truth than you care to know," I say with a hard exhale, then press my lips together.

He places his head in his hands, digesting my words. Finally, he glances up. His expression softens. Then his body slumps forward.

Everything in me constricts. I want to reach out and comfort him, to tell him it will be okay, but I can't convey something I don't believe. How can I tell him I'm scared and failing to protect everyone important from a threat which increases the closer they come? I want to show him what he's added to my life, the changes in me since he waltzed into it and made me feel again. I need him to trust me, yet there's nothing but caution in his eyes.

He rises from the chair, his eyes full of sadness as he stands in front of me staring with a hard intent.

"Do you know what you meant to me?" he murmurs. The pain in his voice is palpable as it flashes across his face. "You are quite the consummate actress, Miss Devereaux. You had me believing you felt..."

"Reece —" I start.

"Don't. Just don't. I've had enough of your cloak and dagger games. You've had a good laugh at my expense. Playing me for the fool."

"It's not like that, Reece."

I stare at him in disbelief. This can't be happening. Everything was perfect and so amazing. Life is finally in full-blown color. Never before have I felt so alive, so connected and open. I want to scream he's got it all wrong. He's everything I ever wanted, but being in my world makes him vulnerable to Edmund's attack. Today's fiasco proves that reality.

"Please tell me I'm wrong," he begs.

You are so wrong — so very wrong — I want to scream. *Please forgive me, Reece. The only way I can protect you is to push you away.* My mind screams to tell him not to go, and I work to force down the roller coaster of emotions. I am devastated by the pain in his eyes. Unfortunately, I can't articulate any of those things.

He closes his eyes and shakes his head once more in disbelief.

"Just as I thought, Miss Devereaux. Your silence speaks volumes. I'd say it's been a pleasure, but I'm unsure that is true."

"You're right. You should go. It's best for all involved," I whisper.

He turns, and out of the corner of my eye I watch him storm back across the room, stopping at Samantha's desk.

"Miss Kingston, inform me of any further developments. I'll be at the Empyrean bar."

Samantha nods, tapping the mute button on her phone. "Of course, Mr. Gabriel."

We both watch Reece walk out the front door.

Samantha's head turns toward me. She stares at me with a look of complete consternation and mouths, *"What the hell was that?"*

I frown and shake my head as I avoid her eyes. Emotions boil, but I refuse to succumb to them.

Today my life ends. I watched it walk out the door with Reece as I sat here doing nothing to stop it.

Suddenly anxious to gain some distance from everyone and unwilling to endure Samantha's interrogation, I walk to my desk, pull my things together, and make my way to the bookcase in the back of the room. The *Art of War* stares accusingly from the shelf as I realize my best strategy and next move. I curl my fingers around the top of the binding, pulling the book toward me. The hidden door slides open.

I sigh, resigned to the fact that after the next step, nothing will ever be the same. Dealing with what is happening to my world because of Edmund has been difficult enough. The thought of him winning terrifies me, and I realize that staying means I will be constantly looking over my shoulder and worrying about the lives of my friends.

***

EVERYTHING IN ME SCREAMS. ALL I'VE WORKED TO ACCOMPLISH is unraveling in slow, insane actions, and I am helpless to stop it.

I sigh and stare out of the window across the upper paddocks of the property. A tear slides down my cheek. I've come so close to having it all, but my ego and pride refused to let me take the leap.

I am a failure. I'm done. I'm alone. All because I held myself separate from my emotions. It is an ironic twist of fate.

There's only one way out of this one. If I can't make the PR firm's target disappear, then I'll disappear. I'll make everything go dark. I'll cut off my tracking and social media and grab enough cash to get me through the next several weeks. By then, maybe Edmund will grow tired of it all.

With solid resolve, I take the phone off my hip. It is my locator to tell my security where to find me. Everything in my world is in it. From it, I control my entire life, and without it I do not exist.

I stare down at it for a long time. I am neither safe in the safety net of my security detail, and I remain vulnerable to the hacks overtaking my automated life.

Everything was so close to perfect.

For the second time in my life I prepare to walk away from everything I love and leave what has become my home.

Tears stream in rivulets down my face, and I savagely wipe them away.

Never be vulnerable, never be weak. The voices of the most influential men in my life runs through my head. I've failed even them. In this moment I am both vulnerable and too weak to do anything about my situation.

With a deep sigh, I place the phone in the middle of my desk and look forlorn around my office. I click off the video camera and take care of my last preparations, then walk out of the door. The soft click of the latch bursts like an explosion in the surrounding silence as I walk away from the world I built.

PLEA FROM THE AUTHOR

I am so glad you've reached the end of the book and hope you enjoyed it. Thank you for giving me your valuable entertainment time. It is readers like you who make writing such an amazing experience.

If you enjoyed the book, I hope you will leave a review.

Be the First to Know

Want more content, news, blogs or early releases?

www.SapphariaMayer.com

Feel free to reach out to me on any of my social media. I love hearing from my readers.

patreon.com/sapphariamayer

bookbub.com/authors/sappharia-mayer

pinterest.com/sapphariamayer

amazon.com/author/sapphariamayer

instagram.com/sapphariamayer

MASTER ME - CHAPTER 1
EMPYREAN CLUB- THE ATLAS COLLECTION BOOK 2

"God, they are hot when they play." Samantha leaned over and nodded her head to a couple playing on the St. Andrew's Cross on the other side of the pool. "I wonder if the hot one swinging the flogger will play with me afterwards?"

"Really?" Sarcasm dripped off her reply as Jillian followed Samantha's gaze. "That's your boyfriend and one of his other partners."

She grinned. "Yeah. Aren't they hot? I'm hoping I can seduce them both in bed."

Jillian shook her head. There was no such thing as too much information between them, but Samantha's extreme love life always made her feel naïve. She guessed it came from the ability to explore everything that piqued her interest.

"Why are people such animals?" Samantha moaned and stood. "Alexandra will be pissed if she comes back to a club that needs repairs. I need to find Kade and see if he can those guys under control. Wish me luck!"

She started toward the pool deck and glanced back with a forced smile. "And stop looking like you're miserable."

Jillian shook her head. For the past two hours, she'd perched on a bar stool watching everyone have a delightful time while she wondered why she hadn't stayed home. With a discouraged sigh, she scanned the club's bar and lounge. The refinement environment sat a juxtaposition with the small groups of people in various levels of undress gathered around the room. In front of the bar, large garage-style glass doors rolled up to make the space flow from inside to the outside. Everything about it was in total opposition to the standard concepts of a BDSM club, but then again, it was one reason Samantha had invited her as a guest. She'd used the excuse of painful elegance as enticement.

On a lounge chair, a muscular brunette caught her attention as his firm hands moved across the body of a woman. He straddled her as he massaged her shoulders. A leather cord with a sterling silver bead hung around his neck in a subtle nod to his position or owner-ship by Mistress or Master. On the bootblack stand, a man in a white tank top and Levi jeans sat while the boi in front of him made his boots shine in the setting sun. In the pool, couples and groups laughed and made out, unfazed by their au natural appearances.

While certain things would signal the obvious, it was often hard to tell who among the groups were dominants. She'd learned long ago that appearances and positions could be deceiving. Just because someone looked like they were the take charge in the bedroom type, it didn't mean it was true. All around her was evidence of someone, no matter how unlikely, falling to their knees for the right person.

Jillian took a long sip of wine. The trouble was finding the right person. To the world, Jillian was a take no prisoners with her shit together type of girl who could take care of herself. On the inside, she knew the right combination would make her melt, but the likelihood of finding him seemed slim in the sea of players.

She set the empty glass down and nodded to the bartender. Her stomach growled in protest against the corset which hugged her body into a tight hourglass figure. A few minutes later, he returned with a full glass of wine and a bowl of bar snacks. He set them down in front of her and smiled.

"I bet you haven't eaten all day," he said.

"How'd you guess?"

"With a corset that tight, you can barely breathe, let alone eat." He shoved the bowl of bar snacks closer to her. "At least eat this. I won't have you passing out on the barstool and leaving me to explain to Security how I fell down on my job. Especially if I let a gorgeously corseted lady land ungraciously on her rump. Besides, I don't want such a report hitting Alexandra's desk. She'd have my hide for it." His Texas drawl was unmistakable and it made her smile at his concern.

From the way Samantha talked, Alexandra was a force to be reckoned with. The club's owner and house dominant was usually at events, but her sudden disappearance had caused quite a stir. The staff did a fabulous job keeping it hushed, explaining she'd taken an extended vacation, but from Samantha's worried expressions and the private conversations carried on in hushed tones, no one had any clue where she'd gone.

On the other side of the room, she spotted Samantha bent toward a guy in a basic T-shirt and jeans, gesturing in her general direction. She'd never been able to convince Samantha she wasn't into the fun and fancy-free ways. It was fun to watch her friend take in the world with such a free spirit, but she could never let herself give up such control.

At the conclusion of their conversation, Jillian watched the man approach. From afar, his wild goatee appeared wicked and sexy. She reached for her wine, straightened her shoulders, and tried to appear calm, cool and confident, even as butterflies assaulted her stomach.

"You must be Jillian." Her name slid off his tongue in a low rumble.

"Um. Yeah," she stuttered.

Up close, he was far less appealing. He was young in the casual way of someone who came into money but didn't care about standard conventions.

"Samantha said I should introduce myself and I am so glad she did too." He leered, appraising her from top to bottom. She wasn't the front of the magazine beautiful, but she expected others to care more about their appearance than the man in front of her. If she put in the effort, so should they.

"And you are?" Her words came out with more distaste than she intended.

"Evan."

"Nice to meet you, Evan." Jillian shifted on her barstool as he moved to take the one next to her.

The potent scent of his cologne almost choked the air from her lungs. Why did guys always think they needed to pour it on to 'smell sexy'?

He looked over to the bartender who nodded and set a glass of bourbon on the bar in front of him.

"What brings you here this evening?"

"Samantha. She dragged me here demanding that I 'make play happen.'"

Jillian forced a smile.

"Well that sounds like a fun proposal. What do you say we find out what that means?"

Her face flushed. When he put it that way, she felt cheap and incapable of finding what she wanted without Samantha's intervention. Or was she being too picky? Wanting a specific type of person who wasn't up for a constant game of kinky catch and release.

Jillian shrugged and let her gaze fall across the room, unsure how to respond. The situation was far more awkward than she could imagine. Couldn't someone approach her like a human? Get to know each other, find out if they were compatible and not just go after the 'fuck me now' parts?

"What things would you like me to get into?" Evan continued, unfazed by her lack of response.

Other than wanting a person who wanted to know her, understood what made her tick, and even realized what would make her melt into a moment of pure bliss, she did not understand what she wanted in the scene anymore. Her private browser was full of darker ideas of domination, and she'd explored areas she never thought would turn her on but made her body race at the mere thought.

Ever since joining social sites for kinksters, she couldn't count the number of cock shots or men begging for her to be their Mistress. Maybe she should take them as compliments because they believed she was hot and a strong independent woman who could handle her own life.

Right next to her sat all of those things in the flesh, and every one of those unsolicited emails was suddenly right in her face. All he was offering her was uncommitted physical play--the thing Samantha told her to embrace with both hands and loosen up.

"I'm not sure what I want," Jillian said, hedging on an honest answer. "I've been out of the scene so long I feel rather like a voyeur and a virgin."

Samantha and her partners were the reason she'd ventured into the club at all. She loved to sit on the sidelines as they played. The dynamics were both overt and subtle. You had to be observant to catch everything that went on between them. Her newest partner, Trey, had a trained eye to keep her to heel. He knew which buttons he could push. The slightest arch or furrow of his eyebrow would cause her cheeky mouth to slam shut or make her walk to him like a magnet when he crooked his finger. Her partner Saul was a sensualist who put her body in a state of pure bliss. His style of domination was soft and subtle, just under the surface. Then there was her girlfriend, Chelsea, who fed her need for the softer, funny, feminine, sexy side. Finally, there was her husband, who had his own set of lovers, and loved to see Samantha happy.

Jillian would never wrap her head around how Samantha juggled so many relationships. Her chosen family seemed functional and contented with the arrangement. On the other side, she couldn't even find one person who filled her baser needs.

Every time she tried to let herself go, her strong, independent, feminist self would yell at her for the traitorous way she wanted to submit to a man. She wanted to let go, to let someone else take control for a while. The word causing her much angst was trying rather than doing. Jillian struggled to be unapologetically in touch with her own sexuality, but doubts always crept in on the idea that another person would earn her submission. Even if those wicked fantasies of force and control starred in most of her sessions with BOB, her battery-operated boyfriend, she'd been in the scene long enough to know that the fantasy and reality were often far apart.

Evan shifted on the barstool next to her, drawing Jillian's attention to him. "Everyone has fantasies they want to live out. We need to find out where to start and go from there. Do you like pain, dominance, being fucked in front of a crowd, sucking lots of men off at once?"

Jillian grimaced at the disconnected images which rose in her head as his words played across her brain. Not the shy and coy type, Evan's directness made her blush, and she grabbed for her wineglass.

"That's a very sex-based place to start," she commented without looking at him.

"Well, Samantha said you were looking for a fun, sexy time. I thought we might skip all the 'Get on your knees' bits and go right to the fun 'do me' parts." He waggled his eyebrows.

She sat there stunned. How had a conversation gone from 'Hi' to 'You wanna fuck?' in record time? Where was the small talk, the personal conversation? She wanted to trust someone to take her anywhere and anytime, inflicting a little pain. Her top ten fantasies whirled through her head, but she wasn't ready for pickup play at the same level.

The photos she browsed of women bound outside, blindfolded and waiting at the feet of a man with her head in his lap, made Jillian hot. The concept of giving control was amazing in theory, but there was no way she could ever make it a reality. It didn't help that she would call someone on their shit and stand toe to toe. No matter how much she wanted the tendrils of dominance to wrap around her once again, the armor she wore did not bode well for any level of deep submission.

Samantha often pushed Trey, but he enjoyed her slightly bratty nature, allowing the cheekiness to go so far before yanking her back to a more submissive place. It was a fascinating process from the sidelines. It often made Jillian wonder what it would be like for someone take her in hand and make her crave the submission. She longed to experience the emotions coursing through Samantha when she had a blissed-out state on her face again. To connect to another person in a way which made the synchronicity appear to happen by magic. A place where, no matter what they asked, her best interests and desires were at the heart of it.

"I don't know. I'm not really the casual fucking type," she answered to fill in the interminable pause.

"Really?" Evan's body stiffened, his shoulders straightening as he leaned in toward her. A glint in his eyes told her he was the type to rise to a challenge, not be put off by it. "I love making a mouthy girl mumble with my cock in her face hole."

Jillian worked to stop the automatic eye roll. Several men she'd encountered on dating and kinky sites seemed to want to break a girl and then leave the pieces behind. They wanted the conquest and not the prize. She didn't want to be with anyone who wasn't invested in her as much as she was invested in him. Was it too much to ask that a man be a gentleman who loved to take control and put her in her place, on occasionally? Too many romance novels let her conjure up the perfect hot bad boy image in her mind, and she sighed. Maybe Samantha was right. She wanted a relationship. Yet she had no relationship. Perhaps she needed to lower her too-high expectations to find one.

"Watch the teeth in that scenario," she warned.

"Mmm. You are feisty. Let's go down to the private rooms and see what it takes to get you on your knees begging for my cock."

"I don't think so." She frowned.

"Why not? The club does free STD testing, they vet everyone

and my status is easy to pull up. You know I'm 'safe.'" His fingers air quoted on safe, throwing an immediate red flag for Jillian.

"It's too soon to just walk downstairs and give you a blowjob, no matter how 'safe' you are," she replied, mimicking his previous movements.

"I thought you were here to have a magnificent time. I can make your body feel so good you will forget your own name when I'm done."

Jillian worked to school the shocked look.

"This could be your only chance to sample all this hot maleness. Live your deepest fantasies with no strings attached. Haven't you wanted to do that for a long time?"

The whole situation was going way too fast and in all the wrong directions. Who just walks up to someone and expects to have sex with them?

"Come on, hot stuff, the private rooms are just down the stairs. I can reserve one and open your eyes to a whole new set of fantasies."

She shook her head. "I'm sure you're a great guy..."

Evan snapped in frustration before she could complete the rejection. "My patience only goes so far, bitch."

Warning bells sounded in her mind and she was glad her wineglass was in her hand throughout the entire conversation. This guy knew nothing about her except the conquest he wanted between her legs.

"Bitch? Really? So not interested." She slid off her barstool, and he followed suit. He was easily three inches shorter when his feet hit the floor.

He looked up and growled. "Yeah. Bitch. I thought this is what you wanted, you cock tease. What's your problem? Not good enough in bed?"

"Isn't it obvious? Her problem is you," a male voice said from behind her and she noticed the body heat radiating off his nearness.

She turned around and let her eyes follow the wall of muscles and tattooed arms up to the face of the man. The angry expression on his face was menacing as he looked down at Evan. Jillian stood, unable to move, between the two men.

"Why don't you fuck off? The lady and I were getting down to some sexy business."

From behind her, the man stepped around Jillian and toward Evan. His body relaxed, but the air rippled with tension as the two men faced off.

After several long minutes, Evan shrugged. "You can have her. She's just a cock teasing mouthy bitch, anyway."

Get your copy now! _Master Me_

MASTER ME (THE ATLAS COLLECTION BOOK 2)

She heals clients. He moves things in the world. When he chains her up, can she tie him down?

Dr. Jillian Hart can read anybody like a book. But her counseling expertise doesn't help fix her own struggles with keeping her love life red-hot. She's hesitant to reenter the world of kink, despite her desires to submit to the chivalrous Empyrean Club security looking for total control.

CEO Ian Breckenridge loves how his persona shifts when he sheds his suit and dons his black club t-shirt. So when the Empyrean Club's owner falls off the map, he's more than happy to lend a hand as a welcome distraction from his business. Though he craves to totally dominate, it makes him ill-matched for the whip-smart woman he saved from unwanted attention. Still he hungers to teach her with his firm touch.

Even though she's sure her new mentor has no explicit interest in anything serious, Jillian can't escape the tightening grip of her attraction to his strong guidance. While Ian fears his needs are too much for anyone to truly accept, he can't hide his growing feelings when someone slips drugs into the gorgeous doctor's drink.

Will his powerful leadership save her from danger and make her beg for more?

Master Me is the second book in the provocative Empyrean Club erotic suspense series. If you like deep relationships, enticing instructors, and steamy scenes, then you'll adore Sappharia Mayer's lesson in discipline.

Buy Master Me ***today!***

ALSO BY SAPPHARIA MAYER

ABOUT THE AUTHOR

Sappharia Mayer's erotic romance comes from years of experience in dynamic and various play in the BDSM/Kink lifestyle. She portrays the dance of power exchange relationships with a passion that pushes her characters, and readers, outside their comfort zone, making them squirm, cry, laugh and learn to see things in a whole new way.

Living around the metro area of the nation's capital gives her an up close view of politics and power on a global scale. She loves to delve deep into her worlds and indulge in her various passions, which may or may not include instigating fun *trouble* with her warped sense of humor. If you love romance based in power exchanges with hot kinky sex, then check out Sappharia's books.

Printed in Great Britain
by Amazon

58900824R00206